33 Years in 3 Days

by

John D'Ambrosio

John D'Ambrosio
johndambrosioauthor.com

Printed in the United States of America First

First Printing 2021
First Edition 2021

ISBN: 978-1-7375327-0-5
Library of Congress Control Number: 2021913608

10 9 8 7 6 5 4 3 2 1

With appreciation:

Structural editing: Erick Mertz (thumbtack.com)
Line editing: Celia Pool (thumbtack.com)
Poems by: John D'Ambrosio
Cover design: John D'Ambrosio
Cover art: Adrianne Shreves
Cover Nordic God drawing: Brigid P. Gallego
Cover Formatted for KDP: Angie Pro_ebookcovers (fiverr.com)
Internal format design: Goran around86 (fiverr.com)

Dedicated to:

My Parents

Who instilled within me passion and spirit, inspired me to explore, encouraged me to succeed, and emboldened me to experience the wonderment of life.

To My Friends

Whether we met growing up, working together, or during my worldwide travels, I thank you for providing your unconditional friendship, enabling me to create memories I will cherish forever.

Acknowledgements

Childhood story inspired by attending the International School system in Southeast Asia: International School Bangkok (ISB) in Bangkok Thailand, International School Philippines (ISP) in Manila Philippines, and the American School Vientiane (ASV) in Vientiane, Laos.

Combat and accident scenes inspired by my brothers in the Special Forces Groups (Airborne), with whom I served, and those who continue to serve proudly, honorably wearing the Green Beret.

Is our past...

truly passed ?...

... or merely resting ?...

...awaiting its re-awakening ?...

... Should we...

... attempt to rekindle our past...?

... or simply accept it...

*...**As passed?**...*

This question

became my quest...

Our Journey / Vår Resan

P

~ Prologue ~

This is a story you may find intriguing, comforting, and heart-warming. The best part of this story is that it's true. Well, it's partially true. Maybe it's merely based on truth. Then again, isn't all fiction based on truth and vice-versa? Anyway, the best part of this story is the journey into which you are guided from the soul-searching, meticulously explored thought process in the beginning to its physical discoveries culminating in the search toward the end of the prose. I won't ruin it by telling you what happens in the end, as you probably won't expect it. And no, you shouldn't skip to the end to find out what happens, because then you'll miss out on the entire journey. The single aspect of this compelling story IS the journey... as it should be. Your search should always be about the journey, otherwise if what you are searching for turns out not to be what you expected, you may consider it wasted time. Who really cares about how the story turns out for these main characters? You'll find out within the storyline what the characters found, and one day you may find for yourself what you find.

Isn't this what life is all about—the journey—the search? With its twists and turns, whether perceived or experienced, within the quest for perceiving, conceiving, finding, learning, and eventually knowing your limits? I like to say that knowing your limits is half the battle; the rest is surviving the discovery process. The goal should in your own search, that you'll be fortunate enough to learn your limits BEFORE you reach them. This is also part of the recipe for a long life.

Experiencing life is about the environment into which you become immersed, the places you visit, the sights (and sites) you see, the pictures you take (both in your mind and with your camera), the sounds you hear, the aromas and odors you smell, the activities in which you participate, the foods you taste, the emotions you feel, the people you meet, the friends you make, the friends you keep, and the memories you create. These are what you'll cherish forever.

Understanding early on that your entire life is a discovery process, may just save you from experiencing the dreaded mid-life crisis. This is YOUR life. Make it what YOU want it to be! I encourage you to live your life and pursue your own journey toward discovery. And the sooner you begin, the better. Enjoy the road to discovery before life becomes too complicated with careers, children, and other commitments. Open your mind and your options as early as possible.

Many people get bogged down in their current lives leaving them merely wishing. Still longing to do what they wanted to do, but only getting as far as wishing they had done it, before deeming it too late. Loving and appreciating life itself somehow becomes a lesser priority. I offer that it's never too late. Many others do it backward, after a tough divorce or breakup. Then their quest may become a series of poor, self-deprecating decisions on a revenge tour, not a quest for unbiased discovery as it should be.

Am I advocating breaking off all ties with those you are intimate with? Absolutely not. Romantic ties are excruciatingly difficult to find. If you've found this and can build on it together, where the two can change together and not grow apart, by all means, take this journey together. Use it to build on what you have. The problem becomes many people don't know themselves well enough to promise the longevity they seek within a relationship. Over time, their discovery process may reveal many differences between themselves as individuals and their partner in the relationship. Eventually, couples may realize that their cores are not compatible, and are forced to decide if they can overcome such a dim prognosis. This is up to each person in the relationship. Although change is good, independent change can create a rift for couples.

This is why I say it is best to learn about yourself by yourself. Nobody truly likes to be alone in life, but we are born alone (except for twins, triplets, etc.), and most likely, we will die alone. So, it makes sense to get used to being alone, doesn't it? However, this process can be more effective, and often emotionally and physically safer to do with a friend of the same gender. Romantic commitments could interfere with or rush the discovery process. Your questions may eventually encapsulate your answers serving as a litmus test for your availability for future relationships—strengths, weaknesses and possibilities of relationship longevity. Which questions you may ask? Questions like: How good am I? What do I want to accomplish? What can I accomplish? What are my limits? Where do I want to go? Which places would I like to visit? Who do I want to help? How do I do this?

Consistent with every mission, expedition, quest, or adventure, within the pages of prose surrounding this storyline, you'll likely learn something new if you're open to it. Challenge yourself to set a course to learn more about yourself, more about others, more about your potential, and more about the possibilities open to you. You're also likely to face the temptation to explore your past in greater detail, to identify and learn from your mistakes, and use that feedback to plan and plot your future. You may embark on your journey out of boredom (hopefully not a mid-life crisis—why wait that long?), confronted by other doors and windows in your life closing, challenged by a friend, or just awake one morning and decide to do it; if you're open to it. As a safe place, I encourage you to use this story as your own starting point. Admittedly, such a journey is safer to read about than to live, but it's a vastly contrastive experience when you live it mentally, physically, emotionally, and spiritually. Why not do it? It's better than wondering your entire life if you should've done something differently. This way you'll know!

As you contemplate your journey in life, especially if it's reflecting into your past, plainly understanding your present, or inevitably planning your future, remind yourself to agree to whatever presents itself, whether your results are positive, negative or indifferent. You must learn to be impartial to your epiphanies. Explore your possibilities. Discover your realities. But do so safely. And until this time surfaces for you, sit back, relax, and patiently enable your mind to contemplate your journey's next steps in the footsteps of the characters as they come alive in this book.

There are few people in life who search to perceive life's events from different perspectives. Who longs to visually discern diverse angles? Who turns the previously unturned? Who notices the neglected? Who inquires into the often ignored? Who explores the existential, the unknown, or the misunderstood? Of all that exists in the external world that is unknown, it is quite possibly matched in comparison with that which lies dormant within each of us. I encourage everyone to enjoy the wonderment of fact, fiction, fantasy, what was, what is, what might, and what could be… this will unfold from the onset of your journey…

May we all continue searching...

finding... discovering... learning...

and our journey never end...

~ 1 ~

In the Beginning / I Början

It was a bright, warm, humid August day in the mid-1970s, between brief bouts of political jockeying, bordering on mayhem in this gentle, yet volatile, complex society in Thailand. My family just arrived in Bangkok. This country was different—it was the most diverse Asian country we lived in up to this point. A country where modern, medieval, and mythical all co-exist within its borders. It was late summer, about a month before school was to begin. Because my Dad's CIA career brought him to U.S. Embassies in Southeast Asia, my sister and I spent most of our childhood growing up among embassy communities (both U.S. and foreign).

My sister Karen and I were used to a nomadic lifestyle. We shared an amazing childhood, and I'm happy to say we both lived to talk about it. We were extremely familiar with moving to new countries and, as a result, to new houses every four years. Returning to the States every two years for "home leave," we felt like foreigners in our own country. We didn't think the same, act the same, speak the same, or dress the same as our American peers. The American kids we spoke with treated us as creatures from another planet. Sure, we spoke English, but we didn't understand the evolving American slang they used. We were unfamiliar with popular television shows, movies, the bands and music they listened to (because Asia lagged behind the U.S. in the entertainment industry), the places they frequented, the sports they watched; even the clothes they wore were different, ours being mostly tailored in Asia. We'd never even seen the latest and greatest technology behind the newest pinball machines with digital sound boxes and LED lighting, prominently displayed in arcades.

While staying in an American motel on home leave, we wandered into a nearby 7-11 convenience store. Hearing an unfamiliar noise taunting us as we entered, we were drawn toward a fantastically designed pinball machine at the back of the store. As a bit of a pinball wizard, I was intrigued and felt goaded into playing. After more than a few spent quarters which didn't last long, I awakened from my trance, gazing at this machine in awe: the voice box, sound effects, bright lights, magnetron ball diverter, pop-out ball traps, invisible travel tubes, and multi-level platforms played simultaneously with multiple shiny silver balls. The technology wrapped into this machine seemed to surpass that of the Apollo moonshots. Karen and I were both astonished.

After grabbing a snack, wandering to the cashier to pay, I said, "That machine back there is one incredible piece of technology! Wow!"

Not sharing one iota of my enthusiasm, she responded, "Yeah, whutevah. Will that be all?"

Back at our real homes in Asia, we attended English-speaking schools within the "International School" system accredited through California. This system in any country is renowned for its high-cost, well-to-do local clientele, and well-connected students and graduates. Regardless of how exclusive it was, it was simply school, to us. Our classmates were just classmates or friends, regardless of what their parents did, what cars they drove or which limousine they had, in which neighborhoods they lived, how many domestic helpers they employed, etc. We all went to school together and made it through classes, extracurricular games and club meetings, inside and outside of school. We mingled with the families of top national and international businessmen, senior-level government officials, and local community leaders.

These were truly international schools where various professions brought these parents to Asia for a few years, after which they returned to their homeland, with few exceptions. Our family was one of those exceptions. We spent our entire childhood in Asia, except for the handful of months of home leave.

Karen got more attention from the locals wherever we were because of her light blonde hair and fair skin, while I fit in like a chameleon because of my olive complexion and dark hair. We both learned to make friends easily wherever we went.

Our lifestyle entailed frequently saying goodbye to our current, soon to be old friends, then going through the uncomfortable and often isolating process of making new friends in a completely new place. Friends would come and go in our lives. We were constantly adjusting to new environments, cultures, customs, social mores, and superstitions of Buddhist, Animist, or Christian religious populations in Asian cities and towns. We adapted to new school dress codes, met new expectations, adjusted to local laws, learned where to go and where not to go, what to do and what not to do. We didn't even have television or radio stations in English until junior high school. The only way to get television in English was to tune a radio to a designated local station broadcasting that tv channel, and then place it behind the television to make the sound projection seem normal. Otherwise, most of the music on the radio was in the local language.

We became accustomed to change and as a result, we remained quite flexible. Each country exposed us to its merits, attractions, detractions, and complications, both cultural and political. We visited some tourist attractions within these countries that were magical, while others we could only tolerate for short periods of time—like the myriad of odors emanating from fresh, aging, soon to be rotten meat, fish, and poultry from the meat sections of open-air markets. Often in these locations, foul odors would stew within the stench of open sewers, becoming quite an abomination to the senses. Here, we learned to breathe through our mouths until we could extricate ourselves from those environments.

On a brighter note, with moving into new houses came new domestic help and new rules for each new household. Dad would go to work at the U.S. Embassy, and Mom was an active volunteer at the American Club thrift shop, managing the household staff (maids, cooks, houseboys, gardeners, drivers, and guards) and doing whatever she did to occupy her time until we got home from school or wherever else we were during the day. Sometimes being invited, and sometimes mandated, we attended State dinners and galas with Embassy or Royal family hosted events, Buddhist festivals within the Southeast Asia mainland, and Christian holiday festivals celebrated in the Philippines. All are memories we will never forget. Each unique, and never again replicated. This cycle was replicated in each country we lived.

Our childhood was definitely one of extremes. From conjuring up mischief derived from sheer curiosity, to hanging out with the local Asian kids who accepted us as their own, to wondering whether we would completely recover from whichever accidents, events, or mishaps we experienced. Initially, the loneliness of living in a foreign land with foreign languages, customs, and food was ours to overcome. Our parents did their best to shelter us from negative events occurring both in the States and those occurring while we were abroad, especially during the Vietnam War. We really only experienced the war when heading to our vacation spots in Thailand, transiting either Udorn or Ubon airfields in Thailand. The eardrum splitting, chest pounding F-4 Phantoms and B-4 Bombers screeching onto the runways, launching as fast as they could, screaming skyward for seemingly endless combat runs, was a 24-hour cycle. This was all we really knew of the war first-hand.

Back then, vacations were typically enjoyed on the U.S. Embassy-owned compound in Pattaya Beach enjoying the crystal-clear, green-blue water and miles of soft sandy beaches, where you could rent horses, speed boats for cruising or water skiing, or fishing boats for day-long trips. Radios on the beach played familiar songs like, "Snoopy and the Red Baron," "Sugar, Sugar," "Brandy [You're a Fine Girl]," and "Hooked on a Feeling."

For those of us who had the experience of living in Burma (now Myanmar) and Laos in the early 1960s, long before the Internet existed, conversing with the local population required knowledge of the local language. This became a bit of a challenge initially, but unlike adults, we were undeterred by making mistakes and, try as we would, eventually we learned to communicate with our domestic help and the local kids. Often, everyone involved in these conversations would end up smiling and laughing as we struggled to figure out what the other was saying. Attempting to order food items or items sold by street vendors was frustrating for the first few months. Sign language was a critical aspect in this communication, especially when bargaining a price down to a reasonable amount at open-air markets. Nonetheless, this was usually a jovial experience. Both the vendor and the purchaser, once satisfied with the price and quantity, each counted their new wares or profits as we parted.

As U.S. Embassy kids in foreign countries, we were encouraged—no, more like forced—to grow up quickly. Everyone expected us to represent the U.S. and our families in a positive light at whichever age. We were expected to act as mature adults, making proper decisions. Indoctrinated on how not to offend local nationals, and how never to embarrass the U.S. Embassy, its staff, or its families, we were acutely aware of the myriad of adverse actions that could get our parents fired and our family PNGed (Persona Non Grata—a diplomatic term for being kicked out of a country). Life happened quickly for most of us. This relegated us to making decisions that would affect us one way or another for the rest of our lives. It was a lot of responsibility, but that was not how we perceived it. To us, this was normal. We traveled from Burma, to Laos, to the Philippines and to Thailand before returning to the States for my last year of high school.

After being adopted at the age of one, a story in itself, I began my formative years overseas in Rangoon, Burma (now Yangon, Myanmar) in the early to mid-1960s. From the age of one to five-years-old, I remember little except our cook, driver, houseboy, gardener, and nursemaids who hovered over us night and day. I do retain glimpses of our household pets as well. I remember traumatic events, like my Dad pretending to leave me in the water in an inner tube at the beach, while he ducked under the waves. This was terrifying. As such, I ensured I never did it to my children. I also remember my older sister Karen, also adopted at the same age. She was a frail rug rat, nonetheless, she earned her reputation as a fearless hellion. One day she naively made her way to the second-floor balcony with her arms outstretched toward our mother on the concrete driveway below. Little Karen's piercing voice blurting, "Mama, I jump, you catch!" Thankfully, her attempt was foiled by the house staff. All was quiet until one night, Dad rushed her to the hospital with a 103-degree temperature. Nobody knew what happened until her nursemaid finally volunteered having seen little Karen snatch the head off a "chinchuck" gecko house lizard, away from one of our house cats. Apparently, she enjoyed the feast as much as the cat enjoyed the lower portion. That snack nearly killed her. But the doctors now had the information they needed to successfully treat her, sending her home shortly afterward.

This was an interesting country. It was here that I first was introduced to Asian Animist superstitious beliefs where it's customary to take children for their first fortune telling. We were no different. Being provided a translation, I kept mine well preserved in my coffers.

It was a structured society wherein the national government did its best to minimize the introduction of foreign products and cultures, and avoided automation to keep employment high. It was hearsay that if a company automated too soon, the government would nationalize its operations. So, Pepsi-Cola for example, maintained hand-blown glass bottles for its soft drink production in Myanmar for years. Also, by restricting foreign tourist travel within its borders to its UNESCO World Heritage sites, these remained well funded, preserved, and maintained. These included the Shwedagon Pagoda (named Shwedagon Zedi Daw officially) and nearby Karaweik Hall Palace (a restaurant on Kandawgyi Lake), well within the Yangon city limits. Other more difficult to reach destinations are either authentically preserved or left to natural decay. Being part of the U.S. Embassy's Diplomatic Corps, our family was able to get diplomatic passes and authorizations to travel the country relatively unimpeded. We enjoyed seeing the multi-ethnic heritage of its people on the pristine beaches of the Sandoway resort area in Ngapali beach, the Royal Palace site of Mandalay (which was completely destroyed during World War II by the Allied bombing operations attacking Japanese strongholds), the ancient towns of Pagan, Pegu and Maymyo (now Pyin U Lwin) with its botanical gardens still amazingly well preserved. We visited many of these remote sites, experiencing them pretty much as they existed hundreds of years ago. In Pagan, we awakened just before sunrise, climbed to the highest point we could on one of the ancient temples watching the orange ball burn through the layer of fog and smoke created by the wood burning fires as they had for hundreds of years; the air was cool and the scent was unmistakenly comforting. We revisited many of these places again as adults, when Dad was once again serving in the U.S. Embassy during our college years in the 1980s.

Moving on to my kindergarten days in Vientiane, Laos during the late 1960s and early 1970s, the goals in our Tom Sawyer lifestyle were simpler than most—reducing the incidence of many cuts and gashes, and staying out of the medical unit or larger hospitals once they stitched our wounds. Unfortunately, I seemed to learn more than others my age how to stay out of the hospital, only after my brief stays there. I still enjoyed a very active childhood, had very patient parents, and was lucky to have a very supportive group of friends. No matter where we went, Dad always encouraged us and sometimes assisted in getting us out of the trouble we got ourselves into—not trouble in the legal sense, but trouble in the physical sense. It's not that we ever looked for it, it just showed up. If we imagined it, we tried it, often suffering the consequences of cuts and bruises accompanying our immature, naïve decisions.

We learned lessons both outside and inside school. This time it would be at the American School Vientiane [ASV—go Cobras] in Laos. Learning the ins and outs of a new school was always a discovery process, but this place from the outset was the most fun. I still remember as we waited for our classmates to arrive under the gigantic banyan tree, we would buy some little round coconut milk pancakes sprinkled with scallions, carefully wrapped in either banana leaves or a newspaper funnel offered by a local vendor. As we cackled our way through adolescent small talk, the air filled with the rustic smell of nearby charcoal fires as shop owners prepared their breakfasts topped with the same scent of coconut pancakes, like those we were munching. Since the American

School was so small, all students rode the same bus to the same school campus regardless of age. We called the bus "Big Red" because it was a long, red school bus. Finally, the bus arrived. With only my lunch box in hand, I stepped through the front door, hopped up the steep stairs past the driver, and jumped up onto one of the open seats. Looking at my short legs with my adolescent feet pointing straight out in front of me, I longed for the day they would be long enough to rest firmly on the floor like the high school and junior high school kids across the aisle. Then I'd be a real grownup. I watched in awe as the high schoolers sat with their homework books stacked neatly beside them. I yearned for the day when I would sit with my feet touching the floor, accompanied by stacks of important homework books beside me just like them; little did I know. But for now, I'd have to sit complacently, feet dangling, with only my cool Superman lunch box beside me.

I stared out the window, passing by the open area of Tat Luang field where we'd often go to carnival and fair type festivals, watch shows with trained monkeys, motorcycle death spiral stunts, and enjoy some rickety carnival rides. It was also here where the U.S. Information Service (USIS) sponsored the Apollo rocket mockup and life-sized lunar module display erected as a publicity stunt to impress the Lao public during the Space Race of the Vietnam War years. I distinctly remember the bus driver yelling out with glee, "APOLLO!! APOLLO!" as he took his hands off the steering wheel, raising them in the air, smiling the entire time passing by this display. After that, it was mostly a silent ride as we stopped for a few more hordes of classmates before reaching the K6 American School campus. In Tat Luang Square, we even attended a once in a lifetime ceremony, culminating in the open-air cremation of one of the nationally ranked monks in 1968. There were local ceremonies at various Wats (Buddhist temples) accompanying weeks of mourning until the public cremation of the body, which we witnessed.

Before class we often played a tackling game we called British bulldogs, which was much like Sharks and Minnows—but on land. The entire school was in the mix from elementary to high school. We little kids all thought it was really cool that the big kids let us play. And it surprised the big kids that us little kids weren't afraid of getting squashed and crushed in the process. Little did the big kids know, the reason we ran so fast was because we were terrified of being squashed! Miraculously, nobody was seriously hurt. Just a few scrapes and scratches from falling into the nearby creek, serving as one of the boundaries. This game often started side skirmishes, a few of which involved me. In one such incident—I remember like it was yesterday, getting my first black eye. Ouch. As it turned out, my classmate and I became pretty good friends, most likely because of the numbers game—we didn't have many potential friends in our grade, so we kept what we had. It was pretty much one classroom per grade. We all learned to get along with each other, playing catch, dodge ball, and another insensitively named game "smear the queer"; playing tetherball, climbing the jungle gym, or riding the giant slide, seemingly for hours on end in the playground in front of school before the bell rang, summoning us for class to begin. And after school, it was back onto Big Red to go home.

Arriving at the bus stop, if it wasn't raining, it was typically hellishly hot. We'd take off our shoes and socks, storing them in our lunch boxes and run barefoot down the sides of the asphalt road, stomping on the tar bubbles for the few miles to the dirt road leading to our house. Once we arrived at the house, we had to clean the bottoms of our feet with a brush and gasoline to get the tar off. Though in our minds, for some reason, this was all worth the trouble. Our cook or houseboy would often supervise this laborious process and inspect our feet before letting us inside the house. I still don't understand why we thought that was fun. But apparently it was.

Like all kids our age, we looked forward to our weekends. And knowing what I know now, our weekends were different—vastly different from what our contemporaries were experiencing stateside. As young kids, however, when left alone to our own devices, we found mud holes to play in, cows and water buffaloes to ride, horses to borrow, bicycle paths to explore, local flora and fauna and insects, fish, creepy crawlies and reptiles to track, catch, and release, and streams in which to while away the hours just exploring. The fact we never really knew exactly what we were doing and lived through these harrowing experiences amazes me to this day.

Sometimes I spent the weekend camping overnight on the rooftop of my friend's house [where I spent the night for two weeks one summer] in a tent with nobody in the house knowing or concerned with where we were, including the driver, houseboy, cook, maid, gardener, and guard. Later, we made makeshift parachutes from bedsheets, jumping from this same rooftop, expecting to land as safely as they did in the movies with real parachutes. Somehow, we broke nothing. We played with all kinds of firecrackers and fireworks, hunted for a special type of ladybug we called "flying turtles" because that's what they looked like to us, or at night wandered through clouds of fireflies, called lightning bugs in the States. Strangely enough, I've never seen those flying turtles in any other country.

We prepared to run, jump, slip, and slide purposefully on algae-covered slick verandas and driveways brought forth by monsoon rains or on soaped up marble floors in front of the colonial French-styled estate houses where we lived. This "slip and slide" game often resulted in more cuts and scrapes. During one such incident at a neighbor's house, I remember being spooked by the first sight of serious amounts of my blood. When I ran home, the wound on my knee most likely opened up even farther. Self-doctoring, as my Mom drowsily suggested, resulted in more than a few band-aids floating down my leg in a stream of blood. I re-entered the pitch-black room where my parents were recovering after yet another late night out, whispering loud enough to be heard over the window-inserted air-conditioning unit, "Mom, the band-aid won't stick, there's too much blood." She switched on the nightstand light, seeing the crime scene in the bathroom, wasted no time getting dressed, and once again rushing me to the U.S. Medical Unit near the Operation Brotherhood (OB) Hospital.

Some of our weekends were spent sifting through the wreckage of abandoned, bombed-out, decrepit buildings, climbing the rickety bamboo scaffold structures to explore Buddhist temples under construction, or wandering for hours in open fields, exploring life, looking for interesting creatures while avoiding the ones we knew were poisonous. Karen and I often climbed into trees or onto the roof of our house, bringing up breakfast or lunch in a bucket, mimicking the characters in the movie, *The Swiss Family Robinson,* while our parents enjoyed another unconscious respite from yet another long night out. When we were good, sometimes they brought us out to "The Spot" night club for special occasions or to the ACA (American Community Association) restaurant after an early movie there.

On nights when we were babysat by our live-in housekeeper, she would flip her eyelids inside out and chase us around the house pretending to be possessed, telling us she'd summon the ghost called "Pii Gasuh" to haunt us if we didn't go to bed when she said. That sent us scampering to our separate rooms terrified, hiding under the covers until we fell asleep. Sometimes Dad brought us out to a bar named "Nicki's" where we would play darts, shuffleboard, watch movies, or just sit and enjoy the awesome freshly made popcorn. Mom was never privy to this place. And as he requested, we never told her. Most often whenever we were, wherever we were, we were told to entertain ourselves. And we did just that.

Sometimes the two of us ventured out on bicycle or moped trips taking an entire Saturday. Again, we passed the time trying to catch creepy-crawlies and release small snakes just to see if we could; unsure if they were or were not poisonous, we assumed they weren't. But if it stood upright, displaying a hood, we knew it was either a Cobra or King Cobra, and we'd get away from those. If it didn't run or slither away, or was bigger or longer than us, it too was not to be messed with. That's about all we knew. Everything else was fair game.

Often our follies met with near tragedy. Like the time we decided to join some local kids swimming in flooded rice fields; I nearly drowned. I was wading in the waist-high water when suddenly I found myself alone, uncontrollably drawn by the raging waters toward a cutout in the dike underneath a low-set footbridge. Instantaneously, I lost my footing, having no leverage and no strength to fight the current. The flowing water took me under and pinned me from my shoulders to my thighs against the cool, sticky clay dike wall. Rushing water surged over my bare shoulders, pressing me down and against the dike wall with interminable force a few feet below the water surface. I heard the garbled yells and screams from the local Lao children splashing in the water now far behind me, as the oxygen in my lungs rapidly depleted, leaving me in a relaxed, dreamy state. There I knelt, trapped, breathless, underneath the water, looking up at passersby just a few feet away crossing the makeshift footbridge, unaware of my perilous situation. They calmly walked past as I quickly faced my demise. I saw a face approaching the water's surface with outstretched arms until I felt myself forcefully plucked out of this potentially murky grave. That earned me the loudest scolding in Lao from the male earth angel rescuing me. I was so grateful. It didn't matter that neither of us understood all or any of the words we exchanged. He understood my rudimentary Lao as I sputtered, "*Khop chai lai lai* [thank you very, very much]!" I completely understood and appreciated his heroic actions. I never forgot that day, nor did Karen. And we never told our parents, afraid of having our wings clipped.

Karen too, had her own childhood moments of fear and trepidation accost her. Early one morning we went to a friend's house to borrow their horses, Zonder and Chestnut, as we often did. While calmly riding in a nearby open field, her horse bucked, violently launching her into the air. After she plummeted to the ground, he kicked her in the forehead so forcefully it left her with a black and blue horse shoe mark on her forehead for weeks. After her own trip to the Medical Unit, she spent days in her room with a concussion, constantly vomiting. I waited outside for her recovery, as the maid inside was nursing her back to health. It seemed like forever to me. I looked forward to her recovery when once again we could climb up to the roof or play with the large black scorpions that appeared after rainstorms, along with the myriad of centipedes and millipedes crossing our paths. Yet another time, she was yelling for me to look at her while she was riding on the back of a water buffalo. Unbeknownst to her, the water buffalo entered a mud hole and all I could think of to say was, "Watch out!" The creature rolled over completely, submerging both of them in the muddy clay pool. All I saw for moments were brown-orange hooves in the air, wide brown horns, and a brown thrashing tail. I watched breathlessly as Karen emerged from the other side of the animal, covered in brown muck from head to toe, standing with her hands and feet spread apart. She stood laughing so loud, she convulsed. We both stood laughing together.

I soon earned more trips to the Medical Unit for stitches, and even to the poison control unit after eating local plants I had mistakenly identified as non-poisonous. I couldn't understand how the Lao kids ate something looking exactly like it, and were okay. They even shared it with me. But when I tried it solo in my backyard, immediately my throat seized up, my eyes burned, and my vocal cords felt as if they had been scalded and stripped out of my throat; I instantly knew this was not right. Darting into the house with my throat on fire… once again I woke up from her slumber, "Mom…" was all I could eke out, pointing to my throat with terror in my eyes, as I struggled to breathe. She understood my message, grabbed the car keys, helped me into the Ford Galaxy 500, and off we went. I survived, resting uncomfortably at home for a few days.

A few times, with a friend of mine on a whim, we took public taxi rides for hours just to visit our favorite playground or visit the National Museum beside the Mekong River. In those days, the taxis were like buses and would stop to pick up as many people as possible along the way to gain extra fares to any destination. Few six-year-olds anywhere would do that. We visited temples and memorials and climbed them as high as possible, even if it was illegal. We would climb until someone screamed at us to come down. Sometimes we climbed thousands of stories into the sky [seemingly]. One such time, atop a Buddhist temple being constructed, a friendly Lao kid at the top convinced me to inhale my first cigarette—to this day, I don't understand why people smoke. I barely made it down to the ground, traversing the loosely constructed bamboo scaffolding while puking my guts up all the way down. The Lao kids thought my reaction was hilarious. Once again, I learned a valuable lesson regarding the criticality of oxygen.

Another time, my parents scolded me after playing with an entire barrel of cooled, yet still semi-liquid asphalt, found during one of our exploratory walks. The barrel was just too inviting for boys my age to avoid flicking the gooey mess onto each other with sticks, until we were nearly completely covered. Bathing in gasoline to remove it from my skin wasn't as bad as dealing with the looks we received from the ACA barber when my Mom explained she wanted him to cut all the tar out of my hair.

Karen and I were always picking up stray kittens and puppies, trying to hide them in our rooms from Mom and Dad, sneaking in food when we could, intending to keep them as pets until discovered. Dad said he brought them to the King's Palace in Luang Prabang, but who knows what he did with them. We rode bicycles, mopeds, and minibikes with no licenses or protective gear. One time, a friend of mine thought it was a good idea to burn straw in a nearby field with a magnifying glass, accidentally burning up the entire dried rice field; that farmer was not happy with us. My second experience with fire happened while playing at a friend's house, jumping and wrestling on the beds one night, while our parents talked in the next room. We placed our sweaty t-shirts over a bedside lamp, moments later bolting out of the room when they caught fire. That was embarrassing. His parents never invited me over to play again.

We learned to make kites from bamboo and wax paper from scratch, avoiding electrified wires and remembering not to run in the way of motor vehicles, which often drove right across the grassy areas in the parks and open fields where we played and flew these kites. One time, we even tried to convince a local business owner that monopoly money was real U.S. dollars to buy gum— he ended up calling a police officer who scolded us. Karen wasn't averse to her own antics. One day, she went to the local outdoor market with the maid and bought some eels, storing them in the large emergency water cisterns in the poorly lit back room of the house. Not realizing this, Mom decided to bathe in one of them— unbeknownst to her, she was swimming among our temporary reptilian pets. Thankfully they were not electric eels like they have in South America.

Enjoying many of our summer days at the pool and snack bar, we whiled away the hours safely in the ACA compound or watching a matinee. Sometimes we'd find our way over to the millions of stacked sandbags stored for either flood control or defense from an air attack. Remember, this was during the Vietnam War, and as Americans, we were targets. This was our enormous fort. We'd play in and around those sandbags for hours on end, as dangerous as it was. When the stacks we climbed tumbled, we'd scramble to the top as fast as we could to avoid being crushed by the hundreds of pounds of sandbags that came crashing down. Amazingly, nobody ever got hurt inside our sandbag city. During the floods at the ACA, we would often grab onto the backs of trucks driving closely by our sandbag city and enjoy being dragged through the water. Ah, the simple pleasures of youth.

Incidentally, it was at the ACA that I saw the movie, *The Green Berets*, starring John Wayne. Little did I know, this movie would shape my future, along with the occasional *James Bond* thriller. I threw thousands of pine cone hand grenades, and stealthily creeped around the house avoiding discovery by our domestic help. After seeing an episode of *Mission Impossible* on home leave, I once accepted a mission to surreptitiously gain access to Karen's transistor radio [which I imagined was a bomb], dismantling it so it wouldn't explode. Putting it back together proved impossible enough that it landed me in a lot of trouble with my parents. That transistor radio never worked again, but it never exploded either! Nobody ever understood my perspective. Sometimes, I myself, didn't understand the purpose of these missions, but that wasn't a license to refuse any mission in the days of my youth. I learned in life, since that time, not everyone would be happy when I accomplished my missions. But, unlike James Bond, at this age, I always got caught… eventually.

Sometimes Dad took me on day-long "don't tell your mother" missions. These were more tangible. We'd take the VW Beetle to the Vientiane airport, make our way to the executive private plane area, and eventually get on small Air America airplanes called *Barons* and *PC-6 Porters.* Parked beside these *Barons* and *Porters,* were *C-7 Caribous, C-123 Providers, C-130 Hercule*s, and even the tail-dragging *DC3s.* The *DC3s* were the workhorses seen in WWII movies, resting their tail wheel on the ground, only getting upright once airborne. These larger airplanes were used as *"milk runs"* to transport us to Thailand for vacations and on the way, often parachuted rice or supplies while airborne. That was fun to watch.

We'd park the car, walk over to the Operations "Ops" shed, meet our pilots, get a briefing, then walk out to the little one- or two-passenger short take-off and landing (STOL) aircraft, climbing in. These light craft were perfect for landing on short, orange-clay airstrips carved out of the jungle. I would crawl into the tail of the plane with the boxes and stacks of mail and supplies, making myself as comfortable as possible for the flight. After a short run-up, the pilot contacted the Ops shed and made our way to the short, perforated steel plate (PSP) runway, bumping down the runway until the ride smoothed, getting airborne. Up higher and higher, the single propeller of the *Porter* whined its way closer to our destination nearing 10,000 feet. We were on our way somewhere near Pakse or Savannakhet among other places, to "meet Dad's friends." I didn't understand why his friends had to be so far away, but it was fun getting there. Peering out the aircraft windows, I never saw the Ho Chi Minh trail that was talked so often about.

The pilot typically would execute a wingover and make dive-bombing type runs toward the orange clay runway in the middle of nowhere to land. They'd take off just as radically too. I thought the pilots were hot dogging and having fun, but later as an adult,

I realized these were maneuvers intended to counter shoulder fired anti-aircraft missiles. We'd land, jump out, and rush into nearby jungle cover. Meanwhile, the plane would take off, never shutting down the engine. We'd wait. And wait. And wait. Dad grew a bit annoyed after I kept asking him when his friends were coming, "They'll be here, Dimitri," he'd say. "What if they don't come, Dad?" I incessantly asked. "They'll be here," he sternly responded. "Now please be quiet and wait," and we waited in the tree line for the sound of vehicle engines of the people he was expecting to come for us. They'd always show up, eventually. And they always drove us to a nearby village, so I could find someone to play with and Dad could talk to whoever he came to meet. Once we all finished conducting our business, we'd get a quick bite to eat and be back in the jungle beside the landing strip waiting, and waiting for the aircraft after the vehicle entourage departed. Eventually we'd hear the plane, it would land, and take us away just as quickly as it came.

Since I was extra cargo, I was left to my own devices, lying down among the parcels inside the tail of the plane, three or four feet behind the pilot. Occasionally, the pilot would me ask if I wanted to fly.

I'd look to Dad for approval and he always granted my wish, "Sure, why not? But don't tell your mother!"

We would jostle around changing seats mid-air, so I could live my dream, and fly the aircraft for about 20 minutes. I attempted nothing radical, and the pilot never encouraged it. After some basic maneuvers with the pilot next to me, instructing, we again jostled around changing seats to land. After returning to Vientiane, we'd go to "Nicki's" to meet more of my Dad's friends from work; I'd watch them play darts, shuffleboard, and had no problem stuffing my face with popcorn before going home. My Dad repeatedly said, "Remember, don't tell your mother." So, I never did.

There were also those long trips out to the ferry station on the Mekong River, to pick up someone we were bringing somewhere to talk to my Dad. Sometimes Karen went too. We kids loved standing up on the passenger seat of our VW Beetle, sticking our heads out the sunroof for much of the highway drive with our hair blowing in the wind. On the return ride, I'd sit in the itchy rear carpeted compartment above the engine just for kicks. You wouldn't be able to do any of that these days. I still remember the story of the impatient driver who honked at water buffalos crossing the road, causing a stampede, crushing everyone inside the vehicle. Whenever water buffalos or cows were crossing the road, Dad never honked his horn. Every other time, like everyone else driving in Laos, the horn was the main means of driver communication.

Everyone seemed to have fun back in those days. One night out on the town with Mom, Dad came home with a large plastic Air India sultan mascot on a flying carpet. He brought it back to the Lang Xang hotel the next day, not remembering having taken it. Mom was always game for nights out with Dad. They often went out with other couples for dinner and drinks or dancing at "The Spot." Whenever they brought us with them for early hour barhopping, we felt really grown up. Although we'd only drink soft drinks or fresh lemonade.

At some point Dad taught us to run a reel-to-reel projector serving as our TV, since in those days Laos had no such amenity. He brought the big cases containing movie reels home and we got all excited seeing which movies they were. He'd let us decide the order in which we watched those movies. He told us he used to bring films with a projector and generator upcountry, showing them to the Hmong or Montagnard villagers in their mountain village. All was well until he showed *The Planet of the Apes*. Villagers were horrified at the notion that American society may really be like that; after all, seeing is believing. It took my Dad days talking to the village chief, convincing the villagers that it was just a movie intended for entertainment, and the U.S. was not really like that. After that experience, he didn't bring any more science fiction movies upcountry.

Learning to make and use slingshots was a staple of our childhood in Asia. As was learning NOT to get a finger in the way of the item being launched—that was a more painful lesson the second time around, for some reason. We also discovered how indefensible plate glass windows are against sling-shotted rocks, or from BBs or pellets launched from air guns. We played with firecrackers, bottle rockets, and a host of other explosives just for fun. We learned how much fun [or trouble] unsupervised kids at our age could muster. This was all commonplace to most of us there. We all thought that every kid our age worldwide got involved in these same "normal" activities. We accepted everything as normal, and never knew otherwise. As we sat down for dinner with our parents at the end of nearly every day, we responded with, "Nothing much," when asked what we did that day. It seemed to suffice.

Four years later, Dad moved us out of Laos to the Philippines in the early 1970s, while he served in the combat zones during the last months of the Vietnam War in Saigon (now Ho Chi Minh City), Tay Ninh, Bien Hoa, and Danang, among other places he mentioned. This was another Asian country where superstitions ran rife. As was customary here, my parents had Asian friends who brought to our house a fortune teller. While shuffling her tarot-type cards when it came to my turn, she shuffled the deck three times and dealt three times. Each time the cards came up pretty much the same, so she collected them up dealing again, until the last time. I asked what they said. She dismissed the result by explaining this was for entertainment only and wasn't real.

"What does it say?" I asked.

Finally, she spoke, pointing to the cards, "You'll be in the government or military for a career, you'll have a large family and… you'll die at a young age."

"How young?"

"Maybe mid- to late 20s. But these cards don't really mean anything. It's just for fun."

The truth was exposed in my mind. I now knew when I was probably going to die and now I had even less time to repay my parents for adopting me and providing me a tremendous life, as they had even up to this point. Now I knew I had less time to be successful, so I began over-achieving. I wanted them to be proud of me.

Karen and I were getting older now, and got into even more trouble. Because of my antics, Dad made more emergency leave trips to the Philippines than he ever imagined, and more than I wanted for him. Participating in countless friendly mud-ball and Chinese firecracker ball fights, I was extremely active in Magallanes Village in Makati, Manila where we lived. There were countless kids our age nearby and many more instigators to encourage us. These activities went on for months, meeting in local parks until one rock-laden flying mud ball struck me in the temple. Blood from the open wound went everywhere; immediately the fun was over for everyone. This experience sent me to Makati Medical Center, completely soaked in blood as Mom and our driver drove me. Our assigned family doctor, named Dr. Ramirez, who had done some minor corrective surgery on Mom, was my attending physician. He sewed me up with nine stitches, barely leaving a scar. Our maid ran over 10 blocks to deliver a clean shirt on a hanger once she received word that I was hurt. It was nice coming back from the hospital in a clean shirt. Eventually, my fun and good luck with firecrackers, bottle rockets, and fireworks came to an abrupt end.

One hot summer day, after my best friend Sebastian and I had as much fun as we could muster blowing up cow pies and mud puddles in a nearby open field, I removed as many black powder sizzlers and firecrackers as I could from the brown bag the vendor put them in. I stuffed them into the front pocket of my tight-fitting cut-off jeans. We intended this to make it easier getting past the guard to our barrio. Sebastian stuffed his pockets too, but his shorts were looser than mine. Avoiding the guard shack, we found an abandoned street where we could crawl under the barbed wire topped fence. Once through, I suddenly felt my body uncomfortably over-heating. Complaining about it, I got up from our shaded perch and walked around in tight circles, fanning myself. The fireworks spontaneously combusted.

I still remember looking at Sebastian, from inside the thick cloud of grayish-white smoke that drenched my nostrils with an overpowering stench of cordite, burning hair, and charred skin. Recognizing what was happening, I violently slapped my front pockets, attempting to put out the blinding flash of flames at the source of ignition. After a few slaps, the searing gun powder spread to my hands from the burst packs of unignited explosives. Despite my attempts to quell the burning, I was powerless to stop it. What seemed like hours, lasted only seconds. Looking down at the carnage of my blackened, numb, open palms, it looked as if I was holding deep fried, burnt pork rinds. We both stared at each other mindlessly in utter disbelief. Unsure what to do, we ran to a friend's house, only to have the maid open and slam the door in shock and disbelief. So, we ran to Sebastian's house where his father rushed to the door hearing our screams and uncontrolled bell ringing at their front gate. Gently he walked me indoors, caring for me until my Mom arrived with our driver to take me to the hospital in our blue, two-door Plymouth Duster. That was an uncomfortable ride much of it sitting in traffic, with an even more uncomfortable exit at the hospital. Our family doctor, once again, was on duty that day. He greeted me in the emergency room as I was lying stretched out on the gurney in shock and excruciating pain under the blinding, round surgical light. It was strangely comforting hearing his friendly voice. I felt a bit at ease knowing he was among the attending physicians.

"Hello Dimitri," his smooth, confident voice whispered. "What kind of trouble did you get into today? Not a rock fight obviously."

"No, I'm sorry, Dr. Ramirez. It wasn't," was all I remember saying. After numbing injections, they peeled the dead skin away until reaching live tissue, then cut it. They did this for my hands, thighs, and stomach. I was hospitalized for nearly three months, which included two surgeries under the skillful hands of Dr. Ramirez to assist growing back the once charred skin on nearly 25 percent of my body. The road to recovery was a slow one.

Once again, Dad sped back to the Philippines on emergency leave. He spent weeks with me in my private hospital room. It was a huge private room. Either Mom or Dad slept with me overnight, so the private nurse wasn't required all night. Sometimes a neighboring patient sent me over ice cream sandwiches, hearing me on those days when the pain of the burns was so overwhelming that I couldn't suffer in silence. This was a lot for a 10-year-old to endure. Eventually Mom and Dad started having parties in the room with friends visiting and playing poker or mahjong. I enjoyed the energy of the company and the festive environment. The parties were always a welcome distraction from my painful healing. My parents never witnessed Karen's terrifying wheelchair rides speeding me down the hallways on nearly every floor of the hospital, getting me out of my room. My parents thought that was very thoughtful of her. I really didn't mind them too much, since she had fun doing it, and I never got more injured. I was becoming hardened at this point in life and somewhat stubborn as a result of my decisions. While still in the hospital, I distinctly remembering my Dad asking me if I learned my lesson through all of this.

"Did you learn not to play with firecrackers anymore?" he asked.

I stubbornly responded, "No. I learned that next time I'll let Sebastian hold all of them!"

Once discharged, I endured about a year and a half of painful physical therapy and whirlpool baths and many more appointments with my favorite doctor. He inspired me, galvanizing me, that all my physical work would inevitably pay off, no matter how difficult it was. Using a form of tough love, he inspired me to learn to walk without a limp and do hand exercises to maintain my dexterity during the healing process. The nightmares about that day lasted for most of that year. Sebastian had the same ones, from his different perspective as a bystander. This was by far our worst experience playing together since our days in Laos, as kindergarten classmates and through the third grade. That day cemented our close friendship and propelled us into the future.

After returning from the hospital, only then did we learn our maid was also a licensed nurse. In the months to come, she was incredibly helpful in applying the burn ointment and changing my bandages, daily. On one of those days, I slipped down the flight of newly waxed teakwood stairs, re-opening my wounds, extending my healing process. When I completely healed from the burns, Karen and I could once again enjoy riding our twin bed mattresses down this same highly waxed flight of teakwood stairs, when Mom was out of the house. I dare not complain about those fun times now. Eventually I was able to walk without a limp and I regained full use of my hands. Though I never had skin grafts, some of my fingers remained tender for years and never grew back the fingerprints which are still blank spots on several fingers. These serve as a testament to my youthful folly.

Life eventually normalized. Once again, I was being struck by flying metal paper clips, and clay and paper spitballs during brief skirmishes inside and outside of school classrooms and on the school bus. It was good to have everything back to normal. These antics were commonplace during my formative years. Among the memories and scars, I had no permanent damage from these brief exploits, and somehow my recovery was always complete. Occasionally we took walkabouts along the tops of the10-foot cinder block walls dividing the middle-class residences. These went on for miles as we braved snarling, barking, jumping dogs, accompanied by the risk of falling. We never did. Once Sebastian returned stateside, I made another good friend in school.

This kid made Ritchie Rich look like a pauper. Whether we were on his private yacht eating lunch, taking week-long vacations aboard their vacation ship to Cebu island with his parents, frolicking in their multi-pooled mansion (often highlighted in Asia Weekly magazine), or wandering around in a chauffeured limousine. Trouble always followed us during those days. We smuggled his dogs into the hospital when his Mom had surgery and we soon were scolded for having syringe fights in the private hospital room. This involved jamming down the plunger on the plastic syringes so hard, it launched the needles off like rockets. Who knew? When he wanted to set up his electric race car set, he summoned one of his father's company electricians to construct it. The massive track took up one entire room — he grew tired of playing with it after four or five hours. Yet, another time, we went to the local market to buy half a dozen ducklings, playing with them in the yards and pools of his mansion for hours. The fun ended in yet another scolding after Ritchie let them swim in his sister's eight-foot long, four feet deep, fresh water aquarium; they gobbled up all her prized tropical fish before we knew what happened. She returned home to the crime scene, shortly afterward. The last thing I remember hearing was her screaming, "Ritchie!!" throughout those vast halls. Those were the days.

We were discovering ours were not typical experiences for the average five to sixteen-year-olds growing up in the States. So long as it wasn't fatal to us, our parents were happy to see us grow up, and gave us the freedom [and funding] to do so. They weren't privy to everything we did and never admonished us when we got hurt, knowing it was unintentional. They provided initial repair, subsequent healing, and encouragement for their little explorers. As life harshly taught us, our injuries always could've been worse. That was enough of a punishment to cauterize our lessons learned indelibly into our developing minds. Remembering the many errors of our youthful past—we never forgot. As adventurers by choice, Karen and I learned our escapades inherently came with bumps, bruises, lessons, and scars, suffering the usual and unusual aches and pains of over-active childhoods. While some took longer than others, our scars healed, our bones mended, and our bodies recovered. We were both older, wiser, and luckier with our hospital days and stays behind us. We learned our physical limits. Before leaving the Philippines, one of our neighbors knew I played guitar and sang. He asked me if I would be interested in appearing on a children's television show, the equivalent of the Muppets. I jumped at the chance. The show was a success and they asked if I could come back as a regular, but we had to leave.

Moving to Bangkok, Thailand in the mid-1970s, once again we were thrust into an historically relevant country that had seen its share of turmoil. Once known as Siam, it changed its name to Thailand in 1939. Dad left Vietnam, joining us there. The less accident-prone part of our growing up would now define our time, as we matured through our most significant teen years here. Despite that, as we sat down for dinner with our parents at the end of nearly every day, we still responded with, "Nothing much," when asked what we did that day. And it still seemed to suffice.

We loved our lives, grateful to have such patient and empowering parents.

I was nearly a teen, and most of my friends outside of school were older locals. My social circles were widening. The world was my oyster. My hobbies became a little riskier, emboldened by years of survival up to this point. They now involved riding bicycles and motorcycles in downtown Bangkok traffic, and firing small caliber handguns and rifles while visiting Mon farmers in the jungles up in the Northwestern province of Kanchanaburi near the Burma border with my Dad. I began riding homemade go-carts, rally cars, or motorcycles owned by these Thai friends. Sometimes I took part in "Fast and Furious" type road rallies and trips, making it to the beach hours quicker than it normally took. We hood-surfed on friend's cars and enjoyed similar types of adrenaline activating activities aboard public trains or buses, especially those heading out of the city on longer trips. I still did whatever seemed to be a good idea at the time, at whatever age I was, whenever I had the opportunity and nerve to experience something new and exciting. But I was getting luckier now.

Here we were once again for another four or five years, in yet another Southeast Asian country. Living in another micro-climate, with another language barrier, another strange diet, and many more pills to take and shots to endure to stave off whatever diseases might afflict or kill us; the list was long. Again, we watched the summer slip by and the school year rapidly approach, as they all inevitably did.

When we first arrived, the U.S. Military still had a large presence that was quickly dwindling, until it finally pulled out. There was still a robust American teen club where American kids and their guests gathered at Soi (street) 21 on the weekends to play indoor games like pinball, video, air hockey, table tennis. There were outdoor pickup games of badminton, tennis, volleyball, soccer, field hockey, and takraw (the Asian game like badminton involving a high net and a straw ball). Here, we could take lessons in many things such as sports, art, and singing to mention just a few. We watched full-length movies on the silver screen offered day and night, and took a break from being teenagers away from our parents. The prices were reasonable, the food was excellent, and most of the staff were American adult volunteers. After the military completely pulled out, taking their families and our classmates with them, the popularity of the club dwindled. The effort to make it self-sustaining failed. We lost our safe-haven and had fewer places to hang out as teenagers.

Karen and I spent our time avoiding the apprehension of attending the International School of Bangkok (ISB – Go Panthers!). We avoided thinking about it by talking to our new friends from the Teen Club and learning our way around our new suburban neighborhood. We lived in the Sukhumvit area, which by local Thai standards was upper class. Food stalls and shops, open-air restaurants, and many mom-and-pop factories were conveniently located down the street. Ten-foot walls of different colors lined the streets, demarcating the boundary lines of each multi-acre property, with broken glass and strands of barbed wire topping the walls for security.

As foreigners in a foreign land, we still got a lot of attention from the local population. We did whatever our hearts desired, based on what we thought was a good idea or what we thought we could get away with. Some of our friends got into gateway drug use, others into recreational use, while most of us merely began experimenting with alcohol at our very young age. The benefit of this was that many of us stopped drinking at the spry young age of 14 or 15, after experiencing alcohol poisoning, or after too many painful bouts with hangovers. At the same time, in the U.S. and in many other countries, our teen contemporaries couldn't legally or ethically start drinking until long after our age. Due to the low standard of living in Thailand, anything and everything seemed available to us, if we wanted it. We went where we wanted, taking taxis, buses, trains, or motorcycles. Klong taxis traversed many of Bangkok's canals or "klongs," through many parts of Bangkok. Many of us could afford to do much more here than in our own countries.

Dad got a membership into the Royal Bangkok Sports Club, or Polo Club, where we met more kids from different walks of life and other Embassies and companies. Eventually this place replaced the Teen Club, once it closed. At night, we started venturing out to many of the night spots and nightclubs the city offered. Some of our friends met with adult trouble, being mugged or beaten while wandering the streets; some were even hospitalized. Yup, we were becoming adults pretty quickly in this city. Karen and I learned to either avoid getting into trouble or developed an inherent ability to talk our way out of it. This was all part of growing up in a fast-paced city. This was completely new to us. Immersed into its unique culture, language, cuisine, and experiences, we loved it. Sometimes we were targets, and sometimes revered by the locals. Whichever it was, it was, and we accepted it without question. Our lives here were much more complex than most anyone our age stateside.

On typical weekend nights, we learned that most of the Embassy kids went to a few local hangouts. The most popular were Crown Pizza (we all called *Crowns*) and *Pop's*; both were devoid of any responsible adult supervision. *Pop's* was where the more adult teens hung out. It was where the older teens went to get away from us younger pre-teens, and we pre-teens went to feel older, and more mature. It was dark, loud, music-steeped and saturated by blacklights reflecting off posters and blacklight-painted graffiti. This was a smoke-filled club where Jimmy Hendrix posters were carefully situated among other popular teen visual aids, edge-to-edge without hardly an inch of empty wall showing. Blacklight signatures of frequent customers adorned the ceilings, bar food was the norm, and virtually any alcoholic drink known to man was prepared with cheap ingredients available at an affordable price to anyone, without regard to age. This practice was customary in most restaurants and clubs in Bangkok.

Known by most parents as the place where the wild kids hung out and where drug use was rampant—they weren't far off. But *Pop's* wasn't the drug den it was reputed to be; technically, all drug use was conducted outside the establishment, as patrons walked down the street to smoke a joint or two. Most of the drug use was marijuana, currently legal in most of the U.S. states; it was fairly harmless. And in those days, the local police didn't bother pursuing such arrests. The few arrests we witnessed involved those who traveled through the gateway to more intense opium-based narcotics like hashish, Buddha grass, heroin and others. Located near the top of a short dead-end street, *Pop's* gained its notoriety mostly due to the two brothers who ran the place.

Many parents encouraged attendance at the tamest option— the Teen Club, with no sanctioned smoking or alcohol drinking. It had adult supervision, a decent snack bar, and games and movies galore. But when this placed closed, the more tame hang-out, *Crowns*, was preferred. Known for its relaxed, casual, cigarette smoke-filled atmosphere, it had a juke box, tables and booths, tasty reasonably priced pizza, and other bites to eat, with cheap beer and Mekhong whiskey. These clubs were an early meeting place to jump off to an exciting evening in Bangkok, where many of us were forbidden by our parents to step foot in, but sometimes did anyway. Often, we ended up at the lounge in the Ambassador Hotel to take in a Bee Gees tribute band, enjoying mixed drinks and munching on snacks. We tried our best to fit in wherever possible, drowned our frustrations and sorrows when we couldn't, and experimented with life, trying to make it more interesting.

In this respect, we didn't really differ from teens in the States, but we had access to much more, as we spread our wings in the sprawling metropolis of Bangkok. The most prodigious difference was that we lived in a country where many of us were under the relative protection of diplomatic immunity (or the perception of it) and the lower standard of living enabled us access to many more instruments of entertainment.

We were as comfortable as newly indoctrinated children into our teen years could be. As for Karen and myself, our parents were quite different. They encouraged nighttime independence within reason and seemed happy to let us engage in whatever activities and lessons our hearts desired, as long as they didn't know exactly what we were doing or where we were going, and were happy as long as we made it home unharmed before our established curfew.

We soon discovered we could easily spend our time exploring Bangkok's canals (klongs) in the cheap fare, eardrum-piecing, wind-breaking, driver-in-the-rear klong boats. Even better was the fact that we had a station at the end of our street. Propelling these boats were unmuffled, race car-like engines that would enable the shallow drafted boats to skim across the canal waters so fast the wind would blow our hair straight back and interlace our eyelashes so tightly it was difficult to see where the boat was heading. Sunglasses were a necessity when sitting in the front seats of these boats.

Besides these economical options, we also rode the local lowest-priced, unairconditioned, no door, "Orange Crush" public buses. These were nick-named based on the poor habits and lack of courtesy exhibited by the drivers. They would often pack in as many passengers as physically possible. We typically traveled with a smidgen of a foothold in the door with 10 other passengers hanging onto a window frame, who were also hoping they wouldn't get crushed against another bus, vehicle, or a myriad of road obstacles. This option seemed better to us than being crushed within the interwoven, sweaty passengers inside the buses, crammed together in the hot, humid weather, plunging through downtown traffic for hours.

Sometimes we deferred to repeating our nostalgic memories of riding the more expensive, air-conditioned, higher-class public buses if we wanted to spend quadruple the ฿1.00 ($0.05 fare). At other times, we elected to sit in traffic inside the open-air, door-less, three-wheeled, sam law, oil and gas mixed motorized taxis (dubbed "tuk-tuk" by Thais because of the sound they made). Sitting in these tuk-tuks with so much noise deafening our ears, along with the purple-smoke air pollution asphyxiating our lungs, did as much damage as being surrounded by hundreds of chainsaws operating at peak rpm. At other times, we traveled in the less noisy, open-air, tiny, four-wheeled Daihatsu pickup truck-type taxis, ("see-law") or the more common air-conditioned or non-air-conditioned taxis.

To this day, I'm amazed how we spent so much time choking on fumes, subjected to the deafening roars emitted by the unmuffled, unregulated cars, trucks, motorcycles and buses of Bangkok traffic, none of which abided by laws and regulations for efficiently flowing traffic. We emerged relatively unscathed. Like the converging, raging waters of ocean, seas, and rivers jockeying for position amidst the chaos in tides and strides of flow, such confluences combined daily to form a mechanical traffic abatis, preventing anyone from getting anywhere in a timely, efficient, safe manner. The modern concept of social distancing is long overdue for Bangkok traffic.

Thailand was such an amalgamation of cultures so diverse, to say we experienced "culture shock" would be a gross over-simplification. Throughout the year, I went over to classmates' houses ranging from American, Indian, Thai, Chinese, Pakistani, Dutch, Afghan, German, Australian, Japanese, Malaysian, Indonesian, and more; they too were foreigners in a foreign country. We all were!

I was shocked one time when one of my friends introduced me to his family members, smiling as he said, "Hey, all of you motherfuckers, this is my friend Dimitri. He's not like any of you shitheads, he's actually a really cool guy, and I invited him over to look at some porn in my bedroom. Bye, bye." As he walked, I followed him upstairs in utter shock. He said a few phrases in Urdu (Pakistan's primary language), and they all answered in unison, "Bye, bye," all while smiling—I was shocked, if not bewildered, to say the least. "You talk to your family like that and get away with it?" "Yeah," he said laughing, "I'm the only one who speaks any English. They're clueless of what I just said." That was hilarious!

Intertwining your life with foreign cultures can be extremely interesting and beneficial. For example, there was a Dutch family whose daughters turned out to be good friends of mine and to whom I owe a great debt of gratitude for teaching me proper table manners. One evening, after spending most of the day working on a school project with my classmate, Sophie, her family invited me to stay for dinner. Formally called to the table, we quickly washed our hands and complied, taking our places, sitting silently.

First, we unfolded our napkins, placing them in our laps. I watched for examples and emulated them. As the servants began filling the water glasses at each setting around the table, they offered food to each of us as they made their rounds. Everything looked purely elegant. We each accepted portions of food from every dish [I knew from a young age it was impolite to deny anything offered]. Once served, the chit-chat started. Next came time to eat. As soon as I grabbed my fork, the subtle dinner conversation instantly ceased. Ten eyes seated around the table were glaring at me in unison, silently burning into my soul. Even the servants stopped dead in their tracks, staring directly at me. Nobody said a thing. Nobody moved. Nobody blinked. Nobody even breathed.

I looked at each one of them around the table and then down at my hand grasping my fork.

I could only muster a quick, "What's wrong?" They looked at me as if I was covered in manure, swaddled by swine. Still, nobody said a word until the father looked at the mother, then back at me, bowing his head in disbelief and total disgust.

He muttered, "You Americans really don't understand the elegance of proper dining, do you?"

I politely asked, "Excuse me, sir? I don't understand." The others remained silent except for Sophie, sitting across from me who cleared her throat trying to get my attention, looking back and forth between me, the fork in her hand, and the fork in mine.

She leaned toward me quietly and innocently said with her cute Dutch accent, whispering, "That's not the proper way how you are supposed to hold your fork. Is that really how YOU hold it?"

"Yeah why, what's wrong?" I naively responded, whispering back.

Both parents bowed their heads down and gasped, "Oh my God. Americans!" I knew I had broken some serious rules at this dinner table, perhaps even some laws, but I had no clue what they were.

Sophie whispered to me with an elegant smile, saying, "Please hold your fork like mine when you eat at this table—and no elbows on the table ever. That's how we do it here."

The father barked with unrivaled authority, "That's the proper way, the European way, and that's the way we do it in this household, thank you very much." I changed my hand position holding my fork using my thumb and forefinger (not grasping it like a machete or a bicycle handlebar) mirroring everyone else's and jerked my elbows from the edge of the table.

Slowly, I took another bite. Sophie smiled and said, "Thank you, Dimitri. Oh, and when it comes time for dessert, you hold the spoon the same way," she whispered.

Whew! All went back to normal after that. The servants started milling around, dinner conversation restarted, and a relaxed mood fell over the table. Why hadn't my parents taught me this? It seemed awfully important to know the proper etiquette in this household, yet I was clueless. I wondered where I'd been my entire life. Why wasn't I taught this "proper" way? Didn't it matter? What mattered was that now, I knew. And I would change my eating habits and meal etiquette forever. This family was full of character. I looked forward to each new moment and new dinner I spent with them.

I was less shocked when attending an event while on a quick trip with my Dad and one of his wealthy Chinese friends invited us to dine at a stag party. I had no idea how my Dad always met with such interesting, well-connected people. Dad and I were the only foreigners in the room with hundreds of people seated around a multitude of round tables, eating with chopsticks. We sat at the head table. The incident started when a gentleman at our table noticed I was holding my chopsticks the wrong way and commented on the inappropriateness of my actions, since chopsticks are never to touch or cross. "What?" I thought. I learned this method from my parents just after I could crawl. They taught me by wrapping a rubber band around the top end of the chopsticks, scissoring them to pick up my food. I quickly disagreed with the instigator, correcting him instantaneously, demonstrating my point. I had to show him I could pick up more with chopsticks using my grasping method than he could with the more conventionally accepted, but weaker, chopsticks grasping configuration used throughout Asia.

I noticed a bowl of snack peanuts on the table. I picked up one of the peanuts with my chopsticks, showing it to my challenger. He was not easily impressed, himself also picking up one peanut. Raising the bar, I picked up two peanuts side by side, displaying them over my head, showing them off to the entire room of diners. He and the surrounding tables applauded as they witnessed my feat; the word spread like wildfire throughout the room of "the young little foreigner's impromptu challenge." My Dad was more entertained by this entire spectacle than I ever remember; sitting beside him, I beamed with pride.

My challenger stood up and clapped while other tables applauded at the two-peanut feat, sitting down shortly afterward. After some serious focus and many more attempts, I placed three peanuts side-by-side in the bowl and eventually was successful in capturing all three peanuts side-by-side, once again displaying my handiwork above my head. The entire head table stood up, not believing their eyes. Standing to join them, I held the three peanuts higher over my head, somehow captured between my chopsticks; one by one, table by table, the entire room rose for a standing ovation, applauding wildly at my feat.

I had proven myself and my chopsticks-grasping prowess to be far superior to any of these challengers and the millions of Chinese throughout history who learned and taught their offspring, blindly passing down their limiting, yet conventional method, of using chopsticks. The challenger applauded at my feat even louder than the first. Suddenly, the entire room began chanting "Gambey, Gambey, Gambey, Gambey, Gambey!" In Mandarin Chinese, this means "bottoms up." The energy accompanying the rolling, thunderous roar in the room was overpowering. My challenger walked over to my seat, placing a large glass of crystal-clear beer in front of me. He cracked a large raw egg into it. Instantly the egg white, yolk, and embryo streamed down to the bottom of the glass, settling into a repulsive mass. I looked at my Dad inquisitively thinking, "Now that's

GROSS!" and he pointed to the glass, yelling over the roar of the crowd as he smiled.

My Dad said, "Bottoms up! Try to keep it down!" as he laughed.

This gave me consent to meet the challenge. I grabbed the glass in one hand, presenting the repulsive concoction overhead as I stood up. The crowd went wild. I gulped down the entire glass of beer as the room reverberated the chant. The beer gushed down my throat followed quickly by the egg yolk, white, and embryo which immediately after reaching the bottom of my stomach attempted to surge back up. It was a tremendous challenge keeping this revolting recipe choked down. But I did it, ensuring my eyes didn't water as my stomach convulsed, trying to expel the foreign matter.

This energized the crowd even more. They repeated the entire spectacle, to which I again complied with another egg-infested beer. That was nasty. Thankfully, they settled down after that; my stomach did as well. Surprisingly, I could eat the full eight-course dinner which followed. I don't know if I could've survived another one of those beers. One by one, the guests came by the table to capitulate; this night would last forever in their minds—bested by this foreign kid. Everyone had a great time. Even my Dad seemed prouder of me than I can remember. So, you see, maturing in this environment had its relevant benefits. The school year rapidly approached as these summer activities waned.

Early the next morning, my Dad took me on a long drive to the Nong Khai border with Laos, explaining very little on the way. I assumed he was helping some Drug Enforcement Agency (DEA) colleagues react to an uncorroborated spot report that members of an international smuggling ring were arriving at the local train station. If they showed up, he wanted me to conduct surveillance... uh... blend into the crowd, watch them to learn what I could, and see where they headed. Maybe we would follow them to determine where they were staying and tip off local Thai authorities. He said nobody would expect a kid to take part in such an activity, so I wouldn't be compromised if I acted normally. Do you know how hard it is to act "normal," when you're doing something completely abnormal? We arrived at the train station and I took my place looking as inconspicuous as possible, pretending to wait on the platform for someone. When the train arrived, I saw what seemed to be the men he described— I tried to determine how many in their group, remembering what I could of the suspects (what they were wearing and their demeanor), the number, size and description of their bags, and the vehicle they entered, to inform my Dad... just like in the movies.

Soon after, I came hurriedly out of the main building and my Dad picked me up in the parking lot to continue following them. Once they arrived at their destination, my Dad pulled over a couple cross streets down and made a few phone calls. We left town. A few days later, my Dad told me the authorities handled it—whatever that meant.

Impressed with my initiation, he later sponsored a trip I always wanted to take to one of Thailand's infamous smuggling points—Ranong, bordering Southern Burma; this time I would go with the Laughing Fox, Chit Sen, on a photographic expedition. Dad dubbed him the Laughing Fox because he always sported that nervous laugh, prone to emanate every minute or so, anywhere he went.

Weeks later, when the time came to go to Ranong, Dad sent me on my way with some cash, a nice camera, about 30 rolls of film, and of course my chaperone, the Laughing Fox. Off to Ranong we went.

Once there, disembarking the train, we settled into an inexpensive hotel and walked around taking photos. The next day, we rented a boat to take us around the harbor and out to the open sea, telling the driver to stay on the Thai side of the water border.

I probably took well over a thousand pictures of boat and ship traffic per my Dad's request. The trip ended abruptly after taking pictures on a local dock a few days later.

Chit Sen said, looking around the dock where I was taking pictures—instantly cleared of people, "Mr. D, we go! We go now!"

"Why?" I asked.

"Look, nobody here anymore!" he ranted. And he wasn't laughing.

He figured we got burned, compromised. We raced over to the restaurant my Dad told us about if we encountered any trouble, using what I learned years later to be a counter-surveillance technique, taking three or four taxis in different directions, ensuring we weren't followed. The restaurant owner fed us and later that night took us to the bus station, putting us on a first-class bus for the nine-hour ride back to Bangkok. Boarding the bus out of the balmy heat of the still air, we were greeted by a stewardess who handed us a box meal, a cold towel, and a cold drink after we sat in our assigned seats. Expecting a relaxing ride once we got out of town, the bus came to an unexpected stop—it was a random border patrol checkpoint.

Chit Sen freaked out, saying he didn't have documentation with him and they would most likely arrest him. Quickly and surreptitiously changing seats to give him the window seat, together we devised a plan of avoidance by pretending that he was asleep. I hoped for the best outcome as the uniformed officials slowly approached the back of the bus toward us. My heart throbbed. To prevent my hands from trembling, I clutched my pant legs with my fingers. My head pounded from the possibility of Chit Sen being apprehended. I didn't know what to do in such a case, as I never imagined such a scenario; apparently neither had my Dad.

I tried to relax myself and remain calm. An officer aggressively approached our seats, asking me for identification. I slowly and as calmly as possible presented my Embassy identification card to him. He pointed his chin toward Chit Sen and asked about him. I muttered in Thai he was my friend and was asleep because he was feeling sick. He stared at the quietly sleeping Laughing Fox momentarily, passing us, heading toward the back of the bus. On his way back to the front of the bus, he continued glaring at us. I ignored him.

As soon as the Border Patrol guards departed the bus, I felt instant relief. Chit Sen didn't move for about ten minutes afterward before sitting upright, ensuring we were clear of the prying eyes of the checkpoint guards. The rest of the night was uneventful, aside from the onboard stewardess clearing the bus out to get the coach cleaned and making sure she seated us appropriately in the open-air restaurant for the all-you-can-eat meal (included in the ticket price of ฿900, about US$40). Reboarding the bus at 0100 am, the next major event was the early morning wake up of coffee or Ovaltine and Thai donut, once again presented by the same lovely stewardess, along with a hot face towel, all-inclusive in the ticket price. This was a successful summer time trip and Dad told me he put the photos to good use.

~ 2 ~

A New Dawn / En ny Gryning

Another tremendous opportunity afforded me was when one of my Dad's sources, I only knew as Mr. Kong, asked if I'd be willing to support his local Rotary Club's foreign student exchange program. He lived in the rural town of Sisaket, in the province of the same name along the Cambodian border. The plan was for me to travel to spend part of my summer with the family who was participating in a foreign exchange program with Australia. Their son would go to Australia, and a girl of the same age would take his place in Sisaket. Like she would do, I was to live with the family, and go to school with their children during my summer break. This would be the entire small border town's first opportunity to meet a foreigner in the flesh.

In typical CIA fashion, I was given a handwritten note to provide the pedicab driver in order to bring me to Mr. Kong's house upon my arrival. One day, off I went by myself on the long train ride. Arriving at the train station, I handed the note to a pedicab driver who nodded his head. I got in. After driving around aimlessly for about 40 minutes, I asked the pedicab driver where he was going, to which he responded, he didn't know. When I showed him the handwritten note, he admitted he didn't know how to read. This was my introduction to the tiny rural town of Sisaket, and this would not be my first surprise. Eventually, we asked around and found someone who could read to get the directions.

Aside from Mr. Kong, nobody in the town spoke any English. They ate only Thai cuisine, watched only Thai programs on television, and only watched Thai movies at the theaters [unless they were dubbed without English subtitles]. During the first week of school, I was invited to eat with the rest of the school at the cafeteria; everyone ate together in an open-air atrium. I was seated at the head table nearest a stage, equipped with a Marshall stacked amplifier, an electric guitar, and a microphone. Toward the end of the meal, I asked the Principal/headmaster if there was entertainment during lunch. To which he responded, "Mr. Kong say you play guitar and sing, so please. Thank you very much," immediately ushering me to the stage. Once the butterflies subsided, I had fun entertaining as best I could. After a few encores, thankfully the Headmaster cut short my impromptu mini-concert telling everyone it was time to go to class. This was great news for me as I was quickly running out of songs.

This school was my first introduction to school uniforms, numerous unique festivals and ceremonies, military-style school formations for the national anthem, often followed by the caning of students to be punished. Life was very different in this extremely rural border area. I enjoyed the challenge and looked forward to the few times Mr. Kong visited, taking me out for day trips visiting ruins and historical sites on the Cambodian border. Except for a bout with malaria and heatstroke, life was good. When it came time for me to return to Bangkok, after paving the way for her, I met the Australian girl, offering as many pointers as I could over the few days I had, to successfully prepare her for what was to come.

Back at home in Bangkok, as usual, mornings entailed a leisurely, healthy breakfast with fresh fruit, cereal, an omelet, juice, yogurt, and cinnamon toast or pancakes prepared by our cook and served by the houseboy. Today was the day I would become an adult—a real, live, grown-up. I finally made it to the big time. Today was orientation day at my new junior high school. Yep, I was a Senior in junior high school now—I would be an 8th grader! This was it! In my mind, I was almost a complete grown-up, though my body still needed to do a bit of growing up!

Today, my Mom and our eternally happy driver, Daen, were taking me on the long, air-conditioned car ride out toward the Don Muang airport near the Bangsue District, where my newest school was located. It was about an hour and a half drive from the sanctuary of our multi-acre-sized yard, artfully landscaped surrounding our Embassy-provided rental house. We would sit in typically heavy city traffic for the foreseeable future. This was long before any of the elevated highways or above ground rail transport systems existed, as they do today in Bangkok. Our time spent commuting through traffic in those days was a much bigger time investment than it is these days.

Taking an air-conditioned private car on the hour and a half long journey to the junior high school campus by the airport was truly a special treat. This ride symbolized to me yet another journey into the vast unknown. I silently stared out the window, wondering what to expect this time at my new school. My Mom accompanying me was as comforting as always during this strange new experience. Next year, I would accompany Karen on her mere 20-minute ride to the high school campus where the real grown-ups went to school—THAT was really going to be a blast! One more year to go! I was twelve-teen now, and next year, I knew I'd surely be an adult; well, once I became a teenager and got into high school I would be, so I thought.

As the driver pushed through the smog in the vehicle log jam, our journey would be prophetically typical and uneventful. Once we arrived at the campus, we drove through heavily fortified, guarded steel gates, opened for visitors that morning. We drove toward the large, white-washed school building sporting a huge gold-embossed Hanuman emblem, a character in Thai mythology which is half-man and half-monkey. The school affixed the emblem to the building above the main entrance, which bore the words the "International School of Bangkok (ISB)." The car stopped and Daen jumped out, opening the door for me. I hesitantly exited then looked up at the tall, wide, white-washed building adorned with the huge gold emblem. I was immediately in awe. "Okay, we're here, let's go, you don't want to be late!" my Mom barked. The driver promptly drove away as we exited, and Mom walked me into the main building, following the signs until she confirmed I knew where to go. She tried kissing me on the cheek as I moved away, looking around to make sure nobody saw. "Mom," I annoyingly whined as she smiled and walked to join the other parents in the parents' refreshment room. She was as patient as always for the few hours I was at the orientation.

I was glad she was there, though I pretended not to know her as all real "grown-ups" do when entering unfamiliar settings in this new "grown-up world." She accompanied me to help me relax and did what Moms do best, just be there. She let me do everything myself once we arrived. I appreciated this, though on the inside I wasn't initially thrilled with the prospect.

There was a lot to do: I found my way to the orientation room following the signs posted in the hallways, listened to the briefings, registered for my classes, got my pre-class reading assignments, participated in a quick guided tour of the broken glass and barbed wire topped, walled campus, got my assigned locker and combination lock, picked up my books and school supplies. I registered for the school bus and got a picture ID card and a bus pass, for use until the bus monitor and driver remembered what we looked like and where we lived along their route. For security reasons in Bangkok, the school bus picked up everyone at their front gates.

I liked the school grounds instantly upon seeing them. Guided into the gym, around the foosball and table tennis (ping pong) tables, badminton, tennis, takraw, and volleyball courts, onto the soccer field, around the lunch area we roamed. I also instantly liked the Vice-Principal, Mrs. Aroon, when we met for the first time during orientation. I would confirm later that year, she never missed an opportunity to introduce herself as the consummate professional she was. A prim and properly educated woman she was a product of formal English upbringing with an influential and well-connected Thai husband. She loved her job and seemed to love being around the youthful, energetic presence of us growing up kids. As far as we were concerned (my soon-to-be-classmates), we liked the bully free atmosphere and seemed to like all those who were soon to be our classmates; I liked most of them, anyway. Black, white, yellow, red, brown complexions, Christian, Muslim, Sikh, Animist, Hindu alike. Animosity and racism didn't exist here. To us, we were all grown-up kids looking forward to a new school year.

This was a completely different world from the months we spent on home leave in the rough Boston suburbs of West Somerville, Massachusetts. The mild-mannered, friendly Lao kids of Vientiane were a far cry from the rumbling, bumbling, rough, tough, street kids of West Somerville who spoke and acted like the thugs their parents were. They admired those who stole and torched cars, got involved in "gang fights," mugged younger kids for their lunch money, beat up other kids because they wanted to, and got arrested plainly because there was nothing else better they could think of to do. Away from all of that, I was now back in a serene international school setting in Thailand; I felt right at home.

I saw a few kids I had met a few weeks prior at the Teen Club, but most were new. I didn't talk to anyone during orientation other than a friendly greeting. We were all inwardly focused and not only apprehensive of the prospect of attending a new school, but this time we would have to find our classes ourselves. Aimlessly wandering through the hallways and byways, finding the right classroom on time would indeed be challenging. In most local Thai schools, only the teachers moved from classroom to classroom.

But like in other schools, we would remain all year in the same classroom and in the same chairs set in stone by the teacher's student desk map, with whoever surrounded us on the first day. This aspect of school wouldn't change, so in every class we prepared to choose who surrounded us wisely, based on peoples' looks and whichever personal profile qualities we could quickly discern. This new environment, while stressful, seemed like it would be much more fun. So far, I looked forward to the start of school this year as much as a grown-up kid could. And I was more excited than apprehensive.

As the formal portion of the orientation wrapped up, I put most of my books and school supplies into my locker, bringing home a few for the homework requiring completion before class began, as shown by the syllabus. I had only a few weeks. Walking back to the car where familiar smiles greeted me, Mom, in her typical motherly fashion, deemed this day a complete success. Convinced now more than ever, to me, this was the merely uneventful precursor to another terrifying ordeal in life where I dare not fail. Soon I would have to face the fact of being less than perfect, judged by others in virtually every aspect of my life. As the summer days drew quickly to their unenviable ends, the fun would soon wane. Today, I looked forward to getting home as quickly as the traffic would allow.

School mornings would begin with either the maid or cook waking me up to start our day and asking us what we'd like for breakfast. House dogs at our feet, parrots and other exotic birds chirping and taunting us from their cages, in the cool comfort provided by the many window-mounted air-conditioning units cooling the tepid, humid air atop the highly polished teakwood floors throughout the house and the cool tiled floors in the kitchen. The household kitchen staff served relatively elaborate meals at our request. This was a wonderful life as it was.

The school bus, like a personal chauffeur, picked me up at the front gate, taking me to school and dropping me back off, where I had to finish hours of homework, sit down for a chef-prepared family dinner, go back upstairs to finish homework, and finally watch about an hour of television Finally, the night would end with a stove-popped bowl of popcorn or a bowl of ice cream before going to bed, starting the entire cycle over again the next morning.

~ 3 ~

Growing Up / Växa Upp

I n a flash, the first day of school was upon me. It was as hectic as any other school morning that year would be, yet I looked forward to many more; mostly because I had no choice. The maid or the cook woke us up at 5:30 am. I jumped up, made my bed, picked up my room (so the maid wouldn't have to - I did this as a matter of pride before their second round of wake-up calls). I showered in my private bathroom, got dressed, made sure I had my homework, and ran down the shiny, waxed teakwood stairs, grasping the banister along the way so I wouldn't slip and fall; I only made that mistake once.

I greeted the maid and the cook with a, "Good morning!" and made sure I greeted the dogs along the way as they took their usual places underneath the dining room table, patiently awaiting morsel treats as they lay on the sparkling clean floor. I sat down alone to my mini feast since my sister could sleep in because she didn't have a long commute to her school. Our cook, wanting to ensure I enjoyed eating her heart-felt creations, peered out the window of the kitchen door into the dining room. I gulped down the culinary delights as quickly as possible, with both the cook and housekeeper providing time hacks for how many minutes before the school bus was expected to be at the front gate ringing the buzzer.

I finished breakfast and quickly yelled out, "Bye Mom!" not that she was anywhere in sight and Dad was long gone to work. I ran out the door as the maid handed me my lunch with the prowess of an Olympic baton runner, preventing me from forgetting the critical package in my haste, attempting to not miss the bus. I snatched the lunch bag from the smiling maid's outstretched arm while she simultaneously held open the door, expediting my swift exit. I barely heard my Mom yelling from the top of the stairs, "Have a good day at school!" As I quick-stepped out the front door I heard the buzzer from the front gate buzzing, which meant the bus was outside the gate waiting for me. I flew down the slick, shiny, concrete front stairs with my book bag on one shoulder and my lunch in hand and after one more quick, "Goodbye!"

I was off running down the acre-long circular driveway which cut across our three-acre well-manicured lawn, hastily heading toward the broken glass-topped, ten-foot concrete perimeter wall. The awaiting bus monitor once again rang the annoying buzzer at the front gate. I opened the impenetrable steel-walled gate with my free hand, ensuring it locked behind me so the dogs wouldn't follow me; this was imperative. I greeted the bus monitor, displayed my school ID card, and jumped onto the impatiently idling school bus. Whew! This was the first of many early morning hour-and-a-half-long bus rides to school.

Upon entering the bus, I had to make a hasty decision which peer pressure would compel me to comply with for the rest of the year. Where to sit? This was a tough decision, as I was only the fifth person on the route. Those already seated were temporarily quiet and shy. Most of the kids on the bus at this point of the route were elementary school kids and way younger than me—

wouldn't you know it! Once they made friends on the bus, their volume of decibels and intensity of interaction would undoubtedly increase. For now, I enjoyed the quiet.

I sat on the right side of the little bus to see my dogs through the ornamental iron gates as we departed. My sister wasn't on this bus, and at this point in my life, I was okay with being on my own. I'd be alone for this upcoming next year anyhow, making new friends and having my own conversations as the bus waded through heavy traffic or flood waters on the way to the junior high campus in Bangsue near the Don Muang International Airport.

A few houses down from me were two kids close to my age, Robert and his sister, Julie. I looked forward to picking them up next. I first met Robert at the Teen Club and since then, we spent a lot of time with each other, becoming best of friends. We both had semi-ferocious Doberman Pincher guard dogs, we both had annoying sisters, and we both adopted our Dads' golf and tennis interests. These similarities significantly solidified our friendship.

When they got on the bus, typically, they were snapping at each other. Robert was smiling most likely because he was ribbing his little sister about something, and she was smirking most likely, envisioning how she was going to provide a full report to their parents upon returning home about how he made fun of her. The multitude of words and actions exchanged by these two were primal and defensive. Julie never really did much smiling so early in the morning—as a little brother myself, I never experienced the luxury of being able to pick on a younger sibling.

At the next stop, Rick got on with his two sisters, Louise and Jean-Marie. Rick was quiet yet full of energy and would soon be the bass player in the rock band we formed with myself as the lead singer and two others, Paul, our very skilled lead guitarist of Filipino descent, and our rhythm guitar and "leader/enforcer/instigator/shyster," Dean.

Incidentally, Dean didn't ride the bus since he lived farther away; his parents had a driver named Chai, who took him to school every day. Extremely spoiled he was. Paul lived in another area and took a different bus. After a short distance, a very attractive, quiet girl subtlety named Stephanie, got on the bus. A delicate girl of Asian and American descent, she was extremely shy, polite, intelligent, health conscious, thin, prim, proper, and always conservatively dressed. She was also in our class, but different, in that she always had something nice to say about everyone she talked to or about, always.

We made a few more stops, picking up a tall, larger kid named Bernard and his sister, Eileen. They never said much and kept pretty much to themselves. By the time these other kids boarded the bus, a few of us were so embroiled in conversation, we didn't really notice anyone else until the last house on the route. All conversations stopped at this house. It was a beautiful, three-story mansion with a professionally landscaped yard, adorned by a Mercedes Benz limousine and a Ferrari parked outside the garage. The gardener opened the gate so the bus could turn around in the circular driveway on this narrow dead-end road. Two gorgeous, much younger, bobble-headed elementary school girls got on the bus at this house, Christina and Jennifer. The older one, Christina, called her sister "The Mexican," because of her tanned complexion. They consistently squabbled between themselves. This completed the students on our bus and at this point, we were headlong into the busy Bangkok traffic, sluggishly moving toward the airport.

This was the first and probably most quiet of the hour and a half long bus rides we'd take to school over the next year. Nobody yet knew what to say, whom to say it to, or what to talk about— thank God for air-conditioning. It drowned out conversations more than a few seats away in the summer months and made the ride quite bearable. I still can't believe with the volume of traffic we faced daily, how we ever got to school or got home on time.

Since ours was an English-speaking International School, as most are, we had a relatively small student body. Few of the Thai public could afford the exorbitant $25,000 per year tuition for primary and secondary schools here at ISB. Who were our classmates? Mostly the children of upper-crust Southeast Asian successful merchants, politicians, embassy employees, airline executives, senior government workers, and children of corporate leaders in blue-chip companies. Also in attendance were missionary family members from a variety of countries, many of whom lived in a boarding hostel near the high school campus. At school, we socialized with all of them, encapsulating a wide diversity of age groups, cultures, experiences, and personalities. Typically, the friends we made in school were the best friends we had. The graduating classes were small, at an average of about 90 students. We cherished our classmates regardless of religion, physical characteristics, clothing style, moodiness, and a host of other factors. Either they were friends, or they weren't. Unbeknownst to us, we would carry many of these friendships into adulthood.

This first ride of the year would be the first of many typical bus rides to school. Along the busy city streets, we would see the occasional store owner rolling up or opening horizontal metal shop doors and shutters for another day of business. Other shop owners busily swept the area in front of their shops, as the dust rose into the already polluted air. Families wandered downstairs from 2nd floor living areas int the shop houses for breakfast. People of all classes and occupations were milling around, going about their daily lives. The bus made its way through the maze of cars, buses, bicycles, motorcycles, tuk-tuks, samlohs, and nearly every type of vehicle imaginable, spewing out 2-stroke and diesel, oily, purple smoke. Newer vehicles sported invisible yet still toxic fumes. The noise outside the bus was deafening, thankfully drowned out by the bus air conditioner.

Jaywalking pedestrians of all ages dotted the streets and byways wherever they pleased to cross. They did so on these insanely busy, crowded streets, crisscrossing virtually everywhere. Typically, we'd see a family of four driving to their destination atop a single motorcycle, with no helmets or safety gear. Screeching tires, the resounding metal to metal thud of two vehicles colliding, followed instantaneously by the shattering of broken glass littering the roadway after impact, became commonplace to us. Sometimes this sound and spectacle involved a motorcyclist scantily clad in street clothes with open-toed shoes sliding across the hard concrete, or similarly hazardous asphalt road surface. Blood residue sometimes staining the roadway and at other times, bleeding victims of such accidents picking themselves up from the street in shock, were also common during our daily commute. Fellow students on the bus either turned away from the wreckage or flocked to the nearest window not to miss a second of the excitement, at the expense of the victims. Otherwise, we succumbed to another dull commute. The memories of a few of these inexpressibly gruesome accidents cross my mind occasionally. Attempting to black out these flashbacks rarely works. These are memories that will never be completely erased, regardless of how hard I try.

The occasional breakfast or fresh fruit carts were pushed to their point of business for the day, completely run by human power. These would provide early morning pedestrians their first few calories of nourishment for the day. Customers would stop to purchase their morning coffee or tea and maybe have a deep-fried donut type pastry to dunk into their hot beverage of choice, usually dark coffee or red Thai tea doused with evaporated milk. Sometimes these drinks were dumped into a plastic bag to go with or without ice, depending on the purchaser's preference, and carried by a rubber band attached to the top of the bag where the vendor inserted a straw for convenient sipping. If you could imagine a complete tiny Starbucks store on a cart, including an enormous pot of boiling water heated by a hand-stoked fire underneath, with serving cups and saucers, and a handful of chairs and tables transported atop, you'd not be far off. Some people milled around talking to others while drinking their hot drinks, others sat down on chairs and stools provided by the vendor. This was the hustle and bustle beginning early on Bangkok streets each weekday. I really don't know how the bus made it to our campus in ostensibly an hour and a half.

After what seemed like forever, the bus arrived at the gated and well-guarded school compound with the large gold embossed ISB Hanuman sign affixed to the main high-rise tower. It felt eerily like watching characters in a movie entering a prison yard as the bus drove past the gate guards and into the motor pool/dismount area. The bus monitor stood up, smiled, and said in English through a cute Thai accent, "Sawadee Kha. Okay, helloooo. Wencome to dah Internatchoonun Schoon of Bangkok. Dis ist duh Bangsue Camput, hab a goos day! See you again in the aptahnoon! If you don lemembuh the numbuh ob da buts, look foh me. Mye nem is KahTehRine. Thhang yoo. Hab a goose daye. Bye, bye." Most of this speech turned out to be the same, day after day, month after month, from every bus monitor. This repetition was strangely comforting in a world so dynamic and new to me, away from my previously restrictive school environment of 7th grade. I came to love being a "senior" here in "junior" high. I believed I hit the big time now, and I was a little adult.

We followed the gaggle of bobble-headed, little people off the bus until they split off toward their elementary school buildings, and we ventured into the large five-story, high-rise building where we pre-teen adults would mold our futures. We were the oldest young students on this campus; this was nice for a change!

"So is the bus monitor's name "KahTehRin" or "KhaTuhRine?"" Robert teased to poke fun of the bus monitor's strong Thai accent as we walked up the stairs accessing any of the five floors, then into the open-air hallways.

"Very funny, it's Catherine," I answered with a smile, "At least she's nice."

"Yeah, she is! Nice tits too!" he grunted.

As we climbed the stairs to our lockers, we noticed students on each floor sitting on long, composite concrete benches, or standing atop these, leaning against the cyclone fencing which protected us from falling or jumping. This fencing allowed plenty of "freshly" polluted Bangkok city air for us to breathe. We had a great view of some nearby green landscaped lots and the highway in the background.

Across from these benches were classroom walls, with naturally stained teakwood doors opening to seemingly hermetically sealed, individually air-conditioned classrooms along the string of open-air hallways. Each floor looked identical, as did each door. Only the tiny numbers atop the door frames differentiated the classrooms. Even though I registered here for school a few weeks ago, to my amazement it looked quite familiar.

We walked up the stairs to the second floor and silently made our way to our lockers, coincidentally, located right next to each other. Somehow, I remembered the combination to my lock and opened it. I double-checked my class schedule with Robert, grabbed the appropriate books, and started the trek to our first class. As we journeyed down the long hallway towards the open-air concrete and composite stairways, we only had to walk up one floor to our first class. I memorized the route to our first class during orientation.

Turning the corner, and as Robert and I continued walking, I remember thinking, "Oh my God..." when I first saw her. There she was. The most beautiful girl I'd ever seen. And she was right in front of me. A tall (taller than me anyway), thin, gorgeous young girl sporting a full head of angelic, naturally blond hair extending barely past her shoulders, almond-shaped piercing deep blue eyes, a soft, gently shaped nose smoothed to perfection, full red lips, a gleaming smile with a full set of pearly white teeth she was not shy to show off, and lightly tanned, baby soft skin. She wore, in contemporary European fashion, extremely tight designer jeans, a tight, light colored buttoned-down blue and white striped, long-sleeved, collared shirt rolled up to her mid forearms. Both stretched across the most amazing perfect form of a human female body I'd ever seen. She was walking by herself, toward us, seemingly in slow motion, smiling.

As she approached, I noticed her beautifully manicured fingers and matching French-tipped toenails peeking out from her flat, brown, leather sandals. Her smile was sensual yet demure. Her aura exuded kindness and friendship, her poise confident and her stride purposeful.

Before that day, I had only glanced at such perfection on the pages of Robert's girly magazines he stashed under his mattress. I stopped dead in my tracks, gazing at her as she approached. My heart stopped. My breath was still in my chest, my lungs quivered for oxygen. I couldn't think of how to spark my brain to communicate to my lungs to draw in another breath or risk passing out. Typically, breathing for me was an autonomic physical response; it wasn't now. Not after I saw this creation of absolute beauty for the very first time. Nor would it be any time after that. I couldn't think clearly. I couldn't move. I couldn't do anything but stare. And stare I did.

My feet refused to move as she brushed by me in the comfortably crowded hallway. Our eyes met, and she smiled and murmured, "Hallo," continuing past, presumably on the way to her first class. I detected a slight scent of herbal shampoo. It was notably overpowering to me, though, most likely quite subtle. My senses were at their peak awareness regarding anything involving her. And just like her, her scent was soft, subtle, and significant. Also, just like her, seemed to disappear as suddenly as she appeared.

My eyes, head, and body sequentially turned to follow her presence. As she passed, I couldn't help myself, I couldn't stop staring. My eyes affixed onto her like a revolving lighthouse light in a dense, foggy night. "WoWWW!" was all I thought and was all I could say. That hair, that face, that smile, that nose, that body, that shirt, those jeans, those fingers, those toes, "WoWWW! Did you see her?" I held my gaze in awe as she slipped by us in the crowded hallway.

I regained a slight awareness of consciousness as Robert's manly, prematurely well-developed, deep voice emerged beside me, verbally slapping me as he playfully nudged by me, chuckling while I still held my gaze in awe. "What's the matter? Never seen a girl before, idiot?" he blurted, following up with an unfettered laugh. I never knew him for his discretion or subtle comments. That's how Robert was. Thankfully, he didn't obscure my view, because that would have abrogated the silent, but sacred, guy code. He turned to join me in gawking at this angelic vision as she floated down the hallway.

"Robert, that's not a girl...that's a woman... an angel... a goddess... WoWWW! Is she real? You can see her, right? Oh my God, I can't believe my eyes!" We both stared in amazement until she turned into a stairwell and was no longer visible. Even as she left our view, I still found comfort in knowing I would most likely see her again; when your entire class is less than 90 people, this is a guarantee. "WoWWW! You saw her, right? I didn't imagine her, did I?" was all I could think of to say.

"Yeah... she's okay." Robert quibbled, "Now we know you're not gay! Hey come on! We gotta get to class... come onnn, let's go, you're gonna make me late, moron. I don't want to get in trouble on the first day of school, idiot!" he muttered as he tugged my shirt toward our intended direction of travel, since he sensed I was in no condition to navigate anywhere independently. Thankfully, we were in the same first class together. Robert had a unique way of snapping me back to reality, as quickly as if he slapped a cold, wet, smelly fish across my face. He did this remarkably well; I think he quite enjoyed it too!

We walked and talked, picking up the pace, now with more purpose. Robert added, "Yeah okay, she's cute, but hey, there are a lot of cute girls in this school," as he oohed and nudged me.

"What?" I blurted, "Cute girls? Not like that! Not like her. She's not cute, Robert; she's absolutely gorgeous! I was still in awe and nudged Robert back.

"She's out of your league," he demanded.

"What?" I asked, pretending not to hear him. I didn't know if I didn't hear him, didn't want to listen, or didn't want to believe it.

"You heard me, she's way out of your league, idiot!" Robert repeated. "Did you see how tall she is?" he added.

I had crushes on Scandinavian-looking girls in my brief past, but this girl was different. Very different. I looked back down the hallway to where I last saw her, hoping to catch another glimpse of any residual energy she may have left behind in her wake. At first, I didn't respond or look at Robert. He probably felt like at that point he finally crossed the line by completely crushing my feelings. Or maybe not, after all, this was Robert I'm talking about.

"Yeah, I saw… so what?" I defended my position.

"Come on, idiot, let's go! Let's get to class; you're gonna make me late. Like I said, I'm not getting in trouble on the first day!"

Robert stepped ahead and led the charge toward the classroom with me in tow close behind, as we speed-walked closer to our goal, attempting to beat the bell. We scooted along on our way, while I remained in awe and still dazed by what I saw. I couldn't believe my eyes.

"WoWWW! Who was she? WoWWW!" Robert ignored my comments.

The bell rang just as we opened the door, crossing the threshold of the classroom. Already seated, our new classmates sat quietly as we entered the room. We froze in place as all eyes affixed on us, as if we busted into a bank brandishing guns yelling, "This is a stickup!" Before we could celebrate our victorious timely arrival with a happy dance, the teacher sternly fixed her eyes, burning with rage right through us.

She cackled, "Gentlemen, the standard in this classroom is YOU are to be seated BEFORE the bell rings... NEVER forget this! Take your seats and don't EVER let this happen again!" pointing to two empty seats next to each other in the middle of the classroom.

Robert leered at me with raised eyebrows, standing motionless, saying nothing, obviously blaming me for our tie with the bell. I silently motioned him with a head nod to go forward. Robert sat down first and I sat in the seat in front of him. Melting into my seat, I silently analyzed the room, noting all the unfamiliar faces, the backs of heads, and then the teacher who was older than I expected. Everyone was silent. There was nothing familiar about this room. I didn't know anyone but Robert. The teacher seemed like she might be nice, once she settled down, but I knew she would be extremely strict. At our age and circumstance, having friendly teachers was critical.

"I trust you've all done your reading assignment... and have your American History textbook with you," she continued.

I turned around in my desk abruptly whispering, "Was she real? Huh? You saw her right, the Angel, right?" I asked Robert under my breath.

"I'm not going to discuss it anymore... shut up! What are you high?" he sparked.

"Yeah... I'm high on the Scandinavian Angel I just saw. WoWWW!" I smirked.

"Give it up, she's out of your league; she's probably dating a tenth grader anyway," he whispered, mocking me. "Like I said, she's way out of your league!" he continued to stammer in a slightly louder tone.

"How do you know?" I quipped.

"Duh, she's taller than you, prettier, and... just forget it, okay? Just accept it—she's out of your league! Turn around already, you're gonna get me sent to the Principal's office, moron! Shut up already!"

"GENTLEMEN! Is this seating arrangement going to be a problem?" the teacher growled. I snapped around and responded.

"No ma'am."

School had officially started. I was in 8th grade... finally a senior in junior high school! I was here! I was a grown-up! This was it!

I kept thinking about the angel throughout class and during the classes afterward. I couldn't get her out of my mind. She was gorgeous and accompanied by an unexplainable positive energy that surrounded her. Her positive aura captured me like a tractor beam. I didn't understand it. I couldn't think of anything but her. It seemed like I'd met her before, yet I hadn't. It seemed I'd seen her before, but I hadn't. It seemed as if I knew her before, but I couldn't have. It felt as if I'd been with her before, but that wasn't possible. Then what could explain this instantaneous, intense reaction to her?

I had a few more classes devoid of Robert's taunting, and I hadn't seen her again. And I wasn't fortunate enough to have any classes with her yet. Maybe it was a blessing, securing my goal of above a 3.0 grade point average (GPA) letting me concentrate, with no temptation or risk of my mind wandering if she was nearby.

As previously agreed, I met Robert at our lockers for lunch. When I arrived, he was putting his books away. Approaching him, I fell against my locker while still standing, playfully fumbling through a few combination sequences on my lock, and pretended to bump into his locker to mess with him.

"Ohhhhhhh, WoWWW! What a woman," I moaned, "I can't think of anything but her! What's the combination to my lock? I can't think… I can't remember… I can't think of anything but HER!" I said as I leaned against his locker.

"OH PALEEZE," Robert groaned. "Let's just go to lunch. SHUT UP! Gimme a break! Are you still ranting on about that foreign girl, AGAIN? Come on, let's go… I'm not waiting for you this time—we're gonna miss lunch! Let's just go—Hey," he sparked, "You might see her at the cafeteria/snack bar or whatever they call it here."

That did it! Instantly convinced, I rushed to open my locker. Without hesitation, I threw my books into my locker, slammed the door, locked it, and hopped down the hallway. I was in the lead for once.

"I thought you didn't remember your combination?" he taunted as he speed-walked to catch up with me.

"I didn't… until you mentioned those magic words, 'You might see her down there!' Come on. Let's go!" Off we went.

"We're all foreigners here in Thailand, you know," I taunted, lambasting his last comment.

"What?" he retorted.

"That gorgeous, perfectly formed, wonder of a woman is a foreigner—like us, you know!"

"SHUT UP! Let's go! Give it a break! Why are you so obsessed?" he verbally spewed.

We wandered downstairs out of the main building, toward the outdoor gymnasium, over to the Foremost brand (found throughout Asia) snack bar/food court of sorts. It was a covered, open-air, outdoor area where the entire junior high population ate lunch.

"Yessss," I said.

My head was on a swivel as Robert sneered at me. He knew exactly who I was looking for. We stood in one of the short lines, bought our food, and went over to a few picnic benches under some picnic tables covered with curved, thatched roofs. Even though I brought my lunch that day, I wanted to seem cool until I knew some people. I could always eat my lunch the cook provided me on the bus ride home or feed it to a stray dog.

It was hot and humid, yet calm, sitting in the shade of the covered picnic tables on this slightly breezy, cloudless day. So many kids were playing so many sports simultaneously. There was the 3,000-year-old game we call soccer, which incidentally is an American aberration to the formal name Association Football [or footbol]. Early Americans referred to the "assoc" becoming "soc" or "soccer" as we call it today—in Thailand, they called it footbol, like the rest of the world. Badminton, basketball, tennis, dodge ball, tether ball, table tennis (ping pong), volleyball, field hockey, and takraw were also being played by these kids.

I'd never seen so many active young adults before in my entire life. They were everywhere. And most of them, well we too, were foreigners. There were Afghans, Persians and other Middle Easterners, Indians, Pakistanis, Sri Lankans, Europeans, Americans, Canadians, South Americans, Russians, Chinese,

Japanese, Guamanians and other Pacific Islanders, Australians, Laotians, Burmese, Malaysians, Indonesians, Cambodians, and of course, Thais. This was probably the most friendly, diverse group of people I'd ever seen, and I spent my entire life up to this point growing up in the U.S. Embassy circuit in Southeast Asia. This group was unique for some reason. But I didn't know it at the time. Robert and I would spend most of our lunch time playing with many of these guys, sharing their food, their customs, their jokes, and their skills at soccer, badminton, volleyball, and table tennis.

For about an hour, I was aghast with the number of kids playing sports, while Robert and I were stuffing our gullets, preparing for the rest of the day's classes. Where was the Viking Princess? It seemed impossible. She was nowhere to be found. Somehow, she just vanished. Once again, my head was on a swivel as I spoke and joked with Robert.

This time Robert did more than sneer, "What's your problem? Whutcha lookin' for, IDIOT?" he teased.

"You know," I snapped as I finished up my lunch.

He snickered, saying, "THAT?" as he silently pointing to the main building behind me where the Princess was coming out of the library, walking down the stairs with her designer jeans, buttoned-down blouse, and flat leather sandals. From this vantage point, I could see her thin, perfectly proportioned legs and once again her amazingly manicured toes coming into focus.

"Shit!" I stood up, grabbing and tossing away my trash and remnants of lunch, making a beeline toward her, blurting, "Come on, we gotta go—damn, check out those manicured fingers and toes!"

"You can't see them from way over here!" Robert jeered, following behind me.

"Wanna bet? Then how'd I know she was wearing sandals? Come on, you're gonna make me miss her—hurry up!"

Launching out of the lunch area, down the covered open-air walkway toward the Princess who now was walking down the stairs toward us, I began trotting, then turned to snap at Robert.

"Come on! You're gonna make me miss her!"

A clearly authoritarian voice with a proper English accent suddenly beamed down from the heavens, attracting our attention, instantly stopping us in our tracks. We slowly turned to face the voice emanating from around a few tall bushes.

"Now, now, boys, please no running. You could get hurt! What's the rush all about? Huh? You've clearly got plenty of time for lunch left to go… the bell won't ring for yet another…" She said, glancing at her watch.

This short silver-haired, tall, slender, pointy-nosed woman close to her 50s continued, "… another thirty minutes. Surely you don't plan on NOT exercising today. You're gonna get fat with such habits, even at your young age. You're not in America anymore, gentlemen. When in Rome…" she snickered. "Go meet some kids, get out and enjoy the sunshine. Get out there and play while you're young enough to enjoy it."

"Yes ma'am," we sang in unison.

That was our Vice-Principal, Mrs. Aroon. We would become quite familiar with her as she would typically pop up in the strangest of places and always with her jovial, yet authoritarian tone of voice. It was like she knew everything! She was careful never to get too close to us emotionally, but she seemed to be everywhere. And she was different. Her concern for us was sincere, for all of us. At first, she seemed a bit like a prison warden who wanted to get to know her inmates. But in time, we realized she reserved a place in her heart for all her students. She encouraged us to be productive citizens of whichever society, motivating us to contribute the most we could. At every opportunity, she planted the seeds for us to be Ambassadors of Life itself, as we all became.

I never knew a Principal, Vice-Principal, or Administrator like her before, and never did again. Everyone liked her, despite her seemingly tough demeanor. She always had our best interests at heart. Until attending this school, I'd never even seen an Administrator unless I was in trouble for some dress code infraction or something. Mrs. Aroon became our ardent, mild-mannered, in-school champion, motivator, rule-broker, dress code, and time enforcer. She never raised her voice, yelled, or was abusive to anyone. We knew her unmistakably as the Headmistress.

We saw no other adults emerge from the Administrative office, and certainly not someone who did rounds among the students, getting to know us all as individuals. She alone seemed to provide leadership and guidance during these formative years, along with a sense of caring and discipline. She kept the leash tight and firm, only to guide us into our futures, as she thought best. Even years later, she was breaking up a fight between one of my soccer-skilled, fearless Afghan friends and a typically renowned high school trouble maker on the high school campus.

Out of nowhere she appeared, sternly stating to my friend who was somehow atop this tall beast of a man preparing to pummel him, "Now, now Kandar, you don't want to hurt him!"

Kandar exclaimed, "Come on, Mrs. Aroon, let me kill this idiot so we'll all be rid of him."

"You know I can't let you do that, Kandar. Come on." Effortlessly, Kandar stood up, moving away from the shocked giant.

Sneering at the fallen beast, Kandar taunted him saying, "You got lucky this time!"

After Robert and I received this first life lesson on this day, we turned and trudged away from Mrs. Aroon, politely making our exit. I picked up where I last saw the Viking Princess, but again she disappeared.

Robert barked at me, "Thanks butt-head! Why didn't you tell her why we were running? IDIOT!"

Suddenly, I caught sight of the Viking Princess disappearing into the outdoor foliage of the gardens surrounding the lunch area.

"Jeez, she's more elusive than Bigfoot," I said.

I was now even more determined to see her, meet her, get to know her, and maybe ask her out—maybe. But she was gone for now. We exited where we saw her enter the foliage and once again, she was gone.

"Awww, shoot!" I said, lightly stamping my foot.

Robert teased, "What were you going to do anyway? Talk to her? Nooo! You're too freaked out around girls anyway."

"I just wanted to see her, okay? Maybe walk by her to see how tall she really is. Okay?" I responded.

Turning away in disappointment, I went out to meet some guys playing soccer, as Mrs. Aroon suggested. Robert and I went to get involved. This was the beginning of our futures as young adults. These were times we would cherish, along with the friends we made, the moments we enjoyed, and the memories we'd remember for the rest of our lives. For now, here we were, in 8th grade!

Inevitably the bell rang, and we joined the muster of young adults running from the hot outdoors into the cool, air-conditioned classroom micro-environments. Even though this was our first day of class, we had no idea our lunch days would pretty much be the same for the rest of the school year. Except for maybe the jokes we told, the friends we made and ate lunch with, and the weather we enjoyed—or didn't. Rain or shine, dark or light, foggy or clear, this was pretty much the way it progressed during lunches that year.

We made our way back into the main building among the frenzied fray of little adults, now crowding the hallways, following routes back to our lockers and on to class, before the next bell rang.

"What class is next?" I queried.

"Algebra, like you didn't know," Robert groaned.

"What books do I need?" I still feigned being in a trance. At least I think I was pretending.

Slamming his locker, locking it in one swift motion, "COME ON, it's math! Let's go!! Geez what's your problem? You're still hung up on HER? She's just a girl!" he screamed.

I grabbed my books out of my locker and followed Robert, "She's not JUST a girl," I raised my voice so he could hear me since he was a few paces ahead of me trying not to be late. "She's not JUST a girl, she's an angel! Hello!? Haven't you heard this is the City of Angels—she's the only one I've seen so far in the months I've been here! She's probably not even real. She's probably a ghost or something... you saw her too! Right?? Right??"

~ 4 ~

Impressing the Viking Princess / Imponera På Vikingaprinsessan

Seeing the Swedish Viking Princess quite a few times during the day for the months ahead just wasn't enough for me. Although I prayed to have a class with her, I also prayed I wouldn't, because I wouldn't be able to think straight in her presence. In the months ahead, I saw her more and more. And when I found out she really was born in Sweden, she intrigued me even more. I became even more enamored. "WOWWW! And she's Swedish—perfect! A real Viking Angel Princess!" I thought.

In time, I discovered her name was Erika. Whenever I saw her walk down the hallway, I stopped everything I was doing for the opportunity to watch her. Her lips, her hair, her smile, her smooth lightly tanned skin, her voice; she was the perfect girl-woman in every way I could imagine. She remained this way to me. When she was nearby, I couldn't think of anything but her... my heart raced, my palms sweated, my every thought was of her. Somehow, I suspected she was untouchable for me, as Robert foretold. Perhaps I didn't want to face ultimate rejection.

She was the most beautiful young woman in the universe to me, and more than anything else, the one person I wanted to get to know, even at my age. That first day she became my dream girl. She became my Viking Angel Princess. How was it contemplating telling her how I felt was beyond the realm of possibility? Perhaps it was fear of rejection of my fragile, near-teen persona I worked so hard to build up with a facade of the tough—though unavoidably shorter—nice guy.

As the year progressed, I looked forward to getting to school every day to see her, to watch her, and be near her. Though I was never lucky enough to have a class with her. Whenever she laughed, her eyes danced. Whenever she glanced my way, I was as astonished with her as I was the first time I set eyes upon her. I couldn't explain it. I didn't understand it, but I enjoyed it.

That year, I had a few of what we called "girlfriends," we hung around with, but none of whom approached how I felt about the Viking Princess. It was quite interesting having so many good friends from different countries around the world. With her being an Angel Princess, though I tried, nothing much seemed to impress her. Nothing worked. I always tried to stay in top physical condition, exercising at every opportunity. She seemed almost oblivious to everyone around her, and to my extreme disappointment, especially me.

Whenever I tried talking with her, I'd count to three, approach her, and just do it. Yet, all I would get from her was a simple "yes" or "no" response to any of my questions. She seemed disinterested in everyone and everything; guys, girls, and—at that age, what else was there? She had her friends, but they were just that, "friends." Disinterested in everything except for schoolwork, she appeared to be an outstanding student.

That first week of school came and went. One day in class during a break, Dean sat down next to me while Paul and Rick surrounded us.

Dean verbally poked me, "Hey! Do you sing?"

"I play guitar," I answered.

"Yeah, but CAN YOU SING?" he again poked.

"Yeah, I guess I can sing." I responded.

Dean quickly introduced everyone, "Cool, you'll be our band singer. This is Paul, he plays drums and keyboard. That's Rick, he plays bass guitar. I play lead and rhythm guitar," Dean added.

They all smiled as they welcomed me into my new role. This day changed my life forever. In time, after what seemed thousands of hours of practice by ourselves, or being invited to join in song with the various Thai nightclub bands, or in the music studios we rented, with top-of-the-line equipment to practice, I became comfortable with my new role. I reveled in my popularity as the lead singer in our young rock band. We all became great friends, and we maintained friendships with many others outside the band individually. Even now as the lead singer in what to me was the most popular rock band in school (of the two we had), this didn't impress her either.

Our band was just that, a group of kids who when together would do many mischievous misdeeds in our quest for thrills. And we'd play music together. We would get the band together for some craziness before or after our nighttime weekend rehearsals. What kind of craziness you ask? Well, none of it involved alcohol, anymore. These guys didn't really drink—they were always too busy doing other stuff. Giving up serious drinking at the ripe age of 12 was easy after realizing it wasn't fun getting sick. We all quickly weaned ourselves from alcohol and weed, and enjoyed life for what it was worth—adrenaline rushes. No more going out drinking to see how much we could drink as we did initially, then suffering from alcohol poisoning. We quickly graduated to more mature ends for fun.

On typical nights when we went out together, Dean got his driver Chai to pick us all up. One Friday night, Paul asked his Dad for some allowance money to go out since it had been a while since he asked. Working for the United Nations, his father was an avid traveler and obliged by leaving us a ₩5,000 note on the dining room table. When we saw it, we all said, "Whoah! Your Dad is soooo cool." We made cursory plans for how we'd spend the money starting with dinner, then a few drinks at a local night club, and take it from there. This would surely be a night to remember! Five thousand of anything had to be at least $100 of American dollars which would be about ฿2,000 Thai Baht. First, we had to jet over to the money exchanger before they closed. Chai hadn't stopped the car when we all bailed out, running inside the money exchanger, slamming doors upon our exit and entrance. There was no Google in those days, so we had no clue how much money we'd get for that night. Paul proudly displayed the note to the exchanger behind the bulletproof glass counter; he promptly looked it up and counted out almost THB฿100.

"Huh? That's it?" we demanded.

"Yes sir, KRW₩5,000 Won in Korean money is THB฿100 Thai Baht or almost US$4.00 including exchange fee.

"Great, Paul—man, your Dad is a real chump! YUP, we'll remember THIS night forever!" was said in grave disappointment.

We all pooled whatever money we had in our pockets, including Paul's tiny contribution. We were still able to go out for a good dinner with some beers at a restaurant owned by friends of Paul's family, but there was no amazing night on the town afterward. Paul's Dad probably got a genuine laugh thinking of our reactions, in whichever country he was that night.

Usually, we'd start with dinner at a local restaurant, stop by a construction site or two to break some bricks, since we all took martial arts after school together. Dean was always the instigator, thinking of some trouble to get us into, and for some reason we all went along with it. There really wasn't much for 12-year-old adults to do in any town at night, and going to *Crowns* to hang out wasn't their scene. Sometimes we'd head down the Sukhumvit main road riding in the car trunk, arbitrarily freaking out cars behind us by plopping our hands or feet out, mimicking dead bodies. Typical reactions were cars placing their high beams/brights on, then dimming them once they prophetically believed they stumbled onto some kind of gangland killings, possibly thinking they would end up the same way if they intervened. These drivers eventually passed us and moseyed along their way. Thankfully, the police never caught us perpetrating that prank. For some reason, this was a blast to us.

We often spent the tail end of the night lighting and throwing firecrackers out of the car windows or roof, surfing atop the sedan, speeding down a deserted back road at about 50 miles an hour like we saw in the movies! Dean would often be heard yelling at his driver from inside the car, "CHAI GO! GO! GO!!" intending to leave us at the end of some abandoned road or "CHAI STOP! STOP! STOP!!" intending to slam on the brakes to send us flying from the roof or hood of the car. Chai was heard yelling back as the wind rushed past our ears and we clambered for suction on the roof with our hands flat out on whichever surface was nearby, or by grasping the antenna stub of the retracted antenna, to stay atop the speeding car.

"No Dean, No! It's too danger! Too danger! No! No!" Thankfully, Chai never succumbed to these dastardly deeds quite as Dean instructed.

On some nights after band practice, we whiled away the hours running around Dean's apartment building, having powdered fire extinguisher fights on several floors, in and out of elevators, and inside the enclosed stairwells, until the fire extinguishers were empty. We never realized those made such an incredible noise and mess! Thankfully, we never had to clean it up. Miraculously, someone refilled these for the next time we got the hairbrained idea of another fire extinguisher fight. Or, the few times we threw water balloons off the roof of Dean's apartment building near or onto passersby; the problems ensued when we graduated from balloons to plastic bags once we ran out of balloons. Not realizing that plastic bags were much more rugged than balloons, one blew a hole right through the roof of the parking garage below. Seeing someone staring up through that hole was shocking. That was the last time we did that!

Pursuing less destructive means of fun, we graduated to jumping off the second or third-floor balconies of Dean's apartment building into the swimming pool below. Sometimes we used balconies of those people he knew weren't home, climbing over from his balcony for jumping angles. Our wet footprints most likely dried before anyone returned, as nobody was the wiser. We never expected, nor experienced, any accidents doing these crazy stunts; for this, we are now extremely grateful. Perhaps if alcohol was involved, we wouldn't have been so lucky.

I was on top of the world, especially when our rock band played together. All four of us were. We thought we were the heat! Everyone seemed to like our rendition of Carlos Santana's "Samba Pa Ti," "Black Magic Woman," Deep Purple's "Smoke on the Water," and others. Every time we attended junior high dances, our classmate fans would play their part and yell for us to play our songs while the professional Thai bands were on their breaks. The Thai bands didn't mind us playing their instruments because we were doing their jobs for them—and they always had the best instruments and sound equipment. So, we always played, and everyone always loved it; or at least they pretended. Strangely enough, I don't remember seeing the Viking Princess at any of these dances.

One song our band played became my trademark. It was a song by the American band *Grand Funk Railroad* called, "Bad Time."

This was my song; and unfortunately, this was my story. I told no one exactly who I was thinking about when singing this song. Little did I know, this revelation would be my life's experience with relationships throughout the rest of my school years and beyond.

No matter how positively other girls responded to me, the Viking Princess was as elusive and disinterested as ever. I was voted into the Student Council, took martial arts after school, played tennis, soccer, ping pong, and was even selected for modeling opportunities in Bangkok. One was a clothing commercial that went national, posting my image on buses, billboards, including in movie trailers in theaters, on full-page magazine and newspaper ads, and even a television spot. I had to hide this from my Dad as long as I could, because he didn't think modeling was very manly. One night, my commercial popped up on the television. I stood up, blocking the screen, asking, "Who wants popcorn?" Stalling as long as I could before having to go downstairs and make it. Despite my efforts, Dad came home one night with a full-page picture of the commercial in the Bangkok Post, a colleague had posted to the bulletin board.

"Do you know who that is?" he asked.

"I do," I responded. Surprisingly, he didn't seem to mind.

I started singing on a semi-regular basis with a Thai pop band named, *King 5,* at a club on the roof of the Chokchai building on Sukhumvit Road. Nothing much impressed this young Viking Princess. Nothing.

Toward the end of the school year, Karen and I began visiting Kanchanaburi, one of Thailand's Northwestern provinces where my Dad's new colleague, whom we called "Uncle Philip," owned a coconut plantation. This plantation was on thousands of acres through which ran the unimproved jungle road to the Three Pagoda Pass on the Thai-Myanmar border to the north. Roughly a thousand subsistence farmers and their families living on the land worked this plantation for decades. Because of their proximity to the border, these people spoke Mon—a dialect of Burmese. We began visiting the plantation mostly during the summers and on long holidays. We always had a blast there. Here, the world was our oyster, whatever that means. This was part of our parents' plan to encourage us to travel to see and experience what we could. Sometimes we traveled with them in Thailand and surrounding countries and sometimes without. To Kanchanaburi, it was typically, without them.

On this plantation I even excavated a once-hidden cave deep in the jungle discovered by farmers. I found artifacts which years later the Smithsonian Institute in Washington D.C. verified the authenticity as being the first of its kind in the area. This excavation yielded stone tools, potsherds, and ancient animal teeth. That accomplishment merely landed me in the school paper. With my parents' support, my endeavors brought me to more of the country than any tourist could've seen.

Experiences like this made our childhood unbelievable to others our age. It usually took us nearly a four-hour train ride, and a three-hour 4-wheel drive ride to reach the plantation in the dry season. Often, we would arrive red-headed, completely covered in orange dust head-to-toe, from the hours it took traversing the clay roads in open-air vehicles. One time during the rainy season, my sister and I went with Uncle Philip in his limousine van. Since this vehicle wasn't expected to traverse the extremely rough, wet terrain, we transferred to a convoy of WWII era 4-wheel drive military trucks at the Sai Yok Noi Falls train station. Here, we also met up with a small band of armed villagers from the plantation sporting guns, rifles, and bandoliers of ammunition; these young men most likely doubled as bodyguards, though they were full-time farmers and hunters.

Something always seemed to happen on these trips. Whether we were standing up in the truck bed overlooking the road, watching a similarly styled vehicle miss hitting us head–on striking the rear of the truck breaking the axle forcing us to a sliding halt, or whether it just got stuck. These trips were always exciting for us. This time, as the 4-wheel truck convoy traversed the slick, saturated roads, we slid back and forth for hours on end through the muddy jungle path, at no faster than walking speeds. At one turn, the trucks got mired in mud so deep that even the front winch couldn't self-recover. We all dismounted while two of the accompanying bodyguards departed our makeshift camp, walking hours into the syrupy darkness. Their mission was to return to the plantation by candlelight, bringing a bigger truck to extricate us. We were trapped there for about 8-hours with nothing but flashlights and candles to light the dark, jungle night. Thankfully, the rain had stopped earlier. While it was too wet to build a fire, Uncle Philip invited us to exit the vehicles and sit on old ponchos atop the spongy wet ground, ferns, and other vegetation, as we tried to fashion someplace flat to sit or lie down.

With nothing else to do but talk the night away, and listen to the sounds of the jungle, Karen and I wondered if we'd be accosted by any of the wild boars, monkeys, tigers, elephants, snakes, or other animals frequenting these parts. There were no lights, no other motor cars, no electricity, and not a single luxury on this flooded path of road. There was darkness, jungle noises, and the occasional snapping of twigs and sounds of something sloshing through mud puddles in the distance. As the night crept on, I was startled by a low growl, I was sure was a tiger stalking us in the surrounding darkness. "—Arrrrck!!" My heart jumped as I tried not to show any reaction from Uncle Philip's guttural outburst. The growling stopped instantly. Uncle uttered a few words in

Mon into the darkness, adding in English, "Stop snoring, you're going to scare the kids!" he shouted out and laughed.

Uncle Philip was an intriguing man. On this night, he introduced me to his mysterious, previously undisclosed past as a private man of Chinese descent. He started early and continued telling stories of his exploits in the rag-tag, desperate-for-recruits, splintering Kuomintang Army when he was growing up in mainland China. He shared that he joined up as a fourteen-year-old child, fighting alongside bands of "guerillas" or "freedom fighters" alongside Chiang Kai-shek's forces. First, they fought against the Japanese, then against the Communist forces toward the end of World War II.

Eventually, he ended up in Taiwan as a young man, years later, emigrating to Thailand. He showed me scars that matched up with all his stories of being stabbed by a bayonet, cut by a combat knife, and shot by a sniper's rifle bullet entering his chest, breaking ribs and partially caving in his chest, before exiting his back—that was a long deep scar. Evidently, it was neither skillfully sewn nor well-healed. The other wounds he displayed looked much like they were scars from bullets. He was a man of many lives. He was tough and resilient, maintaining an attitude that nothing was impossible. Speaking of glory for the goal of unity in a fragile China, not for self-recognition or aggrandizement, he based his philosophy on principles derived from the teachings of Confucius, of which he was fond. My Dad was a Korean War Marine combat veteran, and never spoke ill of Uncle Philip and his stories. Were they true? Who knew? We had no reason to doubt him. He got all those scars from somewhere. Regardless, Uncle was one tough cookie and he looked the part. He even earned the respect of our Dad—a Korean War combat veteran.

In the middle of one of his stories that night, a mosquito circled the flame of the candle he was holding, landing with its legs in the warm wax as we watched. Grasping the candle tightly in his fist, Uncle Philip pushed the flaming wick to the side, away from the struggling mosquito. With the index finger of his free hand, he rescued the mosquito from the fiery liquid wax, and didn't even flinch when we heard the wick searing the fleshy side of his fingertips. Freeing the insect from sure death, he brought it to his lips, lightly blowing while pinching the drying wax between his fingers and thumb. To our amazement the mosquito freed itself, raising its legs, one at a time, out of the solidifying wax, outstretched its wings, flying into the night with another of Uncle's gentle breaths.

"Why'd you do that?" I asked.

He modestly muttered, "There was no need for him to die tonight. Right? I could help him, so I did. At one time or another, we all need such help. So, I helped," explaining his actions as he smiled in the candlelight.

The candle continued dancing shadows across his face, flickering in the night. Uncle continued chanting his memoirs and talking of the Confucius philosophy he held so dearly. To him, there was a lesson in every parable. Whenever we accompanied him to his plantation house, a multi-level, open-air, teakwood house, he'd be up at the crack of dawn practicing his Kung Fu with a Conan-sized sword. There he was in the distance, surrounded by the mist settling at waist level among the coconut trees.

My sister and I had a carte blanche invitation at this plantation house. Electricity was only available until about seven or eight o'clock at night, since Uncle Philip thought it unnecessary to run the village generators around the clock. So, after that time, it was flashlights, candles, and quiet. We often brought whichever friends could convince their parents to let them travel such a long distance by train, bus, or car to accompany us into the middle of nowhere on weekends and for weeks in the summer. Once there, we rode elephants, attended local festivals, avoided the tigers that routinely conducted nighttime raids into the outdoor kitchen looking for food, and we did our best to elude both non-poisonous and poisonous snakes and other critters during our morning, afternoon, and nighttime swims in the stream, a short walk from the house. It was here where we became one with nature. Multitudes of insect sounds filled the night air, often with a powerful shrill pitch temporarily piercing the quiet, as did many other sounds of animals and insects struggling for survival, while others merely went about their chores in the dark. The sounds of nature unfolded outside our nylon-screened, open windows each night, as we attempted to sleep. The jungle was alive with growls, howls, whistles, cracks, thumps, and other sounds permeating the foggy humid nights until dawn. Yet, we felt safe among the plantation's hundreds of coconut trees just outside this teakwood castle.

The villagers who worked the plantation provided us with bullets, handguns, rifles, and motorcycles. But strangely enough, they provided no rules and no adult chaperones. Our only rule meister and chaperone was a man named Chit Sen. He often brought me barefoot wading into jungle streams to toughen me up. We brought nothing but a .22 rifle or M-16s assault rifles for protection, wandering into the still quiet of the daylight, just to see what we could happen across. We dare not venture into these wild lands during the darkness. That would be foolish, if not suicidal.

One quiet summer day, as I was exploring the area on a walkabout with Chit Sen, while wandering along a firebreak between tall ripening cornfields, he jumped on top of me, slamming me to the ground, pushing my face into the hard-packed, orange clay dirt, moving quicker than I ever saw him move. He said nothing, placing his face inches from mine. I saw a terror in his eyes, the likes I'd never seen from this typically happy-go-lucky man. His index finger pressed firmly against his lips, indicating to me not to utter a sound; I didn't. I even held my breath as we both lay motionless in the orange dust, face down. After seconds, which felt like hours as I waited for an explanation, I noticed a few bees hovering around us, then a few more, then even more. A few more seconds brought hundreds more. The buzzing surrounded us and all I heard was the loud vibration, buzzing, and humming outside us, and the thumping of my heart inside my chest. There was nothing we could do but helplessly wait, watch, holding our breath, remaining completely still, hoping this would not turn catastrophic. Millions of bees hovered around us, while what sounded like millions more buzzed above the low-hovering ones. This was serious. The Laughing Fox wasn't laughing now. After what seemed like hours, the mind-numbing buzzing and humming subsided. The scout bees surrounding us finally departed. Chit Sen looked around, at first only moving his eyes. With one side of his face dusty orange, he inched his head upward as the deafening buzzing subsided, getting onto his knees, still leaning on me so I couldn't get up. With effort, he stood up, brushing himself off. As he helped me up, he pointed into the distance down the firebreak to an immense dark cloud we now knew was bees on the horizon.

"Look," he sparked, "The queen bee moving now, and all the hive go with her to find a new home. This is very, very danger for us. Thank you for you listen to me. Sorry for make you all dirty Mr. D. If something happen to you, your father—he kill me!" he said, now laughing it off.

"No problem, Chit Sen, I'll always listen to you. Thank you," I confided. I listened to him a few days later when an unidentified man in a military uniform drove into the village in a ¼ ton jeep. Exiting the Village Chief's house, I struck up a conversation with this man. He explained in perfect English he was going to the Three Pagoda Pass, inviting me to go with him for a few days. This was a place I always wanted to go since it was notorious for the smuggling that went on between Thailand and Myanmar. He was well equipped with radios, batteries, food, water, weapons, ammunition, and other survival items. Was he Thai military, or CIA sponsored, or even part of an Opium Warlord Army? Thinking about it now, inviting me to go with him seems strange since it would cause a rapid, unplanned depletion of his provisions. But I so wanted to go along.

When I asked Chit Sen for permission to go for just a few days, a very serious look came over his face as he explained, "Mr. D, nobody know this man or where he go. Maybe he go to the Pass, maybe not. Maybe he not bring you back!"

I understood his concern, realizing even back then to choose my adventures wisely. If not, any of them could be my last. And I always wanted to live to tell about them.

If he was anything, Chit Sen was kind-hearted, extremely protective, and fiercely loyal. He had no reason not to be. My father employed him as a colleague, often taking me with him on his fact-finding trips. And Dad let him stay in our guest house in Bangkok, as a permanent guest.

We continued on our way as he went on instructing me in the ways of the jungle, between rekindled fits of his high-pitched nervous laughter. Once his laughter started again, it lasted for as long as I can remember that day.

Another time, Chit Sen gave me and Karen shooting lessons outside Uncle's plantation house. Standing on the ground outside, he reached up, opening a lower-level window, and walked about 30 paces, placing a bottle on the arm of a nearby citrus tree. He swung open the wooden-framed screen and continued instructing us on how to shoot with a .22 rifle from inside the window. I was first. As he focused on the task at hand, he crouched out the window beside me. Listening to his words, I first made the front sight blurry, focusing on the target, then made the target blurry, focusing again on the front sight through the rear sight. With the eight steady hold factors in mind, before gently squeezing the trigger and letting out a bit of breath from my lungs, I noticed some movement behind the blurry bottle. Focusing beyond the bottle, I noticed a man walking in the distance outside the caretaker's wooden shack about 50-yards away. I asked Chit Sen about the house and the man outside.

He started laughing and laughing, saying, "Never mind, it just a .22 bullet—it so small. No worry, he move!" He calmly and confidently prodded me to continue as his already high-pitched nervous laughter, became even higher.

"Chit Sen, I'm not going to shoot near that man," I insisted.

Yelling out to the man, saying something in Mon, Chit Sen moved the target out of the line of fire of the caretaker's house. Chuckling and mumbling to himself as he let out a high-pitched whine and more laughter on his way out of the house to move the bottle, he returned saying, "Mr. D, Mr. D, why you so worry about many little things? You not worry so much."

We continued our shooting lesson without incident. Everyday day we spent at the plantation seemed to open a new chapter to another adventure in the jungle; thankfully, none were fatal to anyone.

Back to that night we got stuck. At long last, during the early hours of morning nautical twilight, our rescue party arrived. It was moments before dawn. Human chatter intensified. People milled around, stirring and sloshing about in the partially flooded, muddy, makeshift campsite atop wet leaves and fallen bamboo stalks and leaves. We could hear thumps and thuds in the darkness, illuminated by an occasional oil lantern, flashlight beam, or candle in the distance. Shadows danced everywhere as the activity increased. Uncle stood and muttered commands both in Mon and Thai. After some banging, chain slinging, guttural utterances, overpowering and revving vehicle engines, spinning tires, intertwining diesel and gasoline odors, engines straining and more wheels spinning, a dozen men attempted to free our mired vehicle. Between the manpower, vehicle power, and power of bumper-mounted winches, finally we were on our way again. This was why our parents rarely ventured out to Kanchanaburi with us.

One time the high school's Thai History and Culture club was hosting a trip to the nearby River Kwai, so Karen and I rode our motorcycles down to where the club was supposedly staying. Stopping to talk to a few locals, asking them where "the foreigners" were, they said everybody left earlier in the morning because a student disappeared in the river. He supposedly drowned while many of them were swimming and playing on a rope swing hovering over the river's swift current. They said his name was Rick, and they hadn't found his body. This news devastated me. I thought it might have been our Rick, bass player Rick. That was the last thing I expected to hear. It cast an eerie, worrisome calm over the rest of our weekend. I couldn't verify that it wasn't our Rick until we got back home and could access a landline.

As it turned out, he was a new boy in Karen's class, also barely into his teens. We didn't know him very well; I'd only seen him once or twice. This loss devastated the entire school once the news spread throughout both campuses. The news left us feeling like something was missing for months and months. Even though he wasn't from my specific junior high school ISB campus, we all knew he could've been. His passing forced us to realize our mortality, understanding that even a safe activity like swimming could turn catastrophic. After all the chances we took earlier in our lives, this young, friendly boy drowns while swimming? Facing this tragedy forced us to grow up a little bit quicker, becoming young adults earlier than we should have. Without realizing it, we were enjoying life now harder than most other kids.

Knowing our classmates as we did, we would rather celebrate Rick's memory than mourn his loss. Often our entire school felt like one enormous family; both campuses felt this way, because most of us had a sibling or two at the other campus. We were all a family of equals from varying backgrounds, religions, social and ethnic groups, languages, though from different classes of wealth. Because we were all ISB students, we were open to each other, without prejudice or preformed notions separating students into groups like jocks, geeks, nerds, stoners, and thespians. Our school wasn't big enough to form such strong, isolating cliques. We couldn't afford to exclude anyone. The few troublemakers everyone shied away from as often as possible, were rare. Our classmate passing was an awakening affecting us all.

~ 5 ~

The Catch / Fångsten

Living overseas on the Embassy circuit, we came to understand that any relationship would only last about two to four years at the most, because our parents' jobs would transfer them to another country as part of their usual work rotation. People inevitably came and went, settling into other countries, into other towns, and into other schools. We were no different, continually expected to make new friends. This worked out especially well later in life as I reconnected with one of my best friends, Sebastian. We hiked the Grand Canyon together South to North to South Rim (Rim-to-Rim-to Rim) several times (a 45-mile hike covering 21,000 vertical feet). Over the years, I've also visited many of my international school classmates in their countries of origin.

Since I knew the Viking Princess and her family had been in Thailand for quite some time before my family arrived, I knew her someday would come sooner than mine. And I knew I'd probably never see her again. Once again, I was left with nothing but memories and the few yearbook pictures including her. As the end of the school year approached, I cherished each moment I could see her, and be near her. Moments I could chit-chat with her were like gold. I always appreciated looking at her. As summer approached, I felt like I was on death row facing the final curtain as it neared. I hoped and prayed once school let out that I'd see her in the Teen Club or at the few hangouts we frequented on weekends. I never did. I heard she was the youngest of her siblings and was the only one in Bangkok; apparently her parents were quite strict, and as the baby of the family they didn't let her go out much. When she did show up at one of the hangouts, it was brief and my reaction was still the same... my heart sank, my mind slowed, and I became a bit down, simply because I couldn't muster the courage to get to know her better. I knew I picked a *Bad Time* to be in love, but I continued admiring her from a distance, in silence. I didn't see her at all that summer, and I knew most likely I wouldn't see or hear from her ever again. It saddened my heart to think of this possibility; nonetheless, I realized I had to move on with my life. I knew I didn't have to forget her, nor the memories of her I held so closely.

I looked forward to attending ISB high school at the Soi 15, Bangkapi campus, with the bulk of my new buddies. I looked forward to experiencing the stories I heard from my sister and her friends. I looked forward to meeting my friends at a place called "The Shack" a short walk from the ISB school campus, enjoying a coffee or two inside the restaurant—a large, old, broken down, converted teakwood house. Some students allegedly would go out back and smoke a joint or two before classes started without repercussions. From this location, we could hail and hop aboard a high speed "klong boat" and be off to a nearby market, skipping hordes of Bangkok traffic, and even classes, if we wanted. We could also visit the ice cream vendors, tea and coffee vendors, and fresh fruit vendors parked outside the school grounds selling their wares. They knew exactly when our lunchtime was and we knew exactly where they would be. For less than a dollar or maybe even a little more, we could enjoy our fill of whatever we wanted. Ours would soon be a life of excess and luxury, especially compared to many locals. Would we appreciate our position in life? Perhaps not as often as we should have. But for the most part, I think we did. To this, I was looking forward with great anticipation.

The daily hours of homework after our numerous extracurricular high school activities brought us a more precise focus. We knew these days wouldn't last forever; but we thought they lasted longer than they actually did. The busy school year soon ended. Dean and Rick both left that summer, breaking up our band forever. It wasn't until after the summer when I began high school, that I found out the Viking Princess moved back to Sweden with her family. No longer would I have my head on a swivel everywhere I went, wondering if I'd catch a glimpse of her. Since her father worked for an international company not based in Bangkok, I soon realized I'd most likely never see her again.

I came to understand this chapter in my life involving her was over; completely over. Nonetheless, my life continued, second after second, minute after minute, hour after hour, week after week, month after month, year after year, challenge after challenge, experience after experience, and a busy life it became. It was relatively easy to focus on the multitude of other tasks, hobbies, and accomplishments. Getting lost in my current life, at the time, made the recent past easier to accept.

I thought about the Princess quite often for the remainder of my high school years in Thailand, and filled any possible gaps with travel and activities to take my mind off her departure from my life. My summer weekdays or weekend trips during the school year often included visiting various local Buddhist and Chinese temples, fairs and festivals, and popular landmarks Bangkok offers: the Marble Temple, the Grand Palace, Temple of the Reclining Buddha, Temple of the Dawn, the Giant Swing, the Floating Market, the Morning Market, the Evening Market, the

Weekend Market, the Pat Pong Night Market, Lumpini Park, any of the 5-star hotels, zoos (the Dusit Zoo or the Crocodile Farm) and many, many other places. Photography was my main reason for travel, besides just getting out and about.

Continuing Tae Kwon Do martial arts after school, I was also selected for the school soccer team (Go Panthers), was elected Class President and later Vice-President, appeared as an extra in the Hollywood production portion of *The Deer Hunter,* filmed in various parts of Thailand, starring Robert DeNiro and that grouchy looking mean guy… Christopher Walken or something like that, along with many other classmates. This was a fun experience where I realized I didn't want to spend the bulk of my life pretending to be someone I was not. On top of that, pretending to be that person playing the same scene over and over for an entire day, including up to 45 takes per scene. I actually talked my way into being hired for the filing after being turned away twice by the casting director for being too short.

My persistence paid off when I was called out for the last time I said, "Come on. Like there are no short people in the Army? Practically my entire school is here. Give me a break, pleez?" I was hired!

We traveled on weekends to different shooting locations and had as much fun as one could have spending an entire day shooting a scene. We were paid about $100 a day with room and board while the local villagers were paid only a dollar a day for being background extras. Before the first day of shooting, they gave me a radical haircut being that I would be placed right in front of the camera. Returning home that night, everyone was sitting at the dinner table. Dad just joked, "Excuse me! Who are you? Where is my son, the one with the long hair?" Mocking his efforts of trying to get me to agree to such a haircut since we left Laos. It came to pass that most of us with newly shortened hair were extras in the movie. We enjoyed our new hair style as a badge of honor around school.

Our little junior high school band was my gateway to joining the 10-girl, 10-guy sing-and-dance troupe at the ISB high school campus called, *The Young Internationals*. Paul convinced me to join since he wanted to join too. We both auditioned and both made the cut. This group was very different from anything I experienced, and it was a lot of fun. We learned our routines, practiced daily, and matured quickly, often having to share dressing rooms because the facilities where we toured around the remote areas of Thailand weren't designed for such performances, and surely didn't have separate dressing rooms for men and women or for boys and girls. So, we all changed into our uniforms in the same room; sometimes we changed on the bus. We learned to deal with it maturely. As young pre-teens we came together quickly.

We performed Broadway and Off-Broadway hit songs, and some from Leo Sayer, the Turtles, Three Dog Night, Charlie Brown movies, Jesus Christ Super Star, and Godspell; all were among our repertoire on a variety of stages. In this group, whenever we traveled and got bored, we made up games. There was Bus Surfing.

On one of our trips, our director, Mr. Anderson, realized that some of us were missing from inside the bus, yet the bus hadn't stopped for hours. When he asked the question, "Hey, where is Dimitri, Ricardo, Brandon, Paul, and Sam?" Somebody must have tattled and pointed to the roof because the bus pulled over rather abruptly, and Mr. Anderson stormed out, knowing exactly where to tell the driver to look. The driver swiftly climbed up the ladder at the back of the bus, appearing on the roof rack between the stored equipment and our sun tanning area; we knew we were busted. It was admittedly much easier climbing down the ladder from the roof, instead of crawling out the rear windows of the bus, grabbing the roof rack and pulling ourselves up while the bus was moving at Thai highway speeds. Our method took skill! Completely unimpressed at our newfound skill, Mr. Anderson screamed at the top of his lungs, "How could you be so reckless? What's wrong with you people??? Why can't you just play cards like most kids?"

That stunt earned us a bit of consternation, only to find us hours later caught in the middle of another game we called, Bus Swinging. This game entailed tightly gripping the bar above the opened rear side door of the bus, swinging out between passing telephone poles while the bus traveled at about 60-70 mph. The stakes were high, and our timing had to be impeccable. That had to be quite the spectacle to witness from a rear-view mirror!

As Mr. Anderson was sitting next to the driver looking down the bus in the mirror, seeing us swinging out, he abruptly yelled, "What the fu**?"

What else were we supposed to do while on these multiple day bus trips between performances throughout Thailand? Play cards? It wasn't our fault—we were bored!

While at a train station, we invented yet another game called Train Jumping. In this game, the players boarded an arbitrary train leaving the station—the winner was the last one to jump off and land successfully while the train was moving. We were able to do this because on the local trains the doors and windows either didn't close automatically or were nonexistent. A few contestants spent hours walking back from wherever the train they were riding and were afraid to jump from finally stopped; they were the losers of that game.

Then there was Train Singing where we all sang our repertoire acapella up and down the train, getting the passengers stoked and happy—this was much safer and always worked. And there was Train Surfing... like in the old Western movies, riding atop the moving train, ducking down for tunnels and bridges. On one trip to Chiang Mai in Northern Thailand, many of us bought crossbows from the Hilltribes. So, we invented Train Shooting. This was where we all engaged a tree the appointed targeteer would selectively yell out, and we'd all launch crossbow arrows on cue from the open train windows. Mr. Anderson bless his heart naively saw us as the Partridge Family, while we saw ourselves as Deep Purple, with female performers.

In coming years, I visited many UNESCO World Heritage sites on frequent trips sponsored by everyone's favorite teacher, Mr. Wilson, and his remarkable Thai History and Culture Club. Here, he did such outlandish things like holding classes with us sitting or lying around on the floor on bamboo mats near short tables, taking lecture notes in what he called "traditional Thai style." His primary goal was to ready us for the permissive learning environment of college. So, he adorned his classroom with large floor pillows, on which he encouraged us to lounge around learning. His classes were more fun than any I experienced, even in college.

He often introduced us to exotic foods like Filipino baloot or Asian betel nut. He required us to use positive descriptive adjectives like "different" or "interesting" rather than the usual "gross" or "disgusting." Popular trips were: the Elephant Roundup in Surin, the Candle festival in Ubon Ratchathani, the Loi Kratong Floating Lantern Festival, the Thai New Year Festival Pimai, the Bun Bung Fai Rocket Festival in Roi Et, the Elephant timber farms of Chiang Mai, the ancient cities of Ayutthaya, and Sukhothai historical parks and the temples of Nakorn Panom and Nakorn Pathom, the Nam Tok (water falls) in Kanachanburi where the bridge on the River Kwai is memorialized, Kao Yai national park, and beach activities enjoyed in Pattaya, Hua Hin, Ko Samet, and Ko Samui among others. We stayed busy and learned a lot about this bountiful country.

When the ISB gym teacher and soccer coach, the rough and gruff Mr. Klaus Günter, 1962 German Soccer World Cup team member, converted a local house down the street from the ISB high school campus on Sukhumvit Soi (Street)15, he named the new restaurant and German biergarten, Haus München; this place became more than popular. It was a hit among all of us, as well as the ex-pat community and local pubsters.

His was an establishment themed after a family-oriented Bavarian Grill and Beer Garden with a party room upstairs where we pre-teens and teens could, would, and were expected to congregate away from the customers unaffiliated with ISB. Once it opened, we were all encouraged to go—and we did. Parents loved this place as this was the only location where we had responsible adult supervision away from parents. And this was a place we weren't being preyed on by anyone. Once *Pop's* closed down, or was shut down most likely, teen life become a little less radical and we all came here, getting to know the person under Mr. Günter's gruff exterior as best we could. He looked after us and always wished us well, besides verbally berating those among us who were on his soccer team or in his gym classes.

During my Junior year summer break, I had an amazing opportunity to work in the Refugee section of the American Embassy. It was here where I worked with Peace Corps volunteers and Embassy employees alike. Mom and Karen left early that summer. Dad stayed with me in a hotel so I could finish my summer job. He didn't like the possibility of me working in the refugee camps because in those days they were mostly in denied areas of the country. Roads were often attacked by rogue bands of insurgents affiliated with the Communist Party of Thailand (CPT).

One week, he went to Singapore and I had my chance. I told my supervisor it was okay for me to travel with them to Loei in Northeastern Thailand, so off we went for the remainder of the month. I didn't lie, I could physically go. I took with me whatever money I could muster, leaving a quick note for Dad. He got the note upon his return a few days later, but I was already in Loei.

The train ride to Loei was long and uneventful. The refugee camp, nestled in the hills, was much better than others I'd seen. It was designed to house 10,000 people but when we were there, the tally was over 35,000, increasing daily. Most of the residents lived in single sided UN tents. Theirs was a rough existence. When hiking to the top of the hills surrounding the camp, only at the military crest did the wildlife and birds re-appear. Returning downhill, one could detect a rancid odor in the air from the disease and suffering that was taking place. But we were all there working to improve those conditions.

The detainees were mostly ethnic Hmong Hilltribe villagers who supported the CIA during the Vietnam War and upon the U.S. pulling out, many of them were left behind to fend for themselves. Living up in the mountains, they became fugitives from the new Lao government. Once escaping into Thailand, they were beset upon by thieves and Border Guards who took away all of their possessions, except for whatever silver bars they could hide, which were earned from centuries in the opium trade. They melted down these silver bars to make jewelry and buy cloth and thread for the handicrafts they continued making for their survival. We were encouraged to buy whatever we wanted, with the only stipulation that we couldn't bargain. We had to take their first price. I also used my presence there to practice the Lao language of my youth.

While there, I met Muay Soo, Vang Pao's second in command of the Resistance. He seemed to be a humbly educated man who whiled away the hours at camp working his subsistence garden. I often wandered away from our makeshift interviewing area over to see him during my breaks to learn from him what I could.

Our work hours were long and entailed filling out endless reams of paperwork for new detainees to apply for asylum in a host of countries including the U.S., the United Kingdom, Australia, Germany and France. We interviewed these families to ensure their paperwork was correct. These were people who had no clue when they were born based on our Western linear perspective of life, nor how long they had lived. Having to guess their ages, my supervisor told us to give them birthdays of famous Americans or American holidays to help them out.

Returning for multiple interviews, sometimes with more family members not previously annotated, we were told to give them a break and add them to the family. This often happened when one family was designated before another to depart the camp and children were given away to speed their exit. Being adopted, I knew how difficult it was for parents to make such a decision, not knowing in which country their children would end up or if they would ever see them again. Nonetheless, despite their harrowing past, these people were smiling, jovial, and radiated positivity because they finally had a chance at a future and would someday start life anew. Away from persecution and away from the combat they knew for most of their lives.

Some days, I'd walk around the camp seeing no adult males anywhere. Asking no questions, a few days later, the infirmary would have more gunshot wounded patients. It was clear to me that whenever possible they would leave camp, muster up some weapons and risk their lives returning across the border to fight for their country. A moot fight it was; though their determination was admirable. All our translators sported names like Axe, Mountain, Lake, River which they proudly maintained as their "handles" given to them years prior by their CIA trainers during the war. These were a proud, strong-willed people willing and ready to accept whatever life was going to throw at them with smiles on their faces. Having lost everything physically, I guess there really was no place for them to go but up. And that was the attitude they conveyed. This was one incredibly rewarding job.

I continued going to *Crowns*, making friends, and bidding them farewell until it was our turn to leave the country. Although it saddened me, I knew that getting upset was inconsequential to the inevitable outcome. So, like the Hmong Hilltribe people, I accepted my unknown fate and left for the States with Dad. Had I known how difficult reintegrating back into American culture [or lack thereof] would be, I would've been terrified of the notion of leaving Thailand.

Coming to the Washington D.C. area for my last year of high school was like being crammed into a bottle. The only thing that softened the blow was being selected for the soccer team after talking the coach into a brief trial, since team selections were made prior to the summer. And there was the student rock band which I found my way into somehow. Music and sports seemed to inject me into the culture of the country of my origin better than anything else. And it softened the blow of being a foreigner in my own country. I managed.

The vast expanse of land of the Bangsue ISB campus close to the airport eventually was worth millions of dollars to the business world. In time, the land value led to the complete destruction of both the junior and high school campuses, along with our intimate memories attached to these buildings. Everything was destroyed, paved over with concrete and asphalt, and repurposed in the years that passed. Our only opportunity to physically revisit our common past was replaced by multitudes of nameless, unremarkable office buildings and parking areas. This was the price of progress. Along with relegating the memories of this pleasantly perfect life to some place we could never again physically visit, we were left to recall our memories by glancing through the pages, pictures, and opinions written in our yearbooks by classmates, and in conversations we'd have among our alumni far-ahead in the future at our annual class reunions in the U.S. and Bangkok.

Back then, we attended school in ignorant bliss. Had we known the bleak future of our memory-making fields and school buildings, perhaps our existence would have been marred with depression and pointlessness. Instead, we focused on enjoying every second of our perfectly pleasant present.

~ 6 ~

My Journey / Min Resa

As my life's journey progressed, from time to time I wondered about the Viking Princess. Surviving a failed marriage, seeing my children as often as I could, my life never seemed to slow down. My 20-plus year U.S. military career as an officer began right after graduating from college. It had me traipsing through near-death experiences in training and combat until I retired. These experiences occurred throughout the U.S., Asia, Central America, the Caribbean, Europe, the Middle East, and Africa. I quickly earned a reputation as a "Rainbow Wrestler" with a "can do" attitude, seeking as many life experiences as possible. Some of those experiences nearly killed me. I used to joke with fellow Soldiers, "What doesn't make me stronger... will kill me... but hasn't yet."

Unable to visit the past by physically walking the halls of the old ISB buildings, alumni these days come to association meetings and reunions to reminisce. Here we revisit our memories, rekindling the glory days of our teenage past. The ISB association hosts these every other year, in various parts of the world. How did we all turn out? Some of us became diplomats, Sailors,

Soldiers, Airmen (either officer or enlisted), entrepreneurs, artists, and writers among others. Some even served in primary positions on U.S. Presidential staffs. Three of the four students from our tiny Advanced Placement U.S. History class, ended up serving as Green Berets in the same Special Forces (SF) Group. What are the chances of that happening?

After retiring from the U.S. Army, I finally had the time to attend an ISB reunion dinner organized by some local classmates in the Washington, D.C. and Virginia area. This whet my appetite for reminiscing with my classmates. About a year later, I attended one of the large, national-level reunions convened for all ISB alumni. These include anyone who attended ISB at any point in time, since the individual classes weren't large enough to hold separate reunions. The El Conquistador Resort hotel in Tucson, Arizona was the site for this all-inclusive reunion.

One night, after the primary festivities of the reunion closed down, we were jaw-jacking around the firepit next to the resort pool. We were in various forms of dress, undress, and even bathing suits. A few of us played guitar, while others sang. We all hung out enjoying the clear, cool, star-filled Arizona sky. After enjoying a few more beers in the cool night air, okay, maybe more than a few more, and singing a few more songs, someone invariably brought up Erika. In fact, eventually she became the primary topic of conversation. Somehow nobody knew anything about her. It's like she dropped off the face of the earth.

"Hey D, how is it that you're not married? You're well-employed, in great shape, well-adjusted, and available, right?" someone said in the darkness, as we all stared into the firepit. We watched some toying with embers as we spoke.

Another chimed in, "Hey, do we know any ISBers who aren't married, in acceptable shape, and are still at least fairly active?"

"ACCEPTABLE shape? Why are you lowering MY standards for me?" I asked.

"Come on really? You gotta be realistic, man. It's one thing at your age, being a guy in good shape, but it's a completely different issue expecting a woman within your age range to be. Pffft, yeah right! It's a hormonal thing," he said.

This started a firestorm of gender dissent. For about 15 minutes, they cast slanderous statements across the firepit. Once that tongue lashing died down, a woman's voice in the darkness added, "Oh yeeah... Erika, do you remember her? She was in our class. How about her?"

"Wasn't she that cute, quiet, Scandinavian girl?" someone added.

"Do you mean the tall, beautiful, gorgeous, Swedish Princess with silky blonde hair, the best fitting jeans in the world, perfect eyelashes, blue eyes, slender fingers, and perfectly manicured toes? The one drop dead gorgeous woman who should be and most likely is an international model. You mean THAT Erika?" I boasted in her honor.

"Yeah... her."

"Nope..." I chuckled, "I don't remember her—never heard of her."

"Yes, you do... I'm serious. I heard she's single and she lives in Sweden."

"Gimme a break...forget that...Sweden? That's way too far away. Like that would ever happen," another blurted into the darkness, dismissing the thought.

"Wait a minute! What the hell? Why the fuck not, D? It's Sweden, not the moon!" a Pacific Islander named Jennifer screamed from across the pit.

Jennifer was renowned for speaking her mind. Even without consuming the amount of alcohol she had on this night. She was even more outspoken, and her voice resonated with unbridled passion. We continued launching our words freely across the pit in the cool mountain air, laughing, and egging on each other.

She unexpectedly screeched, "Wait a minute! It's a small world, you know. Sweden is just a few plane rides away, at best! Don't you even have the balls to want to know if she's single? If she's interested in you? She'd be perfect for you! Why the fuck not?"

"Jennifer is right, man!" another said. "Don't be a dick. Sweden is just a plane-ride away. Help yourself out, dude! If you don't do it for yourself, do it for us married folk who want to live vicariously through you."

"Come on. Help your buddies out, man!" said yet another.

"Look man, you need to look her up. You've GOTTA! That's all there is to it! There's no fucking option! You owe it to the perfect order of the universe! Just fuckin' do it! And keep us in the loop! You of all people deserve a chance at happiness. War hero and shit!" another blurted from out of the darkness. I laughed it off without another thought and enjoyed the rest of the evening. That was an awesome night.

A few years prior, home from Operations Iraqi Freedom (OIF) and Enduring Freedom (OEF) in Afghanistan, I became increasingly reclusive. It's a common result dealing with the guilt and anger associated with Post Traumatic Stress Syndrome (PTSS), returning from a war zone with operations unfinished, before the last service member came home. For some unexplained reason, I took it personally. While I was glad to be home after leaving the insanely hostile environment, there was still work overseas left undone. Soldiers, Sailors, Airmen, Marines, and civilians were still risking their lives there. It took its toll on me, as it does for thousands of combat veterans.

I never complained because I always returned from war zones relatively unscathed on the outside. Others died, while many lost much more than they deserved. While shopping at the Post Exchange (PX), I saw amputees barely out of their teens, rolling around in wheelchairs. One time, I heard a young double-amputee Soldier recently returned from Afghanistan talking to a buddy about how his wife had left him. Even people from his hometown shunned him, not knowing what to say or how to react. He felt lost. Hopeless. His life had changed in an instant, both in the war zone and at home. He never saw either coming.

A lump formed in my throat. My eyes welled up, overcome by the emotions of facing the unfairness of life itself. I rushed outside, unable to bear how life had treated this brave young man. Once outside, I felt like the Incredible Hulk was raging within me. I was angry for no apparent tangible reason, with no outlet to calm me down. Soon after this incident, I stopped going out and began staying home alone. After hours and weeks of critical thinking, I diverted my attention by planning house projects, eventually planning and building two patios and a deck. Finally breaking through the plateau, independently I learned how to deal with my feelings. I hunkered down, focusing primarily on finding work, then keeping it, and then excelling at it. In the end, I faced my emptiness and anger by confronting it. I made it a point to go back to the PX, seeking out these young Soldiers. Instead of allowing the anguish that previously overwhelmed me, to overcome and defeat me, I took control. Now I took a few seconds to thank them for their service. Typically, this led to the exchange of a few kind words of appreciation. Taking a few more minutes to share some stories was the medicine we all needed. This was much more productive than abruptly leaving, stewing in anger. Yet, this was no less difficult. The entire time I spoke, I choked back tears and the lump in my throat. Tears wouldn't have helped anyone.

This was my healing process. Wounds on the outside are easy to see. But wounds on the inside, not seen can be just as detrimental and debilitating. I took refuge in nature, connected with Soldiers, traveled, and planned and completed house projects. Everything I could plan and complete based on my vision was MY healing process. I needed it. And if I could share just one of these activities with these young Soldiers, I did.

During one typically lonely night at home, I took a well-needed break from my multitude of planned home improvement projects, in various stages of completion. I sat under the stars, playing guitar with my dogs beside me. I've always said, "Life makes sense the most, when alcohol is the host." Taking my own advice, enjoying a few beers, thoughts of the reunion popped into my head. I logged onto Facebook to explore the possibilities, which before I had only haphazardly considered. Much to my amazement, during one of my name searches, there she was! I saw the angelic smile, surrounded by the same ethereal glow I hadn't seen in 33 years.

Her name was the still the same. And, as my sources that night divulged, she lived in Sweden. My breath stopped and my lungs quivered for oxygen. Memories flooded my mind; otherwise, I felt numb. My feelings remained in neutral. I couldn't do anything but stare at her pictures, enjoying the spectacle in front of me. "WoWWW!!" was my only thought. Still entranced by her image 33 years later. She had changed little; strangely enough, my feelings for her changed little as well. Nothing really changed, except for the time passing between us.

I couldn't think straight. I couldn't move. I couldn't do anything but stare at her picture. My heart raced, my palms started sweating, and once again, my every thought surrounded her. I couldn't believe it. There she was, right in front of me.

I mustered the focus to send her a quick email message, "Hi Erika, it's Dimitri from junior high, are you married?"

I couldn't believe I was so curt and to the point. I didn't want to agonize knowing she probably had a perfect life, was in a perfect marriage, was rolling in money, and was loving life. Even though I hoped all this for her, I selfishly hoped it wasn't true.

Her response was swift and simple, "No, Dimitri, I'm not married. Are you?" My heart stopped. After 33 years, could I once again might have a shot at this perfect form of a woman? Were my years of physical pain and trauma preparing me to finally settle down? Could it be with this living angel, my Swedish Princess? Could I make this happen? Would she want it to happen? After all these years, I felt like I was again back in junior high. I didn't understand it, nor did I want to. What I did want was to revel in comforting memories. I now felt inexplicably, confident.

This time I decided not to be shy, especially not online. And eventually, I'd tell her exactly how I felt, leaving nothing to her imagination and nothing between us unsaid. I vowed if I saw her in person, I would lay it all out for her, explaining everything. At this point though, regarding my feelings, I had more questions than answers.

She quickly and confidently added into her Facebook response, "You'd love it here in Sweden. You should come! The air is so clean, and the forests are so green. The weather is perfect these days. The winters are cold and long, but can be very romantic with a specially prepared dinner including red wine. Afterward, snacking on dark chocolate squares with a mug of hot chocolate topped with whipped cream within reach, is delectable. All this while lying naked under a thick, cozy king-sized blanket in front of a crackling fire, tops off the perfect romantic evening."

We conversed through similarly charged texts during more Facebook sessions in the days to come.

My upcoming business trip to Germany was looming, and my concentration clearly was elsewhere. Based on her sporadic replies, so was hers. Since I traveled nearly monthly for work, I often made my overseas business travel worthwhile by vacationing in surrounding countries afterward. This made sense since I was already nearby and in the same time zone.

This upcoming trip to Germany would be no different. Years prior, I had visited each German border area including: Dresden, Berlin, most of Bavaria to include Stuttgart, Munich, Heidelberg, Frankfurt, Hamburg, Strasbourg, and King Ludwig's castles including Neuschwanstein (the Disney inspired castle), Bad Tolz, Garmisch, the castle town of Rotenberg, and many other towns in between across the vastly beautiful German landscape. I traveled to England, Portugal, the Azores, France, Italy, Croatia, Czech Republic, Hungary, Austria, Switzerland, and Norway. I wanted this trip, like all my previous trips, to be unique and exciting. Now it could be!

I based my first explorations in Europe on the countries where Soldiers I'd served with in Iraq and Afghanistan were from. If I had fond memories of those Soldiers, I'd visit their country. And my internationally minded Dad always weighed in on any of my proposed vacations when I asked him.

During preparations for the war in Iraq, I spent months in Kuwait working with Polish Officers, Non-Commissioned Officers and Enlisted. They were my favorite and the friendliest of those I met. They were intelligent, interesting, and generally a lot of fun. Their doctrine, the immaculate condition of their vehicles, their discipline, even their Battalion structure down to the Safety Officer in each Battalion seemed to mirror what we did in the U.S. Army. The Croatians were a close second; I had already visited Croatia a few years prior when the opportunity arose. My Dad emphasized I shouldn't pass up a visit to Poland. So, there it was. On this trip I would go to Poland. What an exciting life I was having! It was lonely, but it was amazing!

I looked on TripAdvisor.com, LonelyPlanet.com, Viator.com, and a few other travel websites for ideas hashing out a cursory travel plan. Poland's rich history and complex relationship with the Bohemian kings of the past and the Hapsburg Empire intrigued me. So, I planned it out—fly from Germany to Kraków, a semi-mountainous region of Poland's first kingdom, to the capitol Warsaw, which was decimated during World War II with the Nazis leveling it in retribution for its fierce fight against their regime; this city was completely reconstructed in the aftermath. Then, I'd travel Northwest to the seaside town of Gdańsk. I'd fill in the details later, as I always did—I could plan on taking either a train, bus, or airplane or combination thereof, and arrange the lodging later. Sometimes I'd look for a room upon my arrival.

During my first available weekend in Southern Germany (of the two or I had), I could take the short drive once again visiting the lovely Czech Republic with its castle city of Prague along with its bars, restaurants, and clubs like: James Dean, Kožička, Tretter's, and Hemingway. The last time I stayed in a single room at the Prague Hostel it only cost me $10 a night. Or maybe I'd return to Český Krumlov, or Karlštejn Castle. Maybe another visit to the Kutná Hora human bone church was in order. I may even go back to the lush German border town of Flossenbürg, renowned for an ancient castle, now in ruins. I could decide this later based on the weather.

Could I squeeze in a visit to Sweden, too? Should I? Or should I let my memories of the Viking Princess lie quietly dormant in my past? Since all my co-workers at the Pentagon were married, they found my adventures incredibly amusing. The consensus was I should probably go somewhere I hadn't been before, like Poland, and forget about Sweden, since it may be too much time away from work. Even my pinpoint-focused, detailed, demanding supervisor, Daryl, had no problem chiming in on his perspective regarding my vacation planning. He agreed with the consensus. The only person who was excited about this prospect was our supervisor. When this handsome, tall man of Swedish descent jokingly said, "Good for you D. Visiting my people's homeland might do you some good. I hope you do go!" My colleagues just laughed off his comment with sneers and jeers.

The Frankfurt airport was one of my favorite departure points in Europe for both business and vacation travel because it offers so many options. With this in mind, I could defer answering the Sweden question until later. So off I was on another spectacular adventure.

~ 7 ~

The First Landing /
Den Första Landningen

Arriving at the Frankfurt airport mid-morning on a Thursday after the overnight, relatively sleepless, red-eye flight, I went to the first ATM I saw to get some Euros for breakfast. I collected my rental car keys and documentation; Germans do love their paper documentation and tangible credentials. The fact I travel with an international driver's license in my possession is always a plus here. I had a delicious German breakfast at the airport bakery and drove for hours heading south toward the U.S. Army military garrison in Bavaria. It was in a quaint town named Grafenwöhr. The Nazis established a military training area here due to its austere location, difficult terrain, and incomparably, untenable weather throughout the year. This is where I presented my seminars.

Thankfully, in Germany they drive on the same side of the road as in the U.S., and the autobahns have unlimited speeds from Frankfurt to Grafenwöhr which tremendously cuts down on travel time. This helped me get to Grafenwöhr within hours of landing in Frankfurt. There is relative comfort driving as fast as your car can go, realizing there's nothing more you can do to get where you are going any faster. Of course, this requires 100 percent focus; I prefer driving gloves to mitigate sweaty palms, and setting my car up perfectly (mirrors, seat, heat/cool, snacks, etc.) before departure so I don't have to look away from the road for an instant. When screaming down the road at 120 mph, this can be all it takes between life and death.

Upon arriving at the military base, it felt like I spent a lot of time completing the security prerequisites for entry. I got my entrance authorization documentation, and went straight to the building to meet my host for my training venue. I set up the seminar site, downloaded presentation materials to an external hard drive from the local intranet, launched a few emails informing the Pentagon office of my safe arrival, saved a local copy of all my seminar class material and handouts on disk, and was prepared to print the products after lunch, as long as the hosts intended to keep the building open long enough for me to accomplish this. Otherwise, I'd have to complete this task the next morning. All of this could take hours, depending on the state and availability of the IT infrastructure T1 lines (developed by AT&T Bell Labs for transferring data over multiplexed lines). I never wasted any time setting up since this was my primary purpose for being here. At some sites it had taken me six hours just to download and prepare my handouts, so I always accomplished these tasks first. This method was more secure than traveling internationally with official documents. Often this process ran into my weekend hours. Since I knew even the Gasthaus employees didn't particularly enjoy showing up for work on weekends, I had to work fast. This way, I'd have the weekend to myself.

I broke away for a quick lunch and short drive to the military hotel to see if they had any last-minute cancellations. As bad luck would have it, they had none. Staying on the Army garrison saves me hours of early morning driving for the seminar week, and would be safer during foul weather. Even the closer and wondrously comfortable tourist destination of Hotel Am See on the lake in Eschenbach, along with the hotels in Vilseck and Weiden in der Oberpfalz, were completely booked.

I enjoyed staying on the local economy in foreign countries, experiencing the cultural immersion. But inconvenience was an issue here, if not a safety concern; driving in the Bavarian Black Forest during the frigid German winters could be hazardous this time of year. This seminar was a last-minute request, and the only available accommodations within an hour drive was at the Hotel Gasthof Lohbachwinkel. Basically, this was in the middle of nowhere, near the tiny town of Weiherhammer, a 45-minute drive from the Army base (and to any other place in any direction) through the winding back roads of the Black Forest. There's good reason it's named the Black Forest—for its closely planted trees and extreme darkness, causing an absence of sunlight year-round. Driving at night through this area was like driving through visual tar even during daylight hours. In dense fog, it was treacherous.

For this seminar, I arranged for one of my colleagues, Morty, to assist me. He was someone with whom I had a colorful past serving in Special Forces. At this point in our careers, as divergent as our paths were, we had the occasional opportunity of working together. I liked him. He was fiercely loyal, efficient, and an absolute workhorse. Occasionally, we worked in the Washington D.C. area together, even though we consulted for different companies.

Morty had a knack for being quite resourceful, and for knowing where to find the best deals in any country for anything and everything. Somehow, Morty always seemed to find himself the best hotels to stay in and at the last minute would inform me of the deviation in his itinerary. Typically, his explanation would at some point include a story about a wild night, with beautiful foreign flight attendants keeping him up, dancing on tabletops in their drunken stupors. But not this time. He had no choice. This place was very cozy and relaxing—don't get me wrong—but the hazardous drive could take its toll. And as a gasthaus, the only amenities available were a bedroom, and if lucky, a restaurant. Hopefully, the restaurant would be open.

Morty always brought his personal laptop computer with him, so I wouldn't have to bring mine. Having this convenience, I could embark on my side-trips throughout Europe or Asia after the business portion of the trip with only carry-on luggage. I wasn't tied to a laptop with concerns of it being stolen, broken, or hacked. Before departing after my seminars, I mailed back to the States all my business attire and laundry via the U.S. postal service on U.S. bases where I presented. This enabled me to travel streamlined, unencumbered, and light. Morty's presence made it possible this trip.

Before beginning the potentially treacherous driving trek back to the gasthaus/gasthof, I dropped by the German travel agency on post to book my trip to Poland, as I planned the week prior. When I arrived, as bad luck would have it, they were closed. This was much earlier than its posted hours, but this was a German practice I knew well. I'd have to return the next day, Friday, before noon to plan and book my travel. Off I went to the gasthaus to get an early start in my search for the site while it was still light. I had no clue what surprises awaited me on this long, lonely ride through desolate, winding roads, as my stateside GPS with spotty reception translated the route with outdated European maps.

It was a beautiful, smooth drive on well-designed and maintained, yet snow-dusted, minor roads, winding through the German countryside at 50 mph/80 kph speed limits. It was fun twisting in and out of the dark wooded areas at these speeds. Using a slalom driving technique, I progressed closer and closer to the gasthaus as daylight waned. As it turned out, my GPS didn't enjoy the ride as much as I expected it would. After taking an inordinate number of turns within a brief time span, my GPS led me to a dead-end railroad crossing. I stopped dead in the middle of the road since there were no car-crossing areas anywhere in sight—the road abruptly ended with me facing a large German Do-Not-Enter sign affixed to an impenetrable barrier. I was perplexed.

As I sat in my rental car at this dead-end re-tracing my steps mentally, I thought, "What the hell?" There were no roads or bridges crossing over these railroad tracks—the road just ended right at the tracks in front of me. At this very moment it struck me as being very, very strange that just minutes prior, traveling at about 50 miles per hour on this tiny road, I had seen a park bench positioned perilously close to the roadway. I recalled the last few times the sexy-voiced GPS hesitated—it wasn't good. This stupid GPS had me driving down what I now realized was a wide snow-dusted walkway, inside an obscure, poorly marked, countryside park. Upon passing it, I thought it strange some idiot would place a park bench so close to a major road. This thought only entered my mind moments before reaching the railroad tracks and the conspicuously placed sign. "Ah-hah! So that's why it was all so weird! Shit!"

As quickly as possible, I snapped a U-turn, back-tracking my route, covering as much ground as I safely could. And this time it would be slower than 50 mph through the park, that's for sure! I was aghast contemplating the possibilities. The last thing I needed in a foreign country was legal problems leading to a potential international incident with the local police days prior to my seminar. Luckily, it was getting dark and cold enough to dissuade even the staunchest locals from enjoying a walk along this trail during my untimely detour. Once again, I drove past the bench slowly enough not to attract any attention in case anyone saw me.

Returning to the main road, following the GPS re-direct directions, I ended up on the opposite side of a remote German village. I remembered passing through this same village on my way to this very point, from a different direction. This too, perplexed me. Yet I drove on with my frustration level nearing its capacity. Approaching a three-way intersection, I came across some idiot just sitting in a car in the middle of the road with no lights on, with apparently no clue how to drive, and no clue where he was going, or how he would get there.

"Morty???" I thought, "No way!" But it had to be him in his rental car, as he would be searching these same austere roads, for the same gasthaus, at about the same time. And if I knew Morty, he'd be just as frustrated as I was. Judging from the position of his car in the road, it's possible he could've been driving as erratically as I was, spawned from his extreme frustration. It had to be Morty, as ours were the only two cars on the road. And we both would be extremely concerned about not reaching the hotel before dark. Like at the travel agency, it's customary in Germany to have the gasthaus owners simply decide to lock up and go home early or cancel our reservations on a whim if someone showed before us without a reservation. Then what would we do? After already spending hours on these roads before sunset, I couldn't imagine doing this in extreme darkness. We'd never find the place, getting nowhere, except where we had already been.

I approached the car slowly, stopping on the right side of the vehicle, hoping it was Morty. As I rolled down my window, I really hoped it was not some large, very aggressive, German man who may have called the police reporting my extremely erratic driving through their sacred countryside and park. It's times like these I'm thankful for Germany's strict gun control laws, especially in rural areas.

As I peered into the vehicle, illuminating my dome light, I saw the profile of the driver snap his head, looking at me through the dark tint in apparent shock, as if I had materialized out of thin air. He hesitated and after a brief pause rolled down the passenger window, illuminating his dome light. He shouted out the driver's window, "Boy, am I glad to see you! Where the fuck did you come from? You scared the shit out of me!"

"The Frankfurt airport and Grafenwöhr," I responded. "You?" knowing full well that wasn't what he meant.

"Me too. I took a later flight than expected—where the fuck is this place? And where the fuck are we? I can't figure out what this stupid German GPS is saying. I couldn't even figure out how to make the piece of shit speak English!"

Yep! Thankfully, it was Morty. "It doesn't matter, my handheld American GPS is doing the same thing way out here."

After a brief discussion in the middle of the road, we quickly compared verbal notes, discussing where we had been. Relieved to learn we both traveled to this point from different directions, we were left with only one remaining option.

Using deductive reasoning off we drove. I let Morty lead so I wouldn't have to put up with his bitching about my driving or navigating later that night. Eventually, we arrived at a tiny parking lot next to a centuries old quaint, dark wooden structure, we had passed twice. We stopped this time. The building was dark with only a few lights outside illuminating a small sign. The beautifully rustic building on a wooded lot had country charm and was in an extremely remote area; true, even by German standards. Walking up closely, the dimly illuminated, ivy covered sign read "Hotel Gasthof Lohbachwinkel." Whew! We both immediately saved this location into all our GPSs, ensuring we could get back here.

Checking in without incident, it relieved us to learn that the restaurant was open. Settling into our rooms, we agreed to meet downstairs in the restaurant for what we hoped would be an exquisitely prepared German dinner. Dinner with a German bier was excellent, followed by a nightcap which segued into a continuation of our reminiscing and laughing at past escapades. Typically, our conversations began… "Do you remember that guy who was…" or "… that time we…" After that night's intriguing conversation and a few laughs, we paid our bill, planning the next day's start, and settled into our separate rooms for the night. I borrowed Morty's laptop to complete my daily time sheet after the long trip from the States. I was smoked!

After swinging open the over-sized single window the next morning, I awoke to a dense fog peeking at me through the curtains. Breathing in the frigid, fresh air, I did a calisthenics/exercise band workout in the room then went for a quick run outside. I planned on getting to post as quickly as possible after my very satisfying German breakfast, because I had a lot to do. Morty and I took separate cars since we both had separate personal tasks to accomplish. I had to finish setting up the seminar room, then rush to the travel agency to finalize my trip to Poland.

The drive through the forest was uneventful since my GPS didn't forget the way back to the Army post. Setting up for the seminar went quickly, with both of us working it. We called it a day pretty early, wandering over to the post exchange for a quick lunch. Afterward, I popped over to the travel agency; luckily there was no line and I got help instantly upon entering.

Taking a number, after a brief wait, the travel agent called me.

"Hello, I'm Layla. How may I help you?" she cordially said.

During my explanation of my intent to go to Poland to see Kraków, Warsaw, and Gdańsk, but unsure if I should fly, drive, or go by train, she put it clearly and succinctly.

"Go by train?" she laughed. "Zhat is stoopid. Do you know how big Poland is? Why would you even consider going by train?

115

It's a very large, agrarian country. I've been zere and believe me zere's nothing to see at all between those cities… just vegetation— you can see that anywhere! No, no, no, no, no, no—you'll need to fly! Yah, you'll fly or completely waste all your time when you should be touring! And don't even think about renting a car! Driving the roads, the signs, and directions will make you crazy! Poland's public transport is as excellent as any place in Europe, so you can save a lot of time, money, and definitely some frustration there. What else?" she huffed in typical German fashion.

"Well, I was thinking about maybe visiting Sweden after Poland, or I could go in the future on a follow-on trip to Germany. Maybe I could even go next year." I was apprehensive about spilling the beans, explaining my circumstances from my perspective, but I wanted to get a female opinion regarding a potential trip to Sweden and my motivations for doing so.

"Maybe?" she said, "Why maybe. Who maybe goes anywhere?"

I began telling her a condensed version of my story with, "Well, you see there was—there is, this girl I knew in junior high school, 33 years ago and I fell in puppy love with her from the very first time I saw her. I was 12 years old in Thailand where we both went to school, since that's where our parents were working. She left the country before I did so I haven't seen or heard from her until about a week ago, when we briefly communicated on Facebook. She's not married, I'm not married, and she talked me up a bit regarding visiting her in Sweden. She came on quite strong and piqued my interest. She described a Swedish habit of lying by a warm fire during the dark, long nights, drinking hot cocoa, talking, catching up, and taking walks in the woods, visiting sights in her country and stuff like that! That's why I was thinking about going to Sweden… it could probably wait for another time in the future though," I calmly explained.

"You found her again on Facebook? Do you have a picture of her?" Layla questioned.

I showed her the picture I downloaded to my cellphone.

"Are you crazy? Are you really so stupid? You have this opportunity to meet a woman as beautiful as her, who already knows you, and you're not sure if you'll visit her this year or next year? Look at that picture, would you? She's absolutely gorgeous! What is wrong with you? How long do you think a woman who looks like that, in your age range, will be single in ANY country on ANY CONTINENT? Are you crazy? No! YOU MUST go to Sweden! Greta!" she barked. "Are you hearing zis? Look at zis picture, would you? Show her the picture!" she exclaimed, looking over at her non-committing colleagues, inviting them into the conversation. "Helga, you too! Look at zis picture! Do you agree? What would you do? Huh? He needs to go to Sweden as soon as possible, yah?"

Helga, her colleague, chimed in, "Forget about Poland! Go to Sweden dummkopf!! Then after you two get married, you take HER to Poland with you so you won't have to go alone!! What's wrong with you?"

After a few sentences in German, Layla continued speaking, now in English, looking at me, "It's not at all expensive to go from Frankfurt to Stockholm. You're leaving from Frankfurt, anyway; only paying a small change fee is so reasonable. You can't travel from the States any cheaper—from here it might even be half as much! Here, you're in the same time zone, it's not yet winter weather, if you can spare a few days… if I were you, I would do it! If it's that important to you, I wouldn't wait… Maybe she will get married before you have the chance to visit next year. And you'd be kicking yourself once again! But this time, probably for the rest of your life—no? You'll need a rental car in Sweden too. I can get you a good rate from Lufthansa for both the flight and car. I assume you want to arrange your own hotels to save some money? You know there will be no hostels north of Stockholm like you can find in Poland. These two are very, very different countries," she added.

I interjected— "I think you're getting ahead of the situation and assuming a lot about her. I don't even know if she will see me. I wasn't considering going to Sweden for sure until I had THIS conversation with her. I want to visit Poland first, and then maybe go to Sweden. In case Sweden didn't work out, at least I'd have a good time in Poland…"

She continued, "Ahhhh, I'll warn you now. When you go from Poland which is very cheap to Sweden which is one of the most expensive countries in Europe, it will cost you—a lot! But it will be much more expensive next year because the rates go up as they do every year, you know. It will work out better all-around for you to go to Sweden this year, as you wish AFTER, yah AFTER, you visit Poland! Look, I'll run both the Poland trip and the Sweden trip separately since travel rates are especially quite good right now. We are closing soon anyway. Think about it over the weekend and tell me on Monday, so I can book your travel in its entirety. But if I were you, I know what I would do! You know how difficult it is to meet a compatible person these days in any country, I wouldn't recommend you risking waiting one minute more. There's no time like the present, you know! The weather in Sweden is still very nice now, but it's cooling down rather quickly. There should not be much, if any snow, yet. And now, as we are entering what you Americans call 'Autumn,' real winter in Sweden has not yet arrived. You're lucky!" she confidently added. "Will the weather be the same this time next year? Who knows?"

She added, "Have you been to Washington State before? It's like the weather in Washington State at this time of year, right now, sort of…" she quipped. I was shocked she knew about Washington State weather, "So, it's a good time for you to go to Sweden since you're already in the region," she continued.

"You've been to Washington State before?" I asked.

"Yeah, my ex-husband was in the U.S. Military and was from Washington State. We were stationed there for a while."

"So, about taking a train in Poland from the south to the north," I interjected.

"Why? I told you that's an incredibly stupid idea. You'll see nothing and it will take you forever to get absolutely nowhere! Here in Europe, the trains are almost the same cost as flying, anyway. You'll have more time to enjoy yourself by flying. Don't you listen to me?" she insisted. "It's not like taking the Eurail through Germany, Italy, or France. I tell you; you'll see NOTHING!"

You really gotta love the honesty of the German people, but you can't be thin-skinned about it. She wasn't trying to insult me. She fully intended to get her point across in a very direct, efficient German manner. And I appreciated it.

"If you want to see Poland in only one week, you'll have to fly to the major cities with the amount of time you've allocated for your visit… so here we go, fly into Kraków, stay for two-and-a-half days, fly to Warsaw, stay three days, and fly into Gdańsk stay two-and-a-half days, and then fly to Sweden on Lufthansa. It's actually a contract flight from SAS, for four days—we'll do this, ya?"

"Why can't I do it all in seven days?" I asked.

"And Sweden too? Because that's stupid! How can you do that? You'll be traveling the entire time! No, that is really a stupid, stupid idea—you'll hate it, and you'll have no time to see anything. As it is, you'll have to be a lightning speed traveler! If you plan on traveling to northern Sweden, you'll most likely have an issue with the weather on icy roads right now, so I don't recommend you doing that now. If you stay near Stockholm on lowland roads and to the south, you'll be okay."

I remembered Erika saying she lived north of Stockholm in a small town on the water. It was something like Gävle. So, should I decide to take the travel agent's recommended course of action? It sounded like an affordable price because this definitely was not the peak time of year to travel. I wondered.

"Just take all the itineraries and think about it," she urged.

I agreed. She printed me up the itineraries, handing them to me, saying, "Okay, here they are. Don't wait too long to decide or you'll be going nowhere! I'll see you on Monday morning. Early! Don't wait any longer than that because the rates will cancel out on Monday morning and I'm not doing all this work twice. And you can pay for it all on credit card at that time. I'll see you on Monday MORNING! Got it? This is tight planning times already—you will NOT be late on Monday either, ya?!" she squawked. "You got some thinking to do. *Juus*! Goodbye! Now we're closing!" she sparked.

"Sorry, what was your name?" I asked.

"It's Layla," she responded.

"Okay Layla, *juus, danke shen*, thank you," I jovially sung as I walked out the door. "Have a good weekend. I'll be back!"

"You better be!" Layla insisted.

I sped back to the seminar room to re-check the room setup, cast out a few emails to update my stateside office regarding the seminar prep, and then, to Erika, explaining the possibility of me arranging a visit to see her in a few weeks. I completed my time sheet. If, and only if, I was going to go to Sweden would I have to call the Pentagon before missing any discussion windows due to the time difference. I'd have to request permission to take a few more vacation days, and get Security to sign off on it as well. I desperately placed the call to my manager, Daryl; surprisingly, he answered.

After rendering the niceties of the day, I explained my newly emerging potential plans to visit my Swedish Princess in Sweden, possibly requesting a few more vacation days on a whim. This might occur after completing my Poland itinerary. His voice went silent. My stomach knotted up.

After a few seconds, he squeezed out his nasal-pitched, whiney-toned voice he used when he wanted to portray extreme discomfort, displeasure, and complete annoyance with the topic of conversation at hand, Daryl whined, "You wanna do whaaat? You want to maybe might go to Sweden? Aren't you already spending a week traveling through Poland after the training seminar? And now you want to go to Sweden too? You depart to Poland five days from now, and only now you want to change your itinerary? Will the airline even let you change your plans at this point? All this trouble just to see a girl? You'll need to call Lana in Security… tell her you're amending your travel plans and give her the new dates so you're covered there… explain your new plans to George [the office manager]… contact the people attending your Tuesday afternoon meeting to see if someone can take over for you… and contact all the attendees, letting them know you won't be there and give someone the meeting plan so they can chair the meeting… then you'll have to call the travel agency stateside to change your flights because I believe if you originate in the States only they can change your itinerary and if it costs more money for your return, including the U.S. Government per diem rate for your return, you'll have to make up for all that monetary difference out of pocket… for how many days?… four more…?"

"Daryl, is that a yes, or no?" I eked out, hoping he would say it was okay.

I felt like I did in high school when I asked my Dad to borrow the car keys for a date the day after I got a speeding ticket at 0200 am. My heart was dry with anticipation, awaiting his response. I explained to him, as I did to the travel agent stating my case, why I was being so spontaneous for the first time—when in our business, it's severely frowned upon.

Daryl continued, "Really? You wanna do all that for a girl? For a girl you haven't seen in 33 years? You're really stupid! Hahahaha! Aayyy don't care. If you have the vacation time… then yeeeah, I guess so. All this just to chase a skirt? Thaaaaat's craaaaazy! But you better cover your Tuesday meeting or it'll mean your job. Don't you dare push all that over on me on such brief notice! Let me know when you finalize your plans and I'll let Bernie [the Branch lead] know. Good luck… you've got a lot of work yet to do today if you want to add Sweden to your trip here at the last minute! You'd better get busy! And don't forget to let your company know!"

I already knew that wasn't going to happen. I'd let those jealous, superficial idiots know only after I returned.

"Thanks, I appreciate it, Daryl." Deep down, way deep, he was a good guy. I never understood why he made a hobby of making my life so damned difficult. He was always that way.

It was decision time for me. Is this what I really wanted to do? I took the itinerary out of the envelope and looked at it.

The four, well really three days in Sweden, was itself going to be the costliest change to any trip ever and the most expensive vacation I ever took. I couldn't believe my eyes! It would cost $3000 for just three days in Sweden; $1000 a day, minimum, for airfare, rental car, and hotel. Not including gas, taxes, food, etc. I thought for a few seconds—do I really want to do it? I'd really like to try to do it, especially after hearing Layla's thought process and dissertation. I don't know. If I chose not to, I'd show up in the Pentagon having some 'splainin to do, that's all. My contract company would never be the wiser.

As quickly as possible, I made a few more telephone calls and launched more emails, complying with Daryl's instructions. It's a good thing I maintained a great rapport with everyone in my office. The last thing I wanted to do was jeopardize my reputation at work, basically resulting from a whim. The work issues seemed to work out pretty easily; they did in email anyway. I didn't have time to wait or expect any responses because of the time difference from the U.S.

This might work out, if nobody let me down. But if they forgot or reneged, I'd be screwed and maybe even unemployed! The pressure was on! I didn't have time to call regarding the airline reservation changes, so I had to depend on the airline office stateside answering my emails over their weekend, which I knew wouldn't happen.

My seminar host waited impatiently at the door, "Hey! Come on... out, out, out! I promised my wife I'd take her to dinner tonight! Out! I gotta lock up!"

I quickly wrapped up everything, shutting down the computer, closing up shop as quickly as I could, and farewelled my seminar host as he rushed me into the parking lot. Morty didn't come back after lunch; I wasn't expecting him.

I was so looking forward to enjoying a relaxing dinner over a strong German dark/dunkel beer before I became a stress monkey, attempting to resolve how to accomplish all this. What a pain in the ass it was becoming. I risked facing whatever repercussions would result from any of my whimsical plans backfiring if people let me down. What if my plans to see the Princess didn't work out? Then what would I do in Sweden all by myself, out more than $3000, with nothing to do for four, well really—three days? What if she didn't want to—or couldn't see me due to her work or personal commitments or something else? Did I really want to flush over US$3000 and risk having a bad time in Sweden? I didn't know what to do.

As expected, my GPS got me back to the gasthaus without incident, as night fell. I really didn't mind driving at night, especially since I knew the route. Well, the GPS did.

And as expected, when I got to the gasthaus, Morty was already seated in the restaurant, having a beer. He was waiting for another opportunity to razz me about being late, or however he chose to denigrate me for the night, for his own entertainment. I hadn't seen him since we left for lunch. I knew he'd pick something to zing me on. I expected it. He was jealous of me. No, he was more envious of my current life and of my positions during our past military career together. So, I let him enjoy whatever newly found entertainment he would claim at my expense. I really enjoyed his company; he is one of the funniest people I know. I typically found his antics extremely entertaining, even when I bared the brunt of his jokes.

I sat down, seeing the anticipation all over his face. He could not contain himself, so I threw him a bone to gnaw on. I started discussing my firm plans for Poland and potential plans to go to Sweden despite the possible re-arrangements required in the Pentagon. As expected, as soon as I told him the news, he was amidst a deep drink of his beer, which he sprayed on me as he simultaneously choked on it—then burst out laughing.

"Are you serious? You're fuckin' serious?? You're going to do this?! You're really going to do this?? Like, less than a week out?? I knew about Poland... but now Sweden?? Are you serious? When's the last time you saw this girl? Thirty-three years ago? That's the most fucked up thing I've ever heard! Yeah, you're both single, you're both available, and she's going to look just as you said she did in high school? And she's gonna like, no, she's gonna instantly fall in love with YOU!"

"JUNIOR high school," I corrected him.

I should've left that out of the conversation, as this eagerly egged him on to increase his volume and theatrics. To this, he laughed so loudly and so hard, he fell off his chair onto the floor. He probably did this for visual effect, although the numbing properties of the strong, dunkel, Hefeweizen beer could've further intensified and over-stimulated his response. When the hostess rushed over, concerned Morty may have hurt himself, I waved her off, saying Morty always acts like this and he'll be fine.

"Are you seeeeeerious? You're serious…" he murmured again from his position on the floor. "She's probably posted 20-year-old photos or better yet, her daughter's photos! You're AN IDIOT! You're a fuckin' IDIOT!"

Yeah, when he put it that way, I understood his perspective. He wasn't one to mince words or camouflage any of his thoughts. That was his perspective!

"She's gonna be fat, nasty, and ugly, and lazy… oh my God… you're a fuckin' idiot!" he said slathering through his laughter.

Remember, this is the guy with the girlfriend nobody has ever seen. I was glad to provide him a source of entertainment before his dinner; yet, his reactions in the past hadn't dissuaded my actions. If anything, his reaction may have moved me toward forging my intent to go. His laugh attack also attracted the attention of local customers sitting nearby. Undoubtedly, Morty provided them the perfect moniker of the Ugly-American. But he didn't care.

After he settled down, it was time to order our food. The local guests were wondering what the hell was going on between us and began chuckling at Morty's antics, realizing he was harmless. Once he regained his composure and took his place back in his seat at the table, he wiped tears of laughter from his eyes.

"Ohhh to see the look on your face when you see her… Ohhh My God, I wish I could be there… ohhh my God!" he added.

My potential plan truly entertained him. I was glad for him.

"Ohhh my God, now I've heard everything! And you used to be a U.S. Army Special Forces Officer? A real live Green Beret? What an Officer thing to do!!" He continued clucking for a few more minutes.

Understanding that Germans can be quite stoic, serious, and dedicated to near perfection at whatever they do is important. As I surveyed the menu, two items caught my eye—the trout fish and another fish I hadn't heard of. It is called a "Pike." As Morty settled down, the Gasthaus Meister/owner, who also was apparently quite the accomplished chef and doubled as our waiter, came over to take our order. I made the mistake of asking him what the difference was between the Trout and the Pike.

"Ah yez. Ahm glad you asked me zis question. Well, zee TROUT," as his soliloquy began, "is a freshwater fish with white meat. It is quite social a fish, found in freshwater lakes and rivers throughout Churmany and may either live their whole life in fresh water or spend a few years at sea before returning to fresh water to spawn like the salmon fish. The TROUT usually eats shrimp, bloodworms, flies, insect parts, mollusks, and eels. They can grow up to 33 kilos or 66 pounds, as you Americans say. The PIKE fish on the other hand, is also a white meat fish, however, is quite a reclusive fish. It is a predatory fish with spots and stripes along their backs to camouflage themselves in weeds where they live. The markings of the PIKE can be as different as fingerprints for humans. An individual PIKE can grow to about 1.8 meters in length, which is about six feet long. Both fishes are prepared the same way, and you get the same amount in a filet about this long (he gestured about one foot long with his hands); it's a personal preference on which fish you like. If you are staying here in the gasthaus for a few days, which you are, there is plenty of time for you to try both."

"Okay, that's the plan, surprise me for tonight; I'll try both, one today and the other next time. Thank you." I responded.

I had a tough time looking at Morty without laughing; he was biting the insides of his cheeks, tuning red, and holding his breath, preventing yet another outburst.

As soon as the chef left our table and went into the kitchen, I looked at Morty with a straight face and mumbled, "Whut the hell?? Is it me?? I don't want to date the damned fish; I just want to eat it for dinner. Now I feel so sorry for the thing, maybe I'll just have the goulash soup or a salad."

Morty laughed and laughed, staying in his seat this time. "Sweden?? Sweden?? Why not fucking Russia, dude? Wait, I don't wanna give you any ideas! You might lose your fuckin' clearance and your job chasing some filament of your imagination!" he snorted.

"It's figment... not filament idiot, just shuddup and drink your beer," I said in jest.

Dinner was delicious. Morty brought his computer downstairs, and I was able to get online with relative ease in the restaurant. The first message I sent out was another one to the Princess, telling her I was thinking about planning a trip to Sweden. "Hey Erika what would you say if I told you I really was planning a trip to Sweden to see you in a few weeks?"

After sending and reading a few more emails, the Gasthaus Meister explained he had to close the dining area and lock the restaurant, so we had to leave. Morty let me take his computer for the night. The internet connection worked fine in the restaurant, but as soon as I got to my room the internet connection was tremendously degraded, not connecting to anything and then timing out. When I finally got online it was insanely slow, then sporadic. I was wondering if they turned the hotel routers off at night. Then again, we were in a foreign country and Morty had an American laptop, this may be the issue. I completed my timesheet before giving up. I could work my Poland and Sweden itinerary at the Army garrison hotel or library in the morning.

I hit the sack, wondering whether I should go to Sweden, weighing the expense, the timing, the aftermath, my solid reputation as being extremely predictable and having to blaze through the last-minute coordination, the most critical component of which I was missing—a specific invite or an acknowledgement from the Princess herself. If I was going to do it, I'd have to do magic to make it happen. It wasn't going to just happen on its own. Often, I'm quite the pragmatic individual who thinks everything out completely, weighs the risks and rewards, investigates different options, and then arrives at a predictable decision, sometime later. I went to sleep searching for answers.

As the furball in my head became a bit of a distraction, my brain's synapses were working overtime to derive the "best" decision as I lay in bed. It was nearly impossible for me to sleep wrestling with this decision. After tossing and turning half the night, I got out of bed, wandering and stumbling through the darkness to the bathroom for a glass of water. One advantage of being so far out in the country was the water out of the tap tasted fresh, and I could sleep with my windows open, enjoying the cool night air on the second floor of the gasthaus.

I drank my glass of water, looking out the oversized, open bathroom window into the extreme foggy darkness. Then I heard a whisper.

"Do it! Do it now! Go and find!" I looked around and behind me, wondering if someone, like Morty, was messing with me. I looked out the window. There was no balcony. Nobody was outside. It was a spooky experience to have in the heart of the German Black Forest, in an old, history-filled gasthaus nestled deep in the dark, wooded surroundings infused with the foggy, cool air.

The voice repeated, "Do it! Do it now! Go and find!"

A bit freaked out, I closed the window to the already chilly room and went back to bed. I finally got to sleep, not without being awakened several times, hearing the same voice posing me with the single question, "Why not go? Go and find!"

~ 8 ~

A Foggy Dawn /
En dimmig Gryning

Instead of venturing out to the Czech Republic or haphazardly wandering in my rental car across the countryside with my digital SLR camera, as I had done so many times in the past, I slept in the next day. I thoroughly enjoyed a relaxing German breakfast in the gasthaus restaurant. But time wouldn't allow me to relax the entire day. Today was decision time! My impending trips were driving me crazy. What should I do? Would I get another chance to return to Germany next year? I could go to Sweden then. But there was no guarantee this would happen.

I anticipated making the right decision eventually, but expected a bit of trepidation from the stress of running the upcoming week's seminar, deciding where, when, and how to visit various places in Poland. Visiting Sweden was a strong temptation; but was it worth the estimated US$3000 for just three days? I hadn't thought it through completely, nor was I committed to it. Although I mentally worked out my office schedule backup plan, I was still on the fence about it. I had to review the implications and spurious consequences of adding the previously unscheduled stop in Sweden. Everyone I knew thought it was a crazy idea.

Today I was going to spend most of my time online at the Army hotel and in the garrison library downloading documents, soliciting trip plans and recommendations from TripAdvisor.com, Booking.com, Hostels.com and a few other helpful websites to get information on where to stay and what to see visit in Poland and, a few items about visiting Sweden. I completed my analysis on Poland and selected the hotels in each city for the entire week I'd be there. The private room I found, much like an Air BNB, in Kraków, proved to be an excellent choice. The room in the apartment itself was unremarkable—but there, I could focus on the Olde Towne city center, a stone's throw outside the front door to the building.

The Moon Hostel in Warsaw was one place I was looking forward to staying. It promised to be a hotel with the flair and pricing of simple single rooms, and the friendly atmosphere of a hostel. The Olowianka B&B hotel in Gdańsk looked awesome. Built on a private island, it was accessible after a short walk over a tiny car bridge to and from the castle town. This was sure to be an amazing trip, especially with the online winter rates I was getting. And all my bookings included breakfast! I confirmed each stay on my credit card, and printed out a confirmation of each. This was a monumental task. I was ecstatic I finally completed it. But I still had to figure out the significant sights near each location.

I stayed as late as possible to wrap up as many loose ends as I could. I sent a few more messages to Erika on Facebook regarding feasible plans of visiting Sweden, as Erika randomly suggested. I didn't receive a response. I fired off more emails requesting the travel agency stateside provide me a cost estimate and forecast on re-booking my flights, adding the stop in Sweden. With this alternative plan, I would lose my rest day and have to go right back to work the day after returning stateside with no jet lag readjustment time. But I was okay with this sacrifice if it meant seeing the Viking Princess.

Finally, I accomplished everything I set out to do, yet still hadn't made a final decision on Sweden, but it was closing time at the library. With the setting sun, it was time for me to celebrate with a perfect dinner seafood plate of Frutti Di Mare, Italian food cooked the German way at one of my all-time favorite restaurants, Santa Lucia II. This was located in Grafenwöhr, just down the street from the base. I knew it was too late to make it back to the Hotel Gasthof Lohbachwinkel in time for dinner; I would dine here. Whenever in Bavaria I go to this restaurant at least once, as I'm guaranteed a fantastic meal with super friendly service. It has been my go-to favorite German restaurant for over 20 years. And it's one of the many "Mom and Pop-type" German restaurants I adore in this part of the country. The décor is crisply traditional, the food perfectly prepared, the portions almost too big, the prices extremely reasonable, and the staff is world-class friendly. This place always made my trips to Grafenwöhr feel like I was coming home, despite the ever so slight language barrier.

After my perfect dining experience, it was back to the gasthaus. When I arrived, Morty's car was nowhere in sight. I wondered where he went. After a Hefeweizen beer at the gasthaus bar/restaurant, I went up to my room to bed down for an early night. The entire day exhausted me. It could've been the jet lag, but that surely was not the only contributing factor.

The next morning was a lazy Sunday morning. The weather was a perfect 60 degrees Fahrenheit or 16 degrees Celsius. I awoke, exercised a bit in the room and went downstairs to once again partake in a family-style orgasmic, gastronomic experience for breakfast in the restaurant. I noticed outside Morty's rental car still was not in the parking lot. When I asked the co-owner/front desk/barkeeper/chef about him, she said he left earlier right after eating breakfast. I was happy to have this proof of life fact on Morty, since he never missed breakfast, and he was always an early riser. He hated more than anything staying up late. With his lifestyle, I found it strange how he ended up in SF for over 20 years, where most of our surreptitious mission infills [infiltrations] often extended from nightfall well into the wee hours of the morning.

I wanted to take a break and go for a drive, taking in a few sites along the German back roads toward the Czech [previously Czechoslovakia] border, where years ago I stumbled upon the ruins of the medieval castle in Flossenbürg. But I hadn't been there since I purchased my new Canon digital SLR camera. The countryside was perfect this time of year with the green and yellow hues painting the vast farmlands and fields surrounded by lush forests, dashed with white birch trees adorned with a rainbow of velvety wildflowers. These sights saturated nearly every view far and wide in this part of Bavaria at this time of year.

As I drove, the idea of visiting the magical Flossenbürg Castle ruins became a priority. But I'd stay away from the depressing concentration camp in the nearby woods across the ridgeline. I remembered the first time I visited the castle years ago. A Regular Army colleague, Craig, convinced me to go with him to cross into Czechoslovakia, through the heavily fortified border checkpoint, long before it opened its borders to the European Union—perhaps his recollection of history was a bit rushed and flawed.

After the long drive to the border, we were caught in a procession of vehicles, the guards waved us through. "See? It's easy!" he said. Suddenly, one of the armed guards jumped out of the guard shack, blocking our vehicle. He motioning for Craig to pull up and roll down the window. Which he did. The jumpy guard took up a position behind the car.

"Passport…" another no-nonsense guard from the guard shack barked gruffly. Craig surrendered his passport. This guard immediately closed the guard shack, goose-stepping over to the main border office building. Inside the car it was dead silent as my colleague, shocked and dismayed, watched his passport and the guard disappear into the main building.

"What's wrong with you? You never surrender your passport!" I yelled.

"He asked for it," he responded "You're just paranoid."

I grasped my go-to-hell bag in my left hand and the door handle with my right hand, considering running through the one guard behind our vehicle and through two border guard posts. I quickly calculated my options. As I turned around to gauge the security at the two posts, one Czechoslovakian and one German, with the 10-foot cyclone fencing topped with razor wire securing them, my primary question was would they shoot me? If so, who would shoot first? How skilled were they with their weapons? If I made it past the two sets of guards, could I run through the woods and make it back to my hotel within a day? How would the German guards treat me if I ran from the Czechoslovakian checkpoint, if I got through? My questions were limitless and answerless.

Going through my exit planning cycle, a guard emerged from the main building with six more armed guards surrounding the car, yelling for us to exit the vehicle, aggressively pointing their guns at us.

"Great, there go our options," I said.

Once detained, they quickly escorted us out of the vehicle, leading us into the main building. Without a word, we were locked in a detention cell. A border guard with very poor English muttered something, accusing us as U.S. Army officers in civilian clothes illegally attempting to enter Czechoslovakia as spies. Clearly, they intended on impounding our rental car, leaving us in the holding cell for about six hours, weighing our fate.

"You idiot! Go to Czechoslovakia, you said. Now we're in the middle of an international incident, moron! What the fuck were you thinking? I thought you did this before?" I said verbally attacking him.

"I never said that!" he quietly replied. A guard eventually brought in some paperwork, placed it on the table in front of us and said, "Do!"

We didn't. He came into the room a few more times, only looking at the paperwork and said, "Do!" Again, we didn't.

I asked again if they had a guard who spoke English and received no response. So, there we sat.

"You know they can do anything they want to us, idiot! Nobody knows where we went!" I fumed.

Silently, I worried about the gravity of our circumstance, contemplating our future as officers in the Army. I was mortified. What a nightmare! Hours later, an English-speaking guard showed up.

"Major, you must do the paperwork," he demanded.

After some neuro-linguistic programming and silent "mirroring" moves, with my silver-tongued talking, I reached common ground with him. He synched with the fact that we both had children and he had been in the Czech Army. I explained that any paperwork would involve the U.S. Embassy and undoubtedly spark an international incident. Following our embarrassing release from Germany, our return stateside would be met with a quick departure out of the Army, if we were not court-martialed. This would leave my family without a means of support and me with no future.

I added, "Please take the rental car and everything in it. Keep it as a gift!"

"Hey, that's my rental car," my Craig exclaimed.

"Listen, you got us into this situation, I'm getting us out!" I sternly whispered. This is not YOUR car, it belongs to the rental car agency! Just shut the fuck up!"

The entire incident lasted about eight hours. In the end, the English-speaking guard conceded, summoning the other guards to escort us back to the car to collect our personal items from the car before abandoning it. They then escorted us back to the German side of the checkpoint. There was no record of this incident. Which meant no official repercussions, but no rental car either. I thought that was a fair trade for our freedom. I made Craig pay for the taxi the German border guards called for us—that was US$150 he hadn't planned on spending. They thought the whole incident was pretty funny. We didn't.

On the way back to our hotel in Weiden that night, I saw the Flossenbürg castle on the ridgeline as we drove. I vowed to visit someday. That night, I paid for our dinners and drove him to the Frankfurt airport the next day, using my rental car. That was an interesting trip, mostly because my siting of the Flossenbürg Castle ruins, unbeknownst to me, would someday have a profound impact on my life.

Years later, during yet another trip to Grafenwöhr, I convinced another colleague of mine to accompany me to this same castle. We wandered down the back roads following my memory of where I initially saw the castle. We finally caught a glimpse of it through the trees in the approaching darkness. He pulled over to the side of the road in the rainy dusk, where we got out and plodded through the woods to an attack point from where we could approach, based on the lay of the land. It wasn't until circumventing nearly the entire base of the castle that we found the road leading up to it. That was embarrassing.

We weren't in the unrestored castle very long. We had maybe 10-minutes of walking the grounds and entering the dilapidated structure when I suffered a massive headache, with a fever and flu-like symptoms, forcing my expeditious return to the hotel. In a desperate quest for warmth during the bitter German winter, I slipped into the hottest bathwater I could muster. I tolerated the soothing water, attempting to chase away my shivers. With this extremely hot bath nursing my feverish symptoms, I saw a vision on the wall and started reciting what I was seeing in rhythmic verse. I was strangely describing a medieval battle scene circa 948 A.D., I saw playing on the tiled wall directly in front of me as vividly as a movie, as I lay there soaking. Exiting the bathtub to get my tape recorder, I hoped the vision would return. Settling back into the near-scalding water, I was able to resume the vision, reciting the following poem, exactly as it was gifted to me:

Soldier's Cry

So sad to die on the battlefield
All alone, of no more use is the sword or shield
Nobody to comfort, no family to help
Breathing his last of life; without a whimper, without a
yelp...

"...I cannot hear...I cannot feel...I cannot touch, see, or
hold...
...Not a living soul around - or is there?... My breath
draws cold...
...My blood runs as thick as tar in my lungs... I feel death
approaching - can it be...
...Dear God, my God, why is this happening to me?..."

"...Distant sounds, may be help on the way...
...But it too may be the enemy...

...As a professional soldier, never will I plead...
...So, quietly alone, I die, I bleed..."

"...The seed of my sons...as my forefathers were to me...
...My daughters all will come, searching the dead with grief...
...Will I be a desolate soul from a cold, cruel world...
...Will I never see my gravesite, over which, a proud flag is unfurled?..."

"...Tis never good to die alone, so far away, so far from home...
...Will my fellow countrymen ever know, the fervor with which I fought...
...Or will they never care...
....As I clear my throat here on this cold ground, struggling for brief whisps of air?..."

"...My warm blood, once in my veins, now drains from my body...
....My memory is starting to fade...
....Am I an unsung hero...
...Or simply a man whose fate has been made?..."

"...I imagine my tombstone... among the settling dew of the frigid, morning mist...
...A little girl approaches soon... with a single red rose clenched inside her fist...
....As she saunters through the dreary, still air...
...I feel I know this warm, yet inquisitive, stare..."

"...She is gazing at my epitaph... yet I sense no fear...
...Rolling down her satin cheek... a subtle, lonely tear...
...Gliding forever, gently... from her glistening, innocent eye...
...Oh Lord, 'tis never good... when alone a soldier must die..."

"...Then a priest says, to a gathering of a tranquil fest..."
'...Let this soldier go peacefully... with brethren warriors...
... To his final place of rest...
... Have them travel beyond together... with those who have done their best...'

'...I would like to say thank you... from your country...
...Whom may never know your name...
....And may never see your body... or soul...
...We thank you, just the same...'

'... Walk proudly now... toward the light...
...For no more or your days... will you have to fight...
...Thank you my son... you'll have eternal peace and rest...
...With our freedom now safe... to this we can attest...'

"...The little girl, then, kneels beside me... on the wet, spongy ground...
...Placing the rose upon my chest... as it moves sluggishly, up and down...
...She adds a gentle kiss... upon my numbing cheek...

...Her voice quivers, her eyes water... as she humbly tries to speak..."

"...I'm proud of you Daddy... why do you have to sleep...?"
"...She smiles as she whispers... 'I love you, my Daddy...
...And I will tell all the rest...
...I'm proud you were my Daddy... to me you were the best...'

Back to the malaise of the battlefield, on this dreary, bitterly frigid day
With gnashing of teeth, this soldier, was put in harm's way
As the leaves now blow over his lifeless, bloody face
Will he be remembered by the living, or simply find God's grace?'

After this first visit to the Flossenbürg Castle, it became my channeling place of sorts. Whenever in Germany, I would come to this place to resolve any abstract questions life posed to me. This time, I was searching for a similar epiphany regarding my quandary about possibly visiting Sweden.

Should I go? Could I? Should I make this visit happen? Should I risk going there and not being able to see the Princess? Would she even want to see me? I know many people say things online they don't mean or tend to change their minds when confronted with the reality of having to follow through on a commitment. I would be putting it all on the line by going to Sweden. Would this be a critical investment in my future or a complete waste of my time? My colleagues all thought I was crazy; maybe I was... or maybe I was naïve or just plain stupid! I would have to change around my business plans, pay fees, arrange hotels, arrange and pay for new flights to Sweden, arrange and pay for lodging in Sweden, and then plan my return trip home, and risk my reputation of reliability, all at the last minute.

Mine became more than the random thoughts of a man trapped in an emotionally cold, cruel world. These were more than the dreams of a hopeful romantic who wanted to follow his dreams to see where they would lead, if anywhere. I didn't want to wonder for the rest of my life IF—and that was a big IF—something might materialize between myself and the Princess. I wanted to know if there was any chemistry between us... or not. I was available now, and seemingly, so was she. The planets seemed to be aligned for the first time in my life with those of the Princess. I wanted to know. The timing of this trip was crucial. I had to know; it was NOW or never. But this might be the most expensive weekend of my life. I didn't consider it to be a crazy obsession; those dissipate. This became my quest. Was it strange? Was it crazy? Maybe it was.

As I drove through the rolling hills, the morning sun burned through the fog, the blinding light dancing around the driver's visor. I struggled to see as I passed firebreak after firebreak, among the sea of thin, tall green trees. The morning was fresh, the sky new, the weather was clear on the straightaways, and the air pure as my car sliced through the stagnant, thick low-lying clouds on the tight turns through the forest. I opened the windows and then the sunroof to experience nature at its finest. I was at peace. I was completely appreciating life in this moment. I enjoyed being alive. All my senses were alive on this day-off drive meandering through the Bavarian countryside in perfect weather!

Once I arrived at the Flossenbürg ruins, as was typical, I was the only one there. I strolled around aimlessly, thinking, and searching for the answer. In search of the truth, in search of answers, exploring the possibility of a new future, or just trying to uncover what I might find. Mindlessly wandering the hallowed grounds, I posed my questions to the wind. I searched and prayed, mentally, spiritually, and physically.

Eventually, I climbed the stairs to the top of the hill inside the castle walls, visually exploring the majesty of the limitless views in every direction from atop the main tower as I had always done. The weather was perfect and sundown was approaching, but this time I felt nothing. I stood at the very top spire of the ruins, appreciating the unfathomable amount of activity which undoubtedly came to pass at this one site, and in the rest of Bavaria over the centuries. I cast backward in my memory to a very distressing time when I was in a sticky wicket of a situation in my recent experience as a Soldier-warrior. This was one of the many times I thought about the Princess, unsure if I would ever see her, or anyone, again.

The memory returned. This jungle was unlike any jungle I'd seen in Southeast Asia—Burma, Thailand, Laos, Cambodia, Malaysia, and Vietnam. No other jungle was as dense, and none so hostile. No other jungle seemed as crowded and inhospitable to humans. Where peacocks fly out of the dawn overhead like pterodactyls with an overwhelming, bustling, auditory menagerie of fluttering wings breaking the silence, stopping our hearts and breath momentarily. This was in a land that time seemingly forgot. Accompanied on the ground by wild boar, tailed brown monkeys, pit vipers, pythons, king cobras, crocodiles, large monitor lizards, among so many others. In this place, as we silently traversed the jungle, the animals knew we were there. It was their home, not ours. They tolerated us most likely as a source of entertainment. It was the zoo coming to them. Ours was an ominous presence in these lands.

Walking through the dense jungle vegetation in broad daylight, making your way where you could, out of nowhere you'd hear a long, droning, low growl in the distance, getting closer. As the droning growl gets closer, it gets louder. Accompanied by the muffled muster of slow, confident, heavily pounding feet. In a flash, the unmistakable sound of thorny bushes swipes away with the rush of a freight train. A massive, gray wall of darkness occupies your entire foreground. Close enough to touch. In an instant, it disappears into an otherwise impenetrable thorny thicket, a bamboo abatis.

I'd seen these massive creatures from the air while we were flying in the Sri Lanka Air Force's Russian-built MI-17 HIP helicopters. These massive beasts are the true masters of this jungle. They did what they wanted, walked where they wanted, and acted however they wanted. They could hide from sight as easily as they could trample you without warning. When musking, with their eyes weeping, these masters of the jungle played with our vehicles, toppling them over and over like a lawn ornament, leaving them upside down. Flattening manmade obstacles, like perimeter fences, was a sport to these creatures. Every day were reacting to our natural surroundings merely to survive.

Like the wildlife on this island nation of Sri Lanka, formerly the British colony of Ceylon, the Tamil Tiger militant organization, formally the Liberation Tigers of Tamil Eelam (LTTE) was like none I ever contemplated confronting. After 20 years of fighting, these battle-hardened militants were elusive, resilient, ruthless, skilled, and determined jungle fighters.

It was hot and humid. The night was black—pitch black, silent and still. Until it wasn't. Wild animals occasionally screamed out, momentarily piercing the quiet. Lying face down in the prone position on the steamy jungle floor, beads of sweat running from my forehead down my nose, trickling onto the charging handle of my trusty M4 assault rifle underneath my chin. Not a sound. Not even a whisper. Next to me, my team members and next to them was our Sri Lankan SF counterparts; nobody moved. Nobody breathed. Swarms of mosquitos and other flying insects ceaselessly buzzed into our ears, faces, nostrils, and eyes. They bit and stung at will. I heard nobody breathing. None of us moved in the still of the darkness.

Nobody spoke. Not even a whisper. We all waited for our prey to enter our ambush kill zone. We expected the insurgent patrol to appear in our sights sometime that night. As I peered into my night vision device mounted onto my M4, nothing seemed out of the ordinary. The night was so quiet, I could hear a slight ringing in my ears. I was apprehensive that even breathing would cause too much detectable noise. I even thought my eyelids were blinking too loud. Undoubtedly, everyone on the team felt the same. We waited for the fierce, unsuspecting warriors to cross our paths; our counterparts were sure this was the place. So we waited.

I thought of the reputation these ruthless jungle fighters earned. Hopeful for a turnabout of action tonight, it seemed too often before they were hot on our trail, trying to destroy us. Tonight, it was our turn. And it was their turn to see our muzzle flashes first.

A twig snapped—cracking the silence of the night air; the entire world seemed to burst into roaring, imminent destruction. I saw nothing strange through my night vision device even seconds before, and now I definitely couldn't—all hell broke loose. I heard nothing but the deafening sound of gunfire echoing through the jungle. Ceaseless volleys of firepower burst from our M60s, SAWS, and AKs—bam, bam, bam, bam, bam, bam, bam bam, bam, bam, bam, bambam, ratatat, ratatat, ratatat, kapan, kapan, kapan, kaching, kaching, ratatat caching, ratatat, kaching, kaching, kaching as the links and empty brass shattered the once still air, littering the surrounding ground. RPGs exploded—boom, boom, boom. I saw nothing but flashes from gunfire and RPG explosions. I couldn't see shit else! Not a damn thing! My night vision was shot in the first flash. I looked around me and couldn't determine specifically what was happening. I didn't know who was who. Who was alive, and who wasn't? Who was next to me, and who wasn't?

Or, if the friendlies punted, leaving me behind solo, setting claymore mines with timers as they bolted. Each flash blinded me. Closing one eye didn't help in this torrent of explosive metal. It was too late for that. Gunfire complemented by a wall of flashes, enveloping us. Then an unamicable, blaring, blast shattered the night air above the small arms fire—WHA-BOOM!! A kick in the head and chest simultaneously impacted my body. Yep, that was one of our claymores. At least a few of my guys were okay, I hoped. They were raining hell on the enemy, as we did best. Or was it the other way around? We tried to kill them because they were trying to kill us. My ears whined and my head ached from the overpressure.

Wisps of smoke formed a hazy fog from the burning cordite and gunpowder rising in a mist above our heads as we remained motionless, still in the prone position. I knew which guns were ours and which weren't, by how they pierced the silence. If I heard ours, I knew I was beside friendlies. I caught glimpses of people crawling from point to point and back again. Shadows were back-lit by the small arms fire next to me. As my eyes adjusted, our muzzle flashes silhouetted us against the darkness. This was real. People were going to die. And I wanted to make sure it wouldn't be me, my team members, or our counterparts.

A high-pitched deafening whine repeated deep within my ear canal from the endless battery of warfare. My muzzle flash continued as my weapon recoiled underneath me. As the volley slowed, I cautiously closed one eye to ensure I had some remnants of night vision in the seconds that followed. My life depended on it. That is if I was still alive when this entourage of violence ceased; if it ever would. It had to, eventually. Hot metal and shrapnel continuously ripped into the once still night air, bringing destruction and imminent death to anyone in its path. The crack of bullets overhead added to the melee we faced. Someone next to me occasionally hugged the ground, preparing for the enemy to hurl grenades into our position. The expanse of land directly in front of us was completely unsurvivable. The sounds of gunfire ravaged my every thought. My ears were burning with the piercing shrill accosting my cilia, undoubtedly destroying them along with my tympanic membrane. I feared nothing more than imminent death, even more than deafness.

At some point, I heard voices yelling to each other; the ground was shaking in the thunder and lightning of combat. Those with us coordinated and interlocked fires. I didn't know exactly who it was or what they were saying as long as—crack, crack, crack, ratatat, ratatat, ratatat, ratttatttattt—as they continued; I knew they were alive; and so was I.

Loud mumbles soon took over. Gunfire slowed, then ceased as quickly as it began. The piercing shrills in my ears faded. Then started again. I heard—kaching, thump, thump, thud. Something heavy hit the ground, rolling right in front of me. It sounded like a large tree branch hitting the ground—but that wouldn't have made any sense, and it didn't, because that's not what it was. I caught a glimpse of what looked in the darkness like a round metallic object hitting the ground in front of me. Nothing made sense. Everything moved in slow motion. This couldn't be happening. Everything happened simultaneously. It was too real, while at the same time, it felt like I was watching a movie.

I heard the blood-curdling, verbal warning that I've heard a few times before as plain as day, and as clear as an auctioneer sounding off, "Grenade!" I saw what could be a grenade lying on the ground in front of me for a picosecond. As soon as I processed this reality, I rolled away, trying to get as far from this hell-storm bringer as possible. I was up on all fours, scurrying away to escape certain death. The muzzle flashes stopped as everyone scattered. I saw a flash of light like that of an arc welder, accompanied by a powerful force of energy hitting me in the mouth with all the intensity of a baseball bat wielded by a major league player. Thrown backward off my modified stance, a strange sound—pppffffftttt—sliced through the air, nanoseconds before the thousands of screaming, white-hot, imperfectly shaped needles of shrapnel penetrated my mouth, nose, and face. My back impacted the ground first. Surely, I was being ushered to my death. It was sequential at first, then simultaneous, as my mind tried to process what it couldn't and refused to accept. As fantasy, fear, and fact melded into the same dimension, it left me lying there wondering.

Rolling over onto my stomach, gasping for air, trying to grasp my weapon to continue the fight, in case I needed it. A metallic tinge with the sensation of floating chicklets filled my mouth. That recognizable taste of salty iron in my mouth was blood. I knew the taste all too well. I spit down in front of me as I remained in the prone position. Those weren't chicklets—it was bits of leftover shattered teeth inside my mouth in the aftermath of what could've been my death; but apparently wasn't. Not yet, anyway. I made a quick assessment of the damage to my body as I contemplated dying here, as the Soldier did in my poem. Would I die here? Surely a grenade exploding in front of me would destroy much more than a few teeth. Would this be it? A vision of the Princess appeared in front of me. I thought, "No Lord, this can't be it. Not now. Please not yet; I'm not done," I pleaded silently as I realized exactly what had happened, and what was still happening.

The air grew silent, then whispers emerged. The insurgents undoubtedly had the same TTP [Tactics, Techniques, and Procedures] we did, using grenades to break any overwhelming contact and immediately scattering. We consolidated our wits, our weapons, our ammunition, our buddies, and our medical status. I felt the full weight of our medic, atop me now, also in the prone position. His hand slipped on the ground in front of me. His fingers mistakenly felt the slick liquid on the ground beneath me, which he knew could only be blood. "Shit sir, are you okay? Where are you hit?" As his hand felt the bloody mess beneath me, he demanded in a loud whisper, "Where are you hit?... Sir, where the fuck did you get hit? Are you okay?"

As soon as I responded, he knew—it was my mouth. "One fuckin' question at a time!" I yelled back in a loud whisper, at the same low volume that he used to bark at me, in case the enemy returned fire.

"Sir, are you fuckin' okay?"

"No!! I'm fuckin' pissed! God damn it—that hurt! I think my teeth are all fucked up," I said as best I could.

"Lemme see." He turned me over onto my side, covering the two of us with a poncho, rolled tightly atop his med bag. He lit my face with a blue lensed tactical light, since a red light doesn't highlight blood. "Ah... shit yeah, sir, you're not gonna be eatin' any apples or pears anytime soon. That shit looks like it fuckin' hurts. Lemme give you a shot of Nubane to numb you up. Once your adrenaline subsides, that shit is really going to fuckin' hurt! It looks like some of your teeth are fucking sheared off—God damn it! It exposed the roots! Lucky you, sir, a female Air Force Doc is supposed to be coming here in the morning to give us medical support for the remainder of time in country—I hear she's pretty hot!

"How do you guys find this stuff out? How do I not know this?"

"Sir, because you officers don't ask the right questions."

"Well, she's probably not as hot as one I know," I joked.

"What? Damn sir, you're really fuckin' lucky! That shit would've killed a normal mortal," he said, continuing to give me medical attention.

"—Pears!" I abruptly interrupted, still in a loud, forceful whisper.

"What?" he blurted.

"I don't like apples, I like pears, apricots, plums, corn. SHIT—this is really gonna suck! By the way, I'm only pretty lucky."

"What the fuck do you mean, sir?" he demanded as he fumbled in the dark through his medic bag, looking for the Nubane and a syringe.

"If I was REALLY lucky, that grenade would've missed me completely... as it is, I'm only PRETTY lucky!" I chirped.

"Sir, as often as we've been in this position together and you're still alive—I'd say you're pretty God damn fuckin' lucky. And if I were you, I wouldn't fuckin' complain! God is looking out for you, for some reason!" he confided. "You've got something important to accomplish in this lifetime."

"Maybe you're right, Morty! Maybe you're right."

I was lucky as Morty said. I was pretty God damn fuckin' lucky—that's exactly what I thought to myself. Maybe I'm gonna see the Princess again, someday. I've got to get through this. The air was dank with death and destruction. The fog of war dissipated with time. Above us the starlit sky shined brightly, peacefully, light years from where we were. It was peaceful out there. And now it was peaceful here, too. This memory, also, was now worlds away.

Here, atop the Flossenbürg castle ruins, I sat alone on the highest decrepit wall at the apex, looking down about 100 feet from the ground; I dare not fall. The sun dipped below the surrounding Bavarian rolling hills while the air became noticeably cooler.

The air was silent. The visibility limitless. And the endless, green rolling hills rested peacefully in front of the orange and yellow streaks emanating from the setting sun. A few clouds formed a thin opaque belt above the darkened ridgelines in the distance. There was no doubt in my mind why the original builders of this castle chose this site. The once orange, now red-hued streaks filled the bright sky, then became subdued. Only the wind brushing past my ears interrupted the silence. What came to me was the saying, "Red sky at night, sailor's delight. Red sky in the morning, sailor take warning." This was definitely a red sky turning to dusk, soon to be night.

I became impatient, saying aloud, "I get nothing? Nothing? Come on! Give me something! Anything! I came all this way, I need something! Please?"

Suddenly, I felt a presence. I settled into my seated position, ensuring I was stable so not to fall if the wind picked up. The presence left me with an encouraging message as soon as it came, "Explore the unknown, take a chance—just go!" Then I heard a whisper in the wind say, "Do it! Do it now! Go and find! Go and find! Focus on YOUR journey!"

Minutes later my head hit the pillow and this dream entered my mind:

Of the Nordic Princess

From a place of Legends,
Breidablick comes to mind,
True love has eluded me in past forevers
Me thinks, impossible to find

Such a quest for a dear Princess
Long and arduous
Often the road bumpy and unkind
Yet filled with adventure
And high in spirit
If preserving
A positive mind

Mining souls in such a search
For which hides inside layers so deep
Journeying worldwide for the true romantic
It is known, once found, must keep...

~ 9 ~

Divine Words / Gudomliga Ord

That was it—brilliant! I often get burned chasing and wrestling rainbows. The closer I get, the faster they disappear; I can't control them. I can only control what I can—accepting the rest. And this would happen again this time unless the JOURNEY became my focus. This was MY JOURNEY. My rules.

I now knew I HAD to go to Sweden. And I would focus on the best positive outcome. Most people who play out their hand seem to do so mindlessly lock-stepped, moving silently into oblivion, unconsciously expecting disappointment and failure in their pursuits with each step. The philosophy of The Law of Attraction describes this mindset as projecting negative energy into the universe, negatively influencing your future. This is planning to fail, and unfortunately, in these cases, failure will most likely be the result. With a negative mindset, we simply cannot complete the actions necessary to set the conditions for success. We're likely to miss something critical along the way. Setting short, medium, and long-term goals is the best way to achieve success. In my case, long term was only two weeks, so I had to decide, plan, and act quickly, or my window of opportunity would close, maybe forever. I now knew everything I needed to do, to move toward achieving my intended goal of visiting the Viking Princess's land—Sweden. I understood that failing to plan is planning to fail. I had to find what lay ahead, however it may play out!

Within the walls of this castle, I knew it; I felt it—even if Erika wouldn't or couldn't see me, there should be no difference between this trip and any other travel I'd done. And like every other trip, I would be sure to enjoy myself. My focus had to be on the journey, not on the expected outcome. My perspective, however, had to concentrate on the best possible positive outcome. I would go to Sweden, learn about the culture, meet interesting people as I always do, and take hundreds of pictures. If I could see Erika, I would. But I was there primarily to see Sweden.

I had a lot to say, which I left unsaid between me and Erika some 33 years ago! In this perfect storm of frenzied business dealings and rushed international and domestic travels, I wanted to take the time to find, touch, and smell the one rose in my life who got away; if I could. The voices were right; I had to know, so I had to go!

There it was, whether or not I would see Erika, I would go to and have a great time. Who cared if it was one of the most expensive cities in Europe to visit? Who cared if I was going to spend nearly $3,000 for a single weekend? There it was! My journey was on! And my focus was—the journey.

With my deep-seated question now answered, sitting high on this castle wall, with darkness rapidly falling around me, I was hesitant to leave my channeling place. Without a flashlight, I had to use the ambient light left to guide me down the narrow stairway inside the main spire. One misstep could send me hurling perilously down to the hard ground nearly a hundred feet below.

After carefully descending and thanking the spirits for their guidance, I happily returned to the Hotel Gasthof Lohbachwinkel, eager to put my plan into action. As I drove, I wondered if this was why I survived all those close calls I had during my career in the Army.

I remembered the first airborne jump with my newly assigned unit at Fort Bragg, NC after graduating my U.S. Army Officer Basic Course and U.S. Army Ranger School. Everything was normal as parachute equipment jumps went: donning parachutes, jumpmaster checks, loading the plane, more jumpmaster checks, safety checks after taking off, the red lights eventually illuminated, and the jumpmaster started barking his time hacks and commands at the rear of the aircraft. 20-minutes, 10-minutes, 6-minutes, Outboard personnel stand up, Inboard personnel stand up, Hook up, Check static lines, Check equipment, Sound off for equipment check.

"All okay, Jumpmaster!" the first jumper at the front of the stick [the line of airborne paratroopers] closest to the rear doors yelled over the roaring engines to the Jumpmaster, after the "Okay" was sent from the last jumper at the back of the stick [located toward the front of the aircraft].

The rear ramp lowered to nearly flat. Everything went as smoothly as anyone could expect. I clearly see the blue-green horizon 1200 feet above the ground straight out the back of the aircraft. The view was mesmerizing. The Jumpmaster entered the open ramp area to conduct two safety checks, with the Safety controlling his static line. After these 360° checks, he yelled the "One-minute" command then "Stand-by." His last command given was, "Follow me!" And we did as he walked off the ramp's edge.

Out I went as the second jumper with my knees in the breeze. The deafening roar of the engines reverberated inside the rim of my helmet as I counted, "One-thousand, Two-thousand, Three-thousand, Four-thousand, Five-thousand, Six-thousand—I knew this was too long. I should've felt the jarring parachute opening shock at four or five seconds at the longest. Looking up at my parachute for a canopy check, I saw a mangled mess as I was hurled downward by the engine's prop blast. I was not slowing down. Already I was the lowest jumper. Spinning, I placed my left hand over the reserve rip cord grip protection flap, grasping the rip cord grip with my right hand, intending on pulling it for a controlled release of the pilot chute. This would ensure the reserve didn't get entangled in the undeployed main parachute above me. Assessing the situation, trying to prevent myself from spinning, I looked up again, deciding quite optimistically to clear the elongated twisted parachute above me with both hands. Bad choice. Being unsuccessful, I looked down at my reserve parachute once again for a controlled release, instantly realizing all reaction time was lost. I was still plummeting toward the ground, seemingly faster now. The trees got larger and closer at lightning speed. This was the most empty, hopeless, and helpless feeling I'd experienced. All I had time to say was, "Lord, I need a little help here, just let me break my legs—leave my back alone." Somehow, I felt a negotiation in such a situation may be better accepted for some reason. Expecting to die, yet hoping to live, I started hyperventilating to help me focus on the one critical task I had left. My life didn't flash before my eyes, but my choices did. Of which now I had only one—to prepare for the impending impact as best I could. Making sure I had my feet and knees together, with my knees bent, palms up, fingers resting on the rim of my helmet, and my elbows joined together to protect my face. Watching the horizon for the milliseconds I had left prevented me from reaching for the ground with my legs, which would surely snap them off. Hearing only the wind swooshing by my ears and my own hyperventilating, I hit the ground, overcome by a thunderous explosion that rocked my head and entire body. I blacked out.

As I regained consciousness, I did a few snow angels in the deep, soft sand and completed a status check of each inch of my body from my toes up to my head. I mustered the courage to sit up, checking my ears, mouth, nose and eyes for blood. I checked my body for broken bones—there were none. All was normal. Unbelievably, I stood up, thinking, "This is impossible. How do you fall from 1200 feet with the resistance of merely a flag flapping in the wind attempting to slow down. And not die?" This was not an out-of-body experience as I expected—I turned, looking down. There was no body on the ground, just a large divot in the sand about my approximate size. I was still alive and completely unharmed with only a splitting headache. The airplane circled overhead as evidence I had exited that aircraft in the same parachute still attached to me. "Thank you. Life is good," I thought, looking toward the sky, watching the rest of the jumpers depart the aircraft.

At age 29, I was crushed inside a military M939 five-ton truck rollover in the mountains. While serving as the unit Range Safety Officer, I called Range Control, closing down training for that night at about 9 p.m. when the snow and fog led to unsafe conditions for live-fire training. Visibility was at about six feet, so I made the weather call. Severely upset with my action and from ignoring his idea to have our men mount white light strobes to the back of their combat vests to discern them from the pop-up targets marked with tiny red flashing lights [supposedly simulating rifle fire], the Commander made a life-changing decision for all of us. He ordered my team to drive the truck down the mountain road with my entire 12-man detachment in it, despite there being no chains for the tires. I told him we'd stay on the mountain, inside the abandoned Ranger station, until the inclement fog, snow, and icy conditions subsided; we'd join up with the main element as early as possible the next morning. Finding this unacceptable for whatever reason, he ordered my team once again to take the truck down the treacherous icy hill. My objections were now met with direct threats of court-martial. My Team Sergeant who was nobody to object to, physically intervened pushing between the two of us saying, "Sir, you can't reason with this, let's just take the damn truck down the hill as carefully as we can, before we all get court-martialed!"

I remembered the prophesies from years back, both in Burma and in the Philippines. Was this it? Was my time up? As the truck carefully inched down the slick, icy surface through high wind and blowing snow, it suddenly slid uncontrollably down the icy dirt road. Our skilled driver did his best to control the skid, steering into the ditch instead of over the 70-foot cliff on the opposite side of the road. With his last breath he warned every one of our impending doom. "We're going in, we're going in!" His yelling pierced my entire body. The sounds of bumps, thuds, snapping, ripping, and crashing, accompanied by the crushing, twisting sounds of metal and breaking glass, the truck engine raging, overturning multiple times, rested on its top across the ditch. Everything went in slow motion. When all stopped, I was pinned with my face to the frozen ground by the weight of the truck. My head was being crushed. Again, I summoned help from above, "Lord, I need some help here; I can't do this alone." I offered no terms of negotiation this time, saying, "I need time. Please, I need more time. I'm not done here yet," before being rendered unconscious. Regaining consciousness, I was still pinned inside blacked-out cab. Alive and determined to get out to render assistance to the brave Green Beret who had been driving beside me, and to those in the back. As I squirmed for leverage, I felt a lifeless hand next to me, following it to the fingers then working back in search of a pulse; there was none. I called his name, but there was no response. Eventually freeing myself, exiting, I was able to start plucking others from the back of the truck. I distinctly remembered our medic's voice cracking as he spoke, "Sir, he's got no pulse, he's got no pulse. He's...." Rendering to each other whatever assistance we could, while our medic stayed in the cab, we made our way back to the top of the mountain. We completely ignored the empty threats from our career-concerned Commander, who arrived shortly before we departed, ordering us to take accountability of all sensitive items before we left. "Do it yourself!" voices grumbled spewing more appropriate, and uncontrolled adult language fitting this situation. We heard him screeching at the top of his lungs at us as we walked away. The falling snow muted his ranting and foot stomping. Our entire unit had to stay at the Ranger station that night as we waited for the weather to clear, and the air MEDEVAC to arrive. We were now one brave Green Beret down and one truck short. It's difficult losing Green Beret Brothers in combat; in training, it takes an exceptional toll.

Arriving at the gasthaus, the pitch-black darkness of the cool night fell completely into place. As I entered the foyer of this historic building out of the complete darkness, this time, I was bright and brimming with confidence. I sat down with Morty for another dinner ribbing. And yes, for another prolific, yet unavoidable discussion regarding my personal plans for going to Sweden.

Tonight, a new server followed me to the table to take drink orders as soon as I sat down. "*Halo. Darf ich ihnen etwas zu trinken bringen* [hello, may I bring you something to drink]?"

Morty being definitely not the bilingual type decided to impress her with some of his German. He blurted out, "*Krystal vixen err hefferveysin bitter?*"

She smirked, asking him to repeat his answer, "*Kannst du das bitte wiederholen* [can you repeat that please]?" This should've been his first clue.

Soooo… he repeated, *"Krystal vixen err hefferveysin bitter?"*

In perfect English she said, "I'm a little confused, it sounds like you want a clear beer served by a fat waitress. Did you learn to speak German from "Hogan's Heroes" television re-runs?"

Now it was my turn to fall on the floor laughing at this interchange. Morty turned beet red, angered by her comment.

He looked at her and said, *"Vasser bitte* [a glass of water please]."

She jovially confirmed, "All you want is water? You'd better stick to speaking English or you'll starve and become dehydrated here in Germany."

He became even more agitated, never fond of being the victim of practical jokes. "Yup just water, thanks!" he replied blushing. I couldn't contain my laughter, but I didn't fall onto the floor for effect. I probably would've lost a best friend that night; besides, I still needed to use his laptop.

Because of my upbringing I became a human parrot, of sorts, able to mimic nearly any language, yet I kept my order at its simplest. I smiled and said, *"Hefeweisen, bitte* [Hefeweisen please]."

As she went to fetch our order, Morty sneered at her, whispering to me, "Stupid bitch!"

"Lighten up, Francis!" I joked. "At least her English is passable!" I added.

"Shuddup!" Morty demanded, hiding a smile underneath his amusement at the situation. After he absorbed the conversation, he said, "Shit, she shocked me, her English is PERFECT! I'll have to admit THAT was pretty funny." The manager, seeing the events unfold as they did, decided to wait on us for the evening and walked over with our drink orders.

"So…" Morty began the conversation with me, "Did you go anywhere today? Did you make any big decisions?" he asked as he grinned from ear to ear.

"Yes, I did. And yes, I did—I decided to venture out on the wild side tonight and try the Pike for dinner, and maybe later I'll get a *krystal vixen or hefferveysin bitter!*" At this comment I laughed like there was no tomorrow, again staying properly seated. Morty failed to see the humor in my remark. He didn't even crack a smile.

The manager interrupted by placing our drinks in front of us, "Ahh, good choice sir, so it shall be the Pike tonight and for you sir?"

Morty ordered his in perfect English. Surprisingly, the rest of our dinner conversation went extremely well, slightly mellowing from the previous night. I think I broke on through to other side with Morty, and at least half-heartedly gained his support for my trip to Sweden. Out of nowhere he asked with a concerned tone, "Have you received a response from her?"

"Nope, but I'm going anyway. I'm going to focus on my journey, not on her," I closed.

"You're serious?" he asked.

"Yup!" I said. For the first time, Morty raised his eyebrows, moved to silence. I think he felt my potential pain and anguish with my situation.

We finished out the meal with small talk. After dinner, Morty excused himself saying he'd be right back, and returned with his laptop saying, "Here ya go!"

On cue, I sent yet another email to Erika, having received no word from her regarding my plans— "Hey Erika, I'm planning a trip to Sweden in two weeks! Think I'm kidding? What would you say about that?" After some subtle conversation about how

Monday would go, Morty and I finished our nightcaps and bid each other a good night, closing out our weekend.

I woke up unusually early, to get an exercise band and yoga routine knocked out, doing some push-ups, sit-ups, and modified crunches, then out for a quick run in the foggy, cool air. I returned, showered and dressed in my suit, mentally prepared for my early morning breakfast ribbing from Morty; after which, we faced the long drive to the military garrison for the seminar. Again, we drove in separate cars in case of a breakdown or one of us had to leave early.

As scheduled, I was on the platform this entire first day. Morty could pick up where he felt comfortable in the days to come. Throughout the morning in the seminar room, during our breaks, I checked my emails and received no responses from anyone, except from Layla at the travel office. She annoyingly asked me what time I would pay for the trip and pickup my tickets and itineraries. As the day progressed, I kept checking my emails—no word from Erika. We voted to walk across the street and get polish sausage sandwiches and fries from a nearby food truck. This way we could get ahead of our schedule and knock out classes earlier.

Checking once again, I received no new emails at all, except more queries from the local travel office. Their office didn't even open until right before lunch, so I was getting a bit anxious. I finally got through to them on the phone and asked if I could have a bit more time before making my reservations to Poland and Sweden.

In typical German fashion, Layla responded, "Zis is impossible! These trips must be paid as soon as possible or risk losing the Lot [Polish] airline reservations. These are special airfares from Frankfurt to Kraków to Warsaw to Gdańsk and back to Frankfurt and from Frankfurt to Stockholm and return on Lufthansa. This was not easy for me to arrange all these pieces,

Mister [Europeans use "Mister" when they're really annoyed]. Are you willing to risk losing all this? I will not be able to arrange these again!" she said, demanding an explanation.

"I really have no choice. I've heard nothing from the States about changing my return flight— that must take priority at this point or I'll have to pay for the return in its entirety."

"Look Mister, you need to make a decision. If you wait until tomorrow morning when we open, the fares will be gone and I will have to re-book everything. I guarantee you the fares will be much higher; I will see if even some of these fares are available at this point," she hesitantly quivered.

"Can't I pay over the phone with a credit card now or in the morning because I can't get to your office before you close today. Maybe you can stay open a bit later and I can try to leave my seminar early?" I asked in desperation.

"No Mister, zis is impossible! Zis is not the United States. We do things differently here in Chermany, you must pay, sign, process, and obtain your receipts—all in the same transaction day—all in person. Otherwise, it is impossible. It must be accomplished today or you will lose your rates!!"

"Okay, thank you, thank you. Worst case, tomorrow morning, first thing I'll be there as soon as you open—I'll be there! I promise! *Juus, Auf weider sein, danke schoen*," I politely farewelled her on the phone in a bit of a begging tone.

Morty wanted to leave the seminar early to grab some dinner, but before closing the room [which took about 15 minutes] I wanted to check my email. The only responses I had were the official responses from Friday, I'd already seen. There was nothing from Erika. Nothing! And nothing from the U.S. Travel Office; here in Germany I was still eight hours ahead of them, so if I could get connectivity at the gasthaus, I could probably finish this business tonight. The pressure was on.

I bolted out of the seminar facility, begging Morty to lock up with our host since I had to rush to the travel agency. I knew this wouldn't be a popular move. When I arrived, the building was locked down tight as a drum, and lights were off with nobody in sight. I stopped by the Subway sandwich shop on the garrison for a quick dinner sandwich and drove back to the gasthaus, as fast as I legally could. As soon as I arrived, I ran up to Morty's room. Thank God he was in. "The agency on post was closed," I explained. I borrowed his laptop, ran back to my room, and immediately tried to access the internet to work my emails. I wouldn't request the U.S. Travel Office change my reservations adjusting for my trip to Sweden; this time I'd demand it.

The internet was sporadic in my room, so I moved down to the vacant restaurant. After spreading out all my papers on a table, the barmaid approached me, explaining she was closing the dining area and I would have to leave. I collected the laptop and all my papers, rushing back to my room. I desperately took the rickety old German wooden chair from my room, positioning it directly underneath the router located inconspicuously down the hallway in an open closet. I wanted to ensure lack of connectivity was not because of proximity to the routers in this archaic building with its thick concrete walls and hardwood floors. My connectivity faded continually, as did my hopes of finalizing the myriad of tasks requiring coordination.

As I felt my hopes dashed, another guest exited her room, approaching me. I first met her in the parking lot as she gazed at a scratch on her rental car door. I approached, offering the scratch repair pen I keep with me. She was an American Soldier staying in the gasthaus, attending an unassociated conference at the Army garrison. Most likely hearing me pecking away on the computer keyboard, while gasping in complete frustration, she saw I was livid. She asked me what I was doing in the dark hallway, sitting on a wooden chair outside the linen closet with only the light of the laptop screen illuminating my face, attempting to temper my temper, which was surely aglow.

After explaining my dire situation, she told me, "I've got a German Apple laptop with a German air card in it and my connectivity is five-by [military speak for 'unimpeded/perfect' communications]. You can use it if you need. You're having gateway and networking issues stemming from using an American laptop on a German system. I had the same issues after arriving in Germany years ago, so I bought a German laptop. Just give it back to me in the morning, you'll be more comfortable working in your room. I'm in room 4B; I really need to get it back in the morning because I need to leave at 0745 [am]," she said.

She reignited my hopes. "Oh my God, you're a lifesaver!"

The connectivity on her laptop was perfect; she was right. I re-energized and re-connected with my entire professional network. The U.S. Airline Representative completed and verified my transaction—changing my reservations for a $100 nominal fee, since I was no longer traveling on a weekend, it made the fare cheaper for my new departure. I even reserved a rental car for my arrival as a backup to the travel agent's car reservation in Sweden. If not used, it would automatically cancel without a fee. Despite the outrageous prices, I wanted flexibility and found no reliable public transportation conveniently servicing the Stockholm airport. So, the rental car was the option for me. Since I arranged everything else in Poland and Sweden on the garrison computers on Saturday, I required no other coordination for my trips.

Since I heard nothing from Erika, I played it safe, keeping the hotel room I reserved in her hometown. Originally, I was going to stay about 30 minutes away to save a few bucks, specifically Swedish Krona, but then questioned… why? Coming all this way, why spare any expense at this point? In the event I got to see her, I wanted my hotel to be conveniently located. I re-confirmed my lodging for Poland and could complete my tourist research later.

I fired off another email to Erika telling her I would visit her the week after my trip to Poland, not asking. It read, "Erika, I plan on coming to Sweden the week after next. I'll be in Gävle. Is it possible for you to meet for lunch or something? Yes, or no? Think I'm kidding?" I would be ecstatic seeing her after all these years.

One by one in the wee hours of the morning, everyone in my professional network responded. At this time of morning, all I could do was my best effort, and all I could ask of myself was to do my best. Slowly my trips were coming into fruition and my mind was much more at ease, because I was doing what I decided to do, as fast as I possibly could. I confirmed the readjusted stateside meeting schedule with everyone involved. And my office manager finally responded, ending my computer odyssey. Although my brain was fried, I could squeeze out two, maybe three hours of sleep before Day Two of my seminar—it was worth it. For the first time in years, I was the priority, and it felt good. No, it felt great!

The next morning, Tuesday, began like all others. Completing my usual morning routine which I breezed through a bit quicker, checking my emails in between exercises, hoping for some kind of response from Erika, since we were in relatively the same time zone now—still nothing. I brought the laptop back to my Savioress as soon as I finished. Once again thanking her profusely, I went downstairs to meet Morty for his morning chuckles and jeers at my expense. Again, we'd be driving in separate cars, which would be especially helpful for me today since I had to run to the local travel agency expecting them to take my entire lunch period. The travel agency was my top priority, after completing the multitude of seminar tasks, of course.

The seminar went smoothly. We were still in the instructional presentation and discussion phase of the program. I encouraged a vote for an early lunch break and everyone unanimously agreed. At lightning speed, I bolted out the door, making a beeline for the travel agency, driving just fast enough not to arouse attention of the military police. Making the police blotter for speeding would not be good for a person of my stature and responsibility.

As soon as I walked through the travel agency door, Layla, as loud as she was large, exclaimed, "Ahhhhhhh, there you are! Where have you been? Where have you been?? I was expecting you yesterday, remember? YESTERDAY!!! At the latest first thing this morning! Do you remember??? I said we had to do this on Monday! MONDAY was yesterday! I really hope all your flights and prices are still the same! Ahhhhhhhhhh!" she blurted out.

I apologetically explained, "I know, I'm sorry, yesterday got away from me. I was so busy with my seminar and trying to line up my business approvals and return flights to the United States. When I finally made it here, you were closed!"

"Yeah, yeah, yeah, likely excuse, sit down—hurry up!" she motioned me to skip ahead of the line of seated would-be travelers. "Hurry up, hurry up!" as she rushed me to sit in one of the empty chairs in front of her desk, leering at me with her piercing steel-blue eyes. "Now, you still want to do the Poland itinerary with no changes, yah?? And the Sweden trip as well. Yah??" Her fingers typed wildly across her keyboard, as she motioned with gestures for the screen to refresh quicker, typing from page to page, frantically switching from screen to screen. "Naaaaah, come on, come on, hurry up!! I told you!!" She looked around from her screen, glancing at me. "Hurry up computer! Come on, come on! What do you mean NO?? Just do it, you stupid thing!! Come on, come on!" she demanded of the desktop computer as she hammered away frantically on the keys. She rarely looked up or away from the mass of papers sprawled out in front of her. "Oh my God, NO! No-no-no-no-no!" yelling… at her computer screen. My heart was overflowing with such trepidation and hope that I couldn't take my eyes off her. Afraid it might tap her of some of my telepathic positive energy she needed to mainline in order to put this entire trip back together for me.

Scorched by each of her noises, scowls, gasps, and frowns, I sat in front of her desk, silently hoping, praying like an expectant father awaiting the birth of his child. After seemingly the worst emotional journey of her life, Layla stopped what she was doing, closed her eyes, dropped her head, and sighed. She placed her head on her desk in utter defeat.

"WHAT?" I wondered. "WHAT??" I silently screamed as I waited for an explanation, hoping and praying for the best potential outcome.

She lifted her head slowly, opening her eyes, fixating on me with an emotionless, expressionless, blank stare. "Oh my God…I tooooold you. Did I not tell you?"

My heart and mind simultaneously sank into a tar pit of despair. She glared past me as if she'd been struggling through a spiritual exorcism; it appeared she'd been through absolute hell.

"You are so very, very, very, very lucky. You know this, right?!" Then she smiled. "Okay, here's the deal. I got back all your flights on the days you wanted. AND, I got your connections to Sweden and return. You have a three-hour layover in Frankfurt when you come back from Poland traveling to Sweden. That's good. Because you MUST retrieve your bags from Lot [Polish airline] and check them into SAS [Scandinavian airline], because it's a different airline. And you have the time to do it. But when you return from Sweden going back to the States, you need to run like hell to catch your flight, because you have less than one hour to make it. Please explain to the ticketing agents in Stockholm when you leave, that you have a connecting flight in Frankfurt with a separate ticket you purchased on a different airline. Absolutely beg them to book your luggage straight through to your connecting flight. This way if your bags don't get transferred quickly in Frankfurt, the airline will deliver them to your home in the U.S. You won't really need them since you'll be home. Right? If they don't book your luggage properly through to the U.S. from Frankfurt, you'll never see them again. They will be forever lost in the belly of the Frankfurt airport with your personal effects and souvenirs ending up in some former Soviet Satellite state flea market years later. I'll say this again, you won't have time to check your bags in yourself on your flight returning to the U.S., YOU only have ONE hour. If you miss this flight, you might not get a flight out for a week! And I won't be there to do it for you! Now understand, they do not have to check your luggage straight through, because it's a different airline, so be very, very, very, very nice to them. The only thing I must do now is book you a rental car in Stockholm to get you these rates AND YOU HAVE TO PAY FOR THIS TRIP NOW! You have your credit card yah? You don't have to keep this rental car, but you have to make the car reservation now."

"I already made a reservation for a rental car in Stockholm," I proudly reported.

"Áh so, you can cancel mine when you arrive, BUT I must book it here and now to get these rates. They tie this rate to the rental car. And I tell you, it's impossible to beat this car rate because it includes all the insurance and any extra chanrges they will not tell you about online. How much is your rental car you made on your own Mr. Good Deal Hunter?" she joked.

I quickly flipped through some papers and said, "US$443.00."

"No, no, no, no, no are you crazy? Leave this to the experts. Mine is for US$340.00 for all three days with all taxes, insurance, everything. You need to cancel the one YOU made before you get there. They say you don't have to, but do it anyway, or they'll stick you with some made-up fees. Trust me, I know this! I hope you can cancel. Sometimes you can't, if you made it online.

Remember, this is Europe, NOT the U.S.! In a few minutes, we'll be all done here and all you have to do is to arrange your hotels," she said.

"God forbid, you NOT being able to meet your Viking Princess after not seeing each other for so many years and it being my fault? NO sir, it will NOT be my fault! You go see her, even if she is married or has a boyfriend that she is not telling you about. Tell me someday how it works out." I thanked her profusely for her dedication to her work and to me. Wait a minute. What did she mean? Why'd she say that?

Greta and Helga, her co-agents yelled out across the office, "You're lucky you had Layla, I would've had you wait at the back of the line and told you to plan your time better! And you'd be spending another week in your gasthaus here in Grafenwöhr or in the airport in Frankfurt, NOT in Poland and Sweden." They cackled in agreement as they were both probably descendants from the Saxon or Vandal tribes, whichever was the meanest. They added what sounded to be choice sayings in German, cackling once again. I tried to ignore them, clutching my itineraries tightly in my hands as if holding the Holy Grail, handing my credit card to Layla.

Layla didn't laugh or even smile at their outburst. "Don't listen to them," she muttered, "They're just playing." Somehow, I doubted this. I asked for her manager's name and contact numbers so I could voice my happiness with her service. She looked at me with shocking disbelief. "We don't do such things in Germany."

"Maybe not... but I'd like to," I responded.

"When in Germany...," she coyly smiled. Once again, she provided what she promised. "Really the only way you can thank me is to have a great trip. Well, that's it! We're done! Thank you!" she cheerfully added.

As she stood up to bid me *"Auf weider sein,"* I extended my hand politely, shaking her hand; she responded in kind. I wanted to hug her though it would be inappropriate, and would've sent her colleagues, Barbie and Himmler, over in the corner into a cackling, frenzied, hissy fit. So, I refrained.

"Oh, and if you don't have it, make sure you bring at least a warm scarf, gloves, and a hat. Very warm clothing would be good. If you didn't bring them here to Germany… I will tell you those three items are necessary if you want to enjoy your trip to Sweden; otherwise, you'll freeze your ass off, if you dress the way you are now. There's always a possibility it might get a lot colder in Sweden. It's colder than it is here, you know," Layla added.

"Thank you, I'll get a scarf," I said.

After which, I politely left. I had just enough time to swing by the snack bar for lunch before making my way back to the seminar.

The next two days of the seminar went relatively smoothly due to a few good night's sleep and a few more satisfying German meals, after that intense weekend coordination fiasco. I was able to cancel my pre-paid rental car in Stockholm and got a refund as they advertised. I even had time to practice re-packing my luggage, since my airline tickets only included one small checked bag for both Poland and Sweden.

I brought my medium-sized roller bag on this trip which still required me to pack my large duffel bag. Before this trip I lined the duffle bag with a folded cardboard box. Removing it, taping it together, packing it with all of my business attire [suits, shirts, shoes, ties, belts, and laundry] planning on mailing it stateside via the USPS on the Army garrison the day of my departure.

There was still no word from the Princess. I sent her one more email before departing the seminar. It read, "Erika, I decided to take you up on your offer. I've rearranged my entire schedule and

I'll be in Stockholm and then in Gävle the week after next for the weekend of the 21st to 24 September—think I'm kidding? If we could meet, that would be fun; until then, I'll be departing Germany in the morning, touring Poland next week. I will be on email sporadically until then. It would be a shame to come all the way to Sweden and miss you. Truly, Dimitri."

~ 10 ~

Into the Future / In I Framtiden

This portion of my trip was much more stressful than usual. Jetting out of the conference facility I made a stop at the U. S. Post Office. There, I had to wait in a long line to fill out the correct U.S. Customs paperwork, twice. Then I had to undergo a brief interview with the Postmaster regarding what was inside my sealed box of business regalia and laundry, explaining why I was mailing it back to the States, and ensuring the insurance was adequate. Leaving here, I waited in yet another line at the gas station competing with everyone else fueling up before the weekend. Here, I had to figure out which of the six grades of fuel to select, topping off my vehicle. I asked someone which fuel to select for my car, ensuring the autobahn race to Frankfurt would go off without a hitch.

Finally leaving the U.S. Army Grafenwöhr garrison, corkscrewing my way on multiple backroads, working my way toward larger roads, then making it onto dual-lane highway roads, anticipating those road signs that looked like a large bear paw scratching through the speed limit numbers. This is where the road would finally open wide as the autobahn. There it was!

Finally! Ahhh, the autobahn! Pedal to the metal, checking my six in the rear and side view mirrors! I was rockin-n-rollin'! My car screamed through the air toward Frankfurt. I was so looking forward to seeing my best German friend, Hans. He was visiting there for a few hours, from Northwestern Germany to hang out with me.

Palms sweating underneath my driving gloves, I never let my eyes stray from the road ahead. Legally driving like a bat out of hell at NASCAR and Formula One speeds of 160 to 180 miles per hour, I watched my life pass by as vehicles and objects flashed past at lightning speeds. I dared not even blink. Driving at these speeds is one of my favorite hobbies, but takes a tremendous amount of concentration and focus to survive. Even though, knowing I couldn't possibly get to my destination any faster was surprisingly satisfying.

I still had to watch for the highly restrictive speed limit signs that popped up out of nowhere. Before realizing it, you pass one of these round white signs with red borders depicting a large 80, representing 80 kilometers per hour, [a mere 50 miles per hour] and without warning the flash of speed cameras record your unwitting violation. The other traps are the 90-degree turns misrepresenting themselves as exits. These require you to decelerate from Formula 1 speeds to 30 mph to safely exit. One of these exits scared the crap out of me (and terrified my accompanying colleagues) the first time I took one. This experience did permanent damage to the hearts of these passengers, who knew nothing of my training at NASCAR and Formula One racing schools. After my rapid exit and extreme deceleration severely stressing the rental car, I left a few new, long rubber road patches while the odor of burning rubber and brake pads poisoned the air inside the car. Addressing the notably unbreathing, shocked passengers with the thousand-yard stares, in a relaxed, controlled, monotone I joked, "Ahh, no worries guys...

it's a rental!" That was my first experience exiting the autobahn. What a stupid way to slow people down! Now, you too have been forewarned! Without these autobahn lessons and knowledge of the rapid exits, I may have arrived much later meeting Hans, if at all.

Hans was one of my best friends. We had a lot in common. Despite our age difference, we had similar problems meeting women. One of my most cherished memories occurred a few years back when I first met him, staying at the Downtown Backpackers Accommodation hostel in Beijing, China. We attended the hostel's sponsored all-day tour of the Great Wall. This is the longest tour available, requiring hiking the entire day on the walkway linking the only accessible 26 Great Wall watchtowers from Jinshanling to Simitai West. And you can't dilly dally on this hike.

Hans and I first met on the hours-long, early morning minibus ride. There were only eight of us. A tall, slim, handsome, intelligent young man, with short brown hair, 26 years my junior, he was with his long-time girlfriend of five years. She was beautiful, but I purposely paid little attention to her. We all seemed to hit it off instantly. Both Hans and I are approachable, friendly, open to learning about cultures. We both loved martial arts and photography, taking pictures from obtuse angles. Unlike Hans, his girlfriend was standoffish and guarded from the very beginning. Our Chinese minibus host handed out snacks including Oreo cookies, potato chips, and coconut water early in the ride. Hans first broke the ice saying in perfect English, "Hey man, great snacks are these Chinese?" Our Chinese hostel host just laughed. He turned to me with the most welcoming smile saying, "I love your camera. You must be a professional," as he held up his own exact Canon SLR camera, motioning with a thumbs up. The laughter began, and the trip was already a lot of fun.

Soon after we exited the bus, Hans whispered to me, asking to take two sets of pictures while hiking the Wall; one set with his girlfriend in the scenery and one set excluding her. When he requested this, I agreed to oblige, though the comment piqued my curiosity. This was my first clue that all was not well in Camelot.

Hans and I got to know each other better through small talk that afternoon, hiking together, appreciating the many styles of Great Wall architecture. Intrigued, we discovered that the Great Wall initially wasn't designed as one continuous wall. It was a series of shorter walls connecting the 25,000 watchtowers over 20,000 kilometers (12,000 miles) during the 22 centuries (2200 years) of its construction. And yet, it all tied in perfectly. We hiked up and down, over the mountains and rolling hills, over the tower walls, climbed up and down ladders, traversing the elevated paths of old as the day grew long. Hans and his girlfriend seemed to get along as well as any other couple.

Returning from the hike late that evening, I bid good night to Hans and his girlfriend, going back to my US$15.00 single room to take a shower. Then I headed out for dinner alone, down the street. Hundreds of red Chinese lanterns outside and inside one of the open-air restaurants caught my eye. Once inside, I met my other favorite couple from the hostel. After introductions, I invited myself to sit with them for dinner because I didn't really want to eat alone. They didn't mind, especially when I surprised them by surreptitiously paying the very reasonable bill for that delectable meal. An intriguing, young married couple they were. He from South Africa and she from Israel. Upon my return to the hostel after dinner, I headed for the common area where we all congregated day or night. As is typical in most hostels, this is where the Wifi is strongest. It's also where travelers exchange travel ideas and suggestions, and communicate warnings like the rip-off tea ceremonies at popular tourist locations in China, shaking down visitors for hundreds of dollars. And they'll threaten police involvement if you refuse to pay. I mean how complicated is pouring tea? Why does it need a ceremony?

As I entered, Hans immediately stood up, smiling while greeting me, saying, "Ah D, would you like to go purchase some fruits? Let's go purchase some fruits down the street. Yes? We'll go now?"

I whispered, tilting my head in her direction, asking if his girlfriend was going, "Is Emma coming?"

She remained in the corner, head down buried in her laptop, unaware of anyone else's presence.

Hans shook his head quickly and whispered back, "No, we'll go alone, the two of us, please. Quickly…"

As we stepped outside into the darkness, he instantly confided in me, "D, you're the only person in China I can talk to about such a matter." He explained to me what transpired that morning between the two of them. He begged for advice, or at least a sounding board. I obliged.

He started our walk by explaining his request for two sets of pictures on the Great Wall. "Emma and I are college sweethearts, living together in Germany already for five years. We saved all our money for a few years to travel in Asia for five months. China is our first stop before going to India and Southeast Asia. It was on this trip I was waiting for the perfect moment to propose to her. I was going to offer her the engagement ring I brought with me. This morning when she woke up, she told me she doesn't love me anymore. I couldn't believe what I was hearing. And this is only the second week of our five-month trip. Why would she do this? It feels like my entire world is falling apart. What do I do?"

My heart bled for him, even though I'd only known him for a day. He was desperate for a plan of action. He was one of the nicest people I've ever met and didn't deserve this treatment from anyone, let alone from the woman he was willing to entrust with his heart and his future. I tried to distract and console him with an assurance that it was not him who was the problem.

"Well, I will say, it's NOT you. You're the perfect guy! If I was gay, I'd marry you, myself!" he chuckled, then managed to laugh.

"Sorry to disappoint," he joked.

He continued telling me she didn't want to continue their five-month jaunt around Asia together. I had a clue why she wanted to break it off.

"Are you sure that's what she said? Did she say it in German, Italian or English [since they were both fluent in each of these]?" I asked.

"Yah, I know this. She said it in both German and Italian. I understood what she said. There is no confusion," he explained.

As we traveled onward into the darkness, surprisingly, there was a fruit stand still open. Buried deep within the Hutong District, near the main Drum tower, which originally was one of nine gates to the ancient walled city of Beijing. This area was originally home to the artisans who supported the Royals inside the Forbidden City and Royal Palace. Hans was right; the fruit was extremely inexpensive and delicious.

After our purchases, I took a moment to ponder his quandary and told him, "Why don't you pretend she never said it and see how she reacts tomorrow morning?" He agreed.

We planned on talking in the morning after breakfast. Our walk back to the hostel was saturated with natural juicy fruit and juicy conversation, as we tried to apply the best tactics to his quandary should his nightmare continue.

I met them in the adjoining restaurant for breakfast the next morning. Once she ate and left the table, he confirmed what she said. She repeated it once again that morning, and she meant it. I told him he didn't want to hear that she was probably emotionally involved with someone else. And most likely it was the person on the other end of her iPad. There was nothing he could do but agree.

"Hans, you can't always understand matters of the heart, but you have to accept them," I explained, "It's better to find out now than years down the road."

It dumbfounded us both. Why would she embark on such a trip if she obviously changed her mind about him before starting out? In the days following, they both decided to continue their trip, separately. I told him they should travel together through India even as friends, as that was not the country in which to travel alone. But in Thailand and Cambodia he would want to go solo, if she still insisted on separating. These were the places to go solo. And that's how it turned out.

Every time Hans and I meet since then, we pick up right where we left off. He always jokes that although he is well-traveled in most parts of Europe and Asia, he revels in the fact that the only time he sightsees in his own country is when I visit. I'd choose the cities where we'd meet and tour for a few days after each of my business trips. We always have plenty to talk to about, enjoy sumptuous meals, love touring the Olde Towne areas, maintain the same healthy lifestyle, and coach each other in photography angles, shutter speeds, ISO settings and the like. We both enjoy seeing new sights, and he provided me with a German translator for these trips. Over the years we toured Stuttgart, Heidelberg, Dresden, Berlin, Frankfurt, and Hamburg.

Today, Hans was coming to the city of Frankfurt to hang out with me. We were both anticipating this visit since neither of us had seen any of it before besides the airport. I arrived in the early afternoon with plenty of time to meet Hans at the fountain in the Olde Town square. It seemed no time had passed since we last toured. Wandering through the cobblestone streets with its stone walkways and allure of days gone by, we captured pictures of people and places, catching up on the events in our personal and professional lives.

As we traversed out of the Olde Towne and into the areas of modern Frankfurt, we both enjoyed seeing the melding of the architectural styles, often combining the present and past on the same building. I'd never seen such innovation. As we walked, I asked, "So is there anyone new in your life?"

He replied, "No, I wish I could say there was—but no."

We admired the architectural diversity for which the Germans are world-renowned. Passing the European Union headquarters with its droves of protestors outside, we kept walking after snapping a few photos not to attract any attention to ourselves. We talked about our parents and sisters and whatever else came across our minds. All was good in those areas. We also reminisced about other places we visited.

Hans said, "Hey remember that dangerous bicycle ride we took in downtown Beijing with you on back of that rickety bike I rented from the hostel? And when we were in East Berlin staying in that converted boat hostel and those Communist-minded Germans from the East started speaking badly about you being an American? They almost started a fight!"

"Hans, that would've been your fight because I had no idea what they were saying, as you may recall. I really don't speak German. I just sat there eating my breakfast, watching you get your hackles up as they got you agitated. To me, it wasn't worth it getting heated over words I didn't understand. It turned out to be a glorious trip after avoiding that group," I muttered.

While passing other notable area landmarks, with all the sights and sounds of the city, the conversation was focusing on me.

"Oh yeah, did I tell you I'm going to Poland tomorrow for a week, and then to Sweden to meet my dream girl from 8th grade?

We'll meet for the first time in 33 years; we're both single, and I'm going to see what will happen."

"WHAT?? What?? What do you mean? Seriously?" he stopped dead in his tracks with his typically handsome inquisitive smile, eyebrows raised, saying, "You told me nothing of this before."

I had a lot of explaining to do as we walked and talked. "I'm telling you now because I wanted to tell you in person so you wouldn't think I had completely lost my mind. I only got the idea a few weeks ago and decided to pursue it," I said. "And now I'm going to Sweden to see her—well, I'm going to Sweden to see the country, and see her if she is available."

I told him in detail of my history with the Flossenbürg Castle. At first, he was intrigued, and then completely captivated. "How come you never told me of this channeling place before?" he asked.

"Again, I didn't want you to think I'd lost my mind," I said.

"Hey, maybe I should go there to channel romance into my life?" Hans suggested.

"Maybe you should wait until we find out how it works out for me. I don't want you on the wrong channel!" I laughed.

"Great point! I'll wait," he agreed.

We laughed and discussed different scenarios, chuckling through the streets as we typically did, discussing whatever else came to mind as we wandered. With the weather turning colder, we stopped for a quaint dinner. The outdoor restaurant supplied blankets and gas heaters for their guests who elected to dine outside. Those were all reserved or occupied. So, we opted to sit inside a temporarily tented area offering a distorted view of the town square through clear vinyl windows. That was okay, we saw what we came to see.

Dinner here was typically German and tasty. As darkness fell, Hans said he had to get back to his pickup point for his ride back to Essenburg, and I had to drop the car off at the airport. We finished dinner and afterward ducked into a McDonalds for hot coffee. We were soon off in my car to drop him to his ride share stop for his four-hour journey home.

As he exited the car he turned and smiled, saying, "Hey, good luck with your Swedish Princess."

"Thanks Hans, and good luck finding yours." A few seconds later we were again off in different directions. I was going to miss him. I quickly reflected how lucky I was to have a friend like Hans, since few people do. Finally, it hit me, I would be in Poland the very next morning off on another adventure—how cool was that!

After dropping the car at the airport, I took the free shuttle to the hotel, checking in. Dropping my luggage in the room, I went down to the lounge for a libation and some Wifi time on my smart phone. I thought about how randomly a few weeks prior, I found Erika on Facebook. And she began telling me a little bit about her life, what she was doing for a living, eking out sparingly few details as she had done ever since I'd known her. I didn't merely cut to the chase with her, I cut out the chase altogether, without embellishment, asking her during one email exchange, "Are you single?"

"Yes," she responded abruptly, "Are you?"

My heart jumped in excitement just thinking about it again.

Through our sporadic email conversations, she mentioned, "It would be so good to see you after all these years. Wow, I can't believe it's really you. You look wonderful in your online photos," and asking, "Is that how you really look, Dimitri?"

"Yes, it is," I responded.

"It would be great seeing you, Dimitri," she said.

"Yes, it would," I agreed. Then I heard nothing more from her up to this point. Yet off I was going to Sweden, hoping to see her. How crazy was this?

Nothing new appeared in my inbox, though I hoped to get some validation of my feelings and my itinerary. I didn't really need any, since I already made my point-of-no-return decision. Silently laughing at the decision to go to Sweden, purchasing my tickets after what seemed to be a supernatural intervention urged me to do so. If she couldn't or wouldn't see me, I'd change the purpose of my trip from personal discovery to tourism. If I couldn't see her, I'd just drive north until the snow and ice stopped me. Or I could go south or travel west to Norway, exploring parts of that country I hadn't yet seen. The spontaneity of my trip surprised me; this was atypical behavior for me. I laughed at myself. It's a good thing I'm traveling alone. Who else would put up with such uncertainty? But I really wasn't alone, at least I didn't feel I was.

~ 11 ~

Thirty-Three Years Later /
Trettiotre år Senare

I've always enjoyed the pageantry of the past, the prominence of the present, and the magnificence of agrarian scenery on the outskirts of the city-towns throughout Europe. There are clusters of villages and towns across most every country in Europe. They even developed walled cities in the Middle Ages; both protected against marauders.

With an innocence all its own, my eight-day trip to Poland seemed to last forever. Luckily, mine was a remarkable plan, perfectly executed, and the weather cooperated. I planned two-and-a-half days in each city of Kraków, Warsaw, and Gdańsk, hitting the streets with my camera early in the morning. I returned at around 6:00 pm for a brief respite, including a nap. Then I'd head out for dinner and sightseeing, until around midnight. This way, I'd maximize my time and get magnificent day and night shots of the monuments and street activity. Plus, I became familiar with the area quickly.

Poland was uniquely amazing. In each city, I spent my time wandering the clean streets, visiting small cafés, monuments, and castles. I enjoyed seeing the distinctive architecture within each city. It was wonderful. My educational exploration of the Olde Towne and city areas were each uniquely memorable. I enjoyed my first stop in the tiny town atmosphere of Kraków. While historically important to visit at least once, I avoided the depressing and ominous holocaust sites since I'd already seen these in Germany. I wanted this trip to be experiential, positive, educational, and relaxing.

Arriving at the tiny local airport, my first order of business was to find an ATM, since learning during my travels these offer the best money exchange rates. Poland had been a member of the European Union (EU) since 2004, but hadn't adopted the Euro (€) currency, instead keeping its own currency named the Zloty (PLN Zł). I needed to pay local merchants and local transportation in Zloty, so I got my usual US$200.00 for local spending money to begin my journey. It was easy finding the only ATM in the tiny building since it was next to the exit doors.

Exiting the airport, I hailed an airport taxi. The driver was middle-aged, well-dressed, polite, and friendly, but didn't speak a word of English. The 30-minute ride ended at the Stare Miasto Olde Towne area. We stopped right around the corner from the majestic Basilica Mariacka church, driving up to the front door of a building named Pokoje Gościnne Św. Anny. I guessed this was where I reserved the apartment online—the driver knew exactly where it was. Nestled safely inside the city walls, this place was within walking distance to virtually everywhere I wanted to roam at all hours of the day and night. I really lucked out.

Before exiting the taxi, I paid him, tipped him very well, and arranged for him to bring me back to the airport in two days. He immediately jumped from the car, opened my door, grabbing my bag next to me in the back seat. Ensuring I forgot nothing, he swiftly trotted toward the large castle-like wooden wall with my luggage in hand. Wasting no time, he rang the doorbell next to an immense, ancient wooden, barn-type door. This large door included a small access door. The ancient wood looked like many of the castle entrance ramps I'd seen in Europe.

A voice crackled over the wall-mounted intercom box near him. He conversed in Polish for a few sentences, turned to me smiling, nodding his head, and said, "Yes."

I was hoping everything else this trip would be so easy. Communicating to me using his body language and impromptu hand signals, the apartment manager would be down shortly to escort me in. I was so glad he did this for me, as I don't speak a lick of Polish, and English was apparently not a forte of hers.

The last time I received such an energetic reaction from a taxi driver was in Seoul, South Korea when I accidentally handed the driver KRW₩20,000 (Won equaling about US$17.00) instead of the KRW₩2,000 (the equivalent of about US$2.00) he was expecting for the short ride. Both notes were the same size and color. He swiftly drove away sporting an evil grin.

This Polish driver wasn't being nefarious, he was energetic because of his extreme politeness and appreciation. I was thrilled to have a safe guaranteed ride back to the airport, continuing my trip to Warsaw. Now standing outside, looking up at the monumental building, its worn physical appearance told of an ancient, rich past. I hoped this lineage didn't include any restless spirits visiting me during my nights here. Undoubtedly, this would be another interesting experience.

Before the driver left, a polite, elderly woman peered through a tiny peephole in the small access door, and thwacked open an archaic latch. She carefully exited the half-round access door to greet me, as it squeaked open. The driver politely made his intended departure known, again confirming through gestures, that I was in excellent hands.

Before I disappeared through the tiny door, he yelled through the passenger window from the taxi, "Two days!" agreeing to pick me up for my flight in two days.

Then summoning me back to the taxi with hand gestures, "Come... come," as I complied, he handed me his business card with his local phone number to call in case my plans changed. It amazed me how much humans can do with an open mind when confronted by the realization there is no common spoken language between would-be communicators.

The elderly woman escorted me inside the courtyard which was open to the sky above. Confronted by our first obstacle, an old, worn wooden staircase headed nearly straight upward, hugging the steep, cold, stone castle-styled walls in a drawn-out, semi-circular manner. The weakened, rickety structure looked like it was built as a fleeting afterthought centuries ago, providing temporary access to the rooms above. Recognizing this may not be a simple task for either of us, I maintained control of both my travel and camera bags. Approaching, then treading on the bottom stair, she crept along, leading me up the rickety stairway. As she stepped, each stair creaked, moaned, and groaned. I meticulously followed in her exact footsteps. The groans and moans from each stair became louder and much more prevalent with each step. Making our way slowly, higher and higher, up the inside wall, atop this tired, decrepit access way, I peered over the similarly constructed railing. Careful not to lean on it or touch it, I understood it was a long way down to the worn ornate tile, decorating the hard floor far below. Wondering when this stairway had last failed was foremost in my mind, knowing that falling from this height would be a quick, but surely painful way, to reach the bottom.

As we climbed past the second floor looking down, I was in awe of the familiarly unheated indoor courtyards seen elsewhere in European architecture. As we continued to climb, I peered over the fragile railing once again, down toward the ground floor. Again, I hoped the stairway would hold our weight, preventing us from plummeting to an instant death—miraculously it did. Although the higher we climbed, the more space I gave her as I followed. She spoke no English. Occasionally she turned, summoning me to follow with hand gestures. Guided by our positive, open-minded attitudes, we communicated our intent with smiles.

After reaching the apartment door on the fourth floor, she brandished a key, unlocking the door, showing me inside my apartment. The room was simple and comfortable. She offered to let me pay for the next two days using my credit card which she promptly processed on a laptop. Her mastery of her laptop keyboard amazed me. Handing me the room key, and another key to open the wooden access door downstairs, completed the transaction. I thanked her, stashed my luggage in the room, grabbed my camera bag and left with not a minute to waste.

Heading down the wobbly stairway, out through the castle-like ancient wooden access door, onto the cobblestone public streets with my camera in hand, I enjoyed the freedom offered by the fresh, brisk morning air. The breakfasts, lunches, snacks, and dinners I consumed over the next two days were wonderfully refreshing, reasonably priced, and unique. I learned from visiting the multitude of buildings, churches, and museums, Kraków was a splendid, quaint town steeped in a wealth of royal history dating back to the 7th century, as the first capital of Poland from 1038 to 1596. This once leading center of academic, artistic, cultural and economic life, is perfectly positioned along the banks of the Vistula River.

During the day, onlookers basked in the sun, sprawled out on the grassy banks, just relaxing. All of the people I met were friendly. The caretakers maintained the Wawel Castle and museum in pristine condition. Out of personal interest, I attended a church service and wandered through the cobblestone streets in and out of shops, flea markets, bakeries, and typical tourist attractions. My days were long, and the sunsets majestically serene along the Vistula. I understood why this had been such a popular spot for centuries. From my perspective, I was thankful the bulk of commercialism moved with the seat of the capital to Warsaw.

Dinner was within the walls of the city in an outdoor restaurant seating area under umbrellas, space heaters, and thoughtfully provided blankets draped on the back of chairs, as customers dined amidst the candlelit tables. Even my fish was expertly prepared. Alcoholic nightcaps topped off dinner, while the short, quiet walk back to my apartment provided the bit of exercise I needed to get a restful sleep. No restless spirits visited me while in Kraków.

When the morning came that I was scheduled to leave Kraków, I was a bit depressed. Though I looked forward to what else I would discover about Poland in the upcoming days, I would miss this place. The friendly, smiling taxi driver arrived on schedule as I waited outside the wooden access door where he dropped me a few days ago. It felt like I was meeting an old friend who was taking me to the airport. My journey continued leading me to new discoveries ahead, closer to Sweden; I found this thought deeply comforting.

On final approach to the Warsaw airport, out the window, I could see this city was one rife with businesses, public transportation, low-rise buildings, and hordes of activity. As soon as I disembarked the airplane, it felt as if I was back in Dublin, Ireland with all the friendly, smiling people. I gathered my belongings and figured I'd take a public bus for a quick, 30-

minute ride to the Moon Hostel where before visiting the Wifi-free Kraków, I had booked a room online. This establishment was more like a hotel than a hostel, except for the price of $20 a night for my single room. I checked into my room, asked a few pertinent tourist questions of the friendly desk clerk, and as always, immediately grabbed my camera bag and hit the streets on my road to discovery, walking toward the Olde Towne area. There were many more restaurants open day and night, buildings, palaces, and museums to visit and more cobblestoned streets to wander down than there were in Kraków; this made sense since Kraków's population of 770,000 is dwarfed by Warsaw's 1.8 million. I would have a lot of fun exploring this city. As I exited the hostel, my camera was constantly snapping shots. This was proving to be another amazing experience.

Warsaw is an expertly designed city with ultra-wide streets; completely restored, after being leveled during World War II. Seeing the carnage and destruction of many European cities in WWII film footage has always negatively affected me, until one local server conveyed to me in broken English this idea: "When you have an opportunity to redesign your city from scratch, you get it right the second time." They did. Visiting Warsaw these days, you'd never know it had been so ravaged by war. Many museums and building walls depict the stories of war and peace. Occasionally, architecturally engineered, uncovered, unfinished brick windows reveal the past destruction. Others now covered by reconstruction and restoration, the Warsaw population basically buried and erased the wonton destruction the war brought. Destruction not only by the occupying Nazis as revenge against its underground operations, but also by the Allied bombing trying to root out the Nazis. It's comforting to know many European cities have pressed forward, improving its history despite their entangled victimization of war. Warsaw is a prime example of such a possibility.

Meandering the streets of Olde Towne by the Royal Castle in Castle Square until the wee hours of the morning, I felt safe wherever I was. Here, I met many street music minstrels. Listening to their guitars, handpan drums, and flutes reflect off the walls of the tall Olde Towne buildings was heartwarming. After a brief respite taking in their tunes, I often purchased their music CDs and with a nod or simple friendly gesture, continued on my way. I also enjoyed many a thinly sliced, lightly fried and spiced, fish fillet in the sidewalk cafés along the way. Everyone was extremely friendly. Even as I passed the Parliament building, I noticed a large after-hours construction crew repairing the brick paver driveway and walkways adorning the historical building. As I watched intently to learn their techniques, taking some pictures, one worker walked over to me and asked, "You like this? Why?"

"Yes," I responded, "When I go back to the U.S., I will make one like this in front of my house, except much, much, much smaller. I'm trying to learn your method."

He smiled, answering with a thumbs-up gesture and then a bigger smile. When he returned to his group of workers, each of whom was looking my way, he spoke to them briefly. They all cheered in unison and displayed a thumbs-up gesture. After a few more minutes, I waved and continued on my way. They responded in kind.

I immensely enjoyed my visit to Warsaw with the droves of friendly people I encountered; have I mentioned that already? When my time came to a close, once again, I was apprehensive to leave. The same numbered city bus which dropped me close to the hostel, arrived on schedule going the other way, returning me to the airport. It was the easiest, most efficient, and seemingly safest method of travel I ever experienced in Europe. Making my way through the airport was seamless, simple, and relaxing, as I continued toward the flight delivering me to the sea-side, town-city of Gdańsk. With less than half the population of Kraków at 470,000, this is Poland's principal seaport.

Once I arrived at the modern, sprawling Gdańsk airport, I made my way to the indoor arrival greeting area. There were many taxi drivers holding signs with passenger names. One had my name on it. This was the only time I had transportation waiting for me at the airport. And it was a superb idea since Gdańsk is about a 40-minute American interstate-type highway drive away. It was unlike both Kraków and Warsaw.

My "taxi driver" looked more like a wrestler or mafioso than a taxi driver. At approximately six feet tall, weighing in at about 240 pounds, he was wearing a black leather jacket, sporting a smoothly shaved head, atop a wide, stable World Wrestling Federation (WWF) wrestler's physique. I approached him smiling, while identifying myself, he assertively grabbed my luggage and said, "Mr. Dimitri! We go now!" He aggressively and hurriedly led me through the sea of passengers, out into the airport parking lot toward a parked car—surprisingly, it was a Ford Pacifica. Upon approaching the vehicle, he popped the trunk with his handheld key fob and quickly deposited my luggage without hesitation. This was obviously not a registered taxi. There were no taxi signs, no fare stickers, and no visible permits of it being a taxi. He was constantly "checking his six" and the surrounding area as he opened the rear passenger door, skillfully depositing me inside. All he said was, "In!" Against my better judgment, I entered the vehicle. It felt more like being abducted, than being driven to my hotel. This was one of those times I thought of my ex-CIA Dad's immortal words, "It's easy to trust people when you have no choice!" This was indeed one of those times.

He wasted no time starting the car, rushing away from the airport. With the wheels squealing and chirping from the rapid acceleration, deceleration, and G-force turns, he barely slowed for stop signs. He disobeyed all other traffic control signs and signals we encountered, relegating these to mere suggestions. This was quite an uneasy feeling. Within minutes we were onto the highway. He checked his watch incessantly as we sped away. I sat in the back seat in silence, memorizing the traffic signs and our direction of travel as best I could. I was also keen to remember the sights and sounds we encountered along the route. I noticed the back-seat passenger doors had opening handles and power window controls. This was much unlike cars designed to keep people in custody from escaping. But I wondered if they worked.

My curiosity soon got the best of me—no longer would I contemplate this unanswered thought. My fingers approached the switch, my heart rate increased, and my palms began sweating as I depressed the window switch to the "down" position—the window jolted open; the sound of rushing air was deafening.

The driver immediately barked, "No open! No open! I have aircon and heat—you want, I do? No open window! No! Heat!? No open window! I make cold—you want?"

"No, I'm fine," I responded.

In the interest of compliance to calm him down, I immediately pressed the switch forward, closing the window. His continual squinting glare at me in the rear-view mirror was a bit unnerving to say the least, as I answered his demanding question, half-smiling with a shake of my head from side to side.

"It's good," I said.

After a few minutes of silence, he continued staring at me in the rear-view mirror. "You Army?" he aggressively demanded.

"No sir, I was Army long time ago. Now I retired," I responded.

As he sped more uncontrollably down the highway, checking his watch, he barked, "You Special Force—you Green Beret?" he impatiently demanded.

Now he had my complete attention. How could he possibly know this? I immediately became uneasy with his line of questioning. I hiccupped to think all my years of effort and training to operate below the radar in a foreign country were now for naught. I half-expected this to happen in Central or South America or even Southeast Asia or China but not in Poland.

"Shit," I thought. "Now what?" I usually travel unrecognized by most everyone I encounter.

I had a flashback to after our mission in Sri Lanka; our presence there was SECRET. It sparked much concern for the safety of my SF team members when a few of them were visited at their homes by people identifying themselves as Tamil students, once we returned. They were supposedly soliciting monetary contributions for their war effort, even asking a few questions regarding the U.S. Government involvement in Sri Lanka against the separatist movement. This too, seemed highly suspect and too arbitrary to be coincidental.

"You fight Iraq?" he blurted.

"I am retired now. I was in the Army a long time ago. I am working in business now."

"You fight Iraq?" he blurted again as he continued his inquisition.

"Yes, I fight in Iraq, a long time ago," I responded.

He continued speeding down the highway in a rush to get somewhere. He shouted, "My friend fight Iraq!"

Snatching his cellphone from the console next to him, he began pecking intently at the numbers on the keypad. He continued leering at me through the rear-view mirror. Placing a phone call, turning and speaking briefly, he thrusted his cellphone toward me.

"Say hello... You talk... Mr. Dimitri... You talk!"

I complied and heard a voice at the other end, "Hello? This is Michal. Peter tell me you fight in Iraq—Yes?"

"Yes." I responded.

"And you, Green Beret?"

"Yes." Then I expected the voice to tell me, "You are being abduct and soon to take you to undisklosed location, we demand one-million-dollar ransom, you not be happy, you not be komfortable, your government pay or we will kill you!"

"Where inside the Iraq you were?" he actually asked.

"Baghdad and Taji," I responded.

"I too in Iraq. But I in Umm Qasr. I Polish Navy long time. I think maybe we not meet before. But I do meet Green Beret before."

"Probably not me, I was never in Umm Qasr," I said.

"Okay… thank you for talking me… welcome to Poland… Peter is good man… will take care of you."

I knew Peter was a good man. I just wondered how he'd "take care" of me.

"I talk Peter again pleez…" the voice said.

I returned the cellphone to the driver, whom I now assumed was named Peter. After another brief, gruff conversation in Polish, Peter hung up. He continued hurtling down the highway, still looking nervously at his watch. Leering at me through the rear-view mirror, again and again, he snatched up his cellphone yet again, zooming past several potentially close mishaps with other cars.

All I thought was, "What the fu**?"

Again, he pecked out numbers on the keypad, and again he gruffly spoke in Polish.

After another brief conversation in Polish, he thrust the cellphone back toward me, again saying, "You talk!"

"Terrific. Now here it comes," I thought. Now the mastermind of the entire abduction will threaten me."

The calming voice on the phone said, "Mr. Dimitri?"

"Yes." I responded. "This is Jakub. I work Hotel Olowianka in Gdańsk. Peter will bring you to here, in about 20 minutes more you will arrive. Welcome to Gdańsk, Poland."

"Thank you," I dryly responded. This conversation explained a lot. But I had a few more questions about what exactly was going on. I handed the cellphone back to Peter which he stored in the center console.

After a brief silence, he continued peering at me in the rear-view mirror. "You Army, Special Force—you Green Beret," nodding his head, he aggressively repeated to confirm what we discussed just minutes prior.

"Yes, except now I retire," once again I tried explaining.

Without making any adjustment to the speed of the vehicle, he turned toward me, offering his right hand, smiling, "I too, I retire. I, Special Police. I, Gdańsk Special Police, now I retire. I businessman, too! This taxi, my business. My name Peter."

He laughed forcefully, nervously, and uncomfortably. I shook his hand, which he awkwardly withdrew, continuing to drive erratically. Being ex-Special Police explained his driving practices, his comfort with ignoring traffic signs and signals, and with speeding uncontrollably on public highways.

Without adjusting his speed, he opened the console, handing me a leather wallet containing his Special Police credentials, continuing to question me, "You Special Force, you know gun? You have gun? You shoot gun?"

"Yes," I responded smiling.

"I too!" he laughed, as he continued digging into his console, handing me more items, his gun license, his handgun expert rating and training credentials, and finally a replica of his shield. Thankfully, he didn't brandish a gun to show me; that could've ended my vacation. One by one, I looked at each of his credentials, handing them back, not wanting to interrupt his focus on speeding—I mean, driving. Immediately, I let down my guard and felt much more comfortable with the situation at hand, and with him. I then handed him my SF coin I keep in my pocket, saying, "Yes, I am really Special Forces." Immediately he knew what it was.

"Yes, I know. I before… Polish Army too—I know Green Beret… Special Force! Good… Good… very good!" He handed it back to me after a quick look at both sides of the pure silver coin.

"You are Special Police. Were you Special Police a long time?" I asked.

"Yes. Army not long time… Special Police… long time, very long time. Now retire. Now I teach martial art. I drive taxi. I teach my son to martial art. You know?… my son now college… no want to do Police… no do Army… to know woman only. You know?"

Boy, did I know!

"Yes, I have five children. Three girls, two boys. Nobody want to go Army, no Air Force, no Navy, no Coast Guard, no police, only college."

"Believe me, I know. Yes, I know!"

We both laughed. Finally, I felt we were communicating uncoerced.

Nervously checking his watch again, he finally explained, "I am Dragon Boat Captain. You know Dragon Boat?"

"Yes, I know," I responded.

"We practice at Hotel Olowianka in Gdańsk today… at hotel in bottom. I no want be late. We float on canal near hotel. I practice tonight, one hour. You look tonight? You bring camera?" he forcefully added.

"Sure!" I smiled, accepting the less than gracious invitation. Now everything made sense. He was aggressive by nature, and drove similarly, being a retired police officer, and he was rushing so he wouldn't be late for his Dragon Boat rowing team practice. No longer was this reminiscent of traveling in a Humvee (High Mobility Multi-Wheeled Vehicle - HMMWV) outside of Baghdad with would-be informants potentially leading us into an ambush. I felt much, much, more confident about this situation now.

Arriving at the edge of the Olde Towne area of Gdańsk, we drove over a narrow bridge onto a tiny island housing only the hotel. Peter rushed me inside after refusing to take any tip, taking only what he told me the fare was. He ran my bags in to the desk clerk, checked me in, hurriedly bringing my bag upstairs to my room, showing me the way. He dropped the bags in the room as soon as he opened the door.

He barked, "One hour, I back, downstair, you take pictures of Dragon Boat racing here, downstair!" he motioned downstairs.

I agreed. Sure enough, in less than one hour I was ready with my camera and equipment in hand for the town's Dragon Boat racing team to appear in the canal in front of the island hotel's waterway access. And they did. As a leader, there was no doubt in anybody's mind Peter was larger than life. Everyone did as he suggested, and soon the boat was off. I snapped as many pictures as I could. Two canals converged in front of the hotel; this was their practice area. After they put in and started paddling toward the ocean, they were out of sight in no time. This was my cue to start my tour of the ancient city-town.

Back across the tiny bridge, into the town, I meandered. Down the narrow streets, to another bridge leading into the walled city. I met a lot of street minstrels in this city-town as well. And once again, I bought their CDs, now being able to enjoy these local treats forever. As in all other European Olde Towne areas, these artists are often talented and don't mind braving the cool night air. Nearing nightfall close to the arches of the Olde Towne city gates, I found the Chamber of Commerce office. I entered and asked where they'd recommend I visit. "If there is one spot in all of Gdańsk I shouldn't miss, where would that be?"

The two behind the desk answered in unison, "Ahhhh… Sopot. You must take the train in the morning to get there. If you leave now to go there, you would not be able to come back because the train will stop soon." So, there I had it. My plan for my next day's activities. Sopot, it was!

I awoke the next day surrounded by the warmth and comfort of my hotel room, enjoying the window view of the nearby canals—one on each side of the hotel. Readying myself for another wonderful breakfast and the rest of the day, I once again made my way off the tiny island. Watching the swans and ducks frolic in the canal was quite the sight. I walked through both arched stone gates of the Olde Towne area toward the train station. Peeking into a few museums along the way, it took me a while to get there. Once there, it took quite some time to decipher the train ticket machine. I finally bought a ticket for a few US$ in Zloty. Then I realized that train didn't arrive until 5:00 pm.

In complete frustration, I wandered over and stood in a long line of Polish speaking questioners. I asked a beautiful young girl in line in front of me about this anomaly. She started explaining and then said in English, "Stay with me in line and I will ask the clerk. I will do it for you, it can be very complex using these machines. Even for me."

The over-worked, under-appreciated customer service lady behind the glass answered our question. The girl who befriended me rushed over to a machine and bought me a ticket, "You are American, right?"

"Yes," I responded, smiling.

She said, "You bought the wrong ticket before for the passenger train; you needed the express train to Sopot, only for a few dollars more. Now you will have the correct ticket," as she processed the new ticket for me. I gave her the money.

Rushing me over to the train platform to catch the next train due in a few minutes, she said, "Here to Sopot, it will come soon. If you want to get a refund for your first ticket, you can get it after your trip to Sopot. I don't really think it would be worth you standing in another line, though. Plus, you don't speak Polish. Your train will arrive here in a few minutes. I must catch mine too now, it's way over there. They don't arrive as often as yours to Sopot. I'm Kristina, goodbye, enjoy your trip!" After a quick handshake, she was running down to her train platform.

She was right. My train arrived a few minutes later, so I got on. I saw no maps of any sort in the train car and didn't realize there were three such stations with the same name Sopot (I think it was South, Central, and North Sopot in Polish) so I dismounted when we arrived at the first one.

Once outside the train station, I traveled down a few flights of stairs, not understanding which way to walk in this suburban beach area. I knew to head downhill, because that's the way water flows and all water eventually ends in larger bodies of water, so that's where I headed, downhill. Hopefully that was toward the beach. Down the long, pristine streets I made my way, making sure I snapped pictures of the street signs on my cellphone so I could easily find my way back. Eventually, the roads I followed by vast amounts of landscaped yards, behind short see-though fences surrounding beautiful French-styled houses, led to a seemingly endless sandy beach, near the cool waters lapping onto the shoreline.

I chose one of three outdoor beach-front restaurants I happened across, walked inside to the order desk, placed my order, and sat down at a table of my choosing outside in the cool, yet warm air. I enjoyed my reasonably priced seafood linner (lunch/dinner) immensely, as I sat looking, watching, enjoying, smelling the salty air from the Gulf of Danzig.

The sights included small fishing boats and crews and their activities of net mending, boat maintenance, visitors walking in the sand, and flights of the largest variety of water and land fowl/birds I have ever seen flocking together in one place. There were pigeons, ducks, swans, sparrows, and many more birds either fixed, fluttering, flying, or floating together on the beach. No fighting or squawking. Here, unbelievably, I was in Poland sitting, watching the birds on the lapping shores of the Baltic Sea, enjoying an amazing lunch and a tasty beer. This place, the likes before, I had never seen in any of my travels. As I sat watching the rolling waves sneak toward the shore, I wrote:

Poland's Baltic Sea

What a perfect day I had,
Walking on the shores of Poland's Baltic sea,
Snapping photographs of people and animals along the beach,
Missing only the perfect person to be with me.

This perfect woman with whom to share,
This perfect time again,
Yet I do know the perfect woman to behold,
And I know where to bring her, my soon to be best friend.

There are swans on these beaches,

Sharing waters with sparrows, and pigeons, and ducks –
pleasantly un-mean,
All sizes of seagulls, black birds, and crows,
Even one unknown bird to which mine eyes before, forever
remained unseen.

There is magnificent food to be tasted on the shoreline,
Astonishing feelings to me she bestows to someone afar whom
she barely knows,
Wondrous thoughts of this and of her,
Someday soon I hope to be again, with her, seeing the birds of
Poland's Baltic Sea.
I hope someday soon I will revisit this amazing sight,
With the perfect woman in my arms, my new best friend and me,
Who knows what the waters will bring to this beach each day,
I'll see reflecting within her eyes, this sententious sunset by this sea.

After finishing my lunch, I didn't donate any treats to the
wildlife. I remembered my friend, Michael, pointing out a sign to
me while I was visiting him and his wife Kay in England. As we
drove around the seaside towns near Woodbridge, Aldeburgh and
many places surrounding, postings didn't just convey a
discouraging message, "Please don't feed the birds," but a few lines
down threatening, "this will be a £2,000 British pound fine
[US$3,000] to anyone caught." This was a hefty amount for a
simple act of feeding nature. Many seaside towns in Europe and
their surrounding townships previously accosted by these
feathered foes (pigeons and seagulls) aren't very fond of them. So,
I'm careful when I travel. My goal is to enjoy my surroundings,
not offend anyone, avoid any trouble, flying undetected below the
radar. After lunch, I left no morsels, licking my plates clean,
quietly wandering off down the beach toward the distant long
wooden pier.

Arriving at the pier reading the placards and tourist information, it amazed me that this long wooden pier was such a significant site. I only noticed this typical pier from a distance. This is the longest wooden pier in Europe. Its current disposition dates to 1928, however, originally built in 1827. All 1690 feet (or 515 meters) of this pier still proudly rests in front of the Sofitel Grand Sopot Hotel, attracting tourists, picture takers, honeymooners, families, and others from around Europe. It is also here where a proud Adolf Hitler was pictured, walking along these very boards in front of the same hotel, shortly after successfully launching his Navy on its dastardly deed with a surprise attack on the outpost at Westerplatte, near Gdańsk. This was the final act that ignited the whole of Europe into World War II on September 1, 1939.

It was an enjoyable stroll along the planks. There were many people to see, a healthy amount of pleasure craft and yachts, and many pictures to take. Vacationers who appeared to be honeymooners saw my camera and didn't hesitate to ask me to take their photo with their cameras or cellphones. I obliged. Many of them never realized I was not in any kind of rush, determined to take the perfect picture of them they would cherish for a lifetime. Sometimes this took time, especially on a perfect weather day, with ideal light, as this was. I had the best time taking these perfect pictures, regardless of how long it took me. They all seemed to appreciate my efforts.

Venturing close to the water on the lower pier walkway, I dropped my lens cap. I always meant to buy a tether for it but hadn't got around to it. As I fumbled to catch it in mid-air, it slipped through my fingers, bouncing onto the wooden planks, finally slipping between two of them, blooping into the frigid waters below—gone forever, out of my grasp. How symbolic this was to me. After every potentially romantic relationship I had in my life up to this point, all slipped through my fingers, as did my cherished lens cap. This was prophetic.

Working my way back to the train station, I sat on the beach taking pictures of all the different birds frolicking on the pristine sand. Before I knew it, a beautiful, shapely woman sat close by me, watching me snap away at the birds.

"Are you professional photograpfy?" she asked.

"No," I answered, "It's only a hobby. Just for fun."

"I am Stephani, what is your name?"

I wandered over to where she was sitting, joining her in the sand. "Hello, I'm Dimitri."

"Hello Dimitri, do you stay here long?" she seductively asked.

"No, I'm taking the train back to Gdańsk to spend my last night there."

"I see, Dimitri. Well, I hope you enjoy your stay. I must go now. Nice to meet you," and off she went. That was weird. Brushing the sand off myself, I vigilantly set off to catch the train back to Gdańsk.

After arriving, I exited the train station, walking back toward the cobblestones of Olde Towne. This time I attempted to access the one hour of free daily Wifi the city provides each cellphone user on the public streets. As I got online, I hoped I would get a message from the Princess. Wherever and whenever I could that night, I checked my cellphone before and after snacks and dinner, to get some feedback from Erika. After departing Germany, it had been six more days of checking, connecting mostly in airports since my hotels and hostels didn't have Wifi access. Even now, there was no word. Not a one. I continued touring past the steeples and peoples of Gdańsk in the cool night air.

I stopped momentarily by a sidewalk café. Walking by earlier, I paid no attention to this place. Immediately I was spellbound by the unexpectedly full-bodied, warm guitar music emanating from two local guitarists playing inside a plastic, three-inch border set up around them in this small venue. I stood there motionless, mesmerized. Listening to their unique sound as I stood, two women sitting at a table within arm's reach motioned to me to sit and enjoy a beverage of my choice, their treat. At first, they spoke with hand gestures in a rudimentary sign language used to communicate with people out of earshot. As I neared, smiling, they spoke in simple English sentences. I sat down, not understanding the relationship between two, and they soon explained they were discussing the results of a final exam the younger woman had taken in the afternoon from the older one, her professor. I assumed she aced the test by the jovial nature of their discussion.

This hospitality was a mere example of what I experienced during my entire trip to Poland. This portion of my trip, especially to Gdańsk, I would fondly remember as a comforting, friendly visit. After finishing our unremarkable beers and pleasant discussion, the ladies gently excused themselves, using an early morning start as a valid reason for their departure. We all got up, leaving the café. As good luck would have it, the singing duo was taking a break between sets, so I asked them if they had any more of their prominently displayed CDs for purchase. They obliged and even gave me a discount when I took out the remainder of my spending Zloty from my pocket, embarrassingly coming up short.

Smiling they said, "Take it and share." So off I went.

Glancing at the CD, I instantly discovered there was an entire band called, The Acoustic Travel Band, and these were only two of its founding members. This band is one of the most popular bands in Poland. They are on the same popularity level as the band Kerekes, in Hungary. I met that band the year prior as they performed for a sparse crowd in the castle courtyard in the Fisherman's Bastion on the Buda bank of the Danube River. This river splits Hungary's twin cities of Buda and Pest. So impressed with that band, I bought a copy of each of their CDs after their makeshift concert. They, too, were surprised an American would enjoy their music as much as I did. Here in Gdańsk, these musicians were doing what they loved to do, serenading the guests seated at this tiny street-side café where they got their start in the music business years ago. They confided in me this was still one of their favorite venues to play. Learning this only added to the nostalgia and mystique of the night.

Since my last attempt, and again this time, there was no response from Erika. Tonight, would be my last-ditch effort to connect to the internet since I was going to Sweden in the morning. As I wandered through the streets of the Olde Towne in the now cold night air, it wasn't until I was at the outskirts of historic Gdańsk, across the footbridge from my hotel, did I finally connect. Here it was, my last night in Poland; I really wanted a response. FINALLY! I got one.

Her email response: "What? Just like that? You decide to come to Sweden? You're crazy!! Dimitri, it would be nice to see you. However, right now I have so many responsibilities with my work, and I'm having problems getting any time off—I have to work this entire weekend. I also have the kids to think about. I've got a lot going on right now. It would've been better if you visited a few months from now; but, not now. This is not a good time at all! The hotel where you said you are staying is close to my house—so yes, Dimitri, maybe I can try to see you. I can't promise anything at this point. I just don't know if I could see you at all." Her text gave me the impression I may have angered her, or at least made her extremely annoyed at my insistence on visiting.

My heart sank like a lead balloon. This had been such an amazing journey so far, and the spirits in Germany provided me the epiphany, so I couldn't disappoint them. I would do as they said, "FOCUS ON YOUR JOURNEY" staying positive; so I did. Everything lined up—until now.

I darted back my response, "It would only be a few minutes or hours anytime within the next three or four days. I've got my hotel reservations and rental car, so I will be on my own with complete freedom and flexibility. If possible, maybe we could meet for a few hours; or maybe lunch or dinner? That would be great!" I received no further response. Wondering if this was a good idea or if it was after all a crazy, irresponsible whim for all involved. This started driving me nuts! After all, it wouldn't be the first time while visiting a country that "friends" refused to see me because it was inconvenient for them. This could be the one chance in a lifetime, as some are for me. Receiving a "No… I can't make it happen," or as one said, "How about in a week or two?" Her response really disappointed me.

Would she be able to see me? Would she even want to now? I questioned and wondered if it was a waste of time and money— maybe this was a spiritual hoax, of sorts? I stopped the negative thoughts from re-emerging. It wouldn't be a waste if I focused on my journey, stayed flexible, and came up with options, as I usually do. I had all questions and no answers. I had nothing except a realm of possibilities and impossibilities to consider, coupled with more questions upon questions. Only time would tell what lay ahead for me; I'd have to wait and see.

I thought this last night would be the highlight of my trip to Poland. But I was wrong. Every day and night I saw fresh sights, heard unfamiliar sounds, and met sincerely pleasant people. The entire country of Poland and each experience I enjoyed here topped my list. My wartime experience in Kuwait and Iraq meeting Polish Soldiers was merely a premonition of the friendly people I would meet here. The photographs I captured were among my best-ever, both day and night! The walk back to the hotel was a short one, during which I was beaming with contentment at my new music CD relic.

The next morning, I packed my luggage and ate breakfast early. Wandering around the grounds, relaxing, taking a few more pictures on the street, I watched the geese, the swans, the seagulls, and ducks swimming in the canals beside the hotel. I heard a car quickly approaching the hotel over the bridge. It was Peter. But now he was in a new Mercedes Benz.

"Dimitri!" Peter got out of the car and yelled to me.

"Hello Peter, is that a new car?"

"Ahhh, my car broken. No start! This, my wife car," he said laughing. "She not know. We go Westerplatte now, before you go airport! We go now! Quick, quick."

"Do we have enough time? Maybe next visit to Poland I'll go there?" I asked.

He smiled incessantly, "No!" and wouldn't take no for an answer. "You pay me airport. I pay take you Westerplatte. No choice. You Army, You Green Beret. You go Westerplatte. You Army retire, must go Westerplatte! Must go! Must go, yes? Must go now, yes? Hurry! Hurry!" Hustling me back into the hotel to checkout, then running me upstairs, he collected my luggage. He was on a mission.

Because of his police bona fides and credentials with the hotel, I became very fond of Peter. I thought nothing negative associated with another one of his escapades. I wasn't even worried about missing my flight. I knew I was in expert hands. Out of extreme curiosity, I agreed to go. Not that I really had a choice with Peter at the helm. We were off in a flash, and in a flash we arrived.

As we walked the hallowed grounds of the memorial park, I learned first-hand that Westerplatte was the location where the Nazis cast Europe into World War II. Basically, it was the last straw breaking Poland's defenses. Attacking the garrison at Westerplatte with elements of the German Navy, the unprovoked, surprise attack coincided with air attacks, killing many of the Polish defenders. The battle took days and came at a relatively high price for the Nazis; the few surviving Polish defenders surrendered. In an unprecedented gesture among warriors, the Nazis allowed the commanding officer to keep his ceremonial sword while in captivity.

Peter walked me around the memorial explaining everything as best he could even though most of the display placards at each station were in English. I became fond of his accent and his spirited explanations. He reminded me of a Polish version of Steve Irwin, the Australian zookeeper, crocodile whisperer, and adventurer.

Peter was so proud of his own background and country, showing me around the war memorial. He even bought me a few trinkets along the way as mementos of this visit. "Gift! Me to you! No choice!" he said. Like I'd ever forget him, even without the souvenirs.

This experience topped my visit to Poland. What an amazing trip! What an amazing country! What amazing people! What an amazing Peter!

Riding back to the airport with Peter at the wheel, he continually checked his watch, driving at a slower pace today. Thinking how much I would miss it here nearly brought a tear to my eye and a lump in my throat. A tear wouldn't be appropriate for a Green Beret Special Forces Soldier, regardless of how I felt inside. It was easier hiding the lump in my throat. I'd never been treated so well, ever.

These were my last minutes in Poland. I thought of my visit to the old capital city of Kraków, the days spent walking around Warsaw, the quick daylight train trip to the beaches and pier in

Sopot, exploring the seaport of Gdańsk, the music minstrels, churches, museums and buildings of yesteryear, proudly hosting visitors and curiosity-seekers. I reflected on each of my experiences in Poland fondly, even the hour-long deviation to Westerplatte, on Peter's insistence.

Dropping me at the airport entrance in front of a row chock full of no-parking signs, I pointed to them, "No parking?" I asked.

Peter smiled and said, "Arghhhhh," waving with his hands not to be concerned.

I made such a tremendous friend in Peter in such a short amount of time. I regretted having to leave his homeland so soon. When we bid farewell, I truly felt I was leaving a best friend. I never quite made a friend like him in such a short time. Whether he knew me for three days or for thirty years, he was a fantastic person to know. After receiving a quick bear hug and a strong hand shake from Peter, I was off again continuing the rest of my journey... heading into... who knew what!

~ 12 ~

Toward the Edge/ Mot Kanten

L anding in Frankfurt, I had only three hours to make my connecting flight. Three hours seems more than adequate, but not when you're at one of the world's biggest and busiest airports. Two hours is the minimum time suggested traversing this transport hub, if all goes well. And that's just if you're checking in for a flight. I had so much more to accomplish.

Since I wanted to make sure I had my luggage with me, I chose not to attempt checking my tiny 30 lb. bag forward to Stockholm from Gdańsk, as Layla suggested. I checked it to Frankfurt. At least I would be closer to where I last saw it. On one post-business vacation trip to Ireland, my luggage was lost for four days in the dead of the Irish winter. All I had to wear was a suit, dress shoes, and a scarf. I collected my bag at the airport as I was leaving. I didn't want to repeat such an experience on this trip!

After clearing immigration, getting my luggage, and clearing the quick customs check, I had to walk forever to get to the correct terminal. Then, I had to confirm my flight to Stockholm, locate its departure location, find the proper airline kiosk, check-in, print my boarding passes, and stand in one of those Disney World-style long check bag lines which only seem to get longer as you wait. Finally, I dropped the bag for loading onto the aircraft. Whew! I did it! Off on its journey was my bag, and off I was to finish my chores.

Similar to the Mall of the Americas, the Frankfurt airport has three floors dedicated solely to stores and shops. Most of these are high-end stores—Calvin Klein, Fossil, Benetton, Marco Polo, Dior, Coach, and many, many more stores, including the Levi store. Levi Strauss? Really? Yup, in Germany. It's not as high-end, nor is it as low-priced a store as it usually is in the States. Mr. Strauss, a German immigrant, earned his respect among his fellow countrymen after opening his brand in 1853. Who knew? Perhaps the allure of American clothing was a plus.

The Frankfurt airport itself has an integrated Hilton hotel, a large underground railway station for long-range travel (or S-Banh), a subway station (or U-Banh), a main bus terminal, and many rental car companies operating there. The best thing about Germany is not needing a car to get around major cities. Public transportation is primarily rail and bus, going everywhere.

In no other place in the world (except maybe in the Amsterdam Schipol airport) will you see a more diverse amalgamation of people rushing in so many directions, headed for different destinations. Today especially, from my perspective, these people resembled the walking dead, all slogging around in front of me, slowing me down to a snail's pace. Some people had suitcases, some had wedding dresses, some with shopping bags, while others were merely slow walkers or wanderers. So many people were just hanging out at the airport with nothing better to do on a Friday afternoon. This is one massively confusing place to navigate.

Thankfully, as I often do when I travel, I attached a wrist compass to my watchband for an instant magnetic direction check. My three hours there should've been enough time to get everything done, but I couldn't be a dilly-dally diva. I had to spend the entire time busily hopping around, working down my task list. I had to check off as many items as I could as quickly as possible.

My first chore was to get camera stuff. My hunt began traversing the never-ending mall specialty shops. First, I had to get another memory card, since Germany and Poland used up the bulk of my new one. And I had to find a new lens cap with a tether, since the Gulf of Gdańsk swallowed my last one. This was a critical piece of equipment to protect my lens filter from scratches.

And since Layla told me Sweden this time of year might freeze and might even snow, I had to get a scarf. It would be a great addition to the Spring clothes I brought with me. The only other winter apparel I had were my leather driving gloves, doubling as winter gloves for some protection from the cold, the lightweight US$30 microfiber jacket, and a winter cap. My jacket was surely inadequate to face the potential sub-zero cold in Sweden; not designed for winter, it was waterproof, but not cold proof. I bought it a year prior at the Grand Canyon North Rim campground store during one of my hikes with my childhood buddy, Sebastian.

After finishing these chores, I had to make it back through the security checkpoints, buy some gifts for the Princess and her little Princesses at the duty-free stores, maybe grab a bite to eat, and finally catch my flight.

Finding a camera store proved fairly easy. Once inside, I saw some lens solution. Even though I had my powdered graphite cleaner and brush, I wanted to use this with my lens paper in case that alone wasn't good for cleaning the vestiges of the Sopot sea salt off my filters. I wasn't taking any chances with photographing my memories on the next portion of my trip. I spent the money and bought a large memory card and a fitted tethered lens cap, installing it on my camera on the spot. That was fairly quick and easy. Looking for a reasonably priced scarf now would most likely prove to be my most arduous task. I went to the first store, Burberry, and asked the salesperson where they kept their scarfs. She walked me over to a rack and these started at €100 Euro.

"One hundred Euro?" I confirmed with the sales associate. I took out a one Euro coin from my pocket, showing it to her asking again, "One hundred of these?" wanting to ensure there was no miscommunication. Could it be possible, a little piece of straight cloth would cost over US$100.00!

I confirmed again, "So, it will cost for only one scarf €100 Euro?"

"Yes!" replied the saleswoman.

"What does it do?" I asked.

She furrowed her brow and repeated, "What does it do?"

"Yes. I put it around my neck—what else does it do?"

She laughed, "It does nothing else."

I confirmed with her, "I put it around my neck, it does nothing. It doesn't heat up, massage my neck, vibrate, or anything. And it costs €100 Euro?"

"Well… it will make you smarter," she quipped and continued, "Because when you realize it won't do anything but keep your neck warm, remembering you spent €100 Euro more than you needed to spend, it makes you smarter… and warmer… it does nothing else."

"Can I eat it if I get stranded in the snow?" I joked.

"No sir," she laughed and responded, "… Feel it… it's quite soft," she conveyed with her cute German accent.

Then I asked her something which made her nearly fall over laughing, "Do you have any very long socks I could wrap around my neck instead? You see I'm going on an unplanned trip to Sweden to see a woman whom I haven't seen in 33 years and I may not even be able to see her; it will be up to her. I already have many scarfs at home in the U.S. and all I need is a cheap scarf for three days—that's it. I just need a cheap scarf to use for this one trip, so I don't freeze my sensitive neck in the Nordic fiords," I explained.

"Sweden... ahhh... it's quite cold this time of year... and windy too! You should get a scarf and gloves as well!" she touted.

"How about a coat and very warm jacket and boots too?" I added.

"Ah so... of course!" she perked up. We both laughed as she tried to upsell me.

"But if I buy a scarf for €100 Euro, I won't have any money to eat in Sweden."

"Ahhhh yes, but you will look so handsome with your matching hat and coat in your new scarf while you are starving!" she joyfully concluded.

"Greta," as I read her nametag aloud, "It's just a scarf. Do you think I am so ugly that even the most beautiful scarf would make such a difference for me? And it does nothing else but wind around my neck for €100 Euro. All it will really do is physically choke me, as well as financially choke me?" We both laughed.

She said, "You may not be able to find a scarf for less than €100 Euro or maybe even some very long socks."

"Thank you so much for your help. You were so much fun. If it doesn't work out for me in Sweden, I'll be back—you're not married, are you?"

"No, not yet!" she pressed. "Have a good trip and good luck with your girl, and your scarf! "Hopefully I will see you later," she yelled as I rushed out of the store, checking my watch.

In yet another store, I asked again about the scarfs. "Are they made with platinum or gold thread?" These conversations seemed to repeat themselves over and over. I looked in five more stores on my quest. There was no way in hell I was going to pay THAT much for a scarf. The saleswoman heard my frustration as I was mumbling (or more accurately grumbling) under my breath. She approached me. Apparently impressed by my candor, she started laughing, and in English with a heavy Tagalog accent she said, "I know what you mean about these prices. If you go downstairs to the Levi's store you should find something much more reasonably priced—you won't find anything cheaper on this floor. This is veeery expensive here. Go down two floors. It's not far."

I thanked her and, like a marathon walker, made my way downstairs. Hurriedly, I moved closer toward where the Levi store was reported to be. Checking my watch again, I had two hours before departure, and still had no scarf. Now, to find the elusive Levi store, somewhere around here with allegedly the cheapest scarfs in Frankfurt. This way, I wouldn't feel guilty using it just one trip. Down another escalator, I went looking for more stores. Following her general directions, I looked for a store directory. I found many access points to the parking garage, and a few to other stores, but still no directory, and no Levi's sign.

"Great! Just great! It's gotta be here somewhere," I silently huffed as I considered asking someone for either a store directory or the Levi's store, specifically. But my German wasn't much beyond "*Auf weider sein*" and "*Juus*." Even if I knew how to ask someone, I most likely wouldn't be able to understand their colloquial responses. To complicate the situation, most of the people in the airport looked like travelers, and most likely were not from Germany. They may not know their way around this airport as well as I did.

Suddenly, at the end of the longest hallway I have ever walked, short of those comprising the 5-mile indoor outer ring hallway encircling the Pentagon building, I saw the shape of a sign from afar that looked like the Levi's logo. Could it be? Like a wayward wanderer lost in the desert seeing a mirage of an oasis, my heart sped up, my pace quickened, and my eyes squinted trying to focus long distance. This better be it! The red sign transfixed me. Walking so far away from the escalator at this point, remembering the way back would be impossible. And if this was the wrong way, I risked running out of time. Suddenly, there it was! The L-E-V-I's sign and nearby, the store entrance. It was all by itself. They relegated this store to an unknown area in the airport known most likely only to security, maintenance workers, and perhaps other travelers who lost their way.

I rushed into the store, abruptly approaching the saleswoman. The wind my quick pace generated behind me blew the shirts and skirts on the racks as I passed.

"*Hallo. Schprecken zee Inglish bitte?*" I asked.

"Yes, of course I speak English," she said.

My ears rejoiced hearing these words that would otherwise have annoyed me at this point. "Where do you keep the scarves, that are on sale?" I desperately asked.

"Ovar zeyre," she said as she pointed.

Following her directions, I reached the display pawing through the selection of hanging scarfs, "Noooo, no, no, no, no! €80 Euro! Oh no... not this one... not this... not now! No, No, No, No," I thought using my inner, ugly voice. Smiling, I turned toward her using my outside voice, asking, "Do you have anything I could use once or twice just for walking... maybe something not so expensive?"

Undoubtedly annoyed by my "cheap" query, she most likely thought, "Wonderful, one customer this whole week and this guy wants cheap!??" "Ahhh, over there in the basket on the floor. I weel show you."

Despite being a young girl, she walked at a sluggish speed. Soooooooo s-l-o-w-l-y. It tempted me to gently push her by the shoulders, helping speed her along. I really had NO time to spare. She stopped, gently kneeled down, grasped a basket from beneath a display case that was covered by a tablecloth. One by one, s-l-o-w-l-y pulling each scarf out of the basket, handing them to me, describing the colors, as she did. "Heyre is peenk... heyre is yellow... heyre is red... heyre is puhple... heyre is lime green..."

Since I didn't need a lesson in colors, I cut her off realizing I still had to complete my purchase, find my way back through the airport maze of hallways and byways, find the proper security entrance, wade

215

through a sea of passengers, find the gate, buy some presents for the Princess and her offspring, get a bite to eat, and finally board my flight "—is there anything here more masculine... more neutral in there?" I blurted.

Annoyed, she s-l-o-w-l-y rose to her feet, extended her arms handing me the basket saying "Heyre you can look for yourself... perhaps YOU can find something cheap in gray or black?" she condescendingly spouted.

"Okay, thank you."

In just a few scrapes to the bottom of the straw basket, I found a beautifully neutral, gray scarf. It was long, and incredibly soft. And it was only €20 Euro! Woohoo! I found it! I found it! I found it! For some reason, the European scarfs China makes are only sold in Europe. They are longer, wider, and softer than those sold in the States. So now, I'm only €20 Euro into this scarf, and it's unlike any other scarf I have at home. Woohoo! Win-win!

The saleswoman looked at me and said, "Yes, zat will do quite well for your purpose." I didn't know exactly what she meant, but I was sure she wasn't being nice.

Leading me to the cash register like an indignant puppy, "€20 Euro," she said.

I handed her the cash, not wanting to wait to process a credit card. Thanking her, I departed the store faster than I entered, generating even more wind behind me in my haste. With my trophy in hand and my wallet still intact, with credit cards still usable, I made a beeline down the never-ending hallways. Up the escalators I ran, looking for the starting gates, I mean, security checkpoints, ready to run over anyone in my path.

Checking my watch, the harrowing scarf experience took me about 20 minutes. I searched frantically for the security checkpoint, hoping for a short line, hoping to get through the line in time to buy some heartfelt gifts, hoping to find my gate, hoping to get a bite to eat, and hoping to board the silver bird to fly off into the sunset over the horizon to a land far away, that until this point my mind had temporarily forgotten. It surprised me to find the security checkpoint fairly quickly. And no line!

The mood of the security screeners was jovial and light-hearted. As I gained a false sense of satisfaction, hustling into the security check area, as soon as I turned the corner—to my horror—directly in front of me, there were three separate, fully packed, Disney World-style serpentine lines. My heart sank. The old doctor's office trick with the multiple waiting areas! They got me! So here is where everyone in the airport was. I seriously questioned making my connection.

Waiting in line, I shuffled my feet inching forward, line by line, watching the joints in the floor tiles creep past the front of my shoes, among the crowd of fellow plodding passengers. With my stomach knotted, my head pounding, my heart racing, I tried to think of options, of which I had very few. I wondered what I would do if I missed my flight to Stockholm. This was the last departure of the day—I was completely out of options. In Europe, flights to some locations, like in Alaska, can be sporadic; some are even once a week. I prayed silently. What would Layla say if I missed my connection?

Sluggishly rounding yet another corner, a security officer jumped in front of me from out of nowhere, pointing right at me. He lifted a strap out of the stanchion clasp, with a half-smile and tilt of his head, he gestured me to jump the line ahead of the surging crowd, opening a new line into a side room. I was all by myself. Following his cue, I wasn't sure exactly why he singled me out, but I hoped it wasn't to be randomly strip searched. Suddenly, I had a new set of concerns, until he motioned to other passengers to follow behind me. As we exited into another room, there were the familiar walk-through metal detectors (WTMD) and the security screening millimeter wave X-ray-type machines TSA employees call the L3. For once, I was first in line!

"Thank you, God," I thought. I still had a chance of making my flight.

Squeezing through this last vestige of security, I checked my watch once again; I had 40-minutes before boarding. Now to find a few gifts, and get something to eat. Spying a beautifully assembled, brand-new Tesla sports car, I approached, snapping photos, circling it continuously in envy. I joined the circling mass of fellow enthusiasts, gawking at the beauty of such a machine. I wondered who could afford this €200,000 Tesla electric sports car, seeing it was about US $218,177. I wondered about the procedures of getting this dreamy sports car into this cramped area of the airport, past the security gates and lines, without a scratch.

Adrenaline suddenly rushed through my veins as I was dropped back into the reality of the moment. My heart raced, "SHIT! I gotta get presents! This task usually takes me forever! But the saying in SF was, 'When you wait until the last minute it only takes a minute.' Brilliant! There goes dinner!" I panicked. With all this running around I was doing, I couldn't arrive empty-handed! I couldn't do that! I wouldn't.

I only had about 20-minutes before my departure—was the departure time or boarding time printed on my ticket—I couldn't tell which. For some reason these aren't standardized. I couldn't see the gate from where I was, but not wanting to waste a second reconnoitering where the departure gate was, I started shopping. Perusing the lot, I settled on a few single serve liqueurs for my strength and resolve, and to curb my growing appetite. These might be dinner. I also chose a few bags of salted licorice [these are nearly impossible to find back home], raspberry fruit gummies, and Fisherman's Friend cough drops. These were for me. Now for the gifts. Looking over the multitude of choices of chocolates, one of the attendants deliberated aloud over which chocolate I should get.

She walked over to me and said, "Shir, are you lookhing for a ghift of shhoclate shir? I would recommend the Rittahshphort [she was referring to the brand name Rittersport], it 'tis the best." She had a bit of a speech impediment and I couldn't stand listening to the way she said, "Rittahshphort." "Did you know Rittahshphort is da most popular shhocolate bah in Jzhermany?"

I would've done anything just to have her sshtop saying Rittahshphort. "Thank you... I'll get the large sampler box and a few of the other large single chocolate bars. Thank you so much for your help."

So, for the Princesses a huge stacked sample collection of German Rittersport chocolate bars, and a few large single chocolate bars for Erika should do the trick.

Swiftly browsing for anything else suitable for such an unpractical rendezvous as I was facing, I walked with my head on a swivel, I suddenly remembered that when I was in Warsaw, I passed a stall with a woodcarver near the Royal Palace in the Olde Towne Stare Miasto district on Nowomiejska street. He was carving wooden figurines. On display was a three-inch wooden, anciently dressed Polish Soldier, roughly the same size as the angel he was carving. Initially, I walked past him, snapping a few pictures without a second thought. Something made me go back almost as soon as I walked away. I returned to watch him carve the angel and immediately thought this cute angel would be a perfect gift for Erika, potentially my angel. I waited for him to finish, telling him I wanted to buy both. I almost forgot about these little trinkets, tucked away in my camera backpack for safekeeping. Looking into the shopping basket where the salted licorice and raspberry chews were staring back at me; I was so looking forward to eating these. My mouth started watering as I stood in the check-out line.

Amazingly, I still had time to pick up a quick snack and walk leisurely to my departure gate. The gate wasn't far from the restaurant. I couldn't wait for the opportunity to ride the mechanical silver bird which would bring me over the horizon to confront my past, enjoy my present, and venture into my unknown future among the icy fjords of Sweden.

My eyes never left the gate, once I confirmed which one it was. I got a quick meal to go and rushed back to the gate area, finishing it off in no time. No matter how much more time I had, I didn't want to spike it on the 5-yard line and miss this flight! All I could think about was Erika's current Facebook photographs and my memories of her in school in Thailand. Her text about lying under a blanket in front of a well-stoked fire on a snowy night, a glass of wine and hot cocoa within reach jarred me. My memories became so vivid, it was like watching a movie of my past.

For the first time, I was on an emotional journey of my past, coupled with a simultaneous spiritual focus, wondering what the near future would reveal. The discovery phase of my journey would undoubtedly get very interesting once I got to Stockholm, and for the next three days. There was still so much I didn't know. I still didn't know if Erika would or could see me at this point. Regardless of the outcome, I hoped we would develop a closer friendship from this experience. Even this would be better than the intermittent contact we had in junior high. And the lack of contact we had for the past 33 years.

Boarding the ship preparing for departure, I planned on holding nothing back when I saw her; if I saw her. The few single-shot drinks I had after takeoff settled me down and guided me through a few critically needed cat naps. Although I tried to sleep on this four-hour flight through the darkness, I couldn't. I had such a stream of consciousness, like never before. Poems about life and spirituality continually flew into my mind. Was it possible that Erika was my muse? In Greek mythology there were nine muses who were inspirational Goddesses of literature, arts, and science. I already felt happier than I had in a long time; thinking about her breathed new energy into my life and into my creativity.

Once underway, I clutched my camera from the backpack under the seat in front of me. I reviewed the pictures I took in Germany and of the rest of my solo European vacation during the weeks up to this point. Suddenly a poem entered my mind. As I fumbled for my cellphone to write it down, while waiting for my phone to turn on— the poem vanished. It materialized a few moments later once my phone activated. I frantically started typing:

The Future

In two days,
Maybe more,
I'll have an answer,
To the last nearly thirty-four.

Warm food, sensational thoughts,
Will deep feelings within be bestowed?
As the hours pass, soon I'll bask in her glow,
As for the rest... nobody does know.

This journey was such an excitingly refreshing opportunity. What a tremendous idea! I was ecstatic that I revisited those places in Germany and took the time to tour Poland. Even though I was alone, I loved it! And now I looked forward to visiting Sweden, the land of the Vikings and the Norsemen. I looked forward to learning firsthand about their rich, mysterious history, studying the implications that Leif Erikson was really the first to discover America, traversing the vast untempered seas and oceans inside small, compact wooden Viking ships. Many before had undoubtedly attempted and perished from this same feat, solely because they failed to surrender their curiosities. I wondered how large these people were and how they accomplished such feats as navigating through the freezing waters of the North, Norwegian, Baltic, and Barents Seas. These guys undoubtedly had some HUGE cahones!

As I flipped through the pictures on my camera screen, the light emitted made the spectacle of the photos even more captivating, seated in the darkened cabin. The young teenaged girl next to me asked, "Are you a photographer?"

"No, I'm not a professional, I just love taking pictures," I explained.

"That's really a nice camera, it looks expensive. I'll bet you take good pictures with it," she said.

"Nope, I just point the camera. It takes the pictures all by itself." I smiled.

We both laughed.

"I'm never without it when I travel. I named her Cassandra... Cassandra Canon—this way I'm never alone when I travel."

She chuckled, "That's funny. Would you mind if I see some of your pictures?" she inquired.

"No, I don't mind at all, sure you can!" So, I began my photo tour over.

Through my pictures, I brought her on a unique and impromptu tour of the German countryside, across the Bavarian hill country. Moving toward the Czech Republic taking in the sights of the ancient castle towns starting in the southernmost point of the republic of Bohemia, where lie the beauty and majesty of the historic, quaint village of Český Krumlov and the walled town of Ceske Budejovice at the point of convergence between the Vltava and Malese rivers.

I forgot I had these pictures from previous trips still on this memory card. Then, moving north toward the mountain top castle was Hrad Karlštejn, built specifically to store the Czech Royal crown jewels, where they remained for centuries. Further north, we ventured to Prague through its endlessly winding ancient cobblestoned streets, comprising stores, restaurants, apartment homes, churches, and a myriad of other buildings. The short tour continued across the outdoor sculpture-laden Saint Charles Bridge over to both the outside and inside of the Prague Castle overlooking the Vltava River. Scores of wild swans, ducks, and other waterfowl floating in the waters below, begging for food by sticking their heads into my near waterline-level open boat hotel window, when I stayed in the floating barge accommodation named, Botel Matylda.

I also had photos of a tourist sightseeing balloon occasionally soaring above the ancient city. Then aboard a small tour bus, I bumped along the roads Northeast to Kutná Hora, home of the infamous tiny Bone Church. So named being adorned with human bones visibly protruding from the walls and ceiling. Its chandeliers and sconces are made completely of human bones and skulls, making this an experience out of the movies, *Raiders of the Lost Ark*, or *Tomb Raider*. Then showing her photos of the church in Prague where I saw other human skulls embedded into the woodwork of the confessionals. And where I felt an overwhelming urge not to leave until I sat in a pew. Only after seated in a randomly selected pew, I was supernaturally urged to use the kneeler. Once I did, I looked between my hands only to see MY EXACT INITIALS carved into the pew. It had been there for years, and none of the other pews had any engraved initials. I quickly looked above my head making sure a heavy, ancient chandelier wasn't poised to crush me.

"Oooo spooky," she said chuckling while responding to those descriptions.

Winding back across the countryside leaving Prague heading south toward Germany, through the city of Plzeň, home to the 13th century art of brewing the clear, golden-colored Pilsner beer, the true birthplace of both Budweiser and Pilsner Urquell beer. This is also where St. Bartholomew's Cathedral in Republic Square is situated.

Crossing back into Germany is the ancient town of Flossenbürg in Bavaria. This became my channeling place years ago. It's home to a run-down castle, where I was gifted the amazing, perfectly rhyming, 14 stanza-long poem I titled, "Soldier's Cry." I explained that I recorded what I saw in a vision as I spoke. Then were the pictures of the nearby Nazi concentration camp also at Flossenbürg, with evidence of horrifying atrocities occurring there. I explained to her, "This site was unlike Dachau, which also is in Germany. Exuding a somber, peaceful calm associated with it, nestled into and hidden among the peaceful Bavarian rolling hills. These days it's preserved as a museum, though partially developed with residences on one adjacent hillside. You learn of the atrocities that occurred here, but the serene setting sort of takes the edge off that grim reality. Through isolated clumps of trees beyond the ridgeline, are hundreds of old farm sites with their wooden storage buildings, and quaint, quiet German villages connected by tiny roads only large enough to fit an oxcart, leading to the towns of Vilseck, Weiden, Bayreuth, Amberg, and Grafenwöhr." As I flipped through my photographs, she was in awe.

Continuing to guide her on my illustrated photo tour, she looked at each photograph in astonishment, never blinking.

"How long were you in Germany?" she asked.

"Ten days this trip but I've been going there for fifteen years," I replied.

"And you were working too? Wow, you do get around!" she gasped.

"Yes, I do," I chuckled. "This is what you can do when you're all alone, and there is nobody slowing you down. You don't have to stop to eat and take bathroom breaks and such."

"Do you like being single?" she asked.

"No, I pretty much hate it," I responded.

"But you get to see so much," she gasped.

"I see so much because I am single. There is nothing else to do. It's not as enjoyable because I can only enjoy it for myself; there's no sharing it with another person. And I won't be able to play

'Remember when...' with anyone else when I get older, because I was alone visiting all these places," I added.

"So why are you going to Sweden?" she asked in childlike amazement. I told her the brief rendition of the story which led me to this point with Princess Erika, along with my castle experience.

She looked at me with a serious expression and said, "You know, you are the world's perfect man! You're smart, in great shape, loyal, dedicated, full of resolve, and very romantic. When I grow up, I want to meet someone just like you."

"Wow, what a compliment!" I thought. Why women my age can't have the insight this young Viking teen had was beyond my comprehension.

"Thank you. How old are you? Maybe I can wait for you to grow up. If it doesn't work out for me in Sweden, do you want my email address just in case?" I joked.

She laughed, "And you're really funny!"

"How is it you speak English so well?" I asked.

"Oh, my Mom is Swedish and my Dad is from the States. I go back and forth all the time."

"And where are they now?" I asked.

"They're picking me up from the airport in Stockholm. I was in the States visiting friends."

Was this a living oracle providing a glimpse into my very near future? After a while, we stopped talking, and she nodded off to sleep while I stared out the window into the mind-numbing, frigid darkness. As we skirted the dawn of the horizon, the sun's orange glow was visible, abated slightly by atmospheric gases. I stared out the window and occasionally glanced at the teenaged girl leaning her head against the window. I hoped to maintain a childlike curiosity regarding my experiences in the next few days and life in general. These words came to me:

John D'Ambrosio

On the Edge of Darkness*

On the edge of darkness,
Beyond the horizon is light,
The sun peeking over as far away as can be seen,
But not so far as to make it un-night.

What is beyond the vast horizon?
Is it truly dark or light?
You may never know unless to there you travel,
Where eternal rainbows may burn bright.

Whyever travel over the horizon into this unknown?
For you know not which truths it holds,
You may or may not feel the despair of unfamiliar emptiness,
Knowing only then what the unknown may unfold.

Consider the other side of darkness as such,
Past the horizon may be eternal light,
Holding for you what isn't here and now,
Knowing the unknown rainbows of unimaginable height.

Knowing the known knowns is completely safe we contest,
While pondering the known unknowns, may leave one in
frenzied distress,
By reaching across the never-ending horizon,
The known unknowns and unknown unknowns unravel, putting
all unknowns to rest.

*Inspired by U.S. Secretary of Defense Donald Rumsfeld's Speech in FEB 2002, Known Knowns, and Known Unknowns

~ 13 ~

Footsteps Upon Thule /
Fotspår på Thule

The poem was a simultaneous convergence of what I had done, what I would do, what had happened, what might happen, and what was about to happen. Everything in my future was completely unknown to me. I was both apprehensive and anticipatory of the possibilities that were approaching. Maybe the reason that the Vikings took such tremendous risks at hand was to put their unknowns to rest. This thoroughly explained for me the "why" my current journey.

An insatiable joy overcame me knowing that when I visited this strange, far away land, hopeful to meet the Viking Princess, I would come away with answers. The possibility of seeing her, better yet, getting to know her, might end in astounding disappointment if she couldn't or wouldn't see me. My heart began beating rapidly and my breathing critically erratic. I was at this moment, within this moment, and within all three dimensions simultaneously. Somehow, I regained clarity. This was strangely and simultaneously a powerful, yet positive, feeling. Continuing my gaze out the window toward the horizon in front of me, I let my mind wander freely until the sunset crested over the horizon like a solar eclipse. The orange glow on the edge of darkness was fading and soon night would be upon us. Never had I seen such a wondrous spectacle. I realized this was both the single most expensive and intensely compelling voyage of my lifetime. It was already worth it. Perhaps this is why the Vikings traveled into the vast unknown—to experience the great beyond. As my eyes grew heavy and my vision unfocused, I realized I would soon have to press onward, on my own, through the thick night. Perhaps giving my mind some respite before continuing my physical journey tonight would be wise. I too nodded off for a bit.

Outside, bitterly frigid wind and darkness encapsulated the ship as we continued. The dark sky began bleeding through the blanketing cloud cover once the port was in sight. The sun, following us here, occasionally peeking over the horizon, now completely disappeared. Peering outside, I saw my reflection looking back at me. "Am I crazy? Why am I here? What am I doing? What will she look like in person? What will she think of me? Do I look old? Older yes, but do I look old? What if the Princess can't or won't see me? This is crazy!" were all my anxious thoughts. It's a bit late to worry about all that now. I can't believe I might see her as soon as the morning. It was nearly midnight.

At dawn, the captain remarked in a strong Nordic accent, "Ladiis and Zhjentlemen we are beginning our approach to Stockholm, Arlanda Flygplats. It is currently minus 5 degrees Celsius [23 degrees Farenheit], with a steady wind from the west. Da good news is zat it is not raining, or snowing" he chuckled. "Thank you for using our Scandinavian Air Service transport, we hope that we'll be seeing you again soon. Please relax until our arrival. Thank you."

I thought about the tasks I needed to accomplish once the ship docked. I had much to do. Disembark, collect my luggage, get some local currency in Swedish Krona (SEK), secure the rental ground transport with a physical road map, plot my course, and be on my merry way. It was good having my international driver's license with me. Hopefully, they'd have electronic navigators in case my European update didn't load the local maps on my handheld. And I hoped the weather was clear. Although I'd drive carefully to avoid my mechanical transport slipping on black ice in the middle of nowhere, I'd also ask about a local emergency number just in case.

As the ship came to a stop remaining motionless, bright light flooded the passenger compartment, transporting me back to reality where I would have to put into play the myriad of actions I just identified. I stood up, letting the Viking teen exit the air transport, as I collected my thoughts and confidence.

"I hope you have a terrific visit, and good luck with your future—I really hope it works out for you—you deserve it," the young Viking girl said, gathering her personal effects, and departing.

I responded affirmatively saying, "I know you'll do the same."

She was quite mature for her age and had quite the personality. I looked downward grasping my camera bag in hand and when I glanced up to bid her adieu, she had vanished. She was nowhere to be seen. Did she disappear into the sea of disembarking passengers so quickly?

Leaving the ship, I felt uncontrollably cast into the mythical Nordic lands of Thule—the Northern hemisphere's island, where the likeness of the Garden of Eden was guarded by the master society of tall, strong, blond, Viking warriors. It is believed they reigned for centuries in this region. I imagined myself being the living embodiment of the character played by Antonio Banderas in the movie, *The 13th Warrior*, set in A.D. 922. He was an emissary banned from his homeland traveling in a Norsemen caravan. Upon being attacked by a Mongol-Tatar raiding party, the Norsemen saved him along with the rest of the caravan. Taking up refuge with his rescuers, he quickly learned their language, adopted their culture, and became one of them. In my current circumstance, I felt that mythical Viking Norsemen led me to this strange land for a reason. Seeing the many bearded faces, strange money, clothing, language, customs, and seemingly strange courtesies as onlookers greeted their arriving loved ones, I concluded that if things worked one way, I could easily emigrate here.

I was on the ground in Stockholm. I couldn't believe it. I did it! I really did it! Feeling like I was disembarking from a Viking ship of olde. I was entering a wintry wonderland dressed for cool spring, except for my gray knitted woolen cap, and my brand-new, warm, comforting, inexpensive, favorite gray scarf, and my precious, warm driving gloves. All of which I donned with the confidence of an Inuit [formerly known as an Eskimo] in his warmest winter regalia, since it was every bit of warm clothing I had.

Finding my way, squirming between passengers toward the main terminal, like within a school of fish, I rested and caught my breath at a point called the Baggage Claim. Here, I waited for my tiny luggage to be offloaded. I started up a conversation with a friendly gentleman who looked to be an American—he was. I told him a bit of my story after he asked me what brought me to Sweden.

When I asked him if he was visiting, he abruptly said, "Noooooo. I married a Swedish babe I met while visiting years ago. I left the States, moved here and I never looked back. And I never regretted it either." He explained he visited the States once a year to see his adult children. As he put it, "I love my new wife, and my new life in Sweden, and wouldn't have it any other way!"

Perhaps this discussion was another omen for me? I abruptly asked him how much in local cash he recommended I get for my stay. He said, "This is Sweden, man. Get ready to spend bank for relatively little in return! This is the most expensive country in the world to live in!" He was close. I believe Switzerland has Sweden beat in this category, but I understood his message and appreciated his honesty.

"Three days? I'd get US$1500.00 worth of Swedish Krona to be safe. Unless you plan on using credit, if yours work here, which it should, then I'd get half of that in cash. Hey, good luck man, I hope everything works out for you. You never know." I remember him muttering something about spotting his wife just as I turned away for an instant to grasp my arriving luggage.

Leaning down and scooping up my bag only took a few seconds. When I looked up to say goodbye, he too had vanished. Either I was exhausted, these people move at lightning speed, or they weren't really in the physical world as I saw them. What did he mean? Were his words a sign of what was to come for me? Who was he? Why was he really here? Why am I meeting these people so arbitrarily and briefly? Was he an angel or a demon in disguise? Maybe he was just some guy who wanted to mug me in the parking lot after telling me to withdraw US$1500 in cash. Who knows? Though his word selection had piqued my interest, planning this trip had already been a spiritual experience for me. I couldn't let any more unanswered questions into my mind to bother me. I already had too many.

On the way to pick up the mechanical oxcart, I stopped by the automatic money exchanger, verified my credentials, and withdrew the cash. What a relief. I withdrew US$500.00 in Swedish Krona, planning primarily on using my cards. So, credit it was. And if I needed more cash, I was sure I could find a reputable place to get it.

The contemporary, mechanical oxcart clerk was very sweet as she confirmed for me, using credit as a primary source of payment would not cause me any problems anywhere in Sweden. Since it was already further past midnight than I was comfortable with, I knew I had to get going. She confirmed the route I should take, marking a complimentary paper map with my departure and circled my destination. She instructed me how to get my oxcart onto the primary, solidified, gravel path from this port of embarkation. Before explaining how to find the oxcart in the parking lot, she offered use of one of her local navigators for the duration of my trip, ensuring it would speak to me in English.

Another of my standard operating procedures (SOPs) while in foreign countries is always accepting free navigators. But only when they speak to me in English, in terms I can understand. This way, I can use both my handheld and borrowed navigators, lessening the re-directioning experience. Sometimes with two navigators, I became twice as confused, but only for a few minutes at the most. When conflicts arise or if there is any doubt, I learned to defer to the local navigator or passersby—before midnight. Locals should inherently know the route better than we foreigners.

I had a comical flashback of sorts one time in Prague, when I blindly followed the

directions of my navigator while driving at night. Momentarily terrified and bewildered, I ran over a streetcar road divider, which are not tiny bumps—these are like crossing landscape timbers or railroad ties driving at normal speeds. Unbeknownst to me at that time, my navigator was operating in pedestrian mode. Yep, that would've been my fault. I couldn't tell you how many sidewalks, road dividers, pedestrian bridges, and local park sidewalks I nearly drove over in foreign lands, blindly following the misguided instructions of my improperly minded, handheld navigator. I was careful never to repeat that mistake again!

After she wished me well, I was on my way. Leaving the warmth of the well-lit, populated terminal building, I ventured into the darkness, penetrating the frost-laden air. All the while, I kept a sharp lookout for any conspicuous muggers with American accents. I carefully traversed the unlit, desolate, bumpy, icy parking area, to locate my oxcart.

Immediately upon finding it, I quickly and surreptitiously loaded my personal effects, readied myself and the oxcart (mirrors, seat, map, etc.), while contemplating the long journey ahead. Lastly, before departing the relative safety and security of this known point of embarkation into the darkness of the dreary, bitterly cold, clear night, I synched and tested my navigators. Checking the physical map once again, I rolled forward. There was no turning back. Concentrating on the solidified gravel path through the black, still air, the unplowed ice in some lanes made my transport feel as if it had square wheels. I assured myself the wheels were round, pressing forward. Alone and unafraid, I drove into the darkness. Once again, I was on another solo trip heading onto the emptiness of yet another highway. With every mile I drove, I traveled back in time to a place... and... a land I had never known, and which seemingly, time forgot.

Traveling north, heading for the picturesque fishing village named Gävle betwixt the lapping shores of the Baltic Sea and the Gulf of Bothnia, I watched for road signs. Mine was the only oxcart on the road. In the darkness, my mind wandered.

Trying to piece together all the disjointed clues regarding the mystery surrounding Erika, I thought about how she never gave me a definitive answer about anything. I wondered if Swedes were like all those irresponsible Americans throwing around arbitrary statements they didn't mean like, "Hey, we'll have to get together sometime," or "You'll have to come over sometime," and my favorite, "Oh my God, I'd love to see you." Who rearranges his entire professional and personal life over the course of a few days, re-books itineraries to go off the beaten path to another country? On top of that, risks his entire professional reputation on a whim, to meet someone he hasn't seen in 33 years? That's not normal.

I wondered why she didn't answer any of the messages which were critical to my decision making. Either she was impressed with my resolve, or incredibly annoyed at my insistence on taking this opportunity to visit. After all, I didn't try to arrange this visit after months of advanced coordination. Was such little notice a serious upset to her life? It was too late now. Any damage created by my actions was already done. I had to see how it played out and make the best of it. "Nothing to it, but to do it!" I reminded myself. "It's all you! Let's go!"

I watched the entrancing white path markers speed past me. I felt each bump presented by the uneven hardened path. I listened intently to the navigators, occasionally together barking out orders in the form of direction. I was beyond the point of no return, beyond my point of comfort. I was fully committed, and focused on seeing my quest through, whatever it would bring. Strangely enough, I was still the only one traveling on this path, in this direction, at this hour.

The air was cold and still, the path pitch black. What I saw of the geography presented itself with the occasional tunnel carved through the stone atop a sea of endlessly, undulating darkness. Bumps ahead did not appear until I was directly upon them. All I could do was brace myself for the impending impact. Quite possibly there would be many more obstacles ahead which I couldn't predict—this entire experience was quite metaphoric.

As quickly as these bumps were upon me, I could do nothing but maintain course until they passed. I continued forward to learn what I had come here to learn, regardless of the outcome. I would soon verify the known knowns, and the known unknowns, and identify the unknown unknowns, putting all my unknowns to rest just as the Vikings had done and recorded in the annals of their history hundreds of years ago.

All of this was exhausting. Especially realizing how much I had been through in such a short amount of time. I reflected on the characters I'd met, the exorbitant amount of stress I felt, the issues addressed, and actions completed. I was already worn out from presenting my week-long seminar, as I usually felt afterward because presentations have their own inherent stressors. Deciding on and planning my on-again-off-short-term, unknown, undefined, then defined, and then redefined personal travel plans was intense. I had to cope with the failed communications systems, and failed contact with my stateside office and the government travel office, through multiple attempts to contact them, combatting time zones in the U.S. All this was frustrating, worrisome, and nerve-racking. After all this, here I was. Drained, tapped of energy, but somehow still going.

~ 14 ~

Still Going / Går Fortfarande

The pace heading north was much slower than I had anticipated; the road and weather conditions suggested remaining complacent. Still, I saw no reason for dread. I was where I wanted to be, going to where I planned, and I was healthy. So why not simply be happy? Still, I saw no road signs and nor anybody else on the pathway. Surely, I was heading in the proper direction, otherwise my trusty navigators would re-plot my course. We couldn't all be wrong. Everything was consistent. If anything, over the years I've learned to trust my equipment. I knew for certain my map and compass were not wrong. The weather was clear and the travel conditions now perfect, though freezing and bumpy. The air was so cold outside, it permeated the glass surrounding me. The inside of the windshield started to frost. This was easily remedied by diverting warm air from my feet up to the defroster. These conditions were quite the transition from the unlimited autobahn travel speeds on the well-lit roads I enjoyed just a week ago in Germany. I checked my controls again to ensure I wouldn't go beyond the legal limit.

The navigators worked well together, finally providing me checkpoints to which they both agreed. This was comforting. The fact I was still the only one out in the dark remained quite unsettling. I saw dark, hard-packed, gravel pathways, open land, and very few villages or businesses in the direction I traveled. If something happened to me, where would I seek assistance? The words of the American man at the port returned to me. What did he mean he wouldn't have it any other way: marrying a Swedish babe he met while on vacation, leaving the States, moving here, never looking back, and visiting his adult kids in the States once a year? That was a lot to share with a stranger he just met seconds ago. That just wasn't normal. Were his words an omen or spiritual encouragement?

Up to this point, I felt good spirits were pushing me to make this trip to this strange land, while the Norse Gods nudged me with curiosity. I felt similar voices whispering to me in the same manner they had in Germany before booking this trip, "Do it! Do it now! Go and find! Focus on YOUR journey! There is a time for everything. If you don't try or even if you do and you don't believe, you'll accomplish nothing... Do It Now!" What did all this mean? Did it mean anything? So, I chose to follow the rainbow to see where it would lead. My reputation as a "rainbow wrangler" wringing the best potential outcome out of rainbows entered my mind. I was hoping I could follow it this time and it wouldn't just vanish into thin air, as it often would. I didn't hope for the best and expect the worst, as I often had in the past. This time, I expected the best possible outcome, focusing on it. I was enjoying the journey, but I knew I also had to expect the unexpected with an open mind.

Wanting to distract myself by sampling some local music to further enjoy my foreign experience, I scanned the airwaves and settled on one station. It was still pitch-black outside. I saw little of the land ahead beyond the white lines on the roadway. Like much of my travel in the rest of Europe, the only sound of music in my transport was American. I was pestered by meandering metaphors, analyzing every thought entering my mind. I was looking for meaning in everything! At some points in your life, you just roll with it and see what life brings. I continued rolling forward, into the darkness.

Like the Viking explorers of years gone by, I progressed past the point of the known, venturing toward the unknown, entering deeper into the land of the unfamiliar, hoping to arrive at a point of destiny, perhaps of the Thule I would soon come to know and enjoy. I looked toward reaping remarkable benefits in the next three days. This is what I had to believe. I knew what I wanted, but had no idea if it was attainable. This was both the journey and experience I sought; it was here where my focus was transfixed. Undeterred, I progressed. I purged all negative thoughts from my mind that might set me into a quagmire, leading me into analysis paralysis. After all, this was my choice, and it was my planned vacation.

I wondered if the town/village of Gävle was going to be like the tiny town of Moss in Norway. Nobody could accurately predict what I would experience through the darkness of the night just over the horizon. It was exciting and terrifying at the same time. I was filled with an amalgamation of emotions, feelings, and thoughts unparalleled at any point in time during my life prior to this moment. I really couldn't expect anything; that wouldn't be fair to anybody. I simply looked forward to the near future with awe-inspiring anticipation. For now, I just wanted to get to get to the hotel, take a breather, and get as much sleep as possible before potentially seeing Erika in the morning.

Finally, a road sign appeared which proved to be the entrance of the fishing town I sought—Gävle. I took a few unplanned turns to familiarize myself with the immediate area. To my amazement, what I saw in a matter of minutes was about all I needed to know of the "downtown" area. I passed a few businesses, a rotary in the road, a few shops, some charter-type fishing boats at the boat docks and a small attached fishing pier toward the mouth of the river. That was about it. Everything was closed.

She was right, it being a small town. Here I was at the home of Sweden's straw yule goat, Gävlebocken (also known as the Gävle Goat) and the birthplace of the world-famous coffee Gevalia and Ahlgrens Bilar and Läkerol candies. Arbitrarily enough, Cat Stevens at one point was among its 100,000 inhabitants. This old town, first established in 1446, had features which reminded me of my travels through Moss. Though that was a much smaller fishing town of only 36,000 people established in the 16th century, and a mere 360 miles or 550 kilometers to the west. This part of Gävle awakened that memory, making my presence there eerily familiar. Both are comforting and quaint for different reasons. It was late, so I confidently headed for the Elite Grand Hotel, which was supposedly much bigger than the Moss Hotel where I stayed in Norway.

I found the town circle once again with relatively little difficulty. By the time I arrived at the parking lot, it was well past 01:30 am. The weather was nearly clear and still hovering near 0 °F. I was grateful for my new warm scarf and the rest of my warm gear. Signs directed me to a parking lot at the rear of the hotel.

Exiting the car, I heard an overpowering "thump, thump, thump" of club sounds and people yelling and screaming at the top of their lungs at each other. "Greeeat, welcome to rural Sweden!" I thought. I expected this to be a sleepy hollow fishing town on the water. "I don't need this!" Storing my GPSs, I exited and grabbed my camera bag and suitcase from the trunk, working my way toward the front of the hotel, and unfortunately toward the sound of the unruly crowd. As I rounded the corner, the blaring yells and screams indicated to me a riot was brewing. People were everywhere!

Cautiously, I approached the amoebic body of people as more poured out of the nightclub across the street, trudging over the median and onto the sidewalk next to my hotel. We were on a collision course. The crowd seemed to be flowing endlessly from the open front doors, joining the group in front of me. This gaggle of giants was unnerving.

I approached judiciously with my camera bag and small wheeled luggage. There was no way around them. These young people could've grown bored within the walls of the nightclub, seeking more lively means of entertainment, guided by their high blood alcohol levels in the frigid, post-midnight air. Perhaps they were coaxed outdoors by some invisible force, a police entity from within the establishment, or it may have simply been closing time as I've seen at about this same time on 6th Street in Austin, Texas.

The techno, breakbeat sounds blasted from the club, blaring as loudly as if I was inside the club. Though the club doors were propped open, I saw nothing unusual that would cause this level of arousal and commotion. The overly inebriated crowd of youngsters wandered about looking for something to do. And this crowd was growing agitated. They were yelling and screaming back and forth from across the street, pushing and shoving each other as they spilled onto my hotel's sidewalk in typical rave fashion. Drunken people sprawled across every visible surface, casting provocative insults at each other in their aggressive Viking tongue. I couldn't understand a word they were communicating, but their tone made me uneasy. Nonetheless, I pressed forward, guarded in my demeanor. This is the last obstacle I expected to have to navigate tonight. Here goes!

As I approached the periphery of people, I made first eye contact with the females in the crowd, ensuring they perceived me as unthreatening and friendly. I knew looking directly into the eyes of drunken males or angry bulls is both a hostile and provoking gesture. This is universal. As I hoped, the women seemed to appreciate my eye contact, with nobody challenging me as I brushed into the unruly, motley crowd, as smoothly as pouring XO quality brandy gently from its bottleneck.

As I loomed forward, heading for the front door of my hotel, I hoped not to get knifed in the back or blitzed by a bottle before reaching the steps. The crowd continued parting with my slow movement forward. I was careful not to cause a stampede. No sudden movements. I half-smiled as I walked. Not too smugly or aggressively, and not too meekly. I continued moving forward as gently as I could, emulating the Pied Piper, transforming this once raging riot into a calm gathering of sheeple.

I was dumbfounded how this commotion had not drawn even one police officer—there was no police presence anywhere in sight. No police car, no security personnel—nothing. You'd never see this in the States! My focus was complete and undeterred, now on my mission to safely reach the front door. I was ready to use my military training, fighting my way through if I had to, but I didn't want to become involved in an altercation in a foreign country, not here on the doorsteps of Thule. I wanted to remain below the radar, invisible to most. At any other time, in any other country, I could assume such a risk if required. But not this time, not this place, not now. I was too close to completing the first phase of my quest.

The entire situation was surreal. It just didn't fit into my predetermined set of expectations I tried so hard to avoid. "Focus on YOUR journey, Dimitri," I kept telling myself, "Focus on YOUR journey." I was already having enough of a challenge processing the information of where I was, what I was doing, and why I was doing it. Living in the confluence between the past and present, I needed no more challenges dropped into my path.

I ignored the sneers and jeers from some tattooed, rough-looking street tyrants, as they slithered closer toward the hotel entrance as I approached. I continued walking through the amoeba, most of whom loomed over me. "Damn these Vikings are pretty tall people," I thought, "Even the women could probably kick my ass. Drunk or not!"

I continued forward, hoping for the best. The drunken crowd silently and slowly continued parting a pathway for me as I walked. Finally, I reached the hotel steps, walking up the six large stairs to the main landing. Tugging aggressively numerous times on the door handle, I got no result. It was locked.

"Shit!"

Looking through the plate glass door into the well-lit, shiny lobby, I saw no people, no proof of life. The crowd behind me roared. It sounded as if more giants were joining the fiery force of the Nordic God Fray. I'd been traveling for n'ery a fortnight [two weeks], alas experienced no prolonged negativity. Suddenly, a voice crackled over a well-hidden speaker, "Do you have a reservation... excuse me... do you have a reservation?" questioning me.

"God damn it, let me in! Let me in before these people kill me! What the fuck is wrong with you? OPEN the fuckin' door!" I thought with my inner voice. "Uh---yes I do," I responded calmly, with my outside voice. "Do you need the confirmation number?" I confidently added.

"Are you Mister Dimitri?"

"Yes I am."

After a more than unwelcomed, seemingly forever, yet somewhat brief wait outside at the threshold of the entrance, a comforting electronic click echoed throughout the open vestibule. I tried yanking on the door once again; this time it opened. The Norse Gods granted me unfettered access to the safety of Thule.

Magically, a well-tanned foreign assistant appeared from behind a tall counter. I smiled and approached. He was extremely polite in his greeting, "Good evening, sir."

"Quite a crowd [of giants] outside. What's it all about?" I blurted.

"Ahhh yes, nothing. Well, nothing, really. It's always like this on Friday and Saturday nights. Too much alcohol and not enough to do I guess… it's typical. The crowd is quite harmless… but they are quite loud," he explained.

"So that's why the hotel policy is to lock the doors, requiring bona fides prior to being granted access into the hotel at this time of night—ehhh—early morning?" I thought.

He continued, "I assure you; they are completely harmless. But I'll make sure you have a quiet room, well away from the street."

"Thank you." I responded.

He was a young man who spoke with a Caribbean accent, "Will you be with us for the entirety of your original reservation?"

"Yes, I will," I said.

"Is your stay business or pleasure?" he asked.

"It's business… strictly business… at first… but hopefully, it will turn into pleasure," I responded.

I couldn't help but explain, "You see, I've come from the States to visit a woman I haven't seen since we met in junior high school. We went to school together for a few years in Asia. She was the most beautiful girl I had ever seen, since the first time I saw her. Her family left the country before mine did, and I haven't seen her since. It's been 33 years. We've had a few recent exchanges on Facebook, but that's about it. I told her I was coming and asked if she could see me for a few hours or whatever she could spare this weekend, but got no definitive response—I came, anyway. I've always wanted to see Sweden, so here I am. I will either see a lot of it by myself, or a little of it with her. I have no idea what's going to happen or when. So, rather than say this is pleasure, lest I be too assuming, I'll say it's business—personal business." I added, smiling.

He looked at me like I was crazy. Returning the smile, he offered a quick laugh, tilting his head to one side, raising his eyebrows muttering, "Wow, I wish you the best of luck during your stay." He gently nodded, adding, "Please let me know how it goes before you leave, if you would," he smiled again.

"I detect a Caribbean accent—Jamaica? I know you're not from here originally," I said.

"Yah manh, Ima fram Jamaica manh!! Nah, sir I'm just kiddin." He continued laughing. "I'm working here as an intern studying hotel management. I'm originally from the Dominican Republic. My girlfriend is from here. We met in the Dominican Republic. I'm living here with her parents, while she is living with my parents finishing up her schooling. She'll join me here when she finishes. Hopefully someday, I can follow my dream to open my own resort in the Dominican Republic. Well, sir, you look tired. We should get you to your room, you've got a very big day ahead of you."

"That's the truth!" I said, "I'm sure I'll see you again. What is your name please?" I added.

"I'm Nickolas, and you will see me again, since I'm the only one who works the night shift here, that is, until I own my own resort," he snickered handing me the electronic room key. "See you tomorrow, sir."

"Good night," I closed.

~ 15 ~

Swedish Dawn

Making my way from the lobby, up the lofty stairwell to my floor, down the long, non-descript hallway, arriving at my room, I opened the door, entering. I found it clean and appropriate, at $140 dollars a night though, scanning the room, it was nothing more than extremely basic quarters. Surprisingly, it had hardwood floors and Ikea-type furniture with the exception of an intricate wood carving on the ceiling framing a huge mirror which was inexplicably, yet hopefully permanently and intentionally affixed to the ceiling directly above the bed. My first thought was that I hoped it wouldn't come crashing down on me as I slept. As one would expect, the heater was working superbly. Strangely, in this room there were two restrooms, one the size of a closet with a sink and toilet, and the other, a larger room with a sink, toilet, and shower. I realized now why they call the smaller restroom a water closet in Europe. I rushed to unpack my clothes, ironing what I planned on wearing the next morning. Afterward, I showered, brushed my teeth, set the alarm on my phone—strangely enough, this was the first hotel room I'd been in without a clock. But it had a coffeemaker, a top priority in Europe.

I laid out my running shoes—not that I intended to go running in the morning, which may take too much time, and I didn't want to miss any potential phone calls from the Viking Princess. I'd need these for exercising on the slick, faux hard wood floors. Next to a towel, I placed my running shoes, my workout clothes, and my exercise bands for my morning routine. Finally, I settled down on the bed and unavoidably looked at the mirror above me. I contemplated its weight, the physics and mechanics of installing it, and what the requirements of keeping it safely mounted. Somehow, through some feat of human engineering, it hovered over the bed since they'd installed it. It looked incredibly heavy, and I still hoped it wouldn't detach, crushing me!

My overshadowing thought was I needed to get as much sleep as possible so I wouldn't have baggy, saggy, or puffy raccoon-like eyes in the morning. I rolled over, checked the alarm on my cellphone, scratched out a quick time schedule on the tiny pad of paper next to the lamp, turned off the light, and went unconscious.

My cheery alarm tone sounded seemingly moments later. I awoke staring at myself in the mirror above. I was happy it didn't fall on me during my few hours of sleep. I was still tired and didn't much feel like getting up until I realized where I was. I did it! I made it to Sweden! It hit me like a mainlined shot of espresso.

Darting out of bed, I looked out the window since I had seen little but darkness when I arrived. A foggy, dreary Washington State winter view was what I saw, with a backdrop of the nearby bay in the distance lapping through the light fog. The flora and fauna were exactly the same as the Great Pacific Northwest. I loved it here already!

Starting the coffeemaker and turning the radiator off, I plopped onto the towel and in rapid succession knocked out 100 pushups, 100 sit-ups, 100 crunches, plank exercises, an exercise band workout, and closed with a quick pilates/yoga stretching workout. After each exercise, I checked my watch, cross-checking my time with my written time schedule to see how much time I had left.

Since I did not know what to expect, I was on pins and needles regarding the time. I didn't know if I would receive a phone call, a knock on the door, or unpretentiously nothing. Not knowing was killing me. Once again, a thousand questions entered my mind without any answers. Supposing she called while I was in the shower, or walking downstairs, or eating breakfast? What if she called only once and decided to do something else? What if she came by and I wasn't ready, and got upset and left?

Once again, I concentrated on my journey, and on the experience of being in Sweden. I stuck to my schedule. I shaved, showered, and started getting dressed. Assuming she wouldn't call, I weighed my touring options. Drive south to Stockholm, go to the Viking and Vasa museums, or just wander around the Olde Towne of Gamle Stan, one of the oldest and best-preserved medieval cities in Europe. Or I could go local and take a self-guided tour of Gävle, relaxing, wandering around alone as I usually do when I'm in foreign lands, taking pictures of whatever interested me.

Regardless of how I tried tricking my mind, this time was different because no matter what I thought of to do, I had something else [with someone else] that I'd rather be doing. But until I was told otherwise or presented other options, I had to focus on my journey.

I finished getting ready. As I was leaving for a quick bite to eat, the hotel phone on the nightstand rang, piercing the stagnant, cool air. The phone rang again and again in quick succession, interrupting the silence. I rushed to the phone with trepidation, wondering if it could merely be the manager welcoming me to the hotel, as they often do in Europe. Snatching it off the cradle before it stopped ringing, I answered with bated curiosity.

Bringing the telephone handset to my ear, I answered, "Hello?"

A soft, purposeful tone from a woman spoke from the other end, "Hi, Dimitri! So, you're really here! You really, really came! Wow! You're crazy! This is crazy!" she exclaimed. I heard her smiling as she spoke.

I confidently responded, "Hi," then my throat seized. After gaining my composure and taking a few sips from a nearby water bottle, I said, "I told you I'd come. Did you think I was kidding?"

"Listen, I'm at my house now; how about if I meet you in your hotel lobby in about 40 minutes? I'm close by, so I'll just walk," she said.

I was elated. This was the best news I had this trip so far, being on pins and needles up to this point.

"Great! You know which hotel, right?"

"Of course, duh! There aren't many hotels in this town and it's sort of obvious since I called you!" she laughed. "Okay, I'll see you in a bit!" Then she hung up.

I felt my Adam's apple jump into my mouth. I couldn't believe it! After such an emotional buildup and wonderment leading to this moment, here it was! It was unfolding so naturally, as if it had been planned this way all along! 40 minutes? I still had plenty of time to enjoy the breakfast buffet downstairs. I was glad not to miss such an opportunity.

I dashed out of the room, speed walking down the hallway, hopping down the stairs toward the breakfast area. Although I felt like running and jumping over the railing and down the flights of stairs from landing-to-landing yelling, "Parkour," I refrained from doing so. Yet, I could barely contain myself; excitement surrounded me.

Following the aroma of freshly brewed coffee, I made my way toward the source, and found the breakfast buffet tucked away in a small corner room on the ground floor. Upon entering, all the food looked fresh, healthy, and fulfilling. Typically European, and continually re-stocked by the friendly staff who greeted me at the door, my mouth watered with anticipation. Smoked salmon, yogurt, Nutella, fresh tomatoes with sliced mozzarella cheese topped with a fresh basil leaf, freshly baked bread, red and black caviar, fresh vegetables, fresh salad, and a fantastic selection of teas, and of course, there was coffee. There was a cornucopia of croissants, cinnamon rolls, poppy seed rolls, and breads with a variety of butters and cereals beside those. Freshly squeezed orange and apple juices, with tomato juice among others were on display. And there were different weights of milk beside those, even chocolate milk. This breakfast was just as it appeared and smelled—perfect.

I didn't need to rush, but continually kept a sharp eye on my watch. I wouldn't be late for this meeting for anything in the world! I still had a bit of stomach tension, because the Princess might show up with a husband or two, 16 children, neck or face tattoos, piercings, a boyfriend or two, or maybe a girlfriend or two… I didn't know what to expect. I knew she was a bit older now, and so was I. Supposedly, she was single; and so was I. All I really knew for sure was that I didn't really know anything for sure. It was one of those pesky known unknowns I previously mentioned.

Finishing up breakfast, I bid the hostess adieu, returning to my room for one last chance to brush my teeth and freshen up. I made sure there were no poppy seeds in my teeth or misplaced celery strands—all clear. I popped a piece of gum into my mouth, grabbed my camera backpack and the large brown paper bag with the five-pound gift box and loose chocolate treats for the Princess and her little Princesses. I checked on the plainly wrapped little angel and Soldier from Poland, both carefully tucked away in a side pocket of my camera bag. Checking the room one last time before exiting, I made my way down the long vinyl-floored hallway, back down the stairs, and toward the lobby where I would await our fateful moment of meeting.

Once inside the lobby, I waltzed over to the hot drink station in the corner, pouring myself a cup of refreshing hot mint tea. Glancing over to the hotel desk clerk area, Nickolas wasn't working. I was hoping he would be there for a quick confidence boost. I was on my own. It wasn't the first time. Spending a few moments surveying the meet-up location, I mentally blocked out my stage positioning, and decided where my presence would benefit me the most while I waited. Multiple times I analyzed the best angles where I should either sit or stand for her to see my best side. I conducted mental rehearsals to ensure I wouldn't miss her entrance, trip, or mis-speak during this once-in-this-lifetime moment.

I decided I would sit in the lobby on the edge of the couch, so I wouldn't slouch, with the bag of gifts and my camera bag on the floor securely next to me. I positioned them so I would neither forget them, nor trip over them on my smooth, impressive, 33-year later approach. Patiently waiting, my heart was heavy with emotion. A thousand questions once again invaded my serene thoughts. To me, she was still one amazing young girl, but would she still be after all these years? It was as if I buried my emotions in a time capsule, preserved it for 33 years, and in short time the contents were about to be revealed to me. After 33 years, would I still feel the same way? Were my feelings in junior high an extreme form of "like," maybe "a crush," perhaps "puppy love," or was it just a younger form of "true Romantic Love?" Whatever it was, I wondered if I'd still feel the same way once I saw and spoke to her.

Growing up, this was my dream girl. The untouchable one. The mysterious Wondress. My Viking Princess. I repressed these memories for all those years. Tucking them away somewhere in a closet hidden among the halls of my mind. Would she still be the same dream girl? Would she still be the object of perfection for my affection? What if she was tattooed from neck to toe, a practice which I absolutely abhor, except on 300 lb. Harley Davidson HOG bike riders. Then, would she still be my glamor girl?

Ultimately, I dropped into her life wanting to see her, hoping she would spend whatever time she could spare with me. One of my all-time favorite lines is from the movie, *When Harry Met Sally*, when Harry said, "When you think you might want to be with someone for the rest of your life, you want that time to start as soon as possible." I wasn't there yet, but I didn't know—I could've been, eventually. My puppy love grew up and for some reason, never extinguished. It hid for a while, but now was back. In a few moments, I would confront my dream face-to-face. This in itself was exciting. But it was also scary. After all these years, I imagined myself confronting my dream girl with issues of substance, instead of topics of whimsical randomness floating in the minds of 8th graders. Supposing she rejected me? Supposing she didn't? What if there was no chemistry? What if there was? What if my dreams suddenly faded?

I had no idea what to expect. My heart was idling, my mind on hold, waiting for life to unwrap itself. I didn't know which way this would go. I continued just sitting here, wondering, waiting in the lobby, sipping on my mint tea, as would a gentile gentleman of olde would do.

I remembered her being taller than me in 8th grade. Supposing she kept growing into one of those midnight sidewalk Vikings I brushed by last night in front of the hotel, what would I do? If she towered over me, what would I say? If she looked at me in disgust, how would I react? What if she brings children with her? Actually, I'd like that; it would be fun to meet her offspring. What if she could only spend 10 minutes with me? Would she feel about me the same way I felt, or feel, about her? I feared the possibility of all my childhood memories associated with her vanishing in a cloud of disappointment.

Did she have any clue how I felt about her when we were in school? Like many women, she seemed to have terrible taste in boys, and now, most likely, in men. I remember her briefly dating someone way below her caliber for a few weeks. Nobody understood why she did that, as short-lived as it was. Even back then she could've been... no, she should've been a professional model with her choice to date anyone in school. But she never was. And she never did. Her strict parents rightfully were most likely not prepared to accept any risks with her, being the baby of their family.

The thousands of questions rattling around in my head were simultaneously trying to find answers only she could provide. My restless synapses would have to be a bit more patient. What had she been doing for the last 33 years? I imagined this would not be a one-or two-word answer—then again, for her, if history repeated itself, it might be.

I chose my position near the plate-glass windows in the lobby to give me clear visibility down both sides of the street in both directions. Regardless of her avenue of approach, I wouldn't miss her. I sat close enough to the glass to see her, but not close enough for her to see me. I thought it was a good idea to remain seated since I didn't know what my emotional state would be once I saw her. Even after surviving in different capacities, five separate combat zones, hiking the Grand Canyon, the Great Wall of China, the Great Wall of Ston in Croatia, the Inca Trail in Peru, and in training to complete Mount Kilimanjaro, Mount Rainier, and Mount Qumolangma, or as they know it in the West— Mount Everest. I had more than one's fair share of experiences during this lifetime, but my physical accomplishments were far different from the emotional and spiritual gymnastics I was now experiencing.

Keeping myself and my diet in pristine condition, I likened myself to the partying fly in the Smirnoff vodka television commercial sticking to walls watching and partying until suddenly dropping from his perch; with his life cycle abruptly ending. My time could end just as quickly. I wondered if the medical system in Sweden was up to American standards. I did plan this meeting impulsively, not giving myself time to look into any of those factors in the CIA Factbook, or on the U.S. State Department's Safe Traveler Enrollment Program (STEP) website, as I often do when planning a trip.

Sipping my tea, I felt very European. I maintained a sharp lookout down the street, focusing down the street with the concentration, tenacity and acuity of a sniper's eye. Finally, coming into focus I saw what looked to be a tall, blond woman approaching on foot. She got taller and closer, and taller and closer, and taller. Walking confidently down the street, through the icy air with condensation from her breath trailing closely behind. My breathing stopped—I felt my heartbeat slowing until it seemed to come to a complete stop. I was 100 percent focused on this woman. Could this be it—is this what it feels like when your heart explodes? Or maybe this is what a brain aneurysm feels like?

My heart was heavy as my mind raced with anticipation. The golden-haired young woman paused looking both ways before crossing the street, then making a beeline for the hotel door. I watched intently as she glided up the six low-rise stairs. The feeling in the pit of my stomach became much more intense. I watched her every move as she approached. I watched her head, shoulders, chest, hips, legs, and shoes as they appeared sequentially in full view over the top stair. She approached the large glass doors, seemingly in slow motion. I stared as she pranced into the lobby, standing firmly atop the oversized welcome mat. She quickly scanned the large, mostly empty lobby.

Could it be? Was it? I think it is. I hope it is! It's gotta be! As if I was standing on a lowered rear ramp of a U.S. Air Force cargo aircraft C-130 or C-17 at 30,000 feet, harnessing my energy, watching the red light in anticipation of the green light illuminating, ready to jump out on yet another freefall jump. This felt incredibly familiar, but as each jump did, completely different. It felt distant. Adrenaline once stagnant, now surged through my veins.

I sat still. I couldn't believe my eyes, yet I didn't want to rush into her face in case it wasn't her. That might get me arrested, and then I'd never see my Viking Princess. My heart was idle as I watched and waited in anticipation for a sign of confirmation that it was her.

She was well-preserved from every angle. There it was again, the hollow feeling in the pit of my stomach, getting even more intense. I was frozen in time. It was like hearing a sniper's bullet crack in the air overhead searing the surrounding silence, without hearing the explosion of the hammer hitting the primer launching the bullet on its way. Since the bullet travels faster than the speed of sound, the sound follows the bullet's path milliseconds later. That's when you hear the explosion. I waited for my brain to process what I was seeing, what I remembered, what I was thinking, and what I was hearing. "WOWWW!" was the only thought I could consciously form in my overwhelmed brain. In the near past, I could only imagine her in the passenger seat of my car sitting next to me, only to look back at the seat realizing she was never really there. I almost didn't want to face these childhood feelings attached to the wonderment of my Viking Princess, especially if my feelings dissipated over the years.

Her idyllic entrance was nothing like I had ever before witnessed in my lifetime. It was a melding of the past and present, flickering in front of me into a contrived, modified, augmented reality. My concept of reality was speeding up uncontrollably, as the memories of my past were splitting my understanding of the present, creating an alternative reality within another dimension of time, where the end-point was an unknown unknown. My feelings were idle. My mind and heart still raced uncontrollably, embraced by a vortex of blended reality and fantasy. Reality, as I knew it, had stopped. Like the sniper's bullet, I waited for the past to catch up to the present along the same path. Fantasy was about to fill in what I couldn't yet process. I was existing between multiple synergistic planes until no longer transfixed within an alternative reality. Jolted, as if finally hearing the explosion launching the bullet, casting me forward into the present reality I knew would materialize, and with which I would become confidently familiar. The dream girl of my past and the dream girl in front of me, with the same heavenly smile, melded together. Both images merged from two different dimensions in my mind into one. She looked to be the same person. I was now comfortably in the present. We both were. I felt surrounded by life—this was exhilarating.

I rose from my seat smiling and stood completely still. She looked in my direction. I smiled in anticipation. Deciding it was okay to come out into the open, I approached. She left her position atop the welcome mat walking forward, toward me. I enjoyed the metaphor of the word "Welcome" on which she had been standing. I noticed I grew compared to her. She approached with the infamously branded, angelic smile, "Dimitri?" she queried. The closer she approached, the more apparent it was to me, she no longer hovered over me as she had 33 years prior. We now looked into each other's eyes on a nearly level plane; but I had a slight edge. This was one major concern down!

As much as I wanted to experience the magical movie moment where we both run toward each other, drawing each other close, our eyes entranced, arms intertwined, twirling around in a firm embrace, wondering how either of us could've lived without the other for such a long time. This would have been inappropriate. Besides, that really only happens in the movies.

She stood her ground firmly, with her head cocked to one side and her arms raised at her sides, palms facing me, she said, "Hi Dimitri, it's me!"

Nope—they didn't vanish. My feelings were the same. They were intact inside the time capsule, which instantaneously popped open, freeing themselves to roam the earth once again. Hopefully, they'd have the opportunity of growing into a deeply seeded romantic relationship—was this premature?

There she was. Here she was. Here I was. Here we were—after 33 years of complete isolation and separation from each other. She was as angelic as I recalled. Aside from a few light creases near her smiling eyes, nothing had changed regarding her appearance. She was still the same gorgeous young Viking Princess I remembered her to be. I went wild inside. Like a wheat field in a windstorm, my insides were swishing back and forth. I couldn't believe my eyes. Not only was she still beautiful, she was still one of the most beautiful women I'd ever seen—ever. She was undoubtedly the most beautiful woman I'd ever known. Doubt no longer existed in my mind. The emotion I felt in school was real. I came here to find out just how real. In an instant, I knew. I still felt the same way.

As the brain fog clouding my thoughts cleared, finally I comprehended the gravity of this moment. I smiled back at her, offering my open arms with both of my hands at shoulder level exposed while approaching her, showing I had no hidden weapons [similar to what Soldiers do while rendering a salute]. I offered a gesture of peace in the form of a friendly hug.

She accepted. "How long has it been?" she blurted.

"33 years, 29 hours,16 minutes and 32 seconds," I said, glancing at my watch after our ever-so-short friendship hug ended.

"Oh my gosh, I can't believe you are really here! You're crazy! On such short notice, too! Wow, it's great seeing you!" she sparked.

"That makes two of us, gorgeous, and I'm face-to-face with my dream girl, seeing exactly what I saw in you 33 years ago and nothing has changed except a few wrinkles between us," I thought.

"You haven't changed all that much," she exclaimed, "Except for your hair," she said

My hair had thinned over the years and now instead of sporting a full head of hair, I styled it in a Jason Statham close-cut style. Yeah, like I needed to hear that!

"And, you got taller," she said, laughing with the same melodic laugh I adored back then.

Okay, she made up for her first zinger. Though she made no mention of my physique and stature I worked so hard to develop and maintain over the years.

"Sooooo listen, I had to work this entire weekend, but was able to switch with a co-worker, so now I have the entire weekend off to spend with you, and the entire morning on Monday, before you leave for the airport. And my kids are at their friend's house!" she shrugged in excitement.

"I really hope I can show you what you came to see in the few days you have. I hope you won't be disappointed coming all this way. I hope you think it's worth it," she said.

Now I knew she really had no clue how I felt. "I already do," I responded.

"Excuse me?" she asked.

"Uh… nothing… three entire days with you to myself?" I howled. "That's really fantastic! Thank you so much! This is going to be a lot of fun—think I'm kidding? So, how should we start?" I spouted, feeling completely elated.

"I was thinking we go to my house and get to know each other a bit there," she said.

My ears perked up and so did the rest of my emotions. Maybe she knew how I felt, I hoped so.

"So today we can just relax, go for walks with my dog and we can catch up on… wow—how long has it been? I can't believe it! Anyway, then tomorrow maybe we'll go to Stockholm to see the Vasa and Nordiska Museet, museums… you can't come all this way and not see these things, and, of course, downtown Stockholm. I haven't been there in years myself. There are more than a few places you should see… well… aren't you cold? You don't seem to be dressed for this weather," she spurted in perfect English.

"Well, I told you I planned this sort of quickly, with very little feedback, remember? I managed to buy this scarf in Frankfurt. Do you like it?" I said in a joking manner.

"I really can't believe you came all this way. Well, welcome to my homeland of Sweden. I'm so sorry I couldn't come get you at the airport, but I don't have a car. This town is small enough to walk everywhere I need to go. Besides, it keeps me in shape by walking to and from work and everywhere else."

"Ummm-hmmm, yes, you do look like you stay in shape," said my inside voice chuckling.

"What?" she asked.

"That was supposed to be my inside voice," I reminded myself.

"Well, if you came earlier in the day, yesterday, I could've taken a bus to meet you at the airport."

She was her usual beautiful, bright, cheery self from as far back as I could remember. I couldn't imagine who in this world ever would let go of this woman? Over the next three days, as she welcomed me into her personal space, I welcomed her as my guide; physically and spiritually. I silently hoped someday I could return the favor.

"I have a rental car. Should we drive to your house to keep our options open?" I asked.

"Sure!" she cheerfully responded.

Wasting no time I turned, making my way back to the couch, collecting my camera bag and the gift bag.

"What's that?" she questioned.

"Oh, nothing, just my camera and a few things I found."

"That must be quite the camera!" she said.

"And hopefully you'll be quite the model," I joked.

"What?" she asked.

"Nothing," I said smiling, motioning with a quick jolt of my head toward the door.

"And the other bag?" she asked pointing to the other bag in my hand.

"Oh, it's nothing. Just some things I found along the way." I chirped.

"It seems like you've got a lot of nothing with you and you seem to find a lot of it," she joked.

"If only it were true," I peeped.

"What?" she sparked.

I looked into her eyes from our distant stance, we both took a deep breath simultaneously and hesitantly responded, "Nothing." We spoke in unison, smiling and laughing as we turned toward the door, departing the lobby as if the entire scene had been scripted and well-rehearsed. I followed her out the door not being able to take my eyes off her, any of her.

"Nothing, nothing, nothing," she jokingly repeated as we walked.

As I followed behind, I thought, "What a beautiful tail she still has, and she's funny too!" just like I remembered her to be.

Venturing with her around to the back of the hotel, approaching the car, I was the consummate gentleman, as always. Opening her door first, I allowed her entry; placing the bag of treasures and my camera bag behind her seat, before gently closing the passenger door. I took my place in the driver's seat. Thankfully, Sweden drives on the same side of the street as we do in the U.S. and the driver and passenger positions are in the same place, so this took no rehearsal. It was a short drive to her place. I kept looking at the typically empty seat beside me, now filled with the beauty and grace one only experiences in dreams. I couldn't believe this seat next to me was no longer empty. Nor could I believe the beautiful Viking Princess was the one seated next to me. Finally, she let me into her life—if only for a brief time. And now she was leading me directly to her castle.

"How is the hotel?" she asked.

I was thrilled to have her sitting right next to me in the car, for real, for the first time, ever. I was in heaven being so close to her and almost didn't hear her question.

"Uh—the hotel, is nice, nothing fancy. It's clean, and comfortable, but then again, it's just me inside the room. It's all I need. The breakfast buffet is amazing though. I was surprised to see caviar on the buffet and different types at that!" I reported.

"Of course, we have here caviar, Dimitri, you know this is Sweden, right? We're nearly surrounded by water," she explained.

"Apparently, along with the fish, they grow excellent tasting bread, milk, and cheese here too," I added. We both laughed.

"Oh, what's the deal with that huge straw goat down across the Gävlean River I caught a glimpse of last night driving by the town square?" I asked.

"That's our town Yule Goat, I think it's called in English. In Swedish it's called Gävlebocken. It's a big deal here. You know one of the builders years ago had to stop building it because he became allergic to straw. So now, someone else builds it. It's a fairly recent Christmas tradition. It's built with the last straw crop of the summer. It was first built in the late 1960s in an effort to boost Christmas shopping. At 43 feet tall and 23 feet long, it's quite large when you're up close. They start building it in August and hopefully it lasts through Christmas. It has become a bit controversial over the years. Some people love it; some hate it. Vandals typically try to burn it down before Christmas, just to cause trouble. You can go to jail for four years, getting caught trying to burn it down. They've added security patrols, cameras, fences, and everything they can think of to protect it. They even tried using some sort of fire protection liquid one year, but that just turned out to be a different environmental disaster."

"Why don't they just organize a safe controlled burn of it at the end of the Christmas season to save time and money, so they don't have the expense of removing it? Then the pyromaniacs could look forward to taking part in watching it burn. Now that would draw a large crowd! It would be like the American desert celebration called "Burning Man." Some hippies started it in the Nevada desert years ago. They all get together every year, forming a temporary town called Black Rock City, where they celebrate the summer solstice and just hang out. They burn an effigy at the conclusion of that festival, that's why they call it Burning Man. It's quite something to see. And it keeps drawing more and more people each year.

"Burning the Yule Goat would be a pretty neat tradition with a segue into the historical relevance of fire and rebirth in the Scandinavian culture," I said.

"You seem to know a lot about my culture, for never having been here before," she said laughing.

"I did some reading on the internet before coming, as I usually do before a trip," I replied.

"I'd like to see that Burning Man someday," she said.

"Maybe someday you will," I said smiling inside.

Bringing us back to reality, she said, "We'll drive by the Gävlebocken tomorrow on the way to Stockholm if you like, so you can see it in daylight."

~ 16 ~

The New Present

She directed me where to drive until we arrived at her house. I parked in front of a quaint, comfortable home. Hers was a two-story house, looking to be about 1600 square feet. The outside trim was neat and light blue color, with a large picture window overlooking the distant bay sporting a few trinkets in the windows. The front door had a welcome sign posted and a welcome mat in the portico. There were four of these type houses in close proximity to the surrounding larger houses in this neighborhood.

As I exited the car, I ran to her side to politely open her door, easing her exit. I grabbed the paper bag of treasures and my camera bag from behind her seat while she waited. She accompanied me walking slowly uphill toward the front door. I stopped and turned to take in the view of the frigid water and fjords in the distance, among the surrounding greenery. The air was clear and clean, yet crisp and cold, with a slight breeze. The morning fog was well on its way toward lifting. We stood side by side overlooking the bay in the distance. The view was as stunning as the view beside me.

The weather was shoring up to be nothing less than a perfect, cloudless morning.

"It's going to be a perfect day, it's about time too, it's been raining for weeks—this is our first clear day. You brought great weather!" she joked.

"Hmmm," I thought, "A good omen?" I queried.

With my meagerly paired winter clothing ensemble, it would be comforting to get out of the cold and into the warmth of her abode. She took the keys out of her pocket, unlocked the front door and deadbolt, pushing the door open slightly. Out wafted the aroma of breakfast through the early morning mist. Coffee, bacon, eggs, smoked salmon, and a few other olfactory gems I couldn't readily identify. The combination of the scents was both relaxing and invigorating. She invited me inside saying, "Come in for a bit. First, we'll go for a walk with Leif then sit down for lunch when we return. How's that sound?"

"It sounds fantastic!"

"Okay, let's be off. No time to waste."

Suddenly, a big white furry snout of a large furry creature resembling an abominable snowman on all fours, poked out from behind the door. The large snout plunged out of the opening and darted toward me.

"You have a polar bear as a pet?" I joked. We laughed as he nudged past her, jumping on my chest with his front paws.

"Noooo, ooops, this is Leif," she said laughing as she tried pulling him off. She apologetically stepped in front of me grabbing his large white furry mane, rubbing his neck and head. "Big strong boy," she said. Then he jumped over, slamming his large front paws onto her chest.

"Lucky dog," was my only thought.

"Yes, I know, Mama is home after being gone for sooooo, sooooo, veeery long."

She turned to me and muttered, "Come in," as she entered the house, closing the door behind us. "I hope you like animals, because I have a bunch of them."

"I do," I responded, seeing her gaze questioningly out of the corner of her eye.

Seeing the short stack of shoes by the door, I silently took the cue removing my shoes, formally introducing myself to the white polar bear. He was extremely friendly to me as Erika watched in amazement.

"Wow, he usually doesn't take to people this way, especially not for the first time."

"Animals are a good judge of character. They know when they've met a good one," I said.

"You don't have to take off your shoes, we won't be staying very long. Leif really needs to get out for a walk," she stated.

"That's okay, they're easy to put back on. I don't want to make more work for you having to clean up after my footsteps."

"Oh my, you're so thoughtful," she quipped.

Remembering what she was like back in school, I knew I would have to let her take the lead on any conversations we had. Because I had so much to say and only a short time to say it, I was here to get to know her and didn't want to dominate the conversations. Also, because I'd have to frame my thoughts, my words, and my delivery, extremely carefully.

She led the way up a steep, well-polished, naturally stained hardwood stairway; I followed at a polite distance. Her house was warm and accentuated by natural lighting provided by the vaulted ceilings on the upper floor. The scent of pine was everywhere, as was the aroma of food simmering on the stove and in the oven.

She walked straight into the kitchen and pointed for me to go into the family room area. "Go make yourself comfortable and put your stuff down out of Leif's reach please. I'll be right in.

"Just put the bags on a chair somewhere, otherwise Leif will get into it. Since you already took your shoes off, can I get you anything to drink? Beer? Wine? Hard liquor? Water? Juice?" she asked from the kitchen.

I heard the uncovering of pots on the stove accompanied by an increased scent of mixed aromas of allspice, cinnamon, cardamom, ginger, pepper and a few others. As I suspected, she began my visit as the perfect hostess.

I wandered over to the corner of the family room, putting my bag of treasures atop an ornamental chair as she instructed, taking in a brief visual tour of the great room concept design in this relatively large upstairs area. Projecting the ambiance of a ski lodge, sporting a high ceiling with exposed natural wood beams, there were multiple picture windows in the family room, a door leading out to a deck in view of the wooded backyard, a fireplace with a wooden mantle, some large throw pillows on the floor, a couch, a few comfortable arm chairs, a coffee table, and floor lamps. It was artfully decorated with various candles resting on most of the flat surfaces where they could safely be placed. The natural wood dinner table was located close to the kitchen. The relatively large, family room area was centered around the fireplace. It was in European fashion, sparsely decorated and tastefully furnished. This was consistent with what I could see of the entire house.

"I always seem to be cooking something. The girls like it, so I am encouraged daily to come up with something different they might like to eat. I'm making lunch for us to have after our walk. I know you already had breakfast, maybe you'd like a snack before our walk?" she added.

"Which question should I answer first?" I laughed.

Within my new reality, it would take a few more minutes to grasp the concept of where I was, what I was doing, and who I was doing it with. I responded, remaining perfectly within a safe zone of acceptance, not wanting to appear to be high maintenance.

"Uh, I'll have whatever you're having."

A few minutes after the sound of rattling plates, glasses, saucers, and eating utensils subsided, she emerged from the kitchen presenting a bountiful smorgasbord of crackers, cheese, eggs, bacon, caviar, fruit and fruit juice on a large silver tray. She motioned for me to come and sit at the large table as she exited the kitchen.

"Can I help you with anything?" I asked.

"No, don't be silly. You wouldn't know what to do. Besides you're on vacation. Sit and eat," she said.

Getting to know each other all over again with small talk was fun. She got to know me better, anyway. Even before speaking a word, I felt like I'd known her completely, ever since I first saw her back when I was 12 years old. I couldn't explain it. It's just the way it was.

I counted to three a few times before I finally began talking.

"I need to tell you something. Do you wonder why I came here?"

"To see Sweden, right?" she said.

"Yeah, you're half-right," I responded. "I came to see one person in particular in Sweden... and maybe see a bit of the country while I'm here. Over the next three days, I'm going to tell you things I have thought about a tremendous amount over the past 33 years. I imagine some things you hear you may never have expected to hear from me or even remotely thought of involving me in the past. I should've told you this back when we were in school together, but I was apprehensive, or more accurately, scared to death of saying it. I was petrified of rejection. Even though I was one of the most popular kids in school, all I wanted to do was date you."

"Really? I didn't know that," she said as if completely surprised at the notion. "Do you want more juice?" she added, changing the subject.

We enjoyed the mini feast before us, continuing to engage in small talk. When we were done, she got up and started putting everything away in the kitchen and began doing the dishes. She stopped and watched me as I followed her into the kitchen to help her, my arms filled with foodstuffs and plates. I was so smitten with this beautiful, perfect form of a woman in front of me, I didn't know how to deal with my emotions. I never felt this strongly before. Ever! I would've followed her anywhere! As she was busily putting the remnants away in the refrigerator, I stood behind her looking at her soft blonde hair and porcelain smooth skin on the nape of her neck. I so wanted to hug her, but I was afraid of forcing her to deal with potentially unwanted advances inside her sanctuary. It was too soon, anyway. When she faced back toward me, I just smiled and kept my thoughts to myself.

I met her at the sink and asked, "Do you want to wash or dry?"

She smiled from ear to ear proudly in disbelief, cocking her head to one side. "You know, I've never heard a Swedish man ask me that. They would've sat down waiting for me to finish MY job, and maybe even told me to hurry up and get them a beer or something."

"Wash or dry, Princess?" I interjected.

"Wash. I'll wash because I have a certain way I like to have things washed."

So, wash she did, and dry I did. After the cleanup, we moved into the family room where Leif casually and ever so regally lay in front of the fireplace in the combined family and living rooms.

A short break in conversation left the mood in the room ominous.

"So, you're renting this house fully furnished?" I asked.

"No, silly, I bought this house and decorated it myself. It's a bit awkward since it's just blocks away from my ex-, but it's still within walking distance to the kids' school. That was important."

"You decorated this yourself? It looks like you've lived here for years," I said.

"Once I moved out on my own, I decided to invigorate my life as best I could. I studied home décor as another of my passions, and this is how it turned out," she said outstretching her arms up in the air as she turned in a half circle. "I prefer natural wood and simple décor with clean lines and practical, minimal furnishings. It leaves more room to think clearly. Maybe it's a light energy, feng shui thing, I don't know. I just like it," she explained.

"Why don't you go into home or interior design?" I asked.

"It takes special schooling and licensing here in Sweden and it takes time and money, that I don't have right now. I never planned on being single again."

The mood intensified and I sensed the atmosphere was getting tense. Erika probably also sensed this and sparked, "Are you ready to go for a walk now? Leif really wants to go."

Sprawled out in front of the warm glow of the fireplace, Leif probably didn't look like he wanted to go anywhere. But I obliged, "Sure!"

"We'll show you the farmlands and the woods through the rolling hills around here, and walk down to the water's edge, maybe even go to my favorite hidden sandy beach. Hopefully, some of Leif's dog friends will be out too."

"Ohhhh, Leif's a dog?!" I joked, "I keep thinking he's a polar bear," I jovially responded. She got a laugh from that.

She completed a short tour of the upstairs including her bedroom, a bathroom, and then after making our way down the staircase to the lower landing, she showed me the girls' room last. Leif was happily dancing with anticipation, front feet prancing and dancing, twirling in circles, brushing across anything lying in the path of his strong furry beaver-like tail. I donned my jacket as Erika donned hers, and together we both collected our scarves hanging on the wall pegs near the front door. Erika calmed Leif just long enough to attach his leash. As we headed out the door, we both heard a distinct dull snap, and then what sounded like water gushing out of a pipe onto the floor. We looked at each other stunned.

"We'd better check it!" I boldly suggested.

"Ohhhh, just forget it! Then we'll never get out of here. That's where the laundry room is," she gently protested.

I canted my head while looking at her, protesting an apparent lack of attentiveness to what could be a serious homeowner's nightmare, prompting her to lead the way down the short hallway. Also, so I could again gaze at her cute tail as she walked. She turned and trotted toward the back of the house investigating the sound. She momentarily disappeared. Stopping in her tracks, she moaned. I followed closely behind, peeking over her shoulder.

She was audibly upset, "Ohhhhhhhh what now?"

She gasped in disbelief, as if it was just one more of the thousand little paper cuts in her relatively new collection of woes piling onto the turbulent patch of life she was currently wading through. She bent over in total frustration and disbelief as if she had a stomach ache, leaning over the washing machine with her head in her hands. The entire floor was flooded in about an inch of water contained inside the room by the raised threshold.

"God, I don't need this! I really don't need this!!" she gasped, "This crappy old thing has been giving me problems since I bought this place. This stupid washer. Ohhhhhhh!!"

I wanted so badly to hug her and tell her it would be okay and assure her we could fix it. But I didn't want to give her the wrong idea. I just wanted to fix it to make this problem go away for her.

She turned to me demanding, "Forget it! Just forget it! Never mind, just never mind!! Let's just go—you're gonna get your shoes wet. I'll deal with it later. I'll call a plumber on Tuesday to fix it after you leave."

"And you're probably going to talk to the same plumber who installed it in the first place," I prompted in a foolhardy tone. "Just let me look at it. This has to be a simple drainage issue, like a blockage or something. Let me see if I can fix it, it might be something I can quickly remedy."

"No, Dimitri! I don't want you to waste a minute of your time indoors on this trip. This is supposed to be YOUR vacation in Sweden!"

Ignoring her comment, I turned to her and asked, "Did you just run a load of wash?" I asked.

"Yes, this stupid, stupid, stupid thing!" She dared not kick it out of frustration as it might stop working altogether. "Never mind, I'll deal with it later," again she insisted, demanding I ignore the problem.

"No-no-no-no-no-no-no, we should deal with it now, Princess," I sang. "This is water and can destroy a house pretty quickly from the inside out. And it can cause dangerous mold to grow in just a few days. I want you and the kids to stay healthy. It should only take a few minutes—I promise," I said looking into her eyes.

"Famous last words, right?" she sighed.

"Nope. Just my words," I snapped back. "After a few minutes of productive work, we can relax on our walk not having to face this when we get back. All we have to do is contain the water, which pretty much is already done, soak it up, and fix the problem," I added.

I moved the washing machine away from the wall. After a brief survey of the situation, I noticed the water evacuation pipe in the wall from which the pipe in the back of the washer was draining, was too short. This was preventing the evacuation hose from being fully seated so it popped out of place and drained the water onto the floor. I was surprised it hadn't happened before.

"Okay, I found the problem! I can fix this really quickly and permanently; this is easy. Can you get me a few different sized plastic bottles from your recycle bin, a Philips screwdriver, and a knife?" I asked.

"I'm so, so, so very sorry, just leave it! I'll call a plumber later. This is so embarrassing."

"Nope, you couldn't have foreseen this! It's not your fault. I've got this. I'm glad it happened while I was here so I could fix it for free! This is not an option! Chop-Chop! Mush! Go!" I barked.

Rolling her eyes, and sighing, she headed down the hallway at my behest. I yelled a bit after her so she could hear me, "And get a mop and a bucket too!" I playfully added as I took off my jacket and scarf, draping them over the washing machine, ready to work.

She returned with exactly what I asked, along with a semblance of a toolbox. "I don't know where the kids put the rest of my tools, they're around here somewhere… ohhhhh… what a pain."

It was refreshing knowing a woman who knew each tool's name, along with its proper function.

"We're good, these should do it!" I said.

"I really need a man around this house, I hate this!" she insisted.

I stopped working momentarily. "You wanted a man around the house? Now you've got one! And in a few minutes, you'll have a new washer again, working flawlessly," I smiled. "Okay, now all I have to do is cut a length of water bottle to act like a funnel from the water evacuation hose into the house drain line, making sure there is enough pressure to hold the hose tightly and permanently into the drain line. Then I'll tighten the clasp on the washing machine to keep the evacuation hose connected, tighten the clasp on the wall next to the house's drain line, ensuring both are tightly connected, and we're done. Got it?"

She really wasn't amused.

"Come on, it'll take me four minutes—think I'm kidding? You can time me! And this will be a permanent fix! Ready?"

"…Ooookay," she agreed as she started mopping up the water. As I offered to help, "Nope, I only have one mop… and this is your vacation!" she again insisted.

I just laughed, "And a superb one it's turning out to be. There's no place I'd rather be right now!" My comments got her smiling again.

Measuring the distance from the machine evacuation hose to the house drain line with the digits on my index finger, I cut one bottle a third of the way from the top and squeezed it into place midway from the drain line and the evacuation hose, funneling the drain hose into it. Setting the hoses back into place, I tightened the hose clamp to the wall with the screwdriver, and made a few simple torque adjustments. She stopped mopping, watching me work, peering closely over my shoulder. I felt her breath gently brushing across the back of my neck as she exhaled. It was like fresh, clean, puppy breath. I was tempted to stall and work slower to make this moment last, but I didn't want to prolong her agony dealing with the washer.

"See? Everything just popped into place and I didn't even have to remove the hose which is still secured to the wall. Just tightened it up and all done!"

"Just lefty loosey, righty tighty, right?" she said.

"How did you know that?" I asked.

"Everyone in the world knows that," she said surprising me.

Once again, I showed her what I had done and explained how I did it. "There, all done. Permanent, strong, and best of all—free. And you can recycle the remainder of this plastic bottle. How's that for efficiency?"

"Ohhhhh, thank you so much. I'll finish mopping up and we'll be ready to walk Leif," she said.

Her concentration was fixed and unbroken, surveying my quick solution. As I finished checking the connections behind the washer, moving it back into place, I quickly stood up and turned around; she was unexpectedly close to me. We found ourselves face-to-face in each other's personal space.

She jumped back a bit, "Wow, how did you ever think of that?" she blurted.

"It's what I do. I'm a Green Beret, trained to adapt to any situation and overcome adversity."

Then she quickly said again, "Oh my God, you're on vacation. You're not here to fix my house, how embarrassing," apologizing again.

I looked into her eyes and explained, "I'm happy to help. I couldn't imagine letting any water sit there for days. Plus, now you don't have to worry about it ever again! Thank you for letting me feel helpful. You wanted a man around the house, you've got one now, for three more days. What else do you need me to do? Do you have a list?" I laughed.

"Not funny. No, I don't have a list. Let's go!" she said abruptly turning and guiding me into the hallway toward the front door.

We walked out of the room as she summoned the white bear-hund, grabbing his leash. At the time, I thought nothing of her reaction to our close proximity, though it was similar to what in lie detecting is a called a "micro expression." Simply, an autonomic response in the form of a micro-reaction responding to a perceived action. There was none, aside from retracting from our close proximity. We approached the door and once again got dressed for our outdoor trek. Erika attached the long thin leather leash to Leif's collar.

"Wait!" I held a finger to my ear, "Did you hear that noise?" I joked.

"No, no, no, not funny. Let's go before there really is one!" she demanded.

I took my camera out of the backpack, zipping it closed, donning it while slinging my camera over one shoulder around my neck by its specially designed strap.

"Wow, that's quite a camera. And quite a handy strap!" she said.

Camera? This is not just a camera; this is my travel companion. Meet Cassandra Canon. She makes sure no matter which country I visit I always get out to see the sights. She also helps me, when I'm back home from wherever I was, to remember everything I've done and every place I've been by recording it in pictures—what in Europe you call photos. And this strap is designed to ensure the camera stays ready and out of my way until I need it. It stays at the ready, near my hip.

"Ready?" I asked.

"Ready!" she sang in anticipation of enjoying the sensational outdoors.

Leif sensed freedom the second the door was cracked. He followed his nose, rushing out the door as quickly as paratroopers exit an aircraft in flight. Erika was swiftly dragged out the front door, towed behind the once patiently waiting and now sled-dog pulling dog bear-hund.

She yelled to me, "Can you close the door behind you, it's already locked! I have a key!"

I complied, wasting no time catching up to them. Leif chose a quick pace at his level of comfort, strutting regally, confidently leading us on a route he seemed to know like the back of his paw. We walked through a quaint suburban neighborhood, like some in Washington State. Then we traveled down a dirt path etched into the hillside, through some trees, down another dirt path, across a gravel road, down three sets of long concrete stairs, across a public street, and onto a short, graveled entranceway, before a beautifully designed, tree-lined, cobblestone driveway began. The cobblestoned driveway led to an old white mansion that reminded me of something out of the movie, *Gone With The Wind*.

Lush green farmland surrounded the white mansion, now barely visible in the distance. The cobblestone road leading to the mansion was lined with large shade trees on both sides. The trees protected a weathered three-foot stone wall, covered with a thick layer of moss. Surely, we were walking down the same ancient, slightly muddy road traveled by its visitors in the past couple hundred years. Undoubtedly these people crunched the same gravel beneath their feet, before reaching the adorning slippery cobblestones. Erika confirmed this was an entrance to an old Nordic plantation. I stopped to take a few pictures with my camera which patiently awaited its awakening, slung close by my hip.

"You don't mind if I take a few pictures, do you?" I asked, referring to the beautiful moss-covered rocks used to make this wall.

"Nope, as long as I'm not in them. I don't care what you take pictures of," she demanded.

We continued walking and soon passed well-groomed Nordic quarter horses and white sheep in separate pastures along our route.

"Is that your other house?" I pointed to the sprawling white mansion.

"Nooooo, that used to be a privately owned mansion, but now it's a public building and the surrounding land is a public park. They still farm all this land around here. I think they rent out the farmland and pastures to local farmers and herders. There is even a restaurant inside the mansion where they serve breakfast during the week—we can go there on Monday before you go to the airport. The restaurant, or café, as you may call it in English, has amazing breakfast rolls and pastries. It's too bad they're not open on weekends.

"Now it's time to introduce you to my animal friends," she said playfully turning and trotting off, proudly sporting her smile; her tail following Leif's leading the way. Down yet another trail, we ventured, heading away from the mansion.

I struggled to catch up to her and Leif. Once I did, we all walked with the same speed and grace. Using my muscle memory movement, as I did while transitioning to my M4 assault rifle while in the military, I grasped my camera, slung snugly near my hip on its customized shoulder harness. Raising it toward her with the sun highlighting her nearly perfect features, I prepared to click away. I stopped walking. Focusing my camera lens on her, I waited for her to turn in front of the early morning sun, occasionally peering through the trees, reflecting off her natural blond hair like a golden, glowing halo surrounding her face. I watched and waited patiently, peering through the camera's viewfinder, zooming toward her as the two walked ahead.

This took a few attempts. Finally, I snuck up behind them so Erika didn't hear my footsteps walking behind her. I awaited the perfect moment to get this once in a lifetime shot. As she turned to see where I was, in the nick of time I snapped the shot. She heard the unique sound and looked right at me as the camera shutter snapped again.

I exclaimed, "Perfect!"

She immediately objected and snapped, "Please, Dimitri, no pictures. I really don't like how they turn out! Not of me— please... please... Dimitri... no pictures. I'm not in a cheerful place right now and I don't want to remember."

Either she remained extremely humble regarding her looks, as she had when I first set eyes upon her 33 years ago, or she experienced a change in her level of confidence resulting from years of verbal abuse, neglect, or from a series of unhappy personal relationships. She had revealed nothing to me about any of that. She said little about her personal life. For whatever reason, she didn't like what she saw of herself in photographs. What was it that had permanently pierced her confidence? All I could do was speculate. I knew I had to encourage this to change.

"What? This is a beautiful day, you have a perfectly working washing machine, and your long-lost friend is visiting you, bringing you happiness from the land of milk and honey where the streets are paved with gold, from far away over the horizon... and you don't want to remember this time? Are you kidding?

We're going to have a lot of fun in the next few days and I'm sorry, you won't have any choice in the matter. I will capture what I see in you, and I guarantee you'll be impressed with the result. If you don't like any picture I capture, I'll erase it. I promise! Better living through modern technology, right?"

She slowly shook her head from side to side, indicating a NO.

I tried begging. "Please? Please?? Pleeeeeez???"

At first, her facial micro-expressions momentarily displayed anguish… but just as quickly, the corners of her mouth turned slightly upward, transitioning to display no emotion.

"Pleeeez???" I chuckled, smiling from ear to ear.

After a brief, uncomfortable, silent pause, she said, "How can I say no when you smile like that? Okaaaaaay," she hesitantly agreed. Slowly but surely emerging was her angelic heavenly smile I knew from years ago.

"But you'll erase them if I don't like them, right?!" she confirmed in a demanding tone.

"Yes, of course. I'll erase every shot you don't like."

She looked at me silently. Finally, she took a breath and sighed. Again, she smiled, "Okaaaay."

"There's the angel I knew," I sparked.

"I'm hardly an angel," she remarked.

"You are to me and to my camera. A Nordic Angel," I quipped. We both smiled.

I snapped away at this opportunity before she changed her mind. Taking only a few more shots, I didn't want to push my luck and reverse the ground I'd gained. I started walking toward her, attempting to brush past her along the narrow trail.

"Uh-uh-uh-uh, I need to see them first!" she demanded while smiling.

I approached closely, stealing my first opportunity to get close to her. I was careful not to remove the camera strap from around my neck and shoulder, forcing us closer together for her to see the resulting photographs in the camera viewfinder. As I leaned over, I felt her silky, blond hair tickling my nose.

"Yeah, I guess those came out pretty good," she hesitantly reported in her brief commentary.

"Pretty good?" I objected. "They're incredible! They're perfect! How could they not be? They're all portraits of an Angel Princess. Look at all the detail, the composition, the complexity in the lighting, the background... appreciate the entire photograph as a piece of art! Because it is art!" I said smiling.

"Yeah, okaaaay whatever," she snorted. "I like them. You can keep those. Can you send me copies?"

"Of course."

I wasn't about to tell her I was nowhere near done taking pictures of her. Such an amazingly beautiful woman was worthy of capturing from every angle, in every light, in every activity. I hoped I had enough memory cards.

I was living my dream, being with her, basking in the visual relics of my past. I was in heaven with every step we took, with every breath I drew, with every moment in her presence. I was completely fulfilled; completely satisfied in every way possible. Well, almost in every way. It was a feeling I never truly experienced. It was as if I was walking in a dream and feared if I left her presence, I would never experience this elation again. I was afraid I'd wake up nowhere near my beautiful Viking Angel Princess, and this all would have just been a mirage or a dream. At this moment, all my dreams transformed into my present reality.

While we continued walking, I was on the lookout for the silos of sunlight shining through the trees splashing across her hair, face, and figure. I waited for her mind to relax, for her to absorb the moments, basking in the enchantment, before taking another photo. We were surrounded by the singing of songbirds in the crisp cool air, with a slight breeze randomly drifting past. The warm sunlight shining through the trees, sparked distant scratching sounds emanating from the activities of ground-dwelling creatures deeper in the forest. It was serene. I wanted her to feel the relaxation in this moment, especially since it would reflect in my portraits.

As we followed the wooded trail out from under the trees, again I framed my next perfect image of her in the viewfinder and snapped the shutter over and over while she wasn't looking.

"So, when are you going to show me those pictures?" she asked without lifting her head.

Well, I didn't think she was looking. "Right now," I said. I stole another opportunity to get close to her, once again, leaning over to show her the result. I drew as close to her as I could manage.

"Wow!" she chirped, leaning against me looking at the photo, "Now, that's a good picture!"

I sternly interrupted, "Good picture? It's a perfect picture!! They all are!!"

"Yeah, okay you're right. It's a PERFECT picture!" she agreed and coyly, flirtatiously turned her head, continuing to walk. After a few paces, she halted in her tracks.

"Let me see those other pictures again, please," she said as this time, she violated my personal space. I quickly presented the photographic visions of her on my viewfinder, even closer to her this time.

"Wow, they're all pretty good!"

I gawked and squinted at her in protest.

"Okay, okay, they're all PERFECT pictures! Okay??" she exclaimed.

"Yes, they are!" I agreed.

I smelled the sweet scent of her hair from where I stood. This reminded me of the freshly showered heads of long blonde-haired models you see in shampoo commercials. She took a few steps away from me and there it was again... BAM! This was the Erika I knew from long ago. She was BACK! Smiling, confident, glowing, and happy!

Repeatedly, as if now imprinted into our DNA, we revisited the kabuki dance of me showing her the newest pictures.

"Okay, you can keep those too," she continued. "But it's no guarantee of any other future keepers," she added as she continued walking. "I know. I know, YOU'LL SEE... right?" she said, mimicking me.

"Yep, they'll all be keepers!" I tacked onto the conversation.

She turned and snapped mockingly, protruding her head toward me, "Yes, we WILL see!"

She said this just as I captured another and another and another perfect portrait of these moments. I repeated the process over and over and over, as often as possible.

We walked and talked about the birds and the scenery. Loving nature as she did, there wasn't much of anything she missed. She so enjoyed tracking the spectacle of the birds and squirrels frolicking and dancing through the trees. Smiling and laughing as I hadn't heard her laugh before. Her voice echoed through the Swedish wood down every trail we wandered. We were the only humans anywhere within sight or sound. I was completely smitten and she seemed to be too. Neither of us at this moment in time intimated to have a care in the world. We walked and talked about nothing, and about everything, all at the same time. I took pictures of the scenery, of her in the scenery, and of her alone. I was happy to have her trust me so quickly.

As I watched her inside my camera lens, the fluctuating light between the leaves of the trees and the open spaces in the distance brought out the best in her. I listened to every note spoken by her golden voice. Her gentle words floated past my ears; I loved listening to her speak. These very moments were what I dreamed of since the day I first saw her. And now, they were unfolding in front of me. It was later in life than I had both hoped for and expected, but right now I wouldn't dare wish it to be any different. This day was blooming perfectly in every respect. And so was she.

We passed pasture after pasture dotted with grazing horses. She pointed to one beautiful creature looking like someone had bred a Clydesdale gelding and a quarter horse with bright, light blue eyes. These eyes looked like those antique turn of the century glass marbles with the tiny spinners in the middle.

"See that horse over there? That's a Norwegian Fjord Horse," Erika pointed out. "Originally bred by the Vikings in Norway and Sweden, when the two were one country for hundreds of years… it's a tough breed. He's not very tall, but known for having tremendous strength and stamina. We used to ride those when I was a kid, but they can be pretty wild. My parents were uneasy about letting us ride them without a lot of supervision. He's always hanging around here when I walk by. He's handsome, huh? He's lived here ever since I have," she added.

"How do you know it's a 'he'?" I asked.

As we passed, I walked a few steps ahead of her, snapping shots of the sleek, strong, amazingly fit, beautiful creature with the blue marble eyes. Walking over to the fence line, she called to him in Swedish. To my amazement, the bright-eyed Fjord horse walked toward her at his own cool breeze pace, stopping just short of the fence line. My camera continued snapping images of them together. Apparently, something about her aroused him.

"Oh, that's how you know it's a guy—yep, he's a guy," I said.

"What?" she asked because she obviously couldn't see what I was talking about from her angle of view. "What are you talking about?" His penis suddenly fully elongated.

"And he's hung like a horse!" I joked. "Think I'm kidding?" as I pointed to his hindquarters. I laughed and joked, "So, humans aren't the only ones you have this effect on."

As she noticed the change in the horse's anatomy, she playfully slapped my shoulder. She blushed and then her cheeks turned beet red. "Oh paleeeez. I usually feed him crab apples on my walks, so of course, he approaches me. I just didn't bring any today. But I can't explain THAT," she tilted her head and pointed at the spectacle with her eyes.

"Ohhh, I can!" I laughed, "You want me to explain it to you?"

We both laughed. Walking a few steps away from her, I jokingly blurted, "Hey Erika, call me and see if the same thing happens to me."

"I don't think so!" she blushed.

"I know, do you have any crab apples?" I scoffed, "You can feed me one and see what happens!"

"Thanks a lot. Next, you'll say I can make him urinate on command too, huh?" she explained.

"He's not urinating." I bellowed.

After a few seconds, the horse began urinating, the force of the stream loudly impacting the ground beneath him. Her timing was so impeccable we both laughed uncontrollably. She definitely called it.

"Maybe you're a horse whisperer?" I joked.

We walked on, meandering in and out of the wood line on the improved gravel and dirt trail. As we headed back into the forest, we took a detour off the trail taking us to a patch of dark green woods. There was a patch of land completely blanketed with moss, cloaked with an amalgamation of densely populated shade trees overhead. Wild birds chirped loudly and consistently, as they frolicked in the skyways and byways through the treetops. Under our feet, the moss suspended our weight as we walked. We were springing up and down from nature's cushioned moss floor. The sun's rays prominently shone through the treetops, lighting the forest floor with intentional columns of bright white light. The full spectrum of greens on display was breathtaking. This was surely worth another batch of photographs.

As we worked our way back to the trail, we talked about life itself. Passing by more goats and sheep grazing in separate meadows and larger pastures as we roamed. We continued strolling through the forest, passing a small cluster of houses nestled into the wilderness like a "Hansel and Gretel" story [except we weren't in Germany]. Each house style was so different from the next. Some were traditional structures, some looked quite functional, some contemporary, some painted wood, some stained wood, some had grass growing on the roofs for insulation, and some were wood-shingled with wood siding. All were clean looking, surrounded by well-manicured landscaping, skillfully integrated into this natural setting.

Prancing onward, I tagged along behind until Erika finally skipped off the trail, shouting, "Follow me. I want to show you someplace!" as she brushed through some scantily populated young pine saplings.

"Anywhere!" I blurted.

"What?" she grunted.

"Uh… nothing." I hesitantly responded, not believing I confused my outside voice for my inner voice on my response.

She stopped, held Leif tightly by the leash, turned and said, "I heard you. What exactly did you mean?"

"Umm… anywhere… I'd follow you anywhere… anytime… anyhow!" I laughed, "So where are we going?"

I learned this distract and redirect technique from the military. Her eyes continued smiling. Her lips soon followed suit as she playfully shook her head from side to side, quietly snorting her breath through her nostrils.

"Getting tired?" I asked.

As we shuffled our feet, the ground vegetation and moss were growing thicker. Once again, we were floating on a blanket of moss, springing forward with each step.

"Nope, we're just getting started," she exclaimed.

We plodded, then trotted behind Leif for a bit. She explained she wouldn't let him off leash because he might run toward his unseen cousins in the wild. He resembled a mixture of a Malamute and a Husky from the movie, *The Call of the Wild*. She was probably right. From the looks of his physical stature and stamina, he would've bolted, never looking back. Neither of us could've restrained him if he ever had such an epiphany.

Erika slowed as we came to another densely moss-blanketed area. The sun still shone through the treetops overhead, adding hundreds of green hues to the color palette. She stopped. We stood together, admiring God's handy work. Suddenly poised with her arms extended out beside her, she said, "We're heeeeeere," twirling in a circle with her arms out.

"Here, where?" I interrupted. "Where specifically?"

"We're here!" she proudly repeated. "You can't tell anyone what I'm about to tell you—promise?"

"I profoundly promise!" I professed.

"This is where I pick wild Chanterelles."

"What?" I questioned.

"You know, those little brown mushrooms," she patiently explained. "I come here to pick them with the kids, it's a fun place!"

"Shantrelz? "I repeated hesitantly. "They're mushrooms?" I queried. "How do you say that in English?" I asked obtusely.

"Duh, that is English," she laughed. "You know for a smart guy you don't know much about your own language," she quipped.

"Maybe you could teach me," I toyed.

"Ohhhhhhhh, I could teach you sooooo much!" she added in a sultry tone of voice.

"You could? About what?" I begged.

"Duhhhh, about mushrooms," she responded.

"That's not what you meant, and you know it," I countered.

She went silent.

Breaking the awkward silence, I added, "So..." I sparked, "Shantrelz?" I repeated as a question. "What do you do with them?"

"It's not Shantrelz! It's Chan-ter-elles—I find them, pick them, clean them, cook them, and eat them."

"You eat them—the mushrooms you find growing wild in the woods? You're sure they're not poisonous?" I toyed.

"Veeeeery good," she smiled, "Yesssss, I know which ones are edible," she continued.

"How do you know which ones are Chan-ter-elles?" I asked.

"My Mom taught me how to find and recognize them, when I was a little girl."

"Thankfully, she didn't teach you when you were a little boy!" I laughed.

"Hilarious!" she continued. "My Mom taught me, and her Mom taught her. We used to walk for hours in the woods, talking, and picking Chanterelles. She taught me what to eat and what not to eat in the woods."

With my Army Special Forces (SF) background and training, she really impressed me at this point. She wasn't simply a gorgeous-faced Princess anymore. I was discovering she was quite a complex person, with much more depth and intricacy than meets the eye.

"So that's how you know so much about Chanterelle mushrooms and natural cooking," I confirmed.

"My mother's love for pure, healthy food and her love of nature encouraged me since I was a child. After a few years of college and working in the travel industry, I figured that life wasn't for me. Remembering her words and these memories led me to change my focus to attending a culinary school in Stockholm to be a professional chef," she explained. "I like being closer to nature than I could be in the city. So, I moved back here."

"What? You're a school trained chef? A professional chef?" I exclaimed.

"Yes, I graduated from chef school in Stockholm, thank you very much. Why does that surprise you? You didn't think I could do that?" she queried.

"No, no, no, no, it's not that!" I responded, "You're not helping."

"Helping with what?" she demanded.

"Oh, nothing," I said.

She smiled with her happy eyes again—and what a smile she had. Her smile could warm the winter. It was comforting being near her.

"Oh, no you don't, you will not say 'nothing' anymore and let it be the end of it," she demanded. "If you expect me to explain myself, you have to as well!"

We kept walking deeper into the woods, so I assumed we were looking around for more places with Chan-ter-elles.

"So, in your Green Beret training aren't you trained to live off the land, finding mushrooms, living off nature's bounty?" she asked.

"We are. But we're regionally oriented to specific areas of the world. So, of course with my background I was a shoe-in for Asia. We learned plants specific to Asia. But understand, our training is for survival in a tight situation, it's not like we're wandering through the woods looking for items to put into a chef's salad. We stay away from mushrooms. Typically, in a survival situation, nothing good comes from eating that fungus.

"In survival school in North Carolina, for example, I learned what water hemlock and a few other poisonous plants look like. Some candidates in past classes ate those and died. I was careful to memorize those and never harvested them. I spent a lot of time collecting wild onions and garlic, to make a broth using worms, grubs, and flies to survive."

"That doesn't sound very appetizing," she said.

"No, it pretty much tasted like shit. Like most things in nature, either it's sour or bland, without the spices available in a professional kitchen," I explained.

"Well, my Chanterelles won't taste like that. I promise!" she said. "And it's a chef salad... not a chef's salad... just saying," she added.

We got a chuckle out of that.

"I used to bring my kids out here when they were younger. We'd spend hours discovering the forest, picking Chanterelles and just spending time together. Then they got older, they lost interest in taking 'boring' walks with Mom mushroom picking. So now I go by myself."

"So, where are they?" I asked, trying to brighten the mood.

"I told you they're at their friend's house," she responded.

"Not your kids, the Chan-ter-elles," I said.

"They don't grow year-round silly. It's not the season. They're long gone now. But I have some back at the house in the freezer. I'll cook some up for you when we get back... So, what did you mean by that—I'm not helping?" she continued.

"I promise I'll tell you when we get back," I said.

"You'll forget," she demanded again.

"I couldn't forget anything involving you. Especially when you're around," I playfully laughed.

"Okay," she said, "Then I'll ask you again later. I'm warning you; I don't forget anything either."

"I want you to ask me again, because then I'll definitely tell you." We both laughed and continued walking.

"So, what are we looking for now, more Chan-ter-elles?" I carefully enunciated.

"Veeeery good! No! I told you they aren't in season! We're looking for a perfect place," she quipped.

"Ooookay, I'll ask... a perfect place for what?" I questioned.

"We're looking for the perfect place for Leif to poop!"

We both laughed and laughed as I shook my head, "Ohhhh, I walked right into that one!"

"Well, let's hope not!" she snapped.

We laughed more.

Leif glanced back at us briefly before continuing forward.

Erika added, "I've never laughed so much in my life. You're sooooo funny!" she complimented me.

"You know you could laugh like this forever if you wanted to..." I mumbled under my breath.

"What?" she asked.

"Oh, nothing," I cracked.

"Nothing what?" she asked again.

"Nothing... I was just saying—Hey look! Leif found his spot. Leif, don't poop on the Chan-ter-elle beds!" I yelled as my voice echoed through the lush green forest.

"Actually, mushrooms grow much better in poop. It's because of the nutrients and constant moisture it provides," Erika explained, schooling me.

"And they have to be washed after collecting them!" I added, feigning expertise in mushroom preparation.

She continued, "The first rule of cooking is to wash EVERYTHING. That's the first step of preparation. Chanterelles contain a lot of moisture, so you cook them on medium heat, once the water is gone, you add about 4 tablespoons of butter and a few cloves of garlic and VOILA!"

I approached Leif as he was done with his first garden sculpture. Walking in a circle pointing, "Stop, you're making me hungry! Okay... Leif, poop more, poop here... and here... and there... poop everywhere around here. Poop here... Leif, poop here... and here, and here—I don't think he has enough, do you think we should help him out?"

"That's gross! You're crazy! Imagine if some people came by and saw us? All of us pooping out here! What would they say?" she added, nearly falling over laughing.

"We could explain to them we're feeding the Chan-ter-elles. Surely they'd understand!"

"What's the difference? They still have to be washed!" I spouted.

"What's the difference? That's NOT the point!" she squeezed out between her fits of laughter. "This is Sweden NOT the U.S. We don't poop in the woods here! Besides this is MY secret spot!"

We both enjoyed a long laughing fit, convulsing as we laughed.

As our laughter subsided, she said, "That's two things you'll need to explain later. You know, that, right? I'm counting."

"I know…" I confirmed.

I couldn't help but see this teenage girl whom I barely got to know years ago, now standing in front of me, a bit older, a lot wiser, and taller—but thankfully now not taller than me. And just as beautiful as she used to be. Here she was innocently and completely carefree, laughing and laughing as if she hadn't a care in the world. She really had changed little in 33 years. Except now, she was giving me her personal time and sharing her personal thoughts. She wasn't just telling me the time of day, or sharing simple greetings. I looked at her, thinking nobody I met before had this effect on me, ever. I wanted her to be in my life and I really wanted to be in hers. It was crazy; I know. I couldn't explain it. There we were. We only re-knew each other a few scant hours and yet, I felt like I'd known her forever… again, like the years of separation never happened.

This was just Day One of my emotional and spiritual safari with her. I chose not to robotically follow any contrived scripted courses of action. Instead, I'd let it happen, seeing where it would go. I was willfully and joyfully along for the ride. And what a ride this was! I was already happy to let my very near future gently unfold.

Whenever she looked directly at me as we walked, she maintained a vibrant sparkle in her eyes, lit with the passion of dancing flames, highlighting her priceless smile.

"I haven't laughed this much and been this happy in years you know," she finally confided.

"Why is that?" I asked.

"My ex- turned out to be not very nice to me. He used to be… but then he changed. And so went the relationship. Scandinavian men are that way. They're overbearing and controlling. In the end, it was like I just didn't matter. Often it was like I wasn't there at all. If I completed my duties, life was bearable. There was no genuine happiness, tenderness, giving, sharing, caring, or laughing in my life for years and years," she confided.

When I heard this, it pained my heart. She deserved so much more. We both did.

"I know exactly how you feel. But it's not only Scandinavian men, American women can be that way too! People from any country can be like that—and many of them, it seems, I've met," I responded, then hesitated, thinking about my words.

"It's not that people change, but they're natural self comes out. And this is especially prominent if they feel mismatched with their partner. If people don't change together and spend the time together to change, the natural course of events is frustration and anger. Some people may be better off by themselves. I'm not though," I said.

If I'd only asked her out while in school, both of our lives may have been different. I couldn't help but think I could've made her life so much better. And she could drastically have improved mine, especially from a relationship standpoint. We both could have been much happier by this point in our lives than we were. Instead of merely starting out, we could have been progressing through life. It's strange how life takes its twists and turns. But life was what it was, and I was happy for all I did, and had, up to this point.

I explained, "It's all about the thing called 'free will.' You know Cinderella, you're not the only person and yours is not the only relationship where this has happened," I said light-heartedly consoling her.

"I know," she mumbled, "But why did it have to happen to me?"

I comforted her by adding, "It happened to me too! People change their minds, their values, their attitudes, and their preferences. It didn't have to happen, it just did. And it doesn't have to happen again—to either of us," I muttered.

She glanced at me with that sparkle in her eye.

"You think a lot about life, don't you?" she said, though not loud enough to create an echo in the woods enabling potential passersby to delve unwelcomed into what was now becoming a very personal conversation.

"Yeah, sorry… I do that. I have plenty of time for deep thought. I guess I'm just wired that way… I'm rambling," I apologized.

We turned to walk back toward the trail and once again she disclosed to me, "Your perspective is refreshing."

After a few moments of silence, we sauntered back toward the trail where this time she brightened the mood, "That was my secret mushroom place—shhhhh don't tell anyone!"

"No worries, I won't, I promise," I whispered back. "As long as you cook me some Chan-ter-elles as YOU promised," I jovially reminded her.

"I'll definitely do that!" she asserted.

"That would be superb… Chef…" I added.

She turned toward me and smiled. "I still want you to tell me what you meant you know," she added.

"Yup," I agreed smiling back at her.

As we walked, she asked, "Why did people call you 'D' in school?"

"I don't know, I guess they didn't like Dimitri, or they didn't want to say a three-syllable name every time they wanted to address me."

As we walked, I added, "The name fits me though. I'm not Greek, but in Greek it means, Earth Lover… Searcher… it's the male form of the mythological Greek Goddess of corn and harvest. My parents could've chosen another name like Duke—which means Leader, or, Dante—which means Enduring, if they wanted to stick with a name starting with a D. But I think Dimitri suits me, because I love life with everything it offers."

"Come on, let's go D!" she said, also urging Leif to walk faster.

As we walked, I peered through the trees from time to time as we drew nearer to more pastureland. The view was stunning. Traversing over the bright green rolling hills, again we passed pasture after pasture. We continued strolling into a shade-tree canopied, dirt path where a unique mixture of birch, spruce, pines, red alder, and aspen trees dressed the natural walkway. These trees completely blocked the sun's warming rays overhead. I saw the shimmering shores of the Baltic Sea as we ventured out of the wood line toward lower elevations. The water sparkling through the trees shimmered on the horizon. We approached the shoreline, and as if on cue, the sun made its proud presence known. Only occasionally afterward, did it hide behind the cloud banks. It was obtrusive at first, then politely began peering out from the light gray, fluffy clouds. We drew nearer to the water and noticed the glassy movement of the tiny waves provided a stark contrast to the relatively dark wood line from where we emerged. My immediate thought was I had three days of being in this sanctuary, of which this was only the first. I was in heaven.

We followed the shoreline, re-entering wooded trails as the land sloped downward. I became bolder with my camera, snapping shots of her from the front, side, and rear. As we walked through the wooded path, I offered to hold Leif's leash.

She warned, "He won't like it. He doesn't like other people holding his leash. He'll stop, sit, and won't move. Then he'll stare at me until I'm the one holding the leash; you'll see, he's a one-woman man," she chuckled.

"Wanna bet? We'll see about that!" I scoffed.

When I moved toward her, she stopped and Leif sat. I motioned I wanted to hold the leash and she handed it to me.

"Come on, Leif, let's go. Woof!" I barked. He looked at me a bit confused, and without hesitation, he stood up from his proud, regal, seated position picking up a slow walking pace.

In complete astonishment, Erika raised her eyebrows and said, "Wow... that's never happened! He didn't even like my ex-! I'm very impressed!" she chimed.

I smiled, beaming with confidence as we walked.

"I've only begun impressing you," I touted.

"Oh, really??" she questioned.

We both laughed, continuing on our azimuth through the woods toward the shoreline. Occasionally, we wandered off the path onto lighter green patches of thick moss scattered throughout the forest. These sites were amazing. The soft, cushiony, green growth under my feet was spongy and springy. I already felt I had been walking on air while we were on the dirt path, and on this natural carpet made of moss, I truly was.

I so wanted to touch her or brush by her, now more than ever, as we wandered back onto the main dirt path. Leif's ears perked up when something diverted his attention off the trail. I could hear the lapping of the frigid waters of the Baltic Sea shores nearby. Only now it was louder. The waves weren't completely visible to us through the hundreds of brown-barked pine trees and the occasional patch of saplings blocking our view. Leif jerked across the path, crossing in front of us, winding the leash around both of us. He pulled hard on the leash again, attempting to dart away, heading back into the wood line. The long lead wrapped around our legs as Leif pulled away with his powerful bear-like structure.

"Leeeeeiifff!" Erika exclaimed.

He dragged the leash, pulling us closer together—the leash uncontrollably tightened around us. It was surprisingly relaxing, as we were forced together. Perhaps this was fate, but mainly it was Leif. He came to an abrupt stop once the lead couldn't wrap any tighter around us. Though he couldn't drag the combined weight of both of us through the woods, he gave it his best shot. He left us staring into each other's eyes. Our noses touched.

"*Leif gör inte det*! No, no, no, don't do that!" she yelled. Perhaps she was subconsciously translating for me. I loved when she spoke Swedish. This amazed me. Leif didn't let up.

As we stood face-to-face, after a brief hesitation, she turned her face away from mine. As we both looked down at the tangled lead, she worked to unwind it.

I sent Leif a telepathic message, "Good boy Leif, good boy. If you pull the leash making it even tighter, I'll cook you a huge steak, every night for the rest of your life!"

"Oh, Leif..." Erika complained as she strenuously worked to unwind the tangled mess. "Oh, my... I'm so sorry, he's never done that before," she said apologetically.

"I'm not..." I mumbled.

"What?" Erika queried.

"Nothing," I quipped.

"That's three," Erika said.

She suddenly lost her footing during her attempts to unwind the leash, falling over, bringing me down on top of her. I instinctively rolled to one side, protecting my camera and avoiding landing on top of her. As we rolled over together, we were completely, unmistakably, and hopelessly intertwined, entangled within the leash.

I jokingly yelled, "Bad, bad Leif, don't do thaaaat!" in a monotone voice showing severe disbelief in what I was saying.

She looked at me smiling, "Ohhh, you're just loving this aren't you? You probably told him to do that! You guyzzzz!"

"Yes, I am. You should see what Leif and I have planned for us tonight!"

As she worked to unwind the leash, we righted ourselves, sitting up next to each other on the dirt trail... my first instinct was to lie back down on the trail.

"Leif no! Don't move! *Rör dig inte!*" she exclaimed.

He now sat proudly on the periphery on the forest trail hovering over us, simply staring at both of us.

"Thank you, Leif, thank you!" I silently sang his praises.

"Oh no, is your camera alright?" Erika questioned.

"No, I don't think so. Maybe you should give it a crab apple," I joked.

"Get out! It's fine," she snickered playfully slapping me.

I laughed, lying down on the trail as we were still entangled.

"Are YOU okay?" she asked as I laughed.

"I think I need CPR," I joked.

"Get out! You're fine," she said as she playfully smacked my shoulder.

"Got any crab apples," I added.

We both laughed. I wanted this moment to last. She continued laughing. So did I. As we turned toward each other, our eyes locked together. Again, she hesitated, then spun away, finding some space to squeeze between us.

"Are YOU okay?" I asked.

"Yes, I'm fine. Dimitri, I'm so sorry," she apologetically professed.

"I'm not!" I admitted. "I could stay here like this all day and night! Even for the rest of my life!"

Once again, our laughter led to a brief pause. Then it became awkward. We looked at each other; she knew what I meant. I think it scared her. She hesitated and again leaned her head away from me, continuing to untangle us. Again, something caught Leif's attention, and once again he became cluelessly fixated on whatever first captured his attention in the woods. Again, he pulled the leash taut.

"Leif, stop pulling! *Leif sluta dra*—stop pulling!" she demanded as we lay still ensnared in the leash. He finally stepped toward us, giving Erika some slack in the leash; her continual efforts to free us unfortunately began working.

We sat for a few moments looking at Leif as he maintained the high ground. He confidently stared back at us with his large white Malamute-sized head and piercing blue eyes. He appeared to be smiling.

"He's quite the matchmaker," I said.

She looked into my eyes, as we were still nearly nose to nose every few moments through her efforts to untangle the leash, and said nothing. I wasn't sure what she was thinking about, but she was deep in thought.

What a wonderfully awkward moment. In Hollywood, this scene would've resulted in a romantic kiss. But she seemed to be wrestling with some internal demons. And I wasn't about to confront them, trying to rush her into anything. I was happy to be here on the ground with her. She was getting out of a failed relationship and dealing with it in her own way, on her own terms. I didn't want to be her rebound relationship, eventually being cast away among the throngs of exes, once my duties as her muse were complete. I didn't want to push her. It was too bad though; it was a complete waste of the perfect Hollywood moment!

As we finally stood up, brushing ourselves off, collecting our thoughts, Erika finally completed untangling us. She let the leash free for just a second; I saw the leash disappear in front of me as Leif dashed off as fast as he could run, dragging it behind him.

"Oh, no!" Erika barked. "Leif, No! No! No!"

Thankfully, Leif ran to the other side of the trail through the sparsely spaced trees toward the glimmering shoreline, now visible in more than a few glimpses.

"Quick, he's heading toward the water!" Erika yelled as we both ran as fast as we could to intervene in this wild animal's instinct to answer the call of the wild.

As we crested the wood line, Leif was standing on the grassy bank of the shoreline looking back, apparently waiting for us to catch up. We came to a stop next to him, all of us were panting. Our torsos convulsed from the sprint, and our breath visible in the air.

"Whew! That was fun!" I exclaimed, catching my breath. "If Leif wants to go into the water, we should put him on the leash, right?" I asked.

"No, of course not, silly," Erika exclaimed catching her breath as well. She pursed her lips, squinting at me. "He'll pull us into the water with him! You'd love that wouldn't you? We may as well let him frolic off-leash!"

"Spoilsport," I joked.

"Do you know how cold this water is? I'm not walking home soaking wet," Erika jovially responded.

"Just kidding," I reassured her.

"*Leif Gå! Go!*" she said, encouraging him to jump off the bank into the water.

~ 17 ~

Unfettered Discovery

L eif happily jumped from the grassy bank into the shallow, rocky, crystal-clear, frigid waters. He wasted no time frolicking in the gently lapping waves, as if he was chasing hundreds of squeaky toys beneath the surface. The ebbing tide exposed round, smooth melon-sized boulders of various sizes, completely covered with seaweed. Leif used these as perches between play sessions. The shoreline breeze was cold and clammy.

We both sat on the grassy shoulder of the short bank watching Leif. The icy waters rhythmically lapped onto the rocks at our feet. The morning fog was lifting, the air was cool, and the view was crisply stunning. I started snapping pictures again.

She said again, "You know, I really don't like to be in pictures; I hate looking at myself."

I laughed and said, "Funny, I thought you'd be used to it by now. It's already been a few hours. Maybe these pictures aren't for you—maybe... they're for me," I chuckled.

"That's NOT the point!" she exclaimed. "They're images of me and not necessarily for you to have, unless I give them to you. I own them. They're of my image," she retorted.

Enjoying the banter, I added, "You're in a public place. I'm taking pictures of nature, and you just happen to be in the way. It's not my fault. It's not like I could ask you to move out of the way all the time; it wouldn't be practical, nor polite! I can Photoshop you out of them later, if you want. No worries, you'll love these pics!"

"Yeah… you better Photoshop them, whatever that is!" she laughed.

We talked about every topic coming to mind. Reminiscing about the food in Thailand, the traffic we didn't miss, the shopping, and the people we knew in school. We laughed and chuckled the entire time. As we spoke, we watched the waves rolling onto shore, spawned by the passing ferry barely visible on the horizon. The more we talked, the more we both realized we had so much in common. Talking with her was as effortless as talking to myself; her responses were exactly what I was thinking most of the time. I enjoyed getting much more than single word responses during our conversation.

At one point, I convinced her to stand up and lean over onto the grassy bank to strike a few natural poses. She did so jokingly. As she posed for me, I found it difficult to believe that she had never modeled while in Thailand. She was a natural! Even I had taken advantage of the few opportunities presented to me. That one advertisement I did that went viral, resulting in my image being plastered on the sides of buses and buildings, printed on the pages of magazines and newspapers, and even a spot or two on television and in movie theater commercials. Quite the experience that was! Had she modeled, undoubtedly, she would've been a star and her life may have been much different. In fact, had I told her how I felt about her back then, both of our lives may have turned out completely different. Who's knows for sure… I guess that's life.

Occasionally, Leif stood on the rocks nearby shaking his seaweed laden fur to dry himself, sprinkling—no, dousing us in this process. Yep, this confirmed for us, the water was freezing cold! We laughed together at this spectacle.

"Eeek Leif, the water is freezing cold!" Erika yelled.

I leaned over quietly, keeping my distance, saying, "Really? Let me see!" looking at my chest, "Nope, they don't seem to be cold," I blurted, before looking over at hers.

She slapped my shoulder then brought her palms up to her chest, crossing them covering her chest, "There's nothing to see here, pervert!"

We both laughed.

"Pervert," I repeated, "That's harsh!"

"Ohhh, you love it!" she said admonishing me.

The sun was now gaining height in the sky, shimmering off the water. In the distance, another ferry was making its way to wherever it was heading and was the probable cause of the sudden yet constant flow of slightly larger waves preening the shoreline. I stood up momentarily, daring to venture away from Erika's side. Stretching my legs, I balanced myself atop some large rocks watching the waves splash between my legs.

"If you fall into that water, you're going to freeze! Did you bring a change of clothes?" she joked.

"Nope, I'll borrow yours," I responded.

"How are you going to walk back through the woods in soaking wet clothes?" she bellowed as the waves made her words slightly difficult to hear.

"Like I said, I'll borrow your clothes!" I quipped.

"Fat chance!" she snapped. This brief exchange led to an awkward silence. "Come on, let's go!"

She attached the leash and after shaking his fur to his content, off we darted with Leif in the lead. He bounced in and out of the water, onto and off the grassy bank. He knew exactly where were heading.

Following the grassy shoreline, the sun highlighted an area at the edge of the wood line, which ended at a private sandy beach hosting the crystal blue lapping waters. It was low tide. Erika headed toward the beach, exclaimed and pointed, "There it is! The sandy shores of the Baltic Sea like nothing you're going to see anywhere else in the world!"

Leif, still in the lead, walked out onto a sandbar where the quintessential round water-worn rocks lay positioned by time. As the water washed up to us, in seconds it drew back into the sea. A larger ferry was making its way across the calm horizon. I started taking pictures to take it all in. The cool air was crisp and as fresh as inhaling surgical oxygen. This was turning out to one amazing day.

A short pounce away, I was taking pictures. "I'm already looking at the most beautiful sight I might possibly see; the sandy shores merely add to it," I chuckled.

She brimmed at me once again with her angelic smile. "What are you saying?" she asked.

She most likely never had a fan like me before, most people don't. And most likely she didn't know how to handle it. I hadn't either, so I wasn't about to give her any advice. She let Leif loose, and we followed as he explored the frigid-water cresting the beach. After a while, we walked back to the sandy beachhead and sat down. We sat next to each other on the sand, looking at the spectacular view while Leif continued exploring the water. Counting to three, I leaned toward her, entranced by her beauty, getting as close as I comfortably could, feeling awash with her warmth, without embracing her.

I moved closer to her, grasping her hand in mine, as I leaned in closer. I felt the breath from her nostrils like a warm breeze, gently tickling my upper lip; leaning in even closer. Everything was happening in slow motion. I heard nothing, thought of nothing, saw nothing, felt nothing, but her presence getting closer to mine. Here she was. Here I was. Here we were. My childhood fantasies and thoughts were playing out. Whoever said let the past stay in the past never experienced this! Being in this moment was instantaneously mystical, magical, and a bit overwhelming. I felt as if I was being embraced by angels, comforted by spirits, and warmed by her gentle touch. Her silky blond hair gently brushed against my cheek as we sat together in the powder-soft, white sand enjoying the breeze and the view. The cosmos smiled upon us as did her Nordic Gods, hopefully encouraging her to reciprocate my actions. This was my fairy tale, and now it was real. It was really happening!

She looked into my eyes and faintly hinted, "Dimitri... it's been a long time for me."

I wanted so badly to kiss her, but needed to keep the mood light, not wanting to upset her. I gently leaned over, kissing her cheek.

She pulled away slightly and repeated, "It's been a long time, since I..."

"That's okay," I interjected.

I needed to progress slowly. I didn't want any of my actions to confuse her—being just out of a relationship. Suddenly, her words seemed guarded and her movements conservative. I knew in the past she put very little into words, and she needed someone to talk to, but now she most likely needed someone who would listen. Not needing another person in her life jumping into another relationship, she needed to sort things out and firmly grasp her reality. This way she could make positive and lasting changes to her life on the way to awakening and enlightenment. She needed a light at the end of the tunnel. I wanted to be that light. She needed the ability to decide her future for herself. I had to keep the tone light, bright, and fun. So I did.

"Well," I added, "We've got a serious amount of catching up to do! We'd better get moving before this goes too fast, being we're on a romantic beach and all. It could get embarrassing if someone came along and caught us doing whatever in the sand, as hot as this conversation is getting. Though I know, in Sweden they encourage public nudity!"

"Hahaha, veeerrry funny, that's Denmark, NOT Sweden!" she chortled.

I loved seeing and hearing her unbridled laughter. I enjoyed making her feel comfortable and free. I loved doing this for her. She now sounded proud, unafraid, unashamed, and happy. Since I'd known her, she'd always been reserved and stoic. Not now. She was open and relaxed. She was funny and uninhibited. I loved her attitude. Our interchange suggested neither of us had been this happy for a long time. I know I hadn't been. Not like this. Nor had we been together. Not like this. This was magical.

"Shall we go back to the house and make lunch?" she asked.

"Sure!" I happily agreed and got up, and helped her to her feet.

She called Leif and attached the leash, and once again we all continued walking together. The bird songs greeted us as we meandered into and out of the woods, serenading us with different songs as we walked. I watched Erika, wondering what kind of man wouldn't cherish her. Who would risk losing such a beautiful, loving, skilled Wonder Woman? Why would she ever let that happen to her? I was hoping I could find out over the coming days.

There seemed to be much she wanted to say, but after meeting like this for the first time, it was bound to be awkward for normal humans—I had to give her some time; not that I had much to spare. I had to remember we were friends of sorts, long ago. Well, more like acquaintances, due mostly to my powerful fear of rejection.

As we walked, I remembered how our initial internet conversations came to pass. The sun had set and risen time and time again since then. Initially, I pretty much dismissed all that until talking with Layla. It wasn't until I was in Germany trying to plan the specifics of my visit to Poland that I mentioned to Layla about going to Sweden, to see Erika someday.

I remember Layla convincing me to visit, "It's not expensive going to Stockholm from Germany. You'll be leaving from Frankfurt anyway. You can't do it from the States any cheaper, and you'll be in a similar time zone. You should be able to spare a few days... you're both single and she showed some interest. How long do you think your relationship status will last for both of you? You'd be kicking yourself once again, but this time for the rest of your life! If I were you, I would do it! I wouldn't wait!"

She was so right. So, I made it happen; we made it happen. And now here I was walking next to my Viking Princess. The entire experience was surreal. I remembered back to the class reunion, and the comments tossed about across the fire. If only they knew where I was right now! I thought about that fateful night, looking her up on Facebook, laying the groundwork. The one simple message I sent, "Hey Erika! It's Dimitri from Thailand/ISB—how are you?" that changed everything.

Thank you, Facebook! Untimely with her responses; she always had been sparing with her words. These thoughts made me crack up inside. I sought another of life's radically amazing experiences. What if I had dismissed all the input I received—

those at the castle, and the voices in the night? I'd never have come here, that's for sure.

Now here we were. The two of us alone among nature, with Leif, talking about whatever we wanted. I wanted the timing of everything about this experience to be perfect.

Was my time spent in the military, with the many near-death experiences, the myriad complex trials and tribulations I faced continuing but never culminating over all the years, for no apparent reason? Is all of this related to destiny? It was just this morning that we met in the hotel lobby and I now felt like I'd known her for years. The disparate years were completely inconsequential to me, though both of us experienced so much separately. My emotions ran rampant. I felt energized! My insides were on fire! I watched her every move and listened to her every word as if she would reveal to me the secrets to her universe. I was enjoying this roller coaster ride of emotions, in particular.

We walked and talked, tracing our route back by the grassy shoreline, through the moss-carpeted forest, through the pasturelands back toward the house. She confided in me how her relationship staled, and how now her life was seemingly going nowhere. Her ex- had become buried in his work, emotionally distant, and relentlessly selfish with his time and money. Her sole joy rested within her children. Boy, didn't I know this storyline all too well. This seems all too common in many societies, as well. Both of us in our own environments, in separate cultures, in separate countries, were experiencing basically the same turmoil. She exhibited the qualities of someone who felt completely unappreciated.

Why some people, metaphorically, spend so much time grooming their lawns instead of their relationships is distressing. If people treated their lawns as they did their relationships, their lawns would turn brown, dry up and wither away, leaving those left behind destitute, depressed, lacking confidence.

We all deserve much more out of life. I didn't want this perfect form of a woman to feel trapped in a life where she wasn't happy. I didn't want her to refuse to at least try to be happy; it was as if she thought she didn't deserve it! Maybe she had settled for relative unhappiness instead of true happiness, becoming accustomed to it. Her perspective may have become not to expect life to be perfect. Maybe she had nearly given up on having happiness in her life. I'd been through all that. And I knew how it felt!

But I ventured beyond that point, and I now knew that true happiness in life is possible. We merely have to define it and then find it.

I often wonder why some people consistently attach themselves to the same type of people who don't value them. While living for our children is a noble endeavor, it often seems to suspend living our own lives, not improving them. Not knowing how long we have in our one lifetime, it's best not to squander any of the time we have. Maybe it would be best for all involved if everyone lived for themselves, while focusing on their significant others. In doing so, this would benefit their families and their children simultaneously. It would be best to accept the Romantic Love we all deserve... lest we choose to be with the wrong person, for the wrong reasons, and die knowing so.

I wondered if Erika, like so many women, picked the bad boys. Choosing men who don't have the capacity or interest to romantically love them as they need. Not knowing or caring how to express romantic love or even caring to do so. Some people often see only what they want to see in people, not seeing people as they really are, until it's too late; derailing life as we know it and expect it to be. I wanted Erika to have a partner who expressed Romantic Love and could communicate it as she would understand. The book, *The Five Love Languages*, discusses in great detail understanding the qualities of Romantic Love by how we communicate and comprehend it.

A focused search for Romantic Love would yield more than simply playing the childhood card game, Go Fish, with romance, and letting the cards fall where they may. She could improve her world by romantically finding and loving who she should Romantically Love. I wanted her to recognize her relationship mistakes, rectify these as quickly as possible, remember them, and never repeat this cycle. I wanted her to move forward in life, not backward or sideways. I didn't want her to languish in no-man's-land.

I wanted Erika to understand that nothing remains the same within this dynamic universe. Everything is in a constant state of change. With this being said, understanding that relationships are typically in a constant state of change is significant. If they change into something no longer benefiting everyone, or any one person involved, changing it is more significant and necessary than we realize. Eventually, one person begins to divest themselves from this situation. It is accurately described in the sentence, "The one who controls a relationship, is the one who cares least." I'd been there, avoiding: answering the phone, going home, sleeping in the same bed as our significant other, going to school, work, or to social functions in order not to have to face our endlessly grim reality.

Erika was no stranger to knowing that significant life changes can bring forth negative relationship changes. She seemed to prefer to ignore these, rather than confront and process them, to change the result for a better outcome. While I've often told people, "There is great personal merit in living a perfect fantasy, rather than facing a screwed-up reality. Eventually, it's bound to catch up with us." Erika was living in one of these ruts. When I was in a similar situation and had nobody to turn to, this was difficult to process. I'd like to be that someone to help her process this.

The relationship plight becomes especially difficult once a relationship, for whatever reason, starts dying or dies altogether. Moving away from our partners, out of the shared dwelling space, forcing children to process decisions they are neither prepared to make, nor completely understand. As difficult as it can be, it's surely better than living separate lives while bonded together, solely because of the existence of children. This, creating an outward facade of happiness. Many people experience the isolation and desolation inside this no-man's-land of separation and divorce, along with the legal proceedings and emotional baggage that attaches to us like barnacles. It forces us to deal with a confusing, demeaning, enervating, and depressing existence; this is true within most any country or culture in the contemporary world. I wanted to ease Erika's progress, making it a smoother transition once recognizing her circumstances.

We all try making a better life for ourselves—at least we hope this is possible. It became clearer to me as she spoke that I could help her with this. Thinking a situation will NEVER get better, dashing any spark of hope for a better, more emotionally fulfilling life, is a dire circumstance for anyone to face. And it's extremely difficult to face alone. Unfortunately, this seems to be much more prevalent in modern times in every part of the world.

The stress of this situation inevitably takes a personal toll on all involved emotionally, spiritually, and physically. It's imperative to change such a situation before the stress becomes physically debilitating for everyone involved. Sometimes nobody is to blame, sometimes everyone is to blame—life just happens. Whatever the reasons, it's best to bury the negative and search forward for the positive. Admittedly, nobody is going to live forever. Life is short. And it seemed that mine in Sweden was getting shorter every day.

"What are you thinking about?" she asked.

"Nothing really."

"Uh-huh. You were being quiet," she replied.

Once we arrived back at the house, I noticed how dirty and salty Leif was. Without prompting, I took him around to the backyard, asking Erika where she kept the garden hose. Washing this polar bear would be no simple task. It was quite the task with the freezing tap water. Thankfully, he stood still. As I washed him off and cleaned the mud, saltwater, ferns, and moss from his fur, Erika saw me through the window and laughed. She brought me some dog shampoo, along with a glass of freshly squeezed lemonade. I stopped what I was doing, shocked by someone bringing me such a thoughtful gift. I never before experienced this, although I dreamed of it millions of times. At last, he was ready for drying so Erika brought some towels over from her perch on the deck. I dried him while she sat nearby watching the spectacle. It was like washing and drying a horse.

"Thank you so much, Dimitri. You really shouldn't be doing all this work on your vacation," she jokingly sobbed. "Though you do seem to be enjoying yourself," she added.

"I am! This isn't work. This is both heaven and vacation to me. So, would that be a heavenly vacation?" We both got a chuckle.

While I finished towel drying the horse-hund, Erika climbed the stairs up to the deck for a permanently dry perspective. She immediately started laughing at me from her wooden perch overlooking the backyard as Leif sprayed me, shaking off, attempting to completely dry his fur.

"You missed a spot, Leif!" she yelled. "Sorry, I should've warned you he always does that when he's nearly done."

"No, he didn't miss any spots. It merely looks that way from way, way, way over there!"

I sprayed her with the hose but in an instant of clairvoyance she momentarily ran inside. I finished my chore, releasing Leif from my clutches. Up the deck stairs he ran, flying straight through the deck door into the house in a flash. I followed him only part of the way up the stairway, joining Erika, sitting next to her on the stoop.

"Thanks a lot, I hate cleaning him after our walks. That was so helpful! I rarely let him get that dirty. He seemed to have a lot of fun," she said.

"No problem," I confirmed.

She interlocked her arm through mine and lay her head gently on my shoulder. At that inauspicious moment, her cellphone rang and she sprang up to answer it. She became visibly upset as she looked at the caller ID before she answered.

"Ohhhh, arrrgh! I don't need this now," she voiced.

She got up and walked into the yard. It could only have been one person; I knew the look. Even worse, I lived it more than a few times. I heard a male voice yelling through the earpiece from where I sat. Shortly afterward, she answered back. I looked at her blank stare.

She shrugged and mouthed to me, "Sorry."

I reflected on my own experience, wondering what makes Romantic Love turn so bad. Is it a lack of respect? Budding irreverence and animosity? A change of physical or hormonal chemistry? Or simply just relationship burn-out?

I shook my head in disapproval, whispering, "Tell him you're busy and you'll call him back. Be polite, but forceful," I instructed.

She mouthed to me, "I can't!"

Approaching her, I said, "Do it! It doesn't matter who it is! Do it for you!" I insisted.

She looked into my eyes without blinking, as if to muster the strength to do what I suggested… or rather, urged. To my surprise she did it.

She hung up the phone and smiled through her agony, muttering, "Wow, I've never done that before—I don't like being yelled at, especially for no reason," she said.

"Nobody likes it. You shouldn't let anyone make you feel that way," I said. "You don't have to put up with it."

She responded with a simple, "Thank you… that felt good. I won't anymore."

After a few moments of reflection, we returned to the stoop, sitting, enjoying each other's company, along with the view of the grassy hills behind her house. We watched as a deer couple approached, eating whichever vegetation they chose, frolicking in the cool fall air. We watched silently. Once again, she interlocked her arm into mine, gently resting her head on my shoulder.

After the deer departed, she asked, "Why does life have to be so difficult? Why do people have to be so difficult to get along with?"

I paused, thinking briefly, then said, "You're not difficult. I'm not difficult. Not everyone is difficult. I guess those who are, are just wired that way; or at least it's how they react. Nothing is going to change them."

Unfortunately, I knew this universal truth from personal experience! After a time, she led me inside the house, calling out to Leif, explaining to me, "I don't want him on the bed all wet."

I helped her feed Leif and the cats. Thankfully, these were just typical house cats, not little white tigers as I half expected; these cats were invisible and remained undetectable to me. Most cats I know come running when food is poured into their empty glass bowls. Not these cats.

She put on some music, and for our lunch she made the most amazing dish of Chanterelle mushrooms I'd ever tasted. As she previously stated, she really picked them from her secret forest mushroom sanctuary before my visit, storing them in the freezer in a non-descript, zip locked bag. She was careful to hide these from any thieves who may come prowling to steal her secret stash.

"So, what do you think?" she asked as we enjoyed the feast sitting at the modest European dinner table.

"Are you kidding? I could eat this for the rest of my life. Just this!" I admitted.

"They taste even better when they're fresh," she emphasized.

"So, I'll be invited back to discover this through empirical investigation when they're in season?" I pleaded.

She hesitated, "Of course…"

She also served cheese, caviar, smoked salmon, fresh vegetables, fresh bread and wine.

I told her as we sat there eating, just the two of us, "Wow! You're an amazing chef."

"I should be," she snapped, "For all the money I spent at Örebro University getting my culinary degree—I was the honor graduate in my class. I moved to this town by the sea because it was a better environment to raise the kids. My dream someday is to have my own bistro, but we'll see if THAT ever happens!"

"Wow, you're really not helping me," I smiled.

"Yeah?… and what did you mean by those four statements earlier? See? You thought I'd forget," she said poking me.

"No, I didn't think you'd forget, I hoped you would," I jovially explained, continuing the explanation.

"You should really be trying to convince me why I shouldn't be so fascinated by you. With what you say, what you do, and with everything I learned about you today, all of it only makes me want to get to know you even more. Sorry, it had to be said."

Lightening the mood, she jumped up, suggesting, "Let's clear the table and move over to the couch."

I interrupted, "First, let me show you the treasures of the 'nothings' I brought for you and the little Princesses, inside my bag of nothings." I walked over to the corner, retrieving the bag of goodies I left on the chair by the fireplace, handing it to her.

One by one, she revealed the treasures from the bag. Her eyes lit brightly with enthusiasm.

"Oh my God, I love chocolate! Thank you so much!" she said.

The big box is for the Little Princesses and the big chocolate bars are for you," I instructed.

"Nah-ah," she interrupted. "It's ALL for me. I'll be happy to share some of it with them, but only if they're good."

We both laughed.

"Please don't get sick eating all this at once. It's supposed to last all year," I said.

Again, we laughed.

"Come on, let's bring some of these over to the couch and start our dessert feast!" she sparked.

She sashayed with her presents over to the couch. Placing them down on the nearby coffee table, she wandered through the room lighting all the different sized candles, then stoked the fire in the fireplace. The room grew slightly brighter with each candle she lit. I followed her into the dimly lit room, hoping not to trip over any invisible hassocks or kitty cats blocking my path, bringing with me our glasses of wine and water. I set them on the coffee table. She selected some slow mood music, dimmed the lights in the kitchen, and brought a pot of hot tea to the coffee table, seamlessly joining me on the couch.

We sat together enjoying the company, taking in the ambiance of the moment and the aroma of softly scented candles, and opened with a bit of chit-chat.

"How old are the girls?" I asked.

"They're twelve..." she said hesitating, "The same age as we were when we first met in Thailand."

I turned toward her, looking directly into her eyes, saying, "Speaking of Thailand, I've got to tell you a few of my secrets. Please don't say anything, just listen. It's taken me 33 years to get to this point," I pleaded.

I silently counted down from five seconds, whispering to myself, "Here goes!" and I started. "Since the very first time I saw you, not only did I want to get to know you, I felt I absolutely had to. Weird, huh? The past 33 years of my life have really been good, but I've always been missing something. I've been missing someone. Someone with whom to do the things we did today and talk about all the things we spoke about. If we had known each other for those years we missed, I can't help feeling it would've been phenomenal! It still can be! I'd love to have this perfect day last for a long time and repeat it as often as we can. I'd like to see you smiling next to me and in front of my camera. Like you said before, 'Anything is possible.' I want to watch you speak Swedish with your girls. It would be fun to learn to speak with all of you in your native language. And I love this culture. You are quite possibly the nicest person I know... the nicest person I've ever known."

I hesitated a bit and continued, "If I said all this 33 years ago, it might've sounded crazy; it probably still does. Planning my trip to see you in less than a week, was a bit crazy, I'm willing to admit that. But the window of opportunity opened, and I had to enter. Our lives have not worked out in our own countries, within our own cultures, and with the people we've had in our lives. I'm only saying it's something to think about. I know I could make you happier than you've ever experienced before because you deserve it."

Smiling, I added, "Just a thought," chuckling to lighten the mood.

She interjected, "It wouldn't be difficult since I don't remember receiving any heartfelt presents for quite a while."

Her comment nearly brought tears to my eyes and pained my heart. How could she have been treated this way? But, if she hadn't... I wouldn't have been seated next to her, staring into her soulful eyes.

Further lightening the mood, I remembered the wood carvings. "Do you mind if I give you a little something else I picked up for you in Poland? It's just a little something."

"More chocolate? I think we already have enough for the year," she jokingly mocked.

"Nope, it's not chocolate."

"Okay... if you want to," she whispered.

I retrieved the little package from my camera bag, telling her the story of the street artisan I met in Warsaw who carved these wooden characters. I handed her the simply wrapped, carved wooden angel.

As she unwrapped it, I said, "That is you, the Swedish Angel. And this one [as I unwrapped mine], is me—the Silent Soldier."

She immediately sparked, "I know what we can do... why don't you keep the Soldier with you and I'll keep the Angel with me and it'll be our challenge to get them back together again."

She grasped the Angel and playfully walked it across my leg, up my torso, down my hand over to the Soldier in my hand, and started mimicking an Angel's voice. It was so cute. We both laughed and laughed at our impromptu puppet show. I'd never been happier.

We sat on the couch, just the two of us, listening to the slow, modern, jazz music filling the warm air with ambiance. The candles cast a warm glow of light into every corner of the room, reflecting off her pearly white teeth as she smiled. When she moved, the candlelight cast shadows across her shoulder-length blonde hair, as sweet as cotton candy to my senses.

The fire danced in her eyes and crackled as Swedish air embraced us with soothing comfort. A multitude of candles provided heat, ambient light, and romance. The dancing shadows from these tiny flickering flames enhanced the entire experience. Occasionally, we giggled as Leif sighed loudly, a testament to how relaxing and perfect this setting was, even from his dog perspective. After we finished the wine, she poured us some herbal tea.

"Where's the blanket?" I hinted to her.

"Which blanket?" she asked.

"The one you mentioned cuddling under by the warmth of a fire on a cold, winter's night in your Facebook message."

"It's not winter," she laughed. "And it wasn't in one of my messages," she blushed.

"It was too! And as cold as it's getting outside, it may as well be winter!" I responded. "It was in one of your first messages!" my voice danced. Again, we both laughed. I looked into her eyes and softly said, "I've had this overpowering urge to lean over and kiss you ever since I saw you this morning. It's required every ounce of strength and restraint within me not to do it."

"Oh really," she remarked. Quickly standing up she said, "Would you like more tea? We probably shouldn't rush into anything, since we're separated by an entire ocean." She playfully tried to lighten the mood by continuing the conversation as she walked into the kitchen. "You probably couldn't handle me anyway!" she said, peeking around the corner, smiling. I nearly choked on my tea.

"What?" My mind raced to process the images she instantaneously implanted into my mind. I didn't believe what I was hearing within the endless feasibilities of meanings, thinking maybe her translations into English weren't congruent with mine.

"What do you mean—what?" she retorted.

I raised my voice so she could hear me from her place in the kitchen. "I could if you let me! I've heard I'm great—their words, not mine!"

"Maybe you just can't handle the truth, and they didn't want to hurt your feelings!" she yelled from the back of the kitchen.

"What??" I yammered.

"You heard me, and I didn't stutter either!" she affirmed.

I stammered, momentarily thinking of words to follow, "Uhhh..."

She laughed and said, "What's wrong? Cat got your tongue?" gliding slowly back into the family room, taking her place beside me after refilling the teapot and bringing out some more delectable items plus desserts.

"Here, try these. The kids weren't fond of them. Tell me what you think."

"What do you mean I couldn't handle you!?" I repeated.

"I meant you probably couldn't handle me, you know... I can go all night! I know you're in good shape and all, but most guys can't do that! And maybe, I would eventually demand the same of you... every night! You simply couldn't keep up!" she said in a playful, seductress tone of voice, leaning over toward me, displaying her pearly white teeth.

I couldn't believe my ears! "Shut the front door! Excuse me?" I interjected. "My Equestrian Kin we saw in the pasture this morning would vehemently disagree with you! And if you'd care to show me whatever this truth is, you're talking about… I'm sure I could handle you! To both your satisfaction and your udder amazement! With double D's!" I joked.

"What are you talking about double D's? Really?" she smiled, raising her eyebrows.

"Yeah, I meant utter amazement, not udder amazement. You see an udder is a—"

"—I know the difference between the two. I'm not stupid, you know, I'm foreign. Well, not when I'm in this country," she sparkled.

She continued, "And I knew I didn't have double D's, I'm more large C's!" she laughed tugging her shirt away from her body looking down the front of it.

"What are you looking at?" I blurted, "Let me see!"

"Uh-ahhhh!" she coyly snapped her shirt back into place against her chest.

I continued, "You can go all night, huh? What a coincidence! We have all night! Sounds like a challenge to me—I'm up for it! Besides, I need to be given a fair chance to prove myself, especially after such a poor accusation!" I insisted.

"A fair chance?" she asked. "This is not the States, you know. You're in my country now and you don't necessarily get a fair anything in my country. You're a visitor here, remember?"

She voiced a playful "Reeeooor" cat-like sound, and still no cats were in sight. She stood up, slowly crossing over me momentarily straddling me with her legs, instead of walking around the other side of the coffee table as I expected, looking down at me. "I'll be right back," she whispered.

I watched her perfect form inside her tightly fitted jeans, as she walked out of sight and once again into the darkened kitchen. As I watched, she re-appeared into the candle-lit room, sauntering toward me. She brought with her more boiling water in a small pot.

Straddling me once again, standing with the pot of water in her hands, "Careful, this is hot!" she whispered.

"Yes, you are!" I muttered.

"Excuse me?" she said.

Not knowing what exactly to say, I blurted out, "Where did you get those American-sized coffee mugs? Thank you for not using those tiny European thimble-sized, cup-things. I really don't like those—where did you get these?"

Without missing a beat, she leaned over toward me on a kissing-type approach, disclosing into my ear, "IKEA—we have those here in Europe, you know."

We both laughed so hard I spilled a little of my tea as I drank from the mug.

"So, what did you think of the food? You never said," she asked.

"I think the dishes are all fantastic, like you."

It was nearing 9:00 pm, and time for another uncomfortable moment in suspense, as we stared into each other's eyes wondering what the other would do, or say, next.

The deadbolt on the front door thwacked open and the sound of little angels' voices instantly filled the downstairs foyer.

She said a bit surprised, "The kids are back home—I wonder why? They're supposed to be staying at their friend's house tonight. Hmmm, I wonder if everything is okay," she pouted. "Lucky for you! I could've killed you with passion," she said as she playfully pawed at my chest, "Reeeooor!" she purred.

As she stood, I rose to meet her challenge and drew my nose uncomfortably close to hers, as if I was going to kiss her, "And I'd have welcomed it! What a great way to go!" I responded, returning her smile.

She continued teasing and tickling me with her long slender fingers as she moved from the couch, waiting to greet the children from a perch near the top of the stairs. She motioned with her hand at her side for me to stand next to her.

Then she outstretched her hand, clasping my hand in hers in one smooth motion and said, "Come on, you may as well meet them since they're here." As I gripped her hand, I was in heaven. To my amazement, she had initiated this contact.

From our perch she looked down the steep wooden stairs, sleekly yelling downstairs in her native tongue. They both responded.

"Ahhhh," she gasped, "Their friend was feeling sick and, they didn't feel comfortable staying there, so they came back here. It's not a far walk. And it's a safe neighborhood. That's why we live here," she quickly stated as if responding to the surprised expression on my face as I raised my eyebrows.

"I hope it's nothing contagious," I said.

"God, I hope not," she sparked. My, you are a worry wart— that's the expression, right?" she added. You shouldn't put that idea out into the universe."

"Yes, thank you. That's the expression," I added. "Who's the wart now?" I whispered.

Poking me in my side, she laughed.

She laughed after a few exchanges in Swedish with the kids saying, "The kids are really shy to meet you, with you being an American. I don't know why they're like that. But they're coming upstairs. Is that okay?"

"Of course, it's okay," I whispered.

She turned to me, whispering, "They're twins. Identical."

Apparently, being an American still involves quite a mystique to Swedish children their age. She finally coaxed them upstairs. Soon after, the sound of the little teen feet came pounding up the thick wooden stairs. The two beautiful Princesses with long natural blonde hair presented themselves, speaking Swedish as she posed them in front of me.

This is Nora, "Say hello, Nora," and this is Fiona, "Say hello, Fiona,"

"*Hej*," they both said in unison.

She corrected them, "In English, please."

Her demeanor changed immediately, displaying qualities of both the matriarch and a strong patriarch of this little family segment. I hadn't seen this side of her. She always had some unexplainable energy attracting me; she still had it. Again, she impressed me.

"Hello," they streamed in unison and soon melted away into the kitchen where they continually giggled, getting something to eat from the refrigerator.

Erika grasped my hand, leading me back to the couch in the family room, sitting with the little wooden angel in her hand, patting the open seat next to her. "Come, sit. Bring your little Soldier too," she laughed.

"How could I not?" I whispered, as I grasped the Soldier from his place on the coffee table.

She looked shockingly at me, "I know exactly what you mean, you know. My English is pretty good," she said, whispering, squinting at me.

I presented the little wooden Soldier on top of my leg and once again she played with the two figurines before putting them down on the coffee table, then joining the living Angels in the kitchen. While they were working in the kitchen, I sat, looking for evidence of these supposed house cats. They were nowhere in sight. Leif joined me, pawing me for attention. After much discussion, the three came into the family room with mugs of hot chocolate.

"Come, come, my little lovelies, Mr. Dimitri has brought us a bunch of chocolates from Germany!" she reported to the children.

Fiona came the quickest, saying in perfect English, "German chocolate is the best, you know."

"And that's why I brought it. I knew you would like only the best!" I jokingly scoffed.

Erika watched my comfortable exchange with them in amazement. Grasping the wooden angel and Soldier from their perch on the coffee table, she asked in both English and Swedish, "Did you two see these little people Dimitri brought from Poland? Cute, huh?" They both reveled in the lightweight and detail inspiring the creation of the objects.

The two spoke very little English, nonetheless, they attempted. What little they said they spoke in perfect diction and pronunciation. With Erika translating, from time to time intervening into the Swedish sets of conversation, we all had a magnificent time talking, laughing and just hanging out. These girls were fabulous. As I expected them to be.

Erika said, "Mr. D brought his camera and took pictures of your Mamma today. Do you want to see them?" she proudly asked the two. "Would you mind?" she asked me.

Agreeing, Erika and I sat on the couch with the two girls on each of our sides near the coffee table. I grabbed my camera and using the flip-out display, started showing them the pictures.

Erika said, "Hey I didn't know the camera screen could flip out like that! How come you didn't do that before?" she playfully scowled at me as our private joke. Again, she squinted her eyes at me.

Not responding, I just smiled at her.

I showed off the photos I took of their "Mamma" earlier that day and even a few closeups of a banana slug we saw. They were in awe.

"Imagine if you erased them, we'd have nothing to look at," I jokingly scoffed.

The girls said, "Wow! Mamma, these are fantastic. Can we get copies?"

"Yes, of course," I assured them.

In time, they asked to see my photos from Germany and Poland. I also amazed them with those photos. After a while, they went downstairs so "we could be alone" as they explained in broken English. They were so cute as they interacted with us together. This experience instantly transformed our relationship into a solid friendship.

No longer did I need to have her in my life for selfish reasons; now I wanted her to be in it. And, I completely understood the difference.

Seeing it was getting late, I told her she should put the kids to bed and spend some time with them, as much as it killed me to say it. She agreed, "You're the most thoughtful person I know."

Retrieving my camera bag, I headed downstairs toward the door to put on my shoes and make a graceful exit. I really wanted her to stop me. As she followed me to the door, she hastily jumped in front of me, grasping my hand in hers. She turned, facing me, smiling, wrapping her arms around me in a warm embrace. Grasping me in her clutches, she rested her cheek against mine.

Since the front door was right next to the kids' bedroom, she whispered gently, "It's so very good to see you again, Dimitri. I'll be seeing you again soon, okay?"

"Yep, in the morning, right?" I confirmed. I put on my coat, scarf, and hat.

She just smiled as she opened the door. I slipped out into the night. She closed the door behind me so quietly I didn't even hear it.

I made the ever so familiar lonely walk back to the car in the cold, still night air, and endured the short ride back to the hotel parking lot, alone. It was unpleasant at best. I gathered the few items from the car and headed for the front of the hotel. As I entered the lobby, my favorite hotel clerk, Nickolas, greeted me.

"Heeeey manh, how'd it go today?"

My tongue unleashed as I rambled, "It was perfect, everything was perfect. We went for a long walk in the woods for hours and hours. As the weather cleared, I took some amazing pictures of her along with the captivating scenery. We walked and talked seemingly forever; she's in wonderful shape and can even keep up with me. We walk at the same fast pace too! This never happens for me. I met her dog and after the long walk I washed him off since he got dirty walking in the woods and from playing in the water. I mistakenly met her kids, she's an amazing cook—well, she's an academy-trained chef. Lunch was marvelous, as was dinner. And, we have the same taste in music. Her kids are perfect. Everything was perfect. Completely perfect! This never happens to me—ever!" I emphatically explained.

"Sounds great! I'm happy for you—and you have two more days!"

"Thanks! Yup... two more," I answered.

"It's time for you to get to sleep and get ready for another perfect breakfast in the morning to start your day out right! I think it'll work out fer ya," he added.

"Thanks, I appreciate that, Nickolas. You're right, I'd better go upstairs and get ready for tomorrow. I don't want to have puffy raccoon eyes," I responded. "Hey, if she comes by tonight, you know my room number, so you can tell her, right?" I joked.

"Of course, I'll have a key waiting for her!"

We both laughed as I walked up the stairs to my room.

The room was a tad cold, so I took a hot shower before going to sleep. It always feels incredibly exhilarating sliding between fresh, clean sheets after a hot shower. It's especially comforting when it's cold outside. As I completed my nightly routine, I got dressed in my sweats and t-shirt, resting on the bed staring up at the mirrored ceiling thinking, "What a waste of a king-sized bed and a king-sized mirror with only myself to look at." I thought of the perfect day we had, and looked forward to another. Scratching out a few thoughts in rhythmic verse using the notepad on the nightstand, I grew sleepy. Finally, I closed my eyes, welcoming sleep.

~ 18 ~

Swedish Nights In Gale

I hadn't been sleeping long when I heard a soft knocking at my door. Once awake, I waited for verification. There it was again. Turning on the nightstand light, I got out of bed and shuffled to the door. Dazed and groggy, I looked through the peephole and saw Erika smiling. Ever so lightly, she leaned her forehead against the door. Her coat was loosely draped over her shoulders. I couldn't believe my eyes. I grasped the doorknob, slid back the locking bolt, and opening the door, I welcomed her inside.

"Is everything okay?" I whispered.

Without hesitation, she sauntered in with a few steps past the threshold, standing in front of me with a coy smile. She finally whispered, "Everything is fine. The kids are asleep... they're fine. I shouldn't stay too long. I missed you."

As I reached around her, closing the door, she hugged me and nestled her nose into the nape of my neck. Feeling her soft, warm arms embracing me, she whispered, "I needed a hug."

I responded, "You can have as many as you want."

Slipping off her shoes, we stood at nearly the same height, though I was slightly taller. I drew her in. She hugged me tight. I couldn't help myself, turning my head slightly, I gently kissed the nape of her lightly scented neck. She giggled momentarily, pulling away as I breathed lightly and warmly from my nostrils, tickling her ear. Nibbling at her earlobe, tracing my nose downward, gently kissing her neck, we touched noses. Tilting my head while pursing my lips, I closed my eyes and leaned toward her. Our lips touched ever so gently. She drew me in even closer, grasping the back of my neck with her silky palm, gliding her alluring, slim fingers lightly from my hairline to my shoulders. It felt as if a million feathers were brushing over my entire body. She smiled, leaned toward me, offering the tip of her tongue to mine. After 33 years, this was really happening. The moment I hoped for, I prayed for, and waited for was finally here.

I started melting into her presence as she leaned away slightly, looking at my bedroom ensemble in the dim light.

Laughing quietly, she asked, "Is that really what you wear to bed?"

"No," I explained, "This is what I wear to answer the door in the middle of the night."

"Well... well..." she coyly added, tugging at my shirt playfully. "Show me what you usually wear to bed, and I'll show you what I wear," her voice focused and sultry, advertising intent.

Grasping her hand in mine, I led her toward the bed. She sleeked in behind me, removing her coat, draping it loosely over the chair, a few steps from the bed. As I turned to face her, she moved toward me, closer, then closer, saying nothing. She was gorgeous, even in the dim light. She continued to approach until we were close enough to slow dance. With both hands grasping her by the waist, embracing her, I moved us toward the wall a few feet from the bed.

As my lips touch hers, we kissed sensuously, adventurously. Reveling in this experience, the energy between us ignited. We kissed faster and uncontrollably. I felt the crease of her elbow around the back of my neck as she clung tightly to me; I drew her into me.

She smiled gracefully, breathing into my ear. Stepping backward, pulling her close to my chest, we moved together toward the foot of the bed. Our bodies perfectly synched, nesting together with no detectable space between us. She playfully nudged me backward. Sliding her feet forward, holding me close within our embrace. Our bodies mirrored each other's movements in a well-choreographed, well-rehearsed tango. We were inseparable. The warmth of her body emanated through her scantily clothed body. I felt the warmth of her breath prancing across my upper lip. Our tongues gently and endlessly intertwined.

Edging backward as we kissed, when I felt the bedspread brushing at my calves, she stopped kissing me. Gazing into my eyes, poking my chest, with a slight nudge she whispered, "Down." Complying with her directive, I sat on the edge of the bed, drawing her in close. Raising her knees up one at a time, she sat straddling me. Her firm breasts brushed against my face. Looking up toward her, I looked even deeper into her eyes. We were both transfixed.

Provocatively, she unbuttoned her blouse, opening it, wrapping it around my cheeks, exposing her naked upper torso. Pressing her chest into my face, we nestled. Her skin was silky. She was as perfect as I imagined she would be. Without giving me time to respond verbally or physically, she pursed her lips, responding with her dimpled smile and a slight nod of her head. She slid slightly down my lap, grasping the sides of my t-shirt, slipping it over my head, saying, "Off."

She questioned with her eyebrows extended to the peak of their range, her forehead barely wrinkled. "Uh-huh!" she whispered as her smile turned devilish.

Again, she straddled me, peering over me with her soft, sleek, perfectly French tipped manicured fingernails pressing into my back. Her scratching didn't draw blood, but it almost did; I loved the sensation. Her actions spoke louder than her words as she reached down to the bottom of my back with her fingernails. She scratched all the way back up to my shoulders, giving me chills as her fingernails drew close to the base of my neck.

"Reeeooor!" she growled in a cat-like whisper. I'd never seen her like this before, nor had I imagined it—but I loved every second!

Passion and desire embraced my thoughts. I was in this moment touched by her physically, mentally and spiritually. All my senses were alive with energy and awareness. It was amazing to be alive like this. I never felt a supernatural tinge electrifying my entire body. It was magical, intense, and delicately natural, instinctually brilliant as the night crawled on. Hoping, believing, trusting this moment could last forever.

My spirit screamed out to the universe. Her beauty, intensity, and warmth enveloped my body, steeping me in energetic light, perfect passion, and deep desire. Purposeful pleasure and mindful melodies of tranquility and grace caressed my aura. Captivated by animalistic anomalies surrounded in electrifying ecstasy, sparked by this one Viking Angel, drove me to absolute limits within. Her actions touched every follicle, every pore by her presence, every thought by her whispered words, and every hope by her image in the subtle light. This is how glorious life can be. This is the stunning power of Romantic Love, I thought.

Her shoulder-length blonde hair tickled my nose and cheeks. She stared at me with her ocean blue eyes so deep. Arching her back, she let her blouse slide from her shoulders onto the floor behind her. I held her warm body close as she pressed tightly against mine. Leaning forward, pushing me back onto the warm, fluffy, down comforter, neither one of us restraining our sexual excitement with laughter. We giggled, laughed, and kissed, then kissed, laughed, and giggled.

Our breathing was heavy, and our actions silenced our words. I mirrored hers and she mirrored mine. I looked up into the ceiling mirror to watch her naked upper torso in the shadows of the dim light by the nightstand. I couldn't help but take in all of her with each of my senses. I committed to long-term memory every zeptosecond, minute, sight, scent, sound, touch, taste, and feel. I wanted to be perfect for her, and I wanted to be perfect with her. I had no doubts regarding satisfying her—I let my feelings guide my actions, answering her lead.

Casting my view between the ceiling mirror and her perfect form in front of me, I was grateful for it being there. It provided me a 360-degree perspective interlocking heaven and earth in this space. Moving forward straddling my chest, she leaned over me pinning my hands above my head. As she fell toward me, I arched my back spontaneously closing the distance, pressing my lips against hers. As her breasts brushed against my chest, each cell of my body screamed with unrivaled euphoria.

Playfully rolling her over, taking the dominant position enabled her hands to glide wildly all over my back, sides, and chest. Once again, she grasped my naked back with her fingers spread apart, pressing her manicured nails into my skin, slowly, lightly scratching my back from my waist up to my shoulders with erotic flair. As her fingers explored my body, she left not one cell untouched. She pressed away from me ever so slightly as I looked down at her angelic body. Her long, slender fingers scratched over the front of my shoulders, then down my chest, lightly scratching down toward my navel as we kissed. She twerked her hips, then grabbed at the bow knot of my sweatpants, unlocking it, pulling it loose. Penetrating the seal of my waistband with her skilled fingers, she slid them down and away from my body.

Grasping my buttocks with both hands, nails extended she whispered, "I really like that mirror up there," as she looked up at me.

"I do too… as long as it stays up there!" I added.

We both chuckled.

She hesitated, looking back into the mirror saying, "Nah, it'll stay!"

I responded by kissing her wherever my lips could reach. We both giggled, gaining silent consensus. Not wasting any time, I slid my thumb and forefinger into the top of her jeans, unbuttoning them, sliding the zipper down its full length. She inhaled slightly, giving me unfettered access. Her breath quivered with anticipation as my fingers brushed against her waistband. Her abdominal muscles shivered, her legs gently shook, and entire core pulsated, most likely from the butterflies in her stomach. Guided solely by my thoughts, I let the back of my fingers explore her form. Her skin was soft, smooth, and warm. She exhaled gently, her breath quivering stronger now. Her eyebrows pulsed slightly in the dim light and she flash-frowned, looking at me in anticipation of what was to come. I ensured I satisfied her expectations, as she had already satisfied all of mine.

She took the dominant position hovering over me. She sighed, softly groaning. I dared not to miss the slightest sight. The superficial sound of the cloth gliding down her skin, and her overly positive response exposing her naked buttocks, introduced a sensation imprinted on my mind forever. Inhaling to speed and ease the process, she held her breath for just a few seconds, arching her back, in a slight upward dog then downward dog yoga movement, I slid off her pants onto the floor with my feet.

We both smiled at each other, kissing as we explored each other's form with our eyes, our hands, and our bodies. Her soft blond hair again brushed across my face like angel hair. Her voice growled as her breathing increased. The softness of her touch glided across my body as her kisses drew deeper.

We kissed passionately, entranced. Her naked body felt naturally comforting, seamless underneath mine. Crossing her silky legs behind my lower back and her arms behind my neck, squeezing, drawing me closer than I thought possible. She clenched me. We were together in this moment, truly as one. This is what I hoped for, waited for, and longed for.

The down comforter underneath us provided the insulated nest we needed in the cold room air, our naked bodies radiating heat into it, providing the warmth we felt. Our sole intent now was teasing and pleasing each other. Occasionally, I pushed away from her kisses, looking at her perfectly sculpted body and pure skin tone. The sights, scents, sounds, and sensations were even better than I had ever imagined they would be. She smiled in a way I'll never forget. I didn't take my eyes off her, memorizing each pore, and every turn and curve of her perfectly maintained form. I looked deeply into her eyes and again across her body. She purred and growled slightly as she looked back into my eyes, into my mind and soul. As I looked into hers, I could see the reflection of my eyes looking back at me.

We took turns assuming dominance. She was alight with excitement; we both were. Occasionally pausing, I tickled her flat, firm six-pack with the tip of my nose. Our breathing increased. Her lungs quivered with each new breath as they expanded and contracted. I matched her rhythm and mimicked her sounds. I quickly learned her curves as my tongue slalomed the course of her form. This became exceptionally easier each time, as I learned the route.

Kissing her even more energetically drove her further into a frenzied lust. My actions piqued her anticipation. She scratched her fingernails across my back, harder and more passionately when provided the opportunity. Like two snakes intertwined in a mating ritual, each of our bodies were indiscernible from one another; writhing in pleasure over and over, around each other. Slowly, then swiftly, sliding across each other's warm, naked bodies. Kissing her deeply, she twerked in absolute pleasure. I tasted her neck, passionately nibbled and moved to appreciate her earlobes, then gently breathed through my nostrils into each of her ears while the carnival below was in full swing. She was crazy with passion.

Every part of her, physically and spiritually, surrounded me. Her blond hair tickling my nose, her eyebrows tickling my eyelashes, I knew she felt every bit of me. Our bare feet rubbed together. Her body uncontrollably convulsed in ecstasy with the intensity of an Olympic athlete at the pinnacle of performance. She was absolutely stunning. Her beauty was unparalleled and breathtaking, especially in the low light. She was naked with nothing to hide and was remarkably perfect. I caught her occasionally looking into the mirror overhead, smiling.

She was all mine, and I was all hers. And the pleasure was all ours, as was the time. Her efforts mimicked mine and my arousal mimicked hers. We were all that mattered in this world at this moment. Simultaneously, our smiles intertwined. I appreciated all of her efforts, as much as she appreciated mine.

Time drifted slowly. The night was ours. As it wore on, so did we. Her lips remained soft, moist, and smooth. We left no stone unturned, no crevice unexplored, no desire unsatisfied, and no welcomed action left undone. We left nothing untouched, unfelt, uncaressed, unsqueezed, unkissed, or unappreciated. As she moaned and groaned, I matched her pace and passion. Dedicated to pleasing each other, please each other, we did! I was within her, and she within me. She looked into my eyes as she never had before, between her moments of convulsive action. If this was a freefall parachuting competition, we would've earned the world record for the number of points we turned. I grasped her hair as she lay on top of me gazing at my chest, caressing me tightly, with her chest pressing against me. Her nose, now slightly cool, emanated lightly warmed breath. She comfortably nestled into my chest.

In her natural splendor, she shared everything with me, as I did with her. With no physical secrets to hide, no shame to bear, and nothing short of acceptance to provide, our bodies, hearts, and minds were one. Silently sharing our thoughts, our spirits intertwined, and our souls nested. We were completely together, as one.

I cherished the feeling of her hair brushing lightly against my face and over the rest of me. The touch of her soft, long sensual fingers with their warm, slightly harnessed, wild energy, accompanying her body's continuous motion, rocked my world. She writhed in pleasure as I did. Our actions slowed as we completely satisfied each other. Ultimately, she gently nodded off in my arms.

Her naked body resting against me was a feeling I would never forget; one I never wanted to be without. The dim light still softly aglow from the nightstand.

As I lie looking at her, hours had passed. I was afraid to close my eyes—afraid I might open them and she would no longer be there. In the end, I too nodded off for a catnap, purely exhausted, spent, yet, completely satisfied.

When my eyes opened, there she was, still within my embrace. Here we were, both together in heaven, looking up at the dimly lit naked images in the mirror suspended above us. Finally, I appreciated the mirror being there. I buried my face in her hair once again, wanting this moment to last forever. She opened her eyes again, this time looking over at me.

Could all those lone journeys in front of sacrosanct sunsets, subtle sunrises, and miraculously moonlit skies, possibly be shared from this moment forward? My appreciation for life and every circumstance within it could now multiply with each passing day. The limits of natural sensation and boundless Romantic Love could thrive and breathe a life of its own within me. No single feeling could match this amalgamation of consciousness. I was at the pinnacle of an existential experience nobody could or would willingly, nor intuitively, abandon. I released my inhibitions, freed my mind, trusted my future to this flourishing present, welcoming the inevitability of brightly lit days ahead. This could lead me instinctively to protect this relationship and my partner from harm for millennia. This was truly life at its best!

She smiled then whispered, "That… was… absolutely… amazing! I told you I could last all night," she teased.

"And I told you it would be amazing," I responded.

She smiled at me and I smiled back as we held each other sensually, passionately, yet silently in agreement. A little while later I awoke again as she squirmed beside me. Placing an open palm on my chest directly over my heart, she rolled closer, and then on top of me.

"You know, I lo—" I tried speaking as she pressed an index finger across my lips.

"Don't say it," she pleaded, then hesitated.

After a few more moments of silence, she whispered, "You know, I really don't want to… but I've got to go."

All I could say was, "Not yet," hoping to squeeze out as much more time as possible.

She whispered with fortitude in her breath and sighed, "I've got to take care of the kids and get them going. I really have to go. As much as I'd like to stay, I have to take care of my kids."

My present reality was uncontrollably slipping back into a perfect, living fantasy; I was powerless to stop it. Life, once again, would cast me into the lonely labyrinth of chores and obligations I knew it to be.

"Just a few minutes more," I pleaded, "I just don't want this moment to end."

She smiled, playfully pawing at my chest. "I know... I know... me either. Our lives are as they are, and I have my responsibilities to satisfy."

Slowly she rolled onto her hands and knees, hovering over me, kissing me, and rolling over onto one side, posing like the iconic bronze mermaid statue in Copenhagen. She grasped my hand with her fingers intertwined in mine, slowly sliding her palm away until only our fingers touched, whispering, "I gotta go," and slowly rose from the bed.

I watched as her perfect naked form drifted from the faint light into the darkness of the room where the dim nightstand light couldn't reach. She collected her clothes, quietly getting half-dressed, putting on her jeans.

I left the bed coming up behind her, snuggling her, holding her one more time with her naked warm back against my chest. We stood looking at ourselves in the full-length mirror on the wall in the dim light. I was seeing how we looked together. She knew exactly what I was doing, smiling in our reflection. The view was comforting for both of us.

She broke the silence gasping, "Oh God, look at my hair!"

"I love it," I said. "It's supposed to look that way after a play date."

She turned toward me, hugged me tightly and whispered, "You're sooooo warm."

"And you're sooooo hot!" I exclaimed.

As she finished getting dressed, I did too. She asked me, "Are you going somewhere?"

"Yeah, I got a hot date, with a blonde Princess, and I don't want to be late!"

She laughed, "Really? Who could be hotter than this one?"

"No one," I responded, closing the distance between us, playfully tugging on her shirt, "No one in the world is hotter than this one!" I kissed her lips over and over again. "I'm going to take you home to make sure you get home safely."

Turning toward me, grasping my face in her hands, she whispered, "You're completely too nice to me."

"I hope you can get used to it," I said.

"Can we walk? I want this moment to last as long as it can," she pleaded.

"Sure," I said comforting her, "Me too."

Together we finished putting on our clothes. We kissed a few more times.

Exiting the room arm in arm, we glided down the long hallway, down the open staircase, through the lobby, toward the hotel's large glass sliding front door. From the corner of my eye, I caught a glimpse of Nickolas at the front desk. He said nothing, but smiled, motioning to me with his fists extended, gesturing, thumbs-up. I smiled back.

We continued walking into the darkness. Onto the cobble-stoned streets, past the closed shops into the lonely, cold, dreary air of a foggy, biting cold Swedish night, we wandered toward her humble castle. As we walked hand-in-hand, arm in arm, we said nothing, enjoying each other's company. I was exactly where I wanted to be, with exactly who I wanted to be with, steeped in romance within every femtosecond, nanosecond, second, and minute of each step.

As we approached her front door, she turned toward me, grasping my face in her hands, saying, "That was reaally amazing—best ever! Night, night."

Sealing our departure from each other with a deep kiss, she disappeared through her front door. Watching her door close, I was once again alone in the frigid darkness. It was like I'd been torn in half. I walked back to the hotel, overcome by our recent memories, reviewing each of them in my mind. Before I knew it, I was in my hotel room, in my bed, looking up at the mirror... alone... smiling. Comforted by the lingering sweet scent of her perfume, I dozed off.

~ 19 ~

Swedish Dawn Too

I awoke the next day as I had the previous one. My cell phone alarm once again chimed with its bright, cheery tone. I looked up in the mirror, lying in bed alone. Yet again, I was happy the monstrous mirror hadn't crushed me while I slept. Looking around the room, I thought and sighed, "Alone again…"

The bed sheets were completely disheveled; this was quite out of the ordinary for me. My thoughts were as foggy as I expected the morning air to be. I recounted the night's activities and reveled in thought. I did it—I followed my dreams and made it to Sweden. And met Erika. This was amazing! She was no less than I remembered, no less than I envisioned, and no less wonderful than I expected. Relaxing in bed for a few more minutes, I was comfortably warm, wrapped inside the cocoon of the down comforter. I felt complete on this Sunday morning.

Realizing I would see Erika again today was all the motivation I needed to jump out of bed. Investigating the rays of sunshine peering through the curtains, I rushed to the window for a gander outside. Peeling back the curtains, much to my amazement, the view was crystal clear. The sun was shining, not a cloud in the sky, it was already a beautiful day. It's said this was the time of year nobody could accurately predict the weather. I accepted the weather as a sign, a positive omen. I felt hopeful and motivated.

As I did the day before, I started my morning routine with a quick workout inside my room. I showered, got ready, checked my camera, cleaned the lens, and checked the batteries. I headed downstairs for another spectacular breakfast buffet. The powerful aroma of coffee wafted into my room once I opened the door. I became excited following the fruity, herbaceous coffee aroma wafting down the hallway. My mouth watered expecting the smoked salmon with capers, yogurt, toast with real butter and other delectables I feasted on yesterday and would repeat this morning. Entering the room, there was only one seated couple. I sat comfortably a few empty tables from them.

"Good morning!" I said to them as I took my seat.

They were friendly, smiling at me before returning the greeting. "Good morning. Are you American?" the woman asked.

"Yes, I am," I responded.

"Oh, but I don't find Americans typically so friendly," she stated.

"To tell you the truth, neither do I," I said smiling. "I didn't grow up in the States. I'm more of a citizen of the world. I spent my entire childhood in Asia."

"What brings you here to this small town?" she asked.

"I'm visiting a friend I grew up with in Asia. We haven't seen each other for over 33 years. Today is our second day," I explained.

"And you?" I asked.

She responded, "We're celebrating our 30th anniversary. We've come here every year to celebrate, since our honeymoon. Nigel—" she continued, "is from Woodbridge, England, and I'm from Stockholm. We met while he was on vacation with some friends. We love this hotel, the staff, and the food! It's always been wonderful! A great place to get away from it all."

"Congratulations! That's a long time being married," I said.

The man finally responded, "It's been the most wonderful experience I could've imagined."

"What a blessing. You're lucky," I said.

"Oh, it's not luck," she said. "It's patience, understanding, sharing, and caring."

"It's luck!" he interjected. "If I hadn't stopped to talk to her at the Vasa Museum in Stockholm, and been so persistent, we'd never have met. I'd say it's luck!" he smiled. "Have you been there?"

"Not yet, but I hope to go. I'm not sure what Erika has planned for us today. She lives here, so I'm leaving it all up to her," I responded.

"You'll love it. Especially if you have a Swedish guide to show you around, which it sounds like you have. I'm sure you and— Erika?—will have a great time. Who knows, you might decide to stay in Sweden like my husband did."

"Maybe…" I responded.

As expected, breakfast was once again astounding. I especially loved the coffee, lox, salmon, and caviar. The croissants were the freshest, and the juices were all freshly squeezed. Settling down to enjoy breakfast at our respective tables, I looked forward to this day bringing forth many more positive memories. Memories I could hold on to forever, like yesterday. I refused to think of every day that passed as one less day with Erika. Instead, I focused on what each day would bring. Where would we go and what would we do today? What would we talk about? I felt alive and refreshed.

My life took on a unique quality of excitement and renewal since my arrival. Our day yesterday felt longer than any other day

I lived in recent memory. Most likely because I savored every moment, from early morning to the delectable late-night finish. It was something akin to asking if this one day would be my last day on earth—What I you do? Where would I go? Who would I spend it with? How would I feel? Have you ever thought of this? If this was mine, these days are exactly how I would want to spend mine.

Checking my watch, I had 30 minutes until I was to be at Erika's. I excused myself, congratulated the couple once again, and departed the buffet room. I returned to my room, brushed my teeth and grabbed my day pack and camera bag. This started out being a great day already.

I entered the hotel lobby, stopping for a spot of mint tea to go, passing the front desk. Nickolas was busy with guests, so I continued walking past, making eye contact with him. He raised his eyebrows as I passed, saying, "Have another great day, sir... and night!"

"Thank you. You too," I responded, not wanting to interrupt him as I promptly hit the streets.

The weather outside was perfect: clear sky, a slight breeze at 2-5 knots, temperature at about 55 °F or 12 °C. I was upbeat but tired; breathing in the cool air was invigorating. I felt impassioned and reborn.

It was a short drive to her place and I didn't want to be late. But I didn't want to arrive empty-handed either, so I looked quickly for a flower shop. Nothing was open. Even the convenience stores were closed. Ironic that not one convenience store was open on a Saturday morning. Maybe they don't call them convenience stores in Sweden. The entire town was still in bed—on a Saturday morning. I couldn't believe it!

I knew exactly where I was going—which was exactly where I wanted to go, to do exactly what I wanted to do, with exactly who I wanted to do it with, and exactly where I wanted to be. Few people seem to be lucky enough to experience this and appreciate it while it's happening! Life was good. It was better than good, life was magnificent!

When I arrived at her door with my camera slung around my neck, I was a bit early. She answered the door with Leif at her side, bright-eyed and firm tailed—both of them.

"Hi Dimitri, good morning," she motioned me to come inside, keeping out the cold. Wrapping her arms around me, she gave me a powerful hug in the foyer, with the same welcoming smile.

"My, you look so well rested!" she laughed. "You didn't stay up all night thinking about today, did you? Not too much hot chocolate?"

I raised my eyebrows playfully and smiled. Toying with her, looking at her from head to toe and back again, "And you look ravishing as ever this morning, my darling!" I commented in my best James Bond impersonation. "That was quite a night last night!" I boasted, half-whispering.

"What do you mean?" she asked.

"Uhhh—nothing."

"Oh please," she said, "Are you ready? You've had your coffee, right? If not, I'll make you some after our walk. The girls are spending the night with their friends so they already left," she fluttered. "I thought we'd take Leif for a walk first, and then drive to Stockholm, so I can show you the Viking Museum, the Vasa Museum, the waterfront, and downtown Olde Towne Stockholm area called Gamle Stan, and the Royal Palace. You don't want to hang around here all day—maybe this time you'd be fixing my dryer?" she laughed.

"What's wrong with your dryer?" I shockingly interjected.

"Nothing...nooooothing, I was only kidding. This is your vacation. We need to get you out and about," she demanded.

"I have no issue hanging around the house learning about you, your family, and your culture. And helping you with whatever you need."

"Nope, let's walk. Can you get the leash ready while I lock up the house? Now that I know he doesn't mind you doing that."

As we left, I thought it strange after the wild, passionate night we experienced some hours prior, she would be so standoff-ish. Not even a peck on the lips? Maybe she's just shy? Or maybe she felt awkward? Maybe she didn't want any potentially nosy neighbors knowing anything about her personal life? If she didn't bring it up, and her body language didn't portray any evidence of feeling any closer to me after our nighttime Olympic events, I wouldn't bring it up. The welcome hug itself was meaningful, as it was.

"Can you walk in front of us for a few minutes?" I asked.

"Sure, I can. Why?" she asked, hunting for a reason.

"I need bonding time with Leif. If I don't stay on the positive side of a bear-hund like this, it's likely he could eat me!"

"Nah-ahh. Why do you really want me to walk ahead?"

Okay, the gig is up; I continued. "I want to see what Swedish jeans look like from the rear!" I explained to which she roared in laughter.

Squinting her eyes and wrinkling her nose, as she was prone to doing, "Oh, these aren't Swedish jeans, silly," as she started walking, she slapped her open palm across her protruding buttocks simultaneously laughing at herself, "They're Lucky jeans!"

I interjected, "Yes they are, very Lucky!"

"No silly," she explained, "They're made in the USA!"

"Yeah, but they're in Sweden now, so they're really Lucky jeans!" I explained.

"God, you make laugh—even first thing in the morning!" she spouted. She took her place walking ahead as agreed. Suddenly, she spun around slowly in front of me with her hands in the air, her eyes sparkling in the sunlight. "Do these jeans look any different from others you've seen?" she laughed, coming out of her shell.

"Those jeans look better than ANY jeans I've ever seen anywhere—ever! Since I've probably been seeing those same jeans since junior high. They looked as perfect back then as they do now. Some things never change!"

"You're always kidding around," she sparked.

"Do you think I'm kidding?" I challenged.

"Nooooo, don't say that... every time you say that you do something crazy... like coming to see me in Sweden on a whim."

"So, do you regret me coming here?" I asked.

She stopped in her tracks, her expression becoming serious. She ventured, "It shocked me you would come all this way to just to visit me. And on such short notice. Most people say things they never intend on doing. But you are obviously different. I'm glad you came. I needed someone to talk to. It's helpful getting a male perspective. I've been through a lot and am still going through stuff. It's nice to—how do you say it?—get away from the daily grind of life? You're easy to talk to, and you're a lot of fun," she said looked directly into my eyes. "I would never regret having such a good time! This is amazing! I'm glad you're here. Besides, you fixed my washing machine for free!" she laughed.

Her voice echoed down the trail as she spun around and started walking again. "This is amazing weather!" her voice echoed through the woods.

"So, when I ask if you think I'm kidding, you know I'm not?" I asked.

"Nooooo, I don't doubt you! I will never doubt you," she said, her teeth sparkling in the sunlight, complementing her shiny, blond hair. "I believe you now; I'll always believe you!" she lamented.

"Wow, you're a fast learner!" I said, as she glared at me out of the corner of her eye, suddenly I stopped— "Don't move, don't even breathe..."

"Why? What? What's wrong?" she asked, looking from side to side.

Saying nothing, I grabbed my camera from its ready position, brought it to my eye, and started taking pictures.

She immediately objected, "I told you yesterday I really don't like my picture being taken—by anyone's camera! Didn't you get enough photos yesterday?"

"Nope. That was yesterday. We're beyond that, Princess. Come on... give me that smile!" I encouraged. "A camera, you said? This is not a camera. This is a time machine. It captures the lofty beauty of the only Viking Princess I know, within her native surroundings. The Princess I've always seen in you. Do you want to see the results again?" I asked.

"Yes, I do. And if I don't like it... you'll erase them, just like yesterday."

"Erase MY picture on MY camera?" I playfully objected.

"I thought you said it was a time machine?" she sparked.

"Okay, I stand corrected. You're pretty quick-witted!" I remarked.

"If it's an image of me... I own it," she boasted.

"Au contraire, Princess. It may be your image, but it's my perspective and my time machine. You're in a public place and have no reasonable expectation of privacy. We had this discussion yesterday. Technically, you have no rights to the images. Out of the kindness of my heart, I will gladly share them with you—no charge! How many other people can take pictures of you that come out like mine? And how many of MY pictures have you seen that you don't like?" I objected.

"So, I'll get copies of ALL of them?" she asked.

"Yes, you will. No charge," I confidently responded.

"I should charge you!" she boasted.

"And I'd pay whatever you asked," I said under my breath.

"I heard that," she blurted.

The sky was a deep blue, the surrounding greenery dark-green with lofty shades of varying hues interspersed. The light this morning was as perfect as it was the previous day. Again, we were the only humans in the woods.

We walked together side-by-side with Leif in the lead. "Come on!" she said, "I want to show you one of my other favorite places on earth—it's also by the water, you're going to love this place!"

"I already do," I responded.

She turned and coyly smiled and voiced, "I heard that too!"

She and Leif walked ahead of me, as I was taking landscape pictures. The woods parted to reveal a white, baby-powder, smooth beach. Walking on the beach was like walking on baby powder and it slowed our gait. Since we weren't in any rush, I didn't mind. Soon she became part of the landscape.

Looking through the viewfinder, I watched her play with Leif off-leash, throwing a stick into the water, letting the bear-hund fetch it. The sun was gaining height in the sky, shimmering off the water. In the distance, a ferry made its way to wherever it was heading, forming the slightly larger waves careening toward the shoreline. I snapped my camera shutter wildly. Focusing first on the background, then on her. She wore an olive-colored short jacket, a black long-sleeved white designer shirt underneath, with tight blue jeans bottoming out at her faux fur-lined Ugg boots. I snapped intently, trying to capture each movement. In one of my favorite photographs in particular, she had just thrown a stick, her upper torso was facing me, her feet planted firmly in the sand, her head tilted toward me, and she saw just where my focus was, despite the fact that I was wearing tinted sunglasses and was behind the camera.

She let out a loud, "Dimitri!"

This image was picture perfection. With her picturesque smile and body, she was a perfect "10." After a few "landscape" shots, including her, again I couldn't prevent my lens from gravitating to her firm tail. She was well-endowed, well-maintained, and well-preserved. I was happy to know she enjoyed the attention. I still couldn't believe she hadn't graced the pages of magazines worldwide. Her slightly swayed back and broad shoulders highlighted her hourglass figure. Through the viewfinder these photos reminded me of those high-quality photographs seen on the glossy pages of magazines in whiskey commercials.

Despite the separate worlds and the mountains of disparate experience once dividing us, our worlds were now merging, or maybe, colliding. Was it spiritualistic encouragement or fate as I hoped? Before my visit, our worlds seemed disparate and distant. Now they were integrating as one. I was right where I wanted to be, and for the first time I knew so was she. If my camera could do more than just capture moments in time, more like a veritable time machine, it could magically transform our lives into this life, right here and now. I was living my dream.

The Cycle of Life

Yesterday was history
Remembering 'til the day we're old
Tomorrow is a mystery
Waiting, watching it unfold
Unknowing what will happen then
Until it takes place when
We have no choice but to live this way
Until life itself brings its inevitable end.

Throughout my encapsulated presence of thought, Erika seemed oblivious to everything my mind, spirit, and body was experiencing. So, maybe today I'd make it more obvious. Keeping this dream alive, fusing it into reality would be completely fulfilling.

"What are you zooming in on?" she yelled from the firm, wet sand bar.

"Nothing! It's a superb landscape!" I responded.

"Uh-huh...," she answered.

Quickly, I joined her, playing near the waterline with Leif. We began walking and talking, recounting our memories of school once again on the way to another of her favorite spots.

As we walked, I blurted out, "Can I ask you a personal question?"

"Sure," she whipped back.

"Why didn't you ever go out with me back then, or as we say, date me?" I asked.

"I would've, you know. I thought you were so cute!" she divulged.

"I thought you were cute too, but you were much more than that to me," I explained.

"Because you never asked me," she said. "Never once," she emphasized.

"Yeah, but you had to know I was crazy about you—everyone knew. You had to know! I played soccer, took martial arts after school, maintained good grades, and played in a rock band; I was popular... what wasn't to like?"

"You were always doing so much and never seemed to have time to go out... that's what I thought, anyway. It doesn't matter, you never asked me out, and that's that," she closed.

"And what if I had?" I asked.

"Well, I would've gone out with you," she explained.

I added, "And we'd still be together... like now... Well, not exactly, like now. I'd be the father of your kids and they would look like me, but they'd speak perfect Swedish and perfect English without an accent because we'd be a bilingual home," I touted. "We'd be walking arm-in-arm every day, sharing our bed, breakfast, and shower every day for the rest of our lives. I wasn't too busy—"Okay, here goes," I thought momentarily. And then said this out loud, "I thought you were the most beautiful girl I'd ever seen from the very first time I saw you. I thought you were gorgeous, with a pleasing personality. You had a cute figure, smart, and basically, was the perfect young girl. I thought you were shy around me because you didn't like me." I explained. "Couldn't you tell I liked you by the way I acted around you? You were my dream girl!"

"What? Nooooo, I didn't know that. How could I have known that? Why didn't you tell me? I thought you were so cute! I would've dated you!" she repeated.

I added to imprint the idea, "And our lives would be perfect right now! I would've asked you, but you didn't seem interested in me," I added.

"Back then I was shy because my English wasn't very good. That's why I didn't talk much!" she explained.

"You didn't dress like you were very shy in those tight jeans and shirts stretched across your perfect form of a body," I said, begging for an explanation.

She giggled, "That's European-style fashion, duh!" Nudging me with her shoulder as she laughed aloud. "Come on, let's keep walking; we've got a long way to go," she added, "I liked the way you dressed too!"

"You were the ONLY reason I looked forward to school every day," I added. "So, you really would've dated me?" I asked once again, looking for answers.

"If you had the time. I don't know how you fit it all in even back then... I just don't know when you would've had time for me," she explained.

"If you were in my life, I would've made time. I would even have given it all up for you," I defended.

"I wouldn't have wanted you to do that. That wouldn't have been right! Those were your experiences and your memories. And you have a lot of them!" she responded kindly and sensitively.

"I still made time to watch you from a distance," I explained.

"I know, I saw you," she answered.

"Then, I could've squeezed you into my life as my top priority or you could've done it all with me... it's not too late, you know... we're not dead yet!" I begged.

She quickly changed the tone and set a trotting pace to her next favorite place. "Come onnn!"

After a brief bout of Leif prancing, she led us around the shoreline into and out of the woods, back out to a beach. But this one had a rope swing someone hung from a tree along the shoreline. It was in the woods but overlooked the ocean. It swung over the beach using a leaning tree as a natural point of gravitation.

Erika got on it first and I gently pushed to swing her. "You'll forgive me if I touch your tail to swing you. It's an American custom."

She looked back at me and slyly yapped, "No, it's not! I've been to the States, you know. I know, Americans have NO such customs!"

"Yeah, but did anyone swing you while you were there? See? I rest my case. Trust me, I'm an American customs expert. Oops, sorry, that wasn't supposed to be a slap, I lost track of the swinging motion of my hand. I didn't mean to slap your tail, I meant to push you," I laughed then continued, "So you would've dated me back then? And what do you think about me now?" tossing it out there again. I had to know.

"Well," she explained in a light-hearted tone, "Now, you're okay. You're not that bad looking," she said, giggling."

"Thanks for your charity," I said. It felt like she kicked me in the throat and solar plexus simultaneously then thrust a dagger straight into my heart, twisting it. I tried ignoring the comment, camouflaging my disappointment. I hoped she was kidding and would reverse her statement. Or maybe say she was joking, and I was being overly sensitive. She didn't.

"YOU amaze me even now. You always have!" I interjected, breaking the awkward silence. We both chuckled. "Do you think we could ever be together?" I asked.

After a break in conversation I asked, "Would you go out with me now?"

She ignored my question in silence and did well to hide her internally sequestered Muppet mouth, scowl-like reaction. She hesitated as if cornered.

All she said was, "Nothing is impossible," looking back at me flirtatiously smiling, saying nothing more.

"Oh, I must tell you it's also an American custom after swinging you, I'm compelled as the swinger to ensure your tail is swept free of debris, dirt, and pollen, you may have gathered from the swing seat—I must brush you off to my satisfaction," I explained.

She stopped swinging, claiming she was getting dizzy.

"Also, it is customary for the swinger to ensure the person being swung is okay because of the swinging… this is done with a kiss," I said.

"A kiss where?" she asked.

"Remember, I told you about the debris check?" I barked.

"Get out of here!" she laughed.

"Actually, the custom states the swingee shows appreciation to the swinger for doing a super job with a kiss to the lips. That's why American women don't go swinging with just anyone, you know," I laughed.

"But we're not in the U.S.—we're in Sweden," she responded. "Then, I'll be a swinger, and not a swingee," as she started swinging again.

"You can be a swinger with me," I said.

"What?" she asked, obviously unfamiliar with that term.

"So, you ARE familiar with the custom," I laughed enjoying the double entendre.

"No, I'm familiar with YOU!" she loudly retorted still swinging.

At the top of the motion of the swing, she jumped from her perch and landed on the sandy ground after a short freefall. "It's a Swedish custom if you're faced with a custom, you don't understand or believe and you're on a swing... you just jump!" she jabbered.

"Bravo!" I applauded her quick wit and sense of humor. "You're quicker than I expected. You must have had a lot of practice avoiding foreign customs in your past 33 years on swings."

Another of her silent, beautiful smiles acknowledged me.

"You don't waste words do you?" I added.

"No, I don't," she answered.

"Well, that's a trait I'm sure I'll wish you had retained a few months after our wedding," I smiled and celebrated in silence.

"Whaaaat are you saying?" she asked.

"Nothing. Get back on the swing and I'll show you." Was that my outside voice, I wondered?

She giggled, "I'm not sure I like your American customs."

"You liked them last night, without the swing," I added.

"Yes, I did. And the wooden angel you gave me," she answered.

She obviously wasn't tracking our conversation. We laughed incessantly. Leif looked at us like we were crazy. Maybe we were. And why not? It was much more fun than being serious all the time. We sat together on the sand for a while looking out at the water until Leif joined us, and his unmistakably moldy, cardboard, wet dog smell was overwhelming.

"Is that odor from you?" she joked.

"Yep, sorry it always happens when my fur gets wet!" I laughed.

"Come on!" she mustered us up.

We both laughed and stood up from the sandy beach. I leaned over and brushed the seat of her Lucky jeans free from sand and debris. "See, that wasn't painful," I said. "See? It's a win-win!"

"What's a win-win?" she blurted.

"—We both loved that! Come on we're going, like you said," I added.

We followed the trail back into the forest. As we passed some reeds near the sea I asked, "Have you got snakes here in Sweden?"

"I don't know, I don't think so. Maybe snow snakes and ice snakes up in the northern parts of the fjords," she said.

"Very funny… how could you not know?" I queried.

She explained, "Because I don't need to know, that's why! If we have them, they're awfully shy! I've never seen them," she added. We laughed again. She sparked, "With your Army Green Beret training you can tell me when you see one, and then you can catch it. And I can cook it up for dinner with fresh Chanterelles!"

"Okay, it's a deal!" I laughed. Looking at the geese and ducks floating on the water I asked, "Do you cook wild geese and ducks too?"

"Noooooooo. You said YOU don't eat them either," she defended her position continuing, "You said you only eat chicken and fish, including shellfish. Me too! That makes us pescatarians!" she stammered.

"Helloooo? Geese and ducks are forms of chicken. You just don't listen to me," I joked.

"You obviously know little about cooking—besides, they're too beautiful to cook!" she retorted. "I'm only willing to prepare the ugly animals. I know, I know, chickens are cute too, but I gotta eat something! Thank God vegetables don't scream when you cut them or I'd starve!"

She was truly a woman after my own heart.

"And I do remember everything you tell me," she jokingly nagged. Again, we laughed as we all walked back toward the house.

"Since the kids are staying at their friend's place tonight, when we get back from Stockholm, you wanna eat over? Are you getting hungry now?"

"Sure! I'd love to eat now and again back at your place tonight!" I added.

"Me too," she said, "I know a shortcut; Leif knows it too. When we get back, we'll get Leif washed off, get something to eat, and then head to Stockholm."

"Okay!" I agreed. These long days with American summer-style daylight hours were wonderful! The days lasted forever—exactly what I wanted.

During the walk back to Erika's house I asked, "Do you believe in ghosts and spirits?"

"Why do you ask?" she said.

"I'm just curious," I responded.

"Yes, I do," she insisted. "Have you ever seen one?" she asked.

"Yes, I have. I've experienced seeing ghosts or spirits throughout my life, since I was 10," I divulged. "Where was your experience?"

"In my current house," she said.

"What happened?" I asked.

"The first time I saw it I was with the kids downstairs in their bedroom. All the aromatic candles they lit were blown out for no reason. Insignificant items are moved around their room when they're not there. Sometimes harmless items are thrown at them when they are hanging around. They even see strange red or blue orbs of light spinning around their bedroom room at night. It only happens in their room downstairs. It used to scare them, but they never see an actual ghost—what do you call it, a spirit or apparition? Anyway, to them at their age now, it's just a big joke. Thankfully, it doesn't scare them. If they had separate rooms, it might be a different situation."

She related, "I've been upstairs and heard a glass falling off the dresser onto the floor with glass shattering everywhere. But when I went in their bedroom to investigate, everything was in its proper place—nothing was broken. That freaked me out. They've also heard the voices of a little girl talking to her mother in the walls. They say the two talk back and forth sometimes, but I've never heard it, so I don't know if they're—what do you call it—yanking my crank?"

I nearly fell over laughing at her innocence, "No, Erika, that's not what you call it! That's only what YOU call it when you're not in mixed company, with men and women present. YOU should probably just say pulling my leg or joking with me," I bellowed.

"Oh, okay, but you know what I meant."

"Yes, I know EXACTLY what you meant!"

"Even our animals refuse to stay in any of the rooms downstairs by themselves," she continued. "Sometimes when the girls have the cats in their room, for no apparent reason they'll start hissing at the walls."

"These are your invisible cats?" I added.

"They're not invisible cats, you just haven't seen them."

"Yeah—okay..." I joked.

She continued, "One time, even Leif went crazy attacking what he thought was apparently someone in the girl's room downstairs. He was just snapping, snarling, barking, and growling at the wall. This really freaked me out! I've never seen him so vicious before. Well, that's enough of that talk," she closed, "Let's talk about cheerful things."

"You don't want to hear about my experiences?" I asked.

"Nope. Happy thoughts, happy things. Especially when the girls aren't going to be home." As we walked, she said, "I really wish you spoke Swedish."

"I find language fascinating, don't you? The communication of ideas and the translation and mis-translation of thoughts within word selection and sentence structure across cultures is fascinating. It can be as difficult communicating within a single language and culture as it can between or across them. Comprehension can be tricky in any language. Even when translating physical languages," I explained. "So much can be mis-construed. The same is true of non-verbal languages. The language of Romantic Love, for example, can be rife with complexities. We read cues from body language, posture, facial gestures, expressions and micro-expressions, physical distancing, verbal discussion and hints. We get all these signals, some intentional some unintentional, and we try to process all of these into some form of comprehension, but sometimes miss the true intent of the communicator." I had to throw that in there, boy, didn't I know this to be the truth!

"What are you talking about, Dimitri?" she asked.

"It's never too late for me to learn a language. Any language, you know. I even learned a little bit of Swedish from the internet before I came here," I offered.

"You learned Swedish? Like what?" she asked.

"Yeah, like, *Hei Kooshlii*" I said.

She laughed, "What's that supposed to mean?" she demanded.

"You're supposed to know, it's Swedish for 'Hello Darling' darling."

"No, it's not!" she laughed, "It means nothing. That sounds more like an American teaching you a Nordic language. It's sounds like you're talking about "Hygge," not "Kooshli." Hygge is a concept of being comfortable or content in either Swedish or Norwegian. Anyway, in Swedish, 'Hello Darling' is *'Hej älskling'* like that."

"Well, hello to you too, Darling!" I interjected. "So how would I explain to you in Swedish that you've been my Romantic Love interest for over 33 years?" I asked.

"Very funny," she said. "You don't. You've got a lot to learn."

"Like what?" I asked.

"Like the three kingdoms of these Scandinavian countries (Norway, Sweden, and Denmark) were once united as one with a common language. To this day, all three countries are still linked by a common culture and similar, but different languages. And each is still a kingdom. Since Sweden and Norway used to be one country, the language is the most similar, but the spelling of the words can be very different. It's not as easy as you think," she schooled me, "These are very hard languages to learn."

"Difficult."

"What?" she asked

"Rocks are hard, languages are difficult," I said.

"Oh, you're cutting hairs. You know what I meant," she said.

"So *Hei Kooshlii* means nothing. Great, now I'll be like a parrot unable to unlearn what I've learned to say incorrectly from the internet. When I get back to the States, I'll get a real language course and I'll learn Swedish. It'll be fun. You can help me. And I'll learn more than the *'Hei Kooshli'* that I now erroneously know," I promised.

"What else did you learn?" she pressed.

"Okay, no making fun of my accent, I don't really know your Viking languages and I've only learned a little of it since I arrived at the airport a few days ago. Most of you Vikings speak perfect

English and listen to American music on the radio, anyway. That's what I learned," I added.

"You're hilarious," she sparked. "Speaking of Vikings, we need to get back to the house, do lunch, take the trip into Stockholm to visit museums and a few other places. You're going to soooo love Stockholm. Lucky for you, I know my way around there! You've come all this way and you need to see Stockholm. I told you I lived there for a long time and left it to raise the kids away from the city in a small-town environment—you remember that, right?" she insisted.

"Uh… yeah, I remember. Sounds like a terrific plan!" I confided.

We continued gliding through the woods and I still couldn't take my eyes off her. Her angelic voice echoing through the trees was mesmerizing. I still had issues dealing with the surreal experience of my past melding with the present. With what was, what is, what could be, and what I wanted to be. I became concerned that these intense thoughts may cause a brain aneurysm, exploding before my heart did, if this emotional roller coaster journey continued. This was trying and taxing, but it was fun.

Had I left the past in the past and tried to find a new future here, maybe I wouldn't have been so conflicted. I, like everyone else, well, hopefully more people than those I've met or know about, want to find that special someone to settle down with without being confronted with the cheating, drama, and baggage that comes along with many contemporary relationships. Knowing someone from your past, rekindling even the slightest friendship, provides a historical reference point, fueling endless hours of conversational bonding. And it's fun reminiscing together. Had I not contacted her, not spent thousands of dollars coming to Sweden, not searched for my passion, not uncovered my feelings, and not embarked on this physical and spiritual journey, I wouldn't have grown and flourished within myself.

Not that I was falling in Romantic Love all over again, it was that I was uncovering what I covered up all these years. It never vaporized, it was still there, buried deep within me. I wished she would tell me one way or another if it was possible for us to be together.

What did she mean when she said, "Anything is possible?"

I contend, Well, no, it's not. Not if one of us doesn't want it to be. Maybe I didn't really want to know. Maybe I'd rather live in a perfect fantasy than in a dismal reality. According to my empirical Amore principle, the most anyone can invest or control a relationship is 50 percent, at best. And this is true in any relationship. It is said, the one who controls any relationship, is the one cares the least. So far, she seems to be in control. Still, I was looking forward to spending this entire day and night with her.

After we returned to the house, I washed, and dried Leif, making sure he was comfortable inside the house, while Erika was busy in the kitchen. Ensuring I had my trusted time machine bag, Erika grabbed two paper sacks she explained contained a quick snack for us. We got into the car and jetted out.

She directed me to drive past the hotel and the Yule Goat, meandering the back roads until we reached the highway and enjoyed a relaxing drive south. The ride included light-hearted chit-chat, playful banter, and catching up on different aspects of our lives over the past years, as we were now prone to doing.

As we rode south, I mustered the courage to ask if she had anyone special in her life. After a brief pause, in typical Erika fashion with which I was overly familiar, her unmistakable response was just, "No." The rest of the ride we continued to reminisce of our youth in Thailand, and a bit about what we each experienced after we left Thailand.

When we neared the city limits, her tone got more serious and focused, explaining, "Our first stop will be the Viking Museum where we'll park the car. It's a small museum. Then we'll walk over to the Historiska Museet, the Swedish History Museum, and then on to the Island of Museets, or in English, the Island of Museums. There we'll visit the historic Nordiska, the Nordic Museum and then the Vasa Museum—that'll be your favorite. And if we have time, we'll visit the more contemporary Abba Museum. Yes, Abba—that would be the world-famous band from the 1970s, the four-person pop band selling over 300 million albums, the old-fashioned way. Can you believe that their popularity was only second in history to the British band, the Beatles? For some unexplainable reason, it took until 2010 to induct this amazing group into the Rock-and-Roll Hall of Fame. After seeing the museums," she continued, "We can wander around the harbor area, the waterways, the Olde Towne of Gamle Stan, walk by the Royal Palace, and see a bit of downtown Stockholm."

After I parked the car, before exiting to the Viking Museum, she sparked, "Oh, wait, let's eat the snack I brought so we don't get hungry!" She reached into her purse and pulled out two bananas, handing me one.

"Are you serious? Are you kidding?" I blurted. She looked at me completely shocked and astounded as I continued, "Bananas, after yesterday and last night? You couldn't bring apples, or maybe even pears? At least you didn't bring rambutan, you remember those things we called 'hairy cherries' in Thailand." She looked down at the banana she was in preparing to eat, as most people do, peeling it from the top and biting into it. "Oh no, no, no, no, no... don't eat it like that, break it in half or something!" I begged.

She broke out in such hysterical laughter, almost choking on the soft, white, cylindrical portion of the yellow phallic fruit. Again, with her priceless smile aglow, we both laughed until our eyes teared. We finished our bananas and continued to giggle and laugh as we walked toward the entrance to the museum.

"I wasn't even thinking about that," she said multiple times—begging for forgiveness.

I simply responded, "Uh-huh," as we walked. I loved it.

As we entered the small museum, I held the front door open for her, having already thrown the banana peels in the trash can outside. I joked. "In you go!" I was really interested in the Viking displays, since Erika continually touted her Viking past. As we walked, looked, studied, and talked I must've snapped a hundred pictures, some even included the displays.

As I looked at the glass-encased models of the coal and tar pitch encapsulated Viking ships, I remembered seeing the perfectly preserved Viking ships at the Viking Ship Museum in Oslo (part of the Museum of Cultural History), where they proudly boast having the largest display in the world of original small and larger Viking ships. I remembered how these Vikings brought live coals on board these wooden ships with them for warmth and cooking throughout their harrowing journey through the ice-cold seas. They traveled wherever they wanted, often with no land in sight—on relatively small, tar pitched fire hazards! For these mariners, this gave true meaning and responsibility for posting a "fire guard." We spoke of "fire guards" in the military, yet the significance never sunk into my mind until this point.

When I told Erika of my memories of the Viking Ship Museum in Oslo, she shared that she'd been there too and found it as intriguing as I did. She warned me we wouldn't see anything similar until we visited the Vasa Museum—and that's all she said.

"Those Vikings really had some huge balls," I said.

Erika looked at me, her mouth dropping open. "What???"

"Oh… uh, it's uh… an American slang term… it means the Vikings had a lot of courage and confidence traveling the high seas for such long distances so long ago. These guys were tough and fearless!"

"Of course, they were," she stated.

Our banter of the Vikings continued.

As an expert on Viking culture she continued, "The Vikings were really motivated, and didn't seem to have much food or agriculture available to them back then. The Vikings were known as brave warriors."

"They didn't travel for tourism or for fun, you know—in reality they were pirates. They plundered, pillaged, raped and destroyed the lives of many they encountered, stealing what they wanted for themselves. The Vikings were not gracious people… they had a reputation of being ruthless and selfish. You knew that, right?" I said.

"Then I'm a Viking pirate, it's my heritage!" she jabbed. "But I never really thought about it until you just mentioned it. We were told in school about the explorer aspect of the Viking journeys, and even had the discussion about Leif Eriksson perhaps being the first to discover the North America landmass."

"Yup, before 1493, when Christopher Columbus sailed the ocean sea," I responded.

"1492," she exclaimed.

"What?" I asked.

"In 1492, Columbus sailed the ocean BLUE. Jeez—the U.S. has such a comparably brief history and you don't even know it?" she mocked.

"Of course, I do… I was just kidding," I responded.

"Uh-huh," she continued mocking me. "You never know what you know, about who you know, until you know it," she said. I wondered what she meant by this, but sloughed it off as we continued our visit.

We delved further into the rich Swedish history. Through impressive displays historians described the early Vikings as emerging from Germanic tribes that migrated North in the early Middle Ages from the 5th to 10th centuries. Learning this was interesting. Looking, learning, walking and talking, we wandered onward.

I learned that the three Scandinavian kingdoms [Norway, Sweden, and Denmark] were once united in 1397, later splitting in 1523. But Denmark and Norway stayed together until 1814. It's no wonder that Sweden still speaks disparagingly about the other two to this day; but they all reserve a special disdain for the Dutch—we'd find out why just ahead in the Vasa Museum. Finland was even part of the kingdom of Sweden for 700 years from 1150 to their Finnish War in 1809, when Finland joined Russia as an autonomous state.

We walked outside where the air was crisp and cool. Thankfully, the weather in Stockholm this September, though a bit cold in the 40 °F or 4°C range, was still in the fall stages. Colder winter weather hadn't yet set in, not during the day anyway. The thinly populated streets made it seem as if we were one of the few couples in the entire world—technically, we weren't a couple yet, but we were a couple of people walking. As we continued onward toward the Island of Museums, she really played them up.

During our walk, I asked if in the course of her trip to Oslo she had seen the outdoor splendor of the Vigelandsparken, the Vigeland Sculpture Park, which is touted as a "must see." Seeing the locals in their outdoor city life, frolicking among the beautifully manicured grounds with the 212 bronze and granite contemporary sculptures sprawled across the 80-acre Frogner

Park. It is quite a sight for its two million visitors every year. And it's free. As the world's largest sculpture park, this is where you'll see the famous naked, crying, stomping baby, called "Angry Boy" and the granite monolith of 122 naked bodies stacked nearly 50 feet/14 meters high. We both agreed that those places were strange to see. I didn't know what to say after that. I can see the Danes having such a park like that, but the Norwegians? I always thought they were much more conservative. It was weird. Not in a negative way—just in a weird way! She agreed.

Surprisingly, we both took the same route walking around downtown Oslo, past the Parliament building, the official Royal Residential Palace, Oslo Centrum, and then the boardwalk at the Aker Brygge wharf area. We both saw the ferries, the wooden clipper ship replicas, the charter fishing boats, the large clock tower, and the half-scale lighthouse built right onto the wharf. We also ate at the same restaurant located at the beginning of the wharf area, marked with an outdoor awning displaying its name, Druen—right next to a well-camouflaged McDonald's fast-food restaurant. Comparing notes, we had both enjoyed the waterfront view of Akershus Castle, originally built in 1299, and seeing the Oslo Fjord in the distance. What a coincidence!

"While you were there, did you visit the town of Moss, the tiny fishing village about an hour South of Oslo?" I asked.

"Oh, I love it there!" she said. "I have a friend who moved there, I love visiting her! It would be a great place to raise a family and the perfect place to live if you like a small-town atmosphere," she added. "It's weird that you went to all those places too," she said.

"I can't believe you didn't see me there!" I taunted.

We both laughed. "At different times," we barked at each other in unison.

Finally, we reached and crossed the footpath on the Djurgårdsbron Bridge. The view of the Ladugårdslandsviken waterway was spectacular and made for fantastic photos. The Swede developers knew exactly what they were doing when they designed and completed the construction of this boulevard in time for the 1897 World Fair. It is magnificent!

As I stopped to take pictures of all the docked boats, Erika grabbed my arm saying, "Come onnn! We'll come back this same way. You can take as many pictures as you want later, it'll be prettier, once the sun sets."

Our next stop was the Historiska Museet, the large Swedish History Museum. We giggled for a bit before we settled down enough since we had to get serious to purchase museum passes for the rest of the day for both of us. Each museum cost about Swedish Krona (SEK) kr100, about US$12.00. These discounted passes are much more convenient to have, and I didn't want any complications. Purchasing the museum passes and asking the employee for a recommendation on the best route through these museums was a great idea.

We made our way to the Nordiska Museet, the Nordic Museum, an amazing feat of architecture. The museum itself probably didn't take over 30 minutes to see because we were fast walkers and there is really not much to see that we hadn't already seen. Most of those displays are not well explained in any language. Erika kept playing up the Vasa Museum as something we must see "No matter what!"

So off we went, to the Vasa Museum, physically identified by the tall wooden mast protruding from the top of the building. She was right—this was my favorite. They built the museum around the original wooden ship near the harbor waters. Excavating the hull intact from 1959-1961, 333 years after it sank, and they brought up with it, 15 bodies still trapped inside. It has been continually restored since then. The museum wasn't completely built at its current location until June of 1990.

The Vasa ship took two years to build. This ship was ordered built by King Gustav II Adolphus, named after his grandfather, Gustav I or Gustav Vasa. In 1625, this ship was commissioned as the largest, most miraculous warship of all time at 69 meters (226 feet) long, 52.5 meters (172 feet) high, with a crew of 145 sailors and 300 Soldiers. The Swedish Royals invested much of their fortunes into this new symbol of power for the Swedish Empire, amidst wars with Russia, Denmark, and Poland. The shipbuilders were renowned Dutch artisans, the primary designer Henrik Hybertsson died in 1627 before they finished the ship. He found remarkable craft-workers and technicians to adorn this gilded ship, from ornate carved and painted wood carvings to its specially cast, 64 bronze cannons. This top-heavy wooden ship was one of the most heavily armed ships in the world. It is said that there were no detailed plans to provide any guidance to the five teams working on the hull. It is believed that they took smaller ships of that day and scaled them up. Yet, they spared no expense in building this behemoth.

At 4 pm on 10 August 1628, within 20 minutes of starting its maiden voyage after dedication, traveling a mere 1300 meters (1400 yards), a slight breeze caused the ship to list, and it began sinking. Finally sinking below the water, drowning nearly 40 family members who were invited by the sailors onboard; 53 died in total. The family members were invited as a special treat, intending only to travel to the mouth of the bay and then offload. After sinking, the Vasa's mast stuck out of the water as a visible reminder of this national tragedy, until the King ordered it cut below the waterline, removing the reminder of this massive failure. Out of sight, out of mind.

The genuine tragedy was that they built this ship only one meter (three feet) too narrow. But had it not sunk into the depths of the muddy harbor, we wouldn't have it today to gaze upon. The Swedes still aren't happy with the Dutch for creating this catastrophe, though at the time they punished no one.

We wandered around this huge preserved, water-proofed, Vasa ship and its accompanying life boats. She continued explaining this was the ship Hollywood producers used as a model to create their infamous mythical ship named, "The Black Pearl," in the movie series, *Pirates of the Caribbean.*

"People shouldn't be so reckless in endeavors they really know so little about… they should do their research before taking such a gamble," she said in a teasing manner. I sloughed off this comment as her attempt at humor. Politely chuckling, I didn't find it very amusing, since it mirrored my trip to Sweden.

Once we had our fill of the Vasa, we considered rushing toward the Abba Museum, planning on running through it as we did the Nordic Museum.

"The Abba Museum next?" I queried. We looked at each other hesitating. She looked down at her watch then looked back at me.

As we smiled, we simultaneously joked, "Abbbaa. Naaaah."

We laughed at the coincidence.

"Come on!" she taunted, grabbing me by my arm. "Let's go take some pictures!"

Quickly retracing our steps, wandering back over the old stone bridge, we walked around the harbor and stopped for a late lunch at a restaurant hovering over the Ladugårdslandsviken waterway called Ångbåtsbryggan. This restaurant is sandwiched amidst docked fishing boats, private and charter yachts. It was perfect. Although the prices here were most likely quite a bit higher than the surrounding outrageously priced cuisine, the seafood at this restaurant was nothing short of amazing, as was the Swedish dark rye bread called Kavring. This cuisine was heavenly.

As far as the quality of all of our food, the ambiance, and the company I kept, any price would've been well worth it! Our meal was artfully crafted and served, as was our conversation.

After a late lunch, we strolled arm-in-arm down the Strandvägen Boulevard following the harbor waters, stopping for some hot chocolate at a restaurant/café across from the harbor, called Strandvägen. It was next to the Kungliga Dramatiska Teatern, commonly known as Sweden's National Theatre. This Royal Dramatic Theater was founded in 1788 and next door to it, a much less elaborate, but older structure, the historic Musikteater Museet, near where we parked the car.

Every place we visited, my camera constantly fired, both with pictures of the sights and of the contemporary Viking Princess, in the name of whose royal cousins, these ships we saw earlier, were most likely meant to serve.

"Come on, let's walk around the water to the Royal Palace where my 'distant cousins' live, come onnn! We have little sun left," she urged.

As we were skirting the water's edge toward the area known as Gamla Stan, or Olde Towne, we walked down a tiny, meandering cobblestone street, through medieval alleyways dating back to the 13th century. We talked of nothing of any importance, but I was steeped in the topic at hand, whatever it was. Her modelesque leather shoes clip-clopped, echoing through the long, winding, narrow, empty streets as we wandered through hundreds of years of history, taking it all in.

Stopping in front of a restaurant called Gastrologik, Erika sparked, "Come, let's have a quick snack in here. Someday we can come back for dinner, or we can go to the ever-popular restaurant, Tradition Vagastan. We'll try some Kavring in here, everyone makes it just a little differently. You're going to absolutely love it!"

She was right. We had a few baked items from the menu, including croissants and Kavring. They also served the most delectable cup of coffee here I remember ever having.

We departed, continuing to explore the twists and turns of these centuries-old cobblestones. As the sun dropped from the sky, I could capture the spectacle of the changing light on a myriad of subjects, including Princess Erika herself.

We ended our self-guided, day-long tour at the Royal Palace, or Kungligaslotten, walking up the dirt mound toward the contemporary castle. It's reported this building contains 1,430 rooms. We walked toward the wall where I noticed an entranceway in the shadows. Erika drifted toward the guard box. A guard diligently emerged, silently stepping forward to query our intent.

I slowed her gait, waved to the guard smiling, while whispering to Erika, "Nah-uh-uh, what are you doing? I still wanna eat tonight and NOT in jail either!"

"I was gonna toy with him," she stammered.

"Nope! Not worth it!" I insisted as I rushed her away.

Since the Royal Family still occupies the castle as a residence and it was too late to attend a guided tour, surely the guard force wouldn't appreciate any horseplay.

My feelings, conversations, and actions drew me closer and more intensely to her. I continually watched her lips move and her tongue speak. I noticed each time her long slender fingers grasped the railings and rock walls surrounding the harbor walk. Her natural beauty consistently seized me. We finished skirting miles of the entire waterfront; I really hadn't noticed, nor did I want it to end. Beautiful in any light, in any setting, in any weather, and in any location. She nearly eclipsed the spectacular waterfront views of this Nordic gem. She glowed internally with a fire of curiosity burning, much like I had been told I had. Before leaving the area, we saw a beautifully lit clipper ship most likely modeled after the Vasa. Bright and spectacular, it was apparently a dinner cruise type ship. This completed the ambiance and history into which we delved. Unfortunately, it came time to make our way back to the car and drive back to her house. I prayed traffic wouldn't impede our return. It was my intent to spend much quality time at her house. Off we went.

Arriving at her place, the darkness was already well upon us. The subtly set night lights inside cast shadows on the walls, barely visible from the front window. Leif began barking as we approached; most likely he had to go out for a walk. He confirmed this as soon as the door opened. His huge furry white head punched through the opening in the door as Erika turned the doorknob. She reached in, grabbing a leash and a flashlight. Off we went into the darkness, as Leif towed us to his favorite relief place in the nearby woods.

Her voice in the dark was as soft as her words as she spoke of the sights we saw that day, and how she enjoyed city life when she lived there. Her English was perfect, despite a slight hint of her Swedish accent. I didn't know if I would ever be back here again, but I knew I could never return to this moment in time. We all know as fleeting as time is and as dynamic as life is, it's never the same with every breath we draw, with each thought, each scent we smell, and with each star, planet and asteroid passing overhead… life is never the same from second to second. And although I so wanted to relive these moments repeatedly, I knew life would not allow it.

Returning from our short walk, she ginned up another healthy, perfectly tasting meal. Her selection of Chanterelle mushrooms, wine, red and black caviar, a serving of baked chicken, a variety of cheese and crackers, topped off with a Swedish-style chicken stew, was right on target. This woman intrigued me and amazed me, as no one had ever done in the past.

As she spoke, her words were sweet, her lips moist, and her eyes engaging.

They say, "Though you may never remember everything a person says specifically, you will always remember how they make you feel." And I felt great. Here the saying rang true. I held onto every millisecond, nanosecond, and zeptosecond. I valued and cared for this time as I would a jewel-encrusted golden chalice. I looked forward to being with Erika no matter what we were doing. And I feared the passing of another night as we spoke, communicating our thoughts, our memories, our feelings, and our expressions. The array of emotions I was experiencing was completely overwhelming, while insatiably fulfilling. But our time together was dwindling.

"The kids said they are coming back from their friend's house sometime tonight; I'll call them and see what their schedule is. You can come with me to get them. It's not very far from here, we can walk," she said.

"I'd love to," I smoothly responded, without a hint of the excitement I felt.

After dinner, we cleaned up the kitchen where once again she was delighted with my assistance; we readied Leif, donned our cold weather gear, and all three of us headed out into the darkness to get the children. As we walked, we shared more thoughts and memories of times gone by. I don't remember exactly what we talked about, but I remember how thrilled I felt being there.

When we arrived, the kids already placed their bags neatly outside the front door. I grabbed the bags and greeted these shy, young, twin teen girls as they exited. While we all walked back to Erika's, I listened to the Nordic vowels being batted back and forth in the still, chilly night air surrounding the three of them, and Leif. Though I understood none of what was being said, I was grateful for being there in that moment. I felt like the main character in *The 13th Warrior*, as the Nordic language filled the frosty night air. My heart was happy and my soul was filled with Erika and her offspring, as she introduced me to her Nordic lifestyle, walking in the light of the Swedish mornings, soaking up the Swedish afternoon sun, and now walking the streets in the cold Swedish night air. I heard the footsteps of the girls and the white bear-hund, the loose gravel crunching under our feet. Passing under a few streetlights momentarily lighting our path, eventually casting us back into darkness, we walked away from the caressing visual assistance.

Listening to their enthusiastic laughter and giggles in the dark as only the uncomplicated lives of children could reflect, all my thoughts were happy. We all were. I was having the time of my life. Occasionally, Erika would translate snippets of their conversations to me. After a few translations, even Leif turned around and appeared to be snickering at their gentle jokes. Many most likely were at my expense. They were all so cute and funny as they laughed in unison. For the first time in my life, I didn't mind being the center of attention, nor did I mind being the punchline of jokes—I quite welcomed it! In one moment, they simultaneously burst out in hysterical laughter. And these weren't simply chuckles, these were fall-down, belly-aching, bellows of laughter.

Erika once asked, "Do you want to know what we're saying?"

"Yes, of course I do!" I jovially responded.

"They were just saying you were carrying all the bags and holding Leif's leash—which is something you'd NEVER see a Swedish man do, EVER! Unless they paid him as a royal servant or butler."

I chirped mimicking an English accent addressing them, "My dear Princesses, I'm grateful to be of service for each of you, whilst escorting your royal white horse."

They roared with laughter so loudly I heard it echo at the end of the empty street.

Erika said through her laughter, adding, "And they think you're hilarious!"

I happily responded in the same English accent, "Thank you, Princesses. I may not understand the language, but I do quite understand the laughter!"

The roars of laughter continued after that comment. "Ah, I also think you speak harmoniously and delightfully, like music to my ears. Even though I can't see you in the dark of night, I can see your sparkling white teeth shining like the moon and stars above!" I added in an Irish brogue.

After a short translation from Erika, their bellows continued with additional comments in Swedish all the way back to the house.

Occasionally, a fog horn struck its familiar notes, blaring over the waters in the distant bay. This walk represented my emotional journey with Erika. I enjoyed her company and her presence of being. But I hadn't understood the why in what occurred in our past, what occurred along the way, nor where we were going in the future. I was wondering, however, if we'd get to our destination together. Up to this point, I hadn't been given a hint. Nonetheless, I was enjoying my journey.

When we arrived at her humble castle, the kids entered, first heading into their room and then Leif, then Erika, and I followed.

I stopped in the foyer closing the door slightly, turning to Erika hinting, "I should probably head out and let you get the kids settled and ready for tomorrow. You need to complete your motherly duties."

She hushed me, shaking her head from side to side with her eyes closed and to my surprise said, "Nope! First, we'll all have some hot chocolate upstairs. You can go back to the hotel on a warm, full stomach after that." She placed her hand on mine, gently closing the door.

She beckoned the girls from their room and asked them to join us upstairs for a non-alcoholic night cap. I was grateful for this, because Sweden is one of those zero-tolerance countries for drinking and driving. I didn't want to risk driving after drinking any alcohol.

We joined together in the family room around the fireplace, Erika and I sitting on the couch. The flickering glow of the fire danced across our faces, bright with warm reflections. Our hands filled with our bounty, mugs filled to the brim with hot chocolate and whipped cream afloat, stacks of German chocolate bars, and a glass of cold water, all within reach.

"Good luck getting everyone to sleep tonight after this chocolate fest," I said.

Nora and Fiona said concisely in unison, "It's okay, a special treat for us!"

We all laughed. I have always been amazed by the concept of identical twins within the miracle of birth. I still find it so amazing how such a feat could actually come to fruition. I was seeing and hearing in stereo. I could've sat in front of these two, watching and listening to their harmonious voices for hours.

"I thought you two didn't speak English—you were kidding, right?" I asked.

"No, we are speaking English, not too often and not so good," Nora slowly and precisely insisted. "It's good to practice."

We all continued munching, crunching, sipping and laughing. I sipped my hot chocolate, nursing it, once again hoping this night would last forever.

"Did you guys have fun today?" Fiona asked enunciating each syllable.

"We did!" Erika quickly replied. "We walked Leif, grabbed a quick snack [both of us snickering], then went on a magical museum and Olde Town tour of Stockholm, with lunch at Ångbåtsbryggan, a hot chocolate in Strandvägen 1, and a lite Kavring snack at Gastrologik. Then we walked past the Royal Palace, and came back to pick up you two. Dimitri took thousands of pictures."

Fiona carefully said, "You two are so lucky. Next time take me with you! Mamma gave you the BEST tour!"

I turned to Erika saying, "I told you we shudda brought them."

The twins whined in unison, "Mamma!"

"He's just kidding you two. You were with your friends today. Didn't you have fun?" Looking over at me with a wink in her eye, "Thanks!" she said.

I just smiled back at them.

"Yes, we had fun," Nora and Fiona begrudgingly admitted in a monotone response.

Then they begged to see the photos. In order to efficiently share these as Erika suggested, they left their supine position on the large floor throw pillows, joining us on the couch. I flipped out the viewfinder from the back of the camera so everyone could see.

I just smiled. After seeing all the photos, the twins began yawning, and so did Erika. With school right around the corner, I knew I should plan my exit, looking forward to yet another fun-filled morning in Sweden with Erika. It was a somber time for me, because tomorrow would be my last day with Erika, for how long I didn't know; perhaps forever. A lump formed in my throat.

My stomach tightened up, like someone jabbed me. I started feeling anxious, not wanting to leave, not wanting to face the loneliness, or the rapidly approaching unknown. After a count to three I squeezed these words out of my mouth and hated myself for saying them. After motioning with my head to Erika, I mouthed the words, "I think they're getting tired."

She nodded. "Okaaay, you're right. They've got an early day tomorrow," she said, "And that means I do too."

I still hadn't seen nor heard from those cats, though she still insisted she had two of them. The small bowls in the corner were always full of cat food and water. Amazingly, they never appeared to partake in their treats or ours. Maybe the lessons of felines being fearful of humans came early in their lives—if they existed at all. Leif, on the other hand, was always nearby, as polite and diligent as expected, and unintrusive.

We stood together as she led me downstairs until we stood hesitantly in front of the door.

Erika whispered, "I had another magnificent day—I can't believe it. God what fun we had! I really appreciate you coming. Thanks for driving. The weather was perfect. It was great. And I'll see you soon."

I leaned against the door and so wanted to say, "If you were quiet, I could stay with you and we could repeat the hotel experience. Or you could join me again at the hotel." But I bit down hard on my tongue, making sure those words didn't slip out.

The girls clomped down the stairs once they finished the dishes. Heading into their bedrooms they hesitated, turned and said, "Good night, it was nice to meet you. Thank you for the chocolates, and the walk, and showing us the pictures, and the talks," each one adding another event in the series until they finished the sentence, before disappearing behind their bedroom door.

"Erika whispered, "The kids wake up early in the morning for school, so I'll be waiting for you to come by whenever you want. I know you won't be waking up that early. Same time would be good. Give me a hug. I really hate to see you go."

We hugged, and once again, I breathed in a faint whiff of the perfume she applied to her neck early that morning.

"Oh, croissants and cinnamon buns in the morning at the mansion. Night, night," she whispered, raising her eyebrows as she pawed at my chest, "Reeeoooer!" she playfully mimicked a cat, raising her eyebrows as she joked, "I do have cats."

"Night, night," I responded.

Once again, I made a graceful exit as she silently closed the door behind me. Followed by the ever so familiar lonely walk back to the car, enduring another lonely, though quick drive with the empty passenger seat beside me, back to the hotel. Again, as I entered the lobby, Nickolas was there.

"How'd it go today then?" he said smiling, taunting me in a mock Jamaican accent.

Responding somberly, I said, "Today was perfect. If I could have days like this the rest of my life, I'd be in heaven. But for now, I only have one more day."

"What a trip you had though. From the first day, you've come a long way with her. Sounds like you always have an amazing time with her," he said.

"I always do. She could yell and scream at me at the top of her lungs, and I would still enjoy being with her."

He snickered, adding, "I'm like that with my girlfriend. I miss her so much. It's good that I'm living with her parents getting to know them. Having her away at school in a different country is no fun. She should be back soon. It's a rare opportunity when a young man like me can meet such a wonderful woman like her. Someday we plan on moving back there, to open my own resort. You and Erika could visit as my guests of honor. Maybe I could even host your wedding?" he implored, raising his eyebrows while he said it.

"I would love that, but I'm afraid you might be rushing things along a bit, my friend. I so hope you're right, and I'll keep that thought in mind. Thanks Nickolas, you have a penchant for hospitality, you're focused and sincere. You're a fine man, and a good friend. I look forward to seeing your dreams come true. Best of luck," I closed.

We shook hands as I slowly began my departure. He was a welcome and necessary distraction to my hollow feeling. He had a grounding effect on me, by providing me a positive spin on my situation. Without him I may have gone down the rabbit hole of despair and desperation, ruining my last day with Erika.

I wandered over to the tea and coffee table to make myself a cup of hot mint tea, once again, walking the lonely path upstairs, down the hallway and into my room. "One more day," I thought to myself. "I only have one more day. Have I done everything I wanted to do, gone everywhere I wanted to go, said everything I wanted to say, conveyed everything I wanted to convey? Nope! Not yet." I entered my dark, cool room, readying myself for bed.

As I brushed my teeth staring at myself in the mirror, I thought, "Damn, day three—tomorrow—this is it. What to say? When to say it? How to say it?" I thought long and hard, and out it came. I wanted to see how such a soliloquy would sound as I looked at my reflection in the bathroom mirror:

"You know how I felt about you, and how I still feel. Why not be with the only man in this universe who has loved you longer than anyone else besides your parents and grandparents? These past three days have been the best I've ever had." Three days—and proposing already? That's nuts.

Okay, how about, "Erika, I would welcome the opportunity to look at you forever. I want to experience reciprocated Romantic

Love and we have an excellent shot at it. You inspire me. I know this is a lot to absorb after only three days, but this is the truth. I hinted at this to you this weekend, although you seemed uncomfortably distant at first, not that you wanted to be." Or did she?

How about— "Erika, we thought of how many things could make this relationship difficult, and for every obstacle we seemed to have a solution. I'd rather think of how to make us work and not focus on why it wouldn't. These three days could lead to the rest of our lives.

"After 33 years and now three days, these have been the most perfect three days of my life! I can't stop looking at the pictures I have of you in my time machine; our images are frozen in time. Thinking of the past three days, it's not typical to realize the very last of them falls on a Monday. The Monday I'm scheduled to leave. This will have been the best Monday. So far, we've had perfect weather, visited perfect places, saw perfect wildlife, took perfect pictures, had perfect snacks, with the perfect company, and perfect traffic scenarios, during a perfect trip to Stockholm.

"In school, I thought about it but never said it. And now, I've lived before, but not like this. I've felt before, but not like this. I've seen before, but not like this. I feel completely and positively alive and uniquely significant in your presence. I can't keep my eyes off you. You inspire me. Seeing YOU again is one of the most emotionally significant events in my life." Yeah right, I can't say that! She'll think I'm crazy. Remember D, for her it's only been three days.

How about, "You're the same girl I knew 33 years ago. You looked so happy in pictures back then, and you look happy in my pictures now. I can't help but feel I had something to do with this. This has been the most expensive and emotionally charged journey I have pursued. And I'm so glad I did. Our lives have not worked out for us in our own countries, within our own cultures, without each other. I want to have the perfect weekend like this weekend, for the rest of my life! I want to wake up seeing your smile next to me. I want to look into the mirror seeing you next to me. I want to watch you speak Swedish… to experience your culture… learn your language," I closed. "How's that?" I thought.

Nah—it's all too intense to vocalize after only two days. It's too soon! And it's too long. If I said this 33 years ago when I was 12 years old, it would've sounded crazy. It still does. Unfortunately, for some stupid reason you can't rush life, love, or happiness. I've gotta find another way. Ugh! Patience really sucks!

Once again, I rested alone on the king-sized bed, looking up at myself in the mirror overhead. And once again, hoping it wouldn't fall on me. I snickered and sighed as I shut off the light, rolling over to get some sleep. There was no gentle knock at the door that night.

~ 20 ~

The Final Awakening

The next day I the bright, cheery tone of my cellphone alarm startled me awake. Peering out the window, the air was fresh, the sky was blue, the breeze gentle, yet the glimpse of the bay was obscured by morning fog, unlike previous days. I exercised and readied myself as was my routine. But today, my cognitive function was slow. I lacked clarity, mirroring the conditions outside. I felt dazed and distant, yet I couldn't understand why. Most likely because the weight of the world was transferring back onto my shoulders with the ominous feeling of having to depart from the Land of Thule. I became deeply saddened. This was my last shower and the last time I would pack my bag here in Sweden. I went for my last walk down the hotel hallway, down the stairway, eating the last of my buffet breakfasts, enjoying my last great cup of morning coffee, my last cup of mint tea, and my last talk with my favorite desk clerk before departing.

With the passing of each second, I strived to avoid thinking of the looming and foreboding feeling that this was my last day in Sweden. This was the last day with Erika for who knew how long?

Realizing it took me 33 years to get here, not knowing how long it might be before I'm invited to return, if ever? Thinking of my journey up to now, all my energy was focused forward to this point. Now it was focusing backward, a day or two.

I thought of everything I discovered, uncovered, and learned about life, myself, and Erika. I clung to my one positive thought that I still had one more day with her, though realistically it was more like a half-day. I had a bit more than an hour and a half drive to the airport to catch my afternoon flight returning to Frankfurt and then back to the States. I was facing my last drive to her humble castle, and our last walk in the Swedish Wood, to have our last conversations.

Then it would be back to the despair, loneliness, and emptiness of living alone in a hustling, bustling lifestyle. Today felt more like going to the gallows than going back home. Nonetheless, I had to maintain focus on the possibility of a positive future. I had to focus on my journey and focus on the fun I could have. Whether we'd maintain a friendship or develop into more was part of the question only life itself would uncover. I was so hoping this would not be the last I saw of her. Though I knew in the back of my mind the possibility existed.

Walking toward the lobby with my luggage in hand to check out, I was living in a disassociated dream. My disparaged tone, my disheartened feelings, and my desolate mood overwhelmed me with melancholy. These had to be repressed. I had to be positive and hide these feelings as best I could until I was on my way home.

Rushing to bid farewell to my new friend Nickolas, to wish him the best of luck in his new life working in hotel management with the woman of his dreams, his replacement was already there. A gloomy emptiness came over me. This was not the closure I planned. I hoped this was not a sign of how events for the rest of the day would unfold. Walking out of the hotel lobby into the parking lot, I focused on Erika—her smile, her aura, her glow—I felt better already.

Again, I felt alive and refreshed. In her presence, I felt her spirit shining brightly upon mine as did the same young, beautiful Princess Erika 33 years ago. Not much had changed in that realm. For the first time in my life over the past few days, I was experiencing a spiritual inter-aural relationship with another human being. Erika's presence still mesmerized me. I felt complete, relaxed, happy and confident. My every pore was alive and every follicle aware of her presence.

In other relationships I never felt so strongly connected with another; without even speaking a word. I've had girlfriends, and lovers before, but never were my emotions so intense. Never so electrifying. The Erika had eclipsed everyone in my past. It was as if we had been born in another time, been together centuries ago, and now at last, once again talking, laughing, looking, watching, smiling, and eating together—after much longer than the mere 33 years of this lifetime. She was as fulfilling to me as the air I breathe and the water I drink. Wherever we were, there we were, together. Nothing else mattered. Nothing.

As I drove closer to her house, I fixed my focus on her. Knocking on her door, she answered quickly, anticipating my arrival. Opening the door, both her beautifully shaped, flesh-colored nose and Leif's long, strong, white snout greeted me. She hugged me. Leif jumped up on me, not to be left out of the festivities. So I hugged him. Erika didn't correct him because she knew I welcomed his enthusiasm. She merely shook her head and rolled her eyes in disbelief.

"Good morning!" she whispered, her smile brightening my day. Donning her coat not to waste any time, she grabbed Leif's leash from its roost by the door, attaching it, saying, "I want to be quiet because Nora wasn't feeling well this morning so she stayed home from school. Fiona already left. I want to show you more of my favorite places. Ready? Let's go!"

"Do you want to stay here and take care of Nora? "I asked.

"No, she's sleeping now. I'll check on her when we get back."

Once again, all three of us trotted off as we had the past two days. Me with my camera around my neck and her with Leif. As we walked, we talked as we had in past days. I could really get used to this! We talked about the weather, my photography, the trips I experienced, the trips she experienced, the food we tasted, the places we'd like to visit, her house, my house, her children, my children, her aspirations, my aspirations, and the people we remembered from school; as usual, our conversations were all over the spectrum and never repetitive.

She still hadn't mentioned having anyone special in her life and conveyed to me she never connected with anyone on the same level as we did now. She was the most talkative this morning in comparison with past days. As we walked, with each step, and each passing minute, we were getting to know each other better, deeper. We were light-years beyond where we were in school—but I still wanted more. Much more. And my time was extremely limited, waning by the second.

"Thank you for coming with me on all these walks," she said. "I do adore being outside in the fresh air regardless of what the weather is like. I could never again be with someone who doesn't enjoy the outdoors. It has been so wonderful sharing this with you."

We walked by the neatly arranged cottage-type houses deep in the woods, through the trails, in and out of the wooded areas, down the hills toward where the sun glistened on the water in view of the distant fjords, and by pastures empty now of horses, goats, sheep, and cattle that once grazed there. Today our Norwegian blue-eyed Fjord Horse wasn't where he usually was either. I missed him. For some reason, Erika didn't share my concern, so I mentioned nothing of it. The greens were still intensely green. The air was thick, cool, crisp, and clean. The cold nibbled on our noses, leaving a slight hue of red as a reminder and testament winter would soon be making its presence known. Our breath vapor followed closely behind us. Erika remarked the weather had somehow changed completely.

She said, "You know, Dimitri, when you came, the rain, clouds, and cold were chased away. Now that you'll be leaving, it seems the weather is changing too. We'll just enjoy what we have while we have it."

I joked with her, "Of course it was and is. You shouldn't question mother nature or father time. They know what they're doing. You shouldn't mess with the true order of the universe."

Could this have been an indicator of what was to come? I was so going to miss this place. The bold palette of greens splashed across the farm and pasturelands we were skirting, atop the dark brown richly colored dirt trails, through the moss-covered woods, with a slight fog hugging the ground, now lifting into the trees. This scene was reminiscent of a child's storybook tale. The sun occasionally gleaming through the trees overhead as we walked. I raised my camera toward her as I caught the sun highlighting her perfect features once again. I snapped a few more surreptitious and some not so surreptitious shots with my trusty Canon.

She looked into the camera, smiling.

As we walked and talked, I felt important, like I mattered to someone. She was taking the time to get to know me, to talk, to relax, and ask about me.

She asked, "How do you do it, traveling alone for all these years?"

"Well, it's not easy," I explained. "You get used to spending time alone in airplanes, trains, automobiles, and hotels. Get accustomed to walking either crowded or lonely foreign streets, taking public or private forms of transportation, while nobody even notices you. It's like being invisible.

"Once home, you live a life within the seam of two cities. Most of the time during the week is spent commuting five hours a day; two and a half hours each way. You don't really have access to or develop any permanent bond with any social structure, either at work or at home. And home life is a lonely labyrinth of chores and obligations while local friends are mostly acquaintances.

"Work friends live far away, traveling into work from opposite directions, so traffic ensures you never see them in social settings on weekends. While true friends, like You, whom I've known for many years, live off in the distance or over the horizon in different states or countries. These people you rarely see for years at a time. Yet when you do, somehow you pick up where you left off as if time collapsed.

"You communicate where and when you can with people with whom you maintain a spark of commonality. Over time some fade away into their own lives. You communicate while you can, however, and whenever you can."

"Do you get lonely?" she asked.

"It's not as lonely if you make your life your work. And when at work you remind yourself, you only work to live and travel, and not live to work. You avoiding the long interminable commute, by traveling for business as often as possible. You buy yourself a high quality, expensive camera and keep it with you to use as often as you can. You provide it a gender and you even name it, so you never feel alone. You enjoy the partnership binding the two of you together."

"So that's why photography has become so important to you," she suggested.

"You see the sights of life happening around you, while she captures them in her memory, recording it forever—a time machine, preserving life's memories, so I'm able to relive these moments in time forever in my mind, and, posted on my walls for the rest of my life. These are solely my memories; sadly, I can't relive them with anyone else. This is the travesty of my adopted lifestyle—I can tell people about it, talk about it, describe it, but only I can truly relive the sensory experience surrounding these moments. This relegates my photographs to more than mere tangible memories; they are intangible treasures. Is it a life or is it an existence? This is 's a matter of perspective and a daily challenge for me to maintain a positive outlook," I droned.

"Photography has become a critical hobby of mine, because it gets me out of the hotels and hostels, keeps me alert to new things around me, and ensures I stay involved in life. It gives me a purpose while on vacation and keeps me company wherever I go. Oh, and if I get good at it, I may even make some money with it someday," I further explained.

"That sounds intriguing, maybe I should get into that as a hobby. It sounds like a great escape. Nora seems to be interested in your photos. We could use that as a hobby together. Maybe we could take some lessons. Do you get to spend much time at home?" she asked.

"That's a double-edged sword. I make my house both my home and my sanctuary, where I have my tangible toys and joys. I have an irreplaceable relationship with my two dogs and even with the wild birds dropping by to visit my bird feeders and bird baths, the deer who enjoy the salt licks, and the fox, turkey, raccoons, opossum and others who enjoy the sanctuary I provide. When I'm home, I try to make my life as enjoyable as I can until I go back on the road. I rely on family as often as I can to keep my mind straight. They are the only constant in my life."

"So do you like your life?" she asked.

"I have to—it's the only one I have. I like what it can do for me. I like it for everything I've done. I've lived multiple lifetimes in one. It got me here, didn't it?" I laughed. "Times like this, make me love it! Ironically, my entire life has pretty much been this way. And no matter what I do to try to change it, it remains the same."

"Do you get to see your kids much?" she asked.

"Not as much as I used to, and they're getting older now. They've got their own priorities, likes, dislikes, and hobbies. A few of us used to get together for skiing trips; not all of them ski, so that makes it difficult. And they're starting to move to different states, in different directions, starting their own adult lives. We do what we can, when we can," I explained. "I like to travel. Actually, I love traveling. It's not as much fun by myself but it's better than not traveling at all. I've learned to focus on my journey," I shared. "What about you?"

"Have you been to Spain? I love Spain! The food, the land, the moderate weather, the prices, there's so much there to take advantage of," she said.

"I've been to Portugal, right next door. I love it there. It's quaint. With pretty places to visit, plenty of coastline, and good food. I have a friend who just moved there. I go there every year for NATO conferences," I responded.

"We should show each other those countries. I'll show you Spain and you can show me Portugal," she sparked as we walked.

"I'd like that!" I said.

Leif bounded from side to side down the trail. I felt as happy as I had each day here. Minus the ominous shadow surrounding my imminent departure. I felt happy, fulfilled, and spiritually connected with both Erika and Leif.

While continuing to take photographs, Erika becoming unusually quiet. I noticed she, for some reason, didn't have the same sparkle in her eye as I saw in days past. In a few of the pictures, I detected an inward gaze. In other shots, she looked into the camera with an unfocused stare.

It was as if she was trying to lose herself among the spectacle of this natural setting—in the sparkling sun peering through the trees and reflecting off the waters of the frigid Baltic Sea. She was holding her arms close to her body while walking through the wooded trails. Typically, this is a self-soothing gesture, stemming from insecurity. Maybe we both were trying our best to present ourselves as happy and enthusiastic.

She left the trail, stepping out onto the rocky, sandy shore near the water, bent over stepping onto the rocks, grasped a stone, and skipped it across the calm waters. Watching her in the viewfinder, I snapped away. As she grasped another stone, I ensured she saw me doing this. I knew this would bring her back to the normal I now knew.

She yelled at me from the waterline, "Dimitri! Are YOU up to your old tricks again? What are YOU doing?"

Initially, I stammered then gathering my thoughts I said, "Your jeans! I love your jeans—especially from the rear. I'm gonna make my own commercial for those Lucky jeans! Maybe I'll get myself a pair before I go back to the States—just like those!"

"Veeery funny! They won't fit you! They're for girls!" as she smacked her tail.

As she did that, I timed my shot perfectly, yelling, "Got it!" And I captured that angelic smile that followed. I even got an excellent shot of Leif looking back at her skipping stones across the water, as if wondering why she was throwing those perfectly formed chewing rocks into deep waters.

We were now enjoying what started out to be a bit of a foggy, groggy morning. It was becoming a clear, cloudless one. We visited her next "special place" in the woods, then another along the shoreline. Eventually, we took a trail to the old mansion-turned-château, nestled among ancient farmlands where we walked the first day.

As we approached, she turned and smiled saying, "You're going to love this place!"

I again mumbled, "I already do!"

"Excuse me?" she murmured. I returned her smile.

The aroma of freshly brewed hot coffee, coupled with the scent of cinnamon pastries adorned with vanilla and almond toppings, permeated the fresh air, leading the way. Stronger and stronger it became as we emerged from the wooded path. Approaching the château, Erika locked her arm into mine, pulling me toward the café. Her gait sped up as she led the way to the door, opening it for me and Leif.

"Come onnn, I love this place! And so will you!" she urged again.

Once we entered, the warmth of the ovens was unmistakably welcoming. The multiplexed aroma of cinnamon, almond, vanilla, and freshly baked loaves of bread, pastries, and other morning treats were overpowering. There were all types of aromatic breakfast coffees—too many to count. All kinds of soft, gooey, chewy, cinnamon freshly baked breakfast buns, pecan rolls, and the most wonderful doughnuts I'd ever set my nose upon. They also served oatmeal, and malto meal, with a host of freshly squeezed juices for the most discerning breakfast connoisseur.

I leaned toward her and gently spoke into her ear, "So, this is what heaven is like." It was exactly as she described.

"Uh-huh!" she responded gleefully.

Leif was remarkably composed in this carnivalized aromatic cornucopia.

We both picked out a few pastries to share and poured some cups of hot coffee. Placing these items on a tray, we brought our treats outside to enjoy our newfound bounty. We scanned for a potentially open table, though we were the only customers there. It was apparent that the early crowd left all of their used cups, saucers, bowls, glasses and left-over morsels strewn about on every table but one.

As we took our seats, birds of all types [magpies, swallows, sparrows, doves, woodpeckers, jays, swifts, chickadees, larks, titmice, skylarks and others I didn't know], instinctively ignoring us swooping in from every direction. They were singing, chirping, prancing, dancing, fluttering their wings, eating and socializing at every table in this veritable feast that had been prepared specially for them; as far as they knew. Some even took breaks to bathe themselves in nearby puddles before returning for their fill. Our feathered friends obviously grateful for their treats, were in no rush to leave.

This, for Leif, was most likely a front row seat to a live television best of nature presentation. We had this entertainment for our entire snack time. I felt like Snow White in the woodland scene.

I never knew that Swedes were typically such messy people, leaving every table, but one, looking like sunrise after an Irish wedding. I wondered how people could be so reckless in leaving all their dishes outside, as if they had been beamed up by aliens? Or, could they have done this purposefully, for nature's sake?

As we sat, we spent the time laughing, watching the antics of the birds, Leif's reactions to them, talking about our past, and the past days we spent together."

The girls really like you," she blurted.

"How do you know?" I asked.

She laughed saying, "Remember when you washed Leif at the house the other day with the freezing cold water from the hose, removing the mud and seaweed from his fur after our walk in the woods and on the beach? Well, I told the twins about that and they laughed. Nora actually said, 'Gee Mom, no man has ever done that before! And no Scandinavian man is ever likely to volunteer to do that, ever! Plus, he has excellent taste in chocolates. He carried our bags last night AND took Leif's leash—AND, Leif let him! I think he really likes you too! Who would go through this all this for you… or for anyone? Nobody I've ever heard of! I like him! And he takes great pictures. Even Fiona agreed.' I was shocked hearing this since they typically don't take to anyone very quickly," Erika explained.

"You should listen to your children!" I spouted.

"Let's see the new pictures," she suggested.

I pulled my chair close to hers getting as close as I could. Putting my arms around her from the back of her chair, placing the camera in front of her, I extended the display.

Looking back at me she playfully slapped my arm saying, "You sneak."

As we reviewed the pictures on my camera's large screen, suddenly a magpie sat on a chair next to our table, seemingly listening to our conversation, staring at us. Watching the spectacle, we were speechless until I said, "See that black bird with the white markings on its wings staring at us, listening to us? Oddly enough it looks exactly like one I've seen in Korea, China, Thailand, Cambodia, Burma, California, Oklahoma, and well, every state I've been in throughout the U.S. He probably recognizes me. I think he's following me!"

"Get out!" she laughed.

Birds fluttered about filling their bellies with their treats. Going about their daily chores they even ignored Leif, coming within a mere paw's length while he stoically watched. I snapped a few pictures of them feasting on leftovers, gliding and hopping in celebration. I wanted to remember these wild happy birds in this little slice of heaven forever. This day was as perfect as the previous two. The clear weather, the surroundings, the light conversation, and my company; life on earth at this point was more than I expected. I never wanted to leave.

During a lull in the conversation I carefully offered, "You quite possibly are my creativity muse. On my journey here I was gifted a lot of poems."

Changing positions, she leaned over toward me, gazing deep into my eyes with her angelic smile and said, "Would you read some of them for me?" I agreed. Now, instead of the heavy emotional baggage I was afraid to transfer to her from my rehearsed late-night soliloquy, I thought it would be better to let my writing do the talking.

"Really?" I searched for serious interest.

"Really…" she confirmed, looking so closely into my eyes I could see my reflection looking back at me. I'd never seen that before.

Taking my cellphone out of my pocket I started reading, "Okay… here goes," I said. At first, I waffled, then I began reading:

Questioning Life

Who questions why?
With whom and where is too late?
Are we masters of our own destiny?
Or does chemistry determine our fate?

How is it possible?
That chemistry determines fate?
Which decisions will ruin our lives?
When is turnabout too late?

So, who is the One?
Has my beginning, or my end, yet begun?
Is that which is forgotten what you'll be without?
Can that unknown be reborn without doubt?

And on the question of the One?
What if at we first choose the not?
Where and when does our course correct?
Bringing the ship to correctly turn about?

What is the how? Where is the why?
What if we're never beyond comfort, venturing out?
What if we're not really living, while still being young?
Will always we suffer from eternal doubt?

Where is that ONE place of perfection?
For each it's different, no doubt
How do we know when we've arrived at success?
No worries, tis the journey it's about.

Do we ever truly arrive?
Is life consistently evolving to blame?
To stay in touch with the good times?
Can we stop and freeze the frame?

What happens if we become, suddenly one?
How long will we be alone?
Or are we already there?
Strong enough to stand on our own?

She watched me intently as my lips spoke. Once I stopped,
she smiled, faltered and said, "That's pretty deep. There are more,
right? Keep going. Please keep reading." I complied:

The Day We Met

The day we met,
I had no idea what to expect,
What if I didn't recognize you,
What if you saw me and left?

Though these thoughts were lurking in the shadows of my mind,
I was not the slightly bit nervous or depressed,
Waiting patiently for our fateful recognition...
Effortlessly time introduced us, then stood still I can attest.

I felt as if I knew you all along,
Like the decades prior never left,
You said you were running late getting ready,
As I was looking for your number and address.

In truth, we were both a bit late that day,
Not concerned if we looked our best,
We talked revealing our pasts, increasingly more comfortably.
Something in common we had already, I was impressed.

An after-breakfast meeting at first,
It was way too soon for lunch,
We initially settled for drinks of frap and tea,
And together left for brunch.

All in all, so comfortably short a first meet,
From where we saw each other first, most likely we would say,
With a wee bit of caffeine in the mix,
It had been thirty-three years and a day.

With no alcohol, perfume, or cologne,
No fancy clothes or shoes got in the way,
From this day forward we seemed to live,

Learning each other, again, from day to night to day

We caught up together despite all the time that passed,
Thru long walks and talks bleeding into the night,
What we saw and heard of our voices,
Never varied in the day's light.

A remarkable idea on both our parts,
For such a short duration of stay,
May lead to a lifetime of happiness for both of us,
The Angels in heaven might say.

Decades were stolen from Mother Nature,
But she seamlessly covered the debt,
Connecting somewhere in the middle,
But would Father Time lose this bet?

She seemed to enjoy what she inspired in me as my muse, so
I continued...

She Was

We were just children when,
Her smiling, happy eyes looked my way to greet,
She was the perfectly soft-formed image of,
The ONE woman in this world, I'd love to meet.

We came to know each other among friends,
But it wasn't in the cards for us to be,
Even though I felt I quite well knew her,
So much more than an epiphany.

When she brushed by, our auras touched,
My entire presence felt steely,
My heartbeat raced, breath drew short, my palms sweated,

My tongue ceased to work freely.

I wondered where she'd been, since last I'd seen her
33 years prior our friendship started and parted,
A whim, a guess, this Princess I finally found,
Where frigid winds blow, and among fjords they darted.

I wrote to her and, she wrote back,
This went on for not long, never I thought to count it,
Following my dreams, heading toward the arctic sunset,
Atop the mechanical bird, I mounted.

Searching for closure in life
With my idyllic one,
I imagined her smile with more than one dimple,
But perhaps now, she had none

Offering to visit her cold wet lands,
Her responses were n'ery simple.
I planned quite quickly within my silence,
Did my presence cause quite a ripple?

Coming without her knowledge,
The response I received regarding what I'd done,
Unfelt, since my letter of rejection from college.
Though I remember her hair as golden as the sun.

Beaming thru clouds
On a snowy winter's day,
Her skin so softly drawn in heaven,
Her heart kind and pure, as her beauty, dare I say?

Her voice breathed life into angels,
Her mind, sharp and loyal as the day,
Her laugh, simple and pure as the moment first I heard,

These images in my mind, had never gone away.

I dreamt one day I'd find her,
We'd walk with nothing in particular to say,
Would I alone be enamored,
Be it possible she'd feel the same way?

Nearly I had given up on my dream to meet this Viking
Princess,
Sharing her past in the very best of ways,
A second glance, seeing her image unreel,
But quickly vanishing into the light of days.

And now to me she's as real as life,
In her eyes, my reflection looking at me,
She still shines brightly as ever,
Her face as smooth as the waves of the Baltic Sea.

Never give up on your dreams I implore you,
Keep the hope you'll find your Princess someday,
Remember, never to surrender to failure,
Or let 33 years get in your way.

…And then there were the more abstract creations of mine:

Frozen In Time

Our images of each other,
Snapshots forever etched into our minds,
The last moments we remember being with someone,
Will forever, be frozen in time.

People most often will remember,
If you made them feel empty, lost, or sublime,
These may come back to haunt you,

And forever be, frozen in time.

The next time you part from anyone,
Be considerate before being unkind,
Aware that the images you proffer,
Will forever be frozen in time.

...And continuing on:

Partnering For Eternity

How can people limit relationships at the outset?
Don't people want to be a perfect pair?
Life's more difficult, when lived alone,
Do they not know happiness was designed to share?

The sun rises, with each new sunset,
Memories of the mundane unremembered, pass away,
Years may soon find you without that special someone,
Not knowing what you did, just yesterday.

Years of unshared sunsets,
Of beautiful stars and dawns simply gone,
Years to come may soon find you,
Watching the horizon, alone and withdrawn.

You cannot plan for it or time it,
When the perfect person in life you'll meet,
Just pray you'll recognize this bright spirit,
Without letting them pass by your two feet.

Men and women both must know this,
Don't let the golden aura, be the one who got away,
You'll regret that moment for the rest of your life,
With memories, or lack thereof, you'll pay.

When I paused, she looked introspectively yet intently at me, so I continued to dictate, deeper into my lightly charged emotional journey. Because in another 33 years, it would be too late:

Again

I want to love and really live,
I want to trust and lovingly bend,
I want to look deeply into trustworthy eyes,
Knowing this pair will never end.

I believe in the fairytale partner,
I want myself to be one,
I want to start each brand-new day,
Full of smiles, and love, and fun.

To travel with and please each day
Doing as much as could possibly be,
Why grow up and out of fairytale love,
Into adulthood accompanied by misery?

Love should be real and vividly intense,
Able to keep alive its infatuationary flame,
If burning out in just a few years' time,
The lovers simply have themselves to blame.

The two should be one and the best of friends,
Being partners through thick and thin,
Burning with passion, seeking the other's happiness,
Enabling a 'forever love' to begin.

Insulated, protected against the world's upheaval,
So life outside the home is never so dark and dreary,

> This home should become a solid barrier from all evil,
> And life inside burns bright, openly cheery.
>
> This is exactly what I want out of love,
> A true partner and best friend,
> This is exactly what I want out of life,
> For it to be truly wondrous again.

I slowed my speech as she appeared to enjoy what she was hearing. "Wow, those are great!" she exclaimed. "You have quite a talent for writing. Where did you get your inspiration?"

"I think you already know the answer to that question—from my muse," I said smiling.

She promptly got us on our way, distracting me from the sedate rhythmic conversation, once again presenting her modelesque happy smile. In her bubbly, cheerful voice she suggested we lighten the mood, "Are we done eating?" she perked up and grabbed her watch, gasping, "Hey, we've gotta go. Come on! There's someplace else I want to show you! It's my next favorite place in the whole world!"

"You have a lot of those, don't you?" I asked.

"Around here I do!" she sparkled.

We both knew what was foreshadowed in the next three or four hours, and neither of us wanted to rush toward it. Standing up from the table, we were still alone in the garden. I collected our coffee cups and saucers onto the tray bringing them indoors, surreptitiously gathering a few morsels from our plates as a nature donation. When I returned, she was still standing at the table waiting for me. I threw my morsels into the nearby grassy area toward the wild birds so she could see. Silently noticing what I did, thinking I perpetrated this act in a swift, concise, covertly camouflaged natural movement. She displayed her contentment with my action with her smiling, happy eyes. Looking down into her closed fist, she overtly displayed the nature donation she herself had surreptitiously gathered on her own. She threw these in the same direction. Mirroring her contentment with our actions she raised her eyebrows, shrugged her shoulders, and smiled. We both laughed at the coincidence and began walking in the direction she chose. We both knew the morsels wouldn't last long among God's beautiful and free, winged angels.

Again, she locked her arm into mine as we walked, cuddling close into my space. Her deep blue eyes dancing in the sunlight, she momentarily leaned her head against my shoulder clutching my arm firmly. Her blonde hair like a halo, pierced my anxiety. Moments later, I jumped at another chance at capturing such perfection on camera.

I stopped and said, "Don't move." She didn't. I reached for my camera and began snapping the shutter.

She turned as naturally as a professionally trained model, bounced on her toes in her faux fur-lined Ugg boots and then in a bright, bubbly voice she chirped, "Come onnn, let's go." I snapped a few more shots of her natural beauty before following. She extended her arms, smiled, and twirled as if in a professional photo shoot. The difference I made in her life in a few days made me elated. "We're not going to get anywhere by simply standing here," she barked.

She was right. I knew it. But I didn't want to go anywhere. I wanted to stay here and feel this way, forever. I was trying everything to avoid moving, leaving, ruffling this cocoon of happiness. I had to enjoy the time for what it was, at face value.

Walking ahead of me, I watched her bounce down the trail with her once snowy white Leif to her front, carelessly trotting through the residual mud puddles along the trail. I laughed inside, knowing as I did in previous days, once we got back to her house,

I'd be outside washing him. As the woods parted, we stood with our feet again on a different sandy beach.

She sat down and patted the sand next to her. "Sit!" she sparked. I complied. As I bent down to approach the space next to her, she looked ahead at the glistening sun dancing on the water. The frigid waters continuously cleansed the sandy beach, lapping across the sand, gently washing the sparsely spaced boulders securing the shoreline. We sat together with our shoulders touching, both looking forward saying nothing. I was afraid to look at her and risk destroying the moment. Her arm warmed mine as we touched. I leaned slightly into her and she leaned back. Leaning her head over, gently placing it on my shoulder she confided in a gentle whisper, "I'm really going to miss you."

"I'll miss you... I already do," I responded.

"We should keep this light and happy," she said.

We both maintained our gaze toward the horizon just above the glassy water, enjoying the view which again included a ferry in the distance. Part of me wanted to tell her everything I felt, over and over, again making sure she knew how I felt. While another part of me believed I had already done so; so had my poems. I wanted answers, but I knew if I pushed her, the answers I would get would not be those I wanted to hear. I hoped for positive closure. Why had I come on this quest? Was it for the experience or for hopes of a brighter future? Was it for rekindling a friendship? What did I actually expect? Should I expect positive closure or just answers? Or did I come to fulfill some unknown purpose as an unwitting assistant to the forces of the universal order? Or could my purpose have been to help her through whatever issues she wrestled with, never offering specifics? Or was she there to help me with my issues? Did I come to grow, learn, and enjoy myself? Or did I come just because I could? It was all of the above.

I turned toward her, looking into her eyes as she continued looking forward at the crystal-clear view. We said nothing. I broke the silence whispering, "I had an amazing time."

"It was special... very special," she responded still looking at the horizon. Then she hesitatingly whispered, "I don't want you to leave."

I didn't want to either, and if she asked me to stay, I would've found a way. She finally turned to me, looking into my eyes, and said before I agreed not to, "But you need to go. You're an amazing person, Dimitri, and you've got so much to do. People depend on you. I hate to share you with the rest of the world, but I have to."

"You don't have to," I added smiling.

"Yes, I do," she replied hesitantly. She broke her stare and looked back over the water.

"—but..." I tried to respond.

She interrupted me, "We'd better go. I don't want you to miss your flight. Come on, I'll cook you another special something!" she smiled as she stood brushing off her tail with Leif's leash tightly in hand.

"I could've brushed you off—that's my job," I lamented.

She smiled, "Oh, you'd love that, wouldn't you."

"Yesssss, I, would!" I laughed. "It's not too late, here..." I joking motioned toward her buttocks with my hands. We both chuckled as she played along, quickly shifting her weight protruding her hip, offering a single cheek, which I graciously, yet gently, slapped.

As she heard the crack of the slap disrupting the crisp quiet air, she pursed her lips, shrugged her shoulders and brows exclaiming, "Oooooh." We both laughed.

"As I said before—Lucky jeans!" I jokingly and gruffly barked.

"Come on Leif, we gotta go. Dimitri has to eat and then he has to go on a trip," she sighed and pouted. "God, I wish you could stay," she professed.

"Me too. You think I'm kidding?" I said.

"Nooooo, Dimitri, don't say that and do something crazy! People need you and depend on you," she voiced.

"I can come back," I asserted.

"You'd better," she acknowledged, "Come on… let's go eat!"

I watched her bounce down the trail behind Leif with her mission in mind to prepare me another tasty meal.

Entering the wood line, I looked up through the green canopy of the surrounding trees, catching glimpses of the sun occasionally piercing nature's leafy branch dome. We continued walking as I pointed out artfully created dancing shadows performing on the ground. The sun occasionally continued to announce its presence through the trees overhead. As it did, bright light flowed around her blond hair. I captured more pictures of her as we walked. She appeared to be in a daze, barely noticing my actions.

I couldn't help thinking how far I progressed with her in these few days, getting her to relax, leaving the pressures of the world behind, and being comfortable in front of my camera, where she belonged. Because of our time together, she seemed much happier and comfortable. She was noticeably more confident and at ease now, than when we first met. I enjoyed seeing her happy. I wanted this for her. And she wasn't getting any more awkward cellphone calls. Thinking about my impending separation from my muse, I felt dazed and stressed.

The approaching drive to the airport, intending to make my scheduled flights was stressing me out; I was already running behind my schedule. Still, I was completely at peace watching Erika and Leif walk ahead of me. I could only imagine how she would feel when the stresses of her world returned to attack her, once I left. Outwardly, she was happy. I knew my presence for her was a welcome, powerful, and meaningful distraction. It redirected her thoughts and actions away from a dreadfully stressful situation, whatever it was [she didn't say].

My presence brought her hope, focus, fulfillment, awareness and universal promise for a better future. My presence was seemingly as uplifting and positive an experience for her as it was for me. It was fulfilling to know I could do this for another person. So, the spirits in Germany urging me to come to Sweden may not have been solely for my benefit.

We made our way back to the house. Once there, as if on cue, she went inside to cook, while I cleaned off Leif. She prepared another artfully designed meal. Unfortunately, this would be my last meal in Sweden. Following Leif inside, she presented a bountiful buffet of fish, caviar, eggs, crackers, and expertly prepared Chanterelle mushrooms. She added fresh fruit, soup, water, fruit juice and a splash of wine. I watched her every move, trying to take it all in by solidifying these images and actions into my long-term memory.

I knew how I felt, but I didn't know how she felt. I knew she would tell me in time... well, I thought she might—I hoped she might. We kept the conversation light as she watched the clock for me.

Searching for the words, I finally admitted aloud to both of us that I had to leave for the airport. "Well," as we sat eating this wonderfully crafted meal at her dining room table, I stammered, "I hate to do it... but I think I've gotta go. As much as I would love to miss my flight and stay here..."

Erika jumped up saying, "I'll go with you, I can get something for dinner in the town square, for Nora."

"Thank you, God," I thought. It was already like I had a hole in my heart. It would comfort me having her beside me for even a bit longer, avoiding the awkward feeling of not wanting to part from her. I wondered if she thought my most recent approach to discussing our relationship was too aggressive or too serious, or maybe rushing her into another committed relationship, getting too serious too soon. Was it possible for me to "rush" into such a relationship after my explosion of feelings over the past three days that I held so closely for the past 33 years?

Had she thought of me at all? She didn't say specifically. It was doubtful. She still said little specifically about anything in particular. She knew exactly how I felt. I made sure of it this time.

We took a few minutes to clean up the kitchen together. I drifted downstairs, down the hallway, toward the front door, with her close behind. I helped her don her coat, and donned my jacket, then bid Leif a brief goodbye as he waited by the door. Erika checked on Nora in the girls' room, while I checked my camera backpack and secured everything. I still hadn't seen her supposed imaginary cats. Maybe there was more to her than meets the eye?

I was comforted with the fact that she wanted to come with me for the short ride into town; I didn't want to face her closing the front door on me—this metaphor would've skewered my heart! I didn't know what to do when we parted—hug, peck on the cheek, friendly kiss? How does one end such an awkward beginning? It's like she knew exactly how I felt and maybe even felt the same way, but failed to express it. I wanted her to be happy, more than I wanted it for anyone else. I also wanted her acceptance down to my core. If ever a feeling existed where another person could meld together with another body and soul, this was it. Her body language was sporadic and unclear, and her answers short.

So, what better way to remedy an awkward situation than to do it in a public place? Juuust perfect.

She emerged from checking on Nora and we silently made our egress from the house. I led her to the passenger side of the car, opening the door for her, as I had done so many times in the past few days. She stepped in and regally sat as I gently closed the door. I walked around the back, using the tiniest and slowest of steps, taking my place beside her. We traveled toward the tiny downtown area where I would have to leave her in the market square. I felt hollow.

The complexity of actions surrounding my long arduous trip back home to the States began consuming my thoughts. Soon I would be alone with my memories in my mind, images in my camera, and feelings in my heart. I traveled as slowly as traffic would allow. Admittedly, I was procrastinating. Extending this inherently quick trip, staving off my inevitable future, I did my best to stretch out our diminishing time together.

We drew closer to the market square, increasingly aware of the dwindling time we had. With every inch I drove, our immediate future was drawing to an inevitable close. I wanted to say something earth-shattering and profound, but the words wouldn't come. A lump in my throat developed and swelled. My throat drew tight. My mouth went dry. My breath heavy and shallow in my chest. The weight of the world was resettling on my shoulders. I felt a headache coming on. Soon the seat next to me where she was sitting would be empty. I'd be all alone again.

She sat next to me, her eyes focusing forward, down the street. I obsessively glanced toward her, trying to memorize with each nanosecond, her dynamic, intrinsic movements. I captured mental images of the shape of her profile as she furrowed her brow and energized her dimples, preparing to smile. I studied her as she pursed her lips, moistening them in the dry cold air and watched as she used her peripheral vision to see if I was looking at her. I would miss her presence tremendously.

Surveying the action in front of us, her deep blue eyes missed nothing in their path. She inhaled deeply, then blew out a few quick breaths, drew in a long breath, and released it slowly; her breath quivering. She was swallowing excessively, perhaps in anticipation of everything she too had to face alone. Soon she would be expected to stave off the foes and woes of the real world, presenting a strong motherly outward appearance for the twins.

"It's been a delightful distraction having you here. I really enjoyed rekindling the memories of our past. Life may have been busier back then, but it was less serious. It was more fun," she said.

I agreed, adding, "But we didn't know how great we had it."

In a few brief moments, her diversion would disappear and she would once again be expected to face the perceptibly heavy emotions of dealing with her soon to be past, alone. Her cellphone was silent. And so was her voice. Whatever she was thinking, it was intense. The trepidation she undoubtedly felt now would intensify on the heels of my departure. As would mine.

I played the gentle background music of the street minstrel's CD I bought in Poland the week prior; the same music I played on our trip to Stockholm. She caught me looking at her, and smiled as she always did, gently asking, "What?"

"Nothing," I confided, "Well, nothing bad." I shook my head a few times and mustered a closed-mouth smile. She half-smiled in response.

"You know..." I broke the silence, "We can still communicate through Viber, Skype, Facebook, emails, texts, and phone calls. This doesn't have to be the last time we hear from each other. You know, that right?"

In typical Viking Princess Erika fashion as I recalled from school, she regally responded, "I know."

She had a ton on her mind, and she wasn't letting me in. I could sympathize, empathize, and recognize the nonverbal cues, because I'd been there. Hers was not an enviable position. But neither was mine. She couldn't easily camouflage her melancholy, despite her efforts. I hoped for her sake the dark days of her past, along with her bleak outlook regarding her short-term future, would not return. Nothing I could do would change her present circumstance. But I could mitigate her symptoms by consoling her, provide encouraging words. And being strong with her in the last few minutes we were together. My attitude was being affected as well.

"You seem to be deep in thought. Is there something I can help you with?" I asked.

"No."

This perfect time in my momentarily perfect life was coming to an abrupt end. As soon as we stopped, I'd have to let her slip out of my life again; this time possibly forever. I drove past the docks with fishing boats, around the rotary approaching the small downtown area with busy shops and aging buildings close to my hotel. The traffic was perceptibly light, even for this small town. Pointing to the nearby shops where I could drop her off so she could buy groceries, she directed me where to park. I slowed, stopped the car, parking it where she showed me. Exiting sluggishly, almost moping around to the passenger side, I assisted her exit. She looked up at me with those piercing blue puppy dog eyes as I opened the passenger door. Gently, I presented my hand to assist her. With her sultry, angelic demeanor and similarly captivating smile, she said, "Thank you, Dimitri," and glided out into the crisp, chilly afternoon air. I nodded and thanked her by smiling back.

We stood together momentarily in awkward silence beside the car accosted by the frigid air. Her carefree, natural smile I came to know and love in the past few days and captured on my camera, slowly transformed into a concerned, silent, overburdened half-smile. Facing me, she extended her arms out, drawing me in. Placing her chin over my shoulder, grasping me close in a polite, yet meaningful hug, she sighed and muttered, "Thank you so much for coming, Dimitri. Thank you so much for everything."

Like every other moment with her, I wanted this time to last forever. And now it could, in my memories; in my perceived reality, but not in true reality. I told her during the past few days, and this time whispering in her ear using different words, "Focus on your happiness. Focus on your rainbow. Make it happen." I took this opportunity to surreptitiously slip a handwritten note I prepared in the hotel the night prior, into her coat pocket.

Trying to hide the burning lump in my throat, fighting back the tears behind my eyes, I held strong. I knew this point was inevitable and I could only somehow hope my future might include her. No matter how hard I tried, I couldn't alone transform my perceived reality into true reality. These were not the empty feelings of hope I had when I arrived; these were verified feelings from my empirical experience over the past few days. However, like my arrival, I could only set the conditions and await her response. All I said as I looked into her eyes and clenched her hands, "Thank you, Erika. I had an amazing time. I'm so glad I came. I'll miss you. You're an amazing person." I couldn't say anymore, the lump in my throat seized my voice, my throat began aching and a sensation of dry mouth overcame me. I nodded to bid her adieu.

She half-smiled, pursed her lips, and wiped her reddened nose, perhaps moist from the cold. She brushed her hair back away from her watery blue eyes with the back of her gloved hand in the bitter cold, persistent breeze. Nodding her head, whispering back, "Me too, Dimitri. Me too," her voice crackling.

Before she released her grip on my hands, again she half-smiled, saying nothing. She nodded, drawing away slowly, smoothly. We held our gloved hands together for a few moments as our fingers slid apart. Neither of us wanted to face the two divergent paths we were about to travel down; her alone in her country and in her world, and me alone in mine.

Turning abruptly, she walked away with her head down. Her pace was quick and serious, her shoulders drawn up and her arms crossed firmly in front of her. The sun was bright in the cloudless sky, but the air was freezing.

I got out of the cold, sitting behind the steering wheel inside the car. Closing the door, I refused to take my eyes off her as she walked. I was as captivated with her as I was on the first day of my visit, seeing her for the first time in 33 years. Except then she was walking toward me and I was full of excitement and anticipation. Now, she was walking away, and I was full of angst and somber emptiness. She walked at a slower pace than she typically had when she was with me. I so hoped she would turn and look toward me like they do in the movies. I so wanted that Hollywood Farewell. But she kept walking, maintaining her pace intently, and perhaps permanently, head down, focused forward. Watching, as she continued making her way down the sidewalk, her form got smaller. I didn't break my gaze. Again, I hoped she would turn around, even for a moment, for a few seconds, to look back at me one last time before she faded from sight—her breath visibly trailing behind.

Suddenly, as if on cue, she stopped in her tracks and turned. Removing one gloved hand from her coat pocket, her arm tucked closely into her body and hand close to her heart, she presented me with a half-hand wave, moving only her fingers. This wasn't a friendly wave; it was an intimate wave. She managed a half-smile without parting her lips. This was the smile I'd remembered all these years, and now for three more days. "Thank you, Princess," I said silently to myself, watching her. "Thank you for everything." Before she turned for the last time, she mouthed the words "Thank you," then turned and continued on her way. Before life got the best of me, I departed.

Beginning my long journey home, I listened to the music playing in my mind. Occasionally, I checked the GPSs to make sure they were working. Checking the clock, I thought there was no way I would make my flight without speeding. Forewarned when I arrived about the speed cameras and heavy fines waged upon non-conformists, this was classically the time to hope for the best. It was bittersweet. The fact I had to rush to some place away from where I wanted to be, toward some place I knew I had to be, though somewhere I didn't want to go, and inside something I didn't want to take me there, was all extremely troublesome.

My feelings were half-empty as I continued on. I learned from this experience, sometimes life CAN be perfect, just NOT for very long. Looking at the empty seat next to me, remembering how it began empty when I arrived, temporarily filled with hopes and feelings with Erika occupying it, and now—empty again. The process was reversing itself. My new world began to unravel and disintegrate. I thought about her looking at me as she sat beside me. Then how she turned back to look at me one more time before walking away, touching my soul with her smile. I no longer wondered about my dream girl—now, I knew. And I knew her. And she knew me. Undoubtedly, she was thinking of me—I didn't know to what extent and in which capacity. This was why I felt only half-empty. The Erika I knew went through a metamorphosis during my visit. And she was real to me now. I recalled looking into her eyes, seeing myself looking back at me— that was a first.

Although I wanted another week, or even another weekend with her, deep down I knew I wanted a lifetime. It seemed I'd been in Sweden for months, not days. My reality and fantasy were fused, just as the past and present had been during my entire visit. My power of perception was expanding. Encroaching into my present, my awareness of her morphing pressed forward into a perceived, yet all too believable reality.

As I watched the mesmerizing lines in the middle of the road whisk by, I came to realize I had no more control over my life with her than I had over these lines. I knew my established limits, but the lines I had no control over. I couldn't move them or change them, much like the Erika over whom I had no control or influence as she whisked by in my life. In the bright light of the afternoon sun, I really had not a care in the world. I traveled with all the grace, energy, and natural beauty of a wild mustang running on the open plains with his mane flowing in the wind. I knew I'd no longer wish, wonder, hope, and pray about the "what if" of my visit. I did it! I made it happen, against all odds, against all logic, and against the advice from others—I did it, I was ecstatic that I had. I was exceptionally free to let my memories and my emotions roam, silently. Knowing what I accomplished from conception to completion was fulfilling. I took astounding pride in thinking, "Mission accomplished!" I smiled as I traveled forward through the frigid air.

Grateful for having the capacity of feeling the way I do, I question why so often in the past my feelings were left unfulfilled and unreciprocated. I wanted someone to care about me as strongly as I cared about her. I wanted someone to truly miss me, as much as I missed her. I wanted to be a priority in someone's life, not a mere afterthought or simple distraction. I wanted to be cherished, not merely tolerated. I wanted someone to think of me and buy me tiny trinkets, no matter how insignificant. I wanted someone to want to share my life, as much as I wanted to share it.

How could I have survived my experiences of war and suffering, happiness and celebration, dark and light, at home and far away, only to yield no emotional relationship of any significance at this point in my life? I thought about how lucky emotionally shallow people must be, never feeling tremendous emotional stress or debilitating loneliness. Never knowing the overwhelming need for spiritual fulfillment, or even harboring a comprehension of reality within the multitude of dimensions in life itself, as I do. I wondered if it was better to traverse life with minimal downs and minimal ups? Within such a perspective, life would most likely never be too terrible. However, it would never be great either—life would be relegated to always being merely "okay."

Up to this point in my life, the only thing I really wanted to come into fruition, was to find and become involved in a relationship where Romantic Love was the primary mutual focus. I needed a break from the material world of disappointment. I needed a best friend. I needed a partner to relax with and help me explore the world and my feelings. I needed an eternal romance. Erika appeared to me to be the perfect woman I knew years ago, and our relationship was developing into what I had imagined it could be.

Was this a crazy conclusion to reach after only one three days... well, there were the 33 years prior. I knew it was crazy, but I've heard of plenty crazier! It was about time a relationship worked out for me. I paid my dues. Here I was traveling the world, doing everything I dreamed of doing, seeing amazing sights, learning unbelievable facts, seeing mind-blowing landscapes, tasting orgasmic food, but having nobody significantly special to share it with. In my mind, this was only half a life. It was a life somewhat unfulfilled, despite all the successes I attained. Now I had this one amazing life-changing weekend. Mentally, spiritually, physically, and emotionally, I had a fantastic journey; that's all that mattered. I planned my journey, and I did it! I made it happen! I did it! I really did it!

Arriving at the Arlanda airport grounds, I passed the Jumbo Stay, a converted 747 aircraft now a hotel at the far end of the runway. I hadn't seen that when I arrived, possibly due to the late hour, but most likely because I was mentally exhausted. Everything was easier now, because I'd done it all just 96 hours prior.

Once onboard the aircraft, I kept glancing at the empty seat next to me. Though it was empty, my euphoria would last for my entire journey back to the States. My recent experience completely overshadowed each nanosecond, minute, and days of the past 33 years. My most recent memories consumed my thoughts of this perfect weekend. My dreams transformed into reality. I didn't have all the answers I wanted, but then do we ever? I had something better—the memories and photographs accompanying those memories I could cherish forever. Plus, I had a happy near future to look toward.

I wore down all four of my camera batteries looking at the photographs on my camera; mostly the ones I took in Sweden. Occasionally, these memories brought a tear to my eye. I missed her. Now knowing exactly what I was missing was tortuous. But I was in awe of these new images. She truly was as beautiful as I remembered 33 years ago, now just a little bit older.

I made my connecting flights all the way home. Now I had to catch up with all that I had temporarily ignored. Unfortunately, my life would soon go back to normal; well, as normal as it could be. Normal as I knew it to be. Ultimately, it would seem like I never left; but my photographs would prove otherwise. None of this mattered to me now. I was enjoying the ride!

~ 21 ~

Chasing Ghosts

The week I returned home after all was said and done, I settled into my routine, except I had a few activities to add. Sooner than I realized, life was back to the normal daily grind with the round-trip five-hour car, train, and metro/light rail commute, returning from the Pentagon to my countryside retreat daily, until my next business trip.

Initially, Erika and I communicated daily. We both looked forward to it. We texted, Skyped, Vibered, spoke on the phone, and emailed. We took advantage of every aspect of modern communication afforded to us. It seemed we had everything in common: likes, dislikes, diet, movies, activities, humor, philosophy, spirituality, and hobbies. I was still in heaven. I looked forward to the seconds, minutes, and hours until our next contact. That was a routine I truly cherished and was the priority in my life.

I whiled away the time both at work and at home, awaiting the next opportunity to talk to her. Sometimes she'd call me first thing in my morning and I'd give up my workout, or miss my train commute, having to drive three hours to work in heavy traffic by myself. But I was okay with this. Sometimes we'd talk until the wee hours of the morning when I'd try to squeeze in a few hours of sleep before running to catch the train to D.C. for work. I was okay with that too, for I was in Romantic Love and nothing else mattered.

Conversing with her brought me to a much better place mentally and spiritually. She had her carved, painted Polish wooden angel, and I had my carved, painted Polish wooden Soldier. Each of us carved and painted smiles into the faces of our somewhat expressionless wooden figurines. We did this at the same time without coordination. Both of us surprised the other. When we discovered this, we were equally amazed and amused. I made a small wooden pedestal for my figurine Soldier, where he could watch over me from his perch in whichever room he was. I held close to her words, "It would be our challenge to find the means to reunite them." These words played over in my mind. We began all our video chat sessions by mimicking these figurines talking. We often ended our conversations deciding which movies to watch, looking forward to the upcoming weekend.

We had movie night, despite the six-hour time difference. Knowing the other was watching the same movie worlds away on the same day was comforting. The following day, we'd discuss the movies we saw. This was fun. It still seemed like we had watched the movie together, without interrupting each other by talking during it.

I bought a new watch with world time zones to always accurately know what time it was in her time zone. My buying a video language training program to learn Swedish since she mentioned wishing I could speak her language, was a big surprise to her. Certainly, this wasn't too much to expect of me. I scoured department stores for items to purchase and snail mail to her at astronomically staggering prices. I compiled gift baskets for the day she may decide to visit. I continued serving as her muse, and she as mine.

She remained tight-lipped regarding most of the details in her personal life and I didn't think it was my place to pry; not yet, anyway. I wanted to give her the space she needed. I felt this was an intense time in her life. She needed a friend. And, I didn't want to interfere in whatever healing she needed. I was honestly interested in helping her find her the happiness I felt she so richly deserved. My motives were pure and unselfish.

We talked so she could vent on her terms, when it was convenient in her time zone. I wanted to help her get focused, absorb some of my energy, and derive the motivation to move forward through her quagmire. For about a month, we spoke daily. Eventually she missed a few contact windows, and then missed more and more. Soon, our contact became sporadic. Our charted rituals quickly faded. I spent hours waiting for the phone to ring, texts to chime, or emails to arrive.

One night, I noticed my carved Soldier wasn't on his perch. I looked everywhere—under, over, inside, outside, beside all the furniture throughout the room. I extended my search into the rest of the house and inside every bag I owned. I even queried the dogs about chewing him up. One of them, in the distant past, ate a prized, carved, wooden decoy that cost me hundreds of dollars— as I looked at them accusingly, they both turned toward each other and then back at me, repulsed by the thought of being wrongfully accused; I soon thought otherwise. I continued looking—even checking inside my vacuum cleaners.

This wooden Soldier was the one item I couldn't afford to misplace, since it was critical to the beginning of all our video conversations. Between the loss of the Soldier and her sporadic contact, I began feeling a deep emptiness inside. Day after day, night after night, I unsuccessfully searched for my little wooden friend. I wondered what happened to him—he simply disappeared. More and more time passed since my last communication with Erika, and since my carved wooden friend vanished. His absence became an ominous omen.

Though I tried, my video chat attempts and phone calls went unanswered. Even the voice messages I left fell on deaf ears, unacknowledged. My texts and emails remained still in the silence of their outboxes, unseen by blinded eyes. Surely, it had nothing to do with the loss of my little wooden friend. Or did it?

I continued calling, leaving messages, texting and e-mailing, receiving no response. Like my little wooden friend, one day she too vanished from my life. My new best friends and muse were nowhere to be found. I became completely hollow; my world devastated. My confidence and self-worth crushed. I was no longer counting the seconds, minutes, and hours, between our contact; I was dreading more time passing, because I knew what it meant. Waking each morning into this nightmare of reality became excruciatingly painful. My meagre existence with extremely limited human interaction outside of work became excessively grueling.

My sleepless nights dragged onward into sleepless days. A few more weeks, then a month passed before my hopes of any contact were realized. Finally, on one of my long train rides home, it came as a brief, impersonal text message, without context.

"Hi, how are you? I've been really busy! Ciao!"

Without warning, I felt as if my stomach had been punched, wrenched, and ripped from my body. My heart fluttered with anguish. I sat on the train keeping it together, awaiting arrival at my station. The minutes crawled by as I stared out the window, trying to vanquish negative thoughts of what was happening. She was a shadow fading from my life.

I wasn't prepared for these endless days of hollow, shallow emptiness, filled with the loneliness, I now came to know as normal. I went from being her muse, and a priority in her life, to being utterly insignificant. I wasn't even an afterthought. I was nothing. Occasionally, I received a few simple texts like the previous one, but no direct responses to my messages.

Months later, when work was sending me on my bi-annual trip to Hawaii, I sent her an invitation to meet me there. My treat. I offered staying in separate rooms, and even suggested she bring the twins. After about a week, she politely wiggled out of this invite with only two words,

"I can't."

Opening fresh wounds in my heart, my hopes rekindled within me as I waited for another response. It never came. All my hope was eventually squeezed dry. The raging fire of Romantic Love was still smoldering inside me. I never wanted to give up hope. Her words that "Nothing is impossible," kept echoing in my mind. As did her once clear intent, "Why don't you keep the Soldier with you, and I'll keep the Angel with me. It'll be our challenge to get them back together."

I began questioning everything associated with my journey. Ultimately, as a means of self-preservation, I matched my actions and reactions with hers. My phone calls stopped, my writing slowed—as did the texting, emailing, and letters I once wrote. She stopped answering, so I stopped initiating. One day everything just trickled away. She muted all positive vibes and feelings regarding our newfound friendship. I placed my Swedish language CDs into a giveaway box. The most difficult fact to accept, was that I wasn't everything to her she was to me. I wasn't the person to her I wanted to be. I wasn't the one I hoped to be. I wasn't the one I expected to be, despite my thoughts, hopes, and prayers, that I could be. I was nothing to her.

At first, this was a complicated and difficult reality for me to face. The possibility of being completely insignificant to the one person in the world with whom I felt to be perfectly matched, though physically separated by the expanse of seas, oceans, and time zones, was difficult at best. She relegated me from daily personal contact as a top priority, becoming routine to both of us, to no longer even an after-thought. This was quite the emotional storm to wrestle. In the end, I realized there was nothing I could do, but accept it. Whatever it was. I was completely dumbfounded regarding her actions and reactions. This wasn't the first time for such an occurrence in my life, and it probably wouldn't be the last. However, it would probably be the last from Erika.

Countless questions remained in my mind. Was her heart so broken and irreparable that she lost faith in the possibility of finding Romantic Love with the probability of happiness, or was it just with me? Was she apprehensive of a long-distance relationship or already committed to another person without telling me? Was there something else she refused to tell me, or did she need to be single for a while longer, capturing space to breathe and think? I contemplated taking the advice I gave Matt years prior. Maybe there was someone else in her life.

She once believed in my words and in me... but for whatever reason, she couldn't... she wouldn't... or at least didn't vocalize it now. Was she choosing not to be honest with me, or being purposely evasive because it was easier for her? Or was it? Maybe it really wasn't easier for her. I didn't know. But I wanted to know, unequivocally.

On one typically lonely night in my house nestled deep in the woods and rolling hills of Fredericksburg, I returned from yet another frequent visit to Ferry Farm. This was George Washington's boyhood house where he lived from age six to 22-years-old. It hit me. Why not go where I initially found her? I went online, checking her Facebook page. She had changed her relationship status. It now read, "In a relationship." Did she make a decision greatly affecting me without even a mention? Or did her status change not involve me? I sent a quick note on Messenger since she seemed to be actively communicating there. Without elaboration my note read,

"I assume your change in relationship status has nothing to do with me."

Days later she responded, "I suppose I should've told you."

Perhaps at first, without communicating how she felt, she enabled my thoughts to wildly generate feelings for her. Cultivating a lush landscape of Romantic Love among rolling green hills, fertile with plant life. Then later, on this cue, the rolling hills instantaneously withered without the water of encouragement, and the fertilizing words of affirmation. No longer was time and sunlight provided for uninhibited growth. Maybe it would've been easier if I was the one who lost interest. Within me, the fields of hope were drying into a desert of despair, at long last decaying into dust, blowing away into the winds of time. Although I knew the result, I didn't know the why. I may never know.

Accepting as fact, that nobody wants to be a consolation prize—least of all, me, I began my acceptance of true reality. I hoped she would soon fade from my thoughts and dreams. I felt as lost as a priest discovering irrefutable evidence disproving the existence of God—except I still worshipped the idea of Romantic Love. I lost faith. I lost hope. For now, I lost focus in my quest for Romantic Love.

I also knew irrefutably that "Everything is impossible," if your Romantic Love Interest doesn't feel as you do. Because each of us is only half of the Romantic Love equation. The challenge would now be mine alone to foolishly pursue, if I elected to do so. I felt compelled to thank her for the feelings she birthed with fire within me years ago. And for the creativity she recently sparked within me; but I never got the chance.

What did I write on the note I slipped into her coat pocket during our last moments together? The message was quite simple. I wanted her to know I was ready and willing to accept my role in her life as her muse. It was my responsibility to return the favor, as we should all strive to help each other when called upon. My note read:

Being The True Optimist

One person looks at the world
Seeing the destruction and suffering
Thankful for the situation...
Knowing that it could always be worse.

Another person looks at the world
Seeing the destruction and suffering
Thankful for the situation...
Knowing that it could always be worse...
Hoping that it will get better...

Yet another person looks at the world
Seeing the destruction and suffering
Thankful for the situation...
Knowing that it could always be worse...
Hoping that it will get better...
Expecting it to get better someday...

And yet another person looks at the world
Seeing the destruction and suffering
Thankful for the situation...
Knowing that it could always be worse...
Hoping that it will get better...
Expecting it to get better someday...
Knowing that it will get better someday...

The True Optimist looks at the world
Seeing the destruction and suffering
Thankful for the situation...
Knowing that it could always be worse...
Hoping that it will get better...
Expecting it to get better someday...
Knowing that it will get better someday...
And decides to make that day TODAY!

Hoping, knowing, and expecting are NOT courses of action.
They are courses of inaction.
Make the decisions for YOUR life, or they will be decided for
YOU.
Without YOUR action in YOUR life, nothing is likely to change
for YOU.
Plan, decide, and act!
Be the better optimist!
Be the TRUE OPTIMIST!

I later came across a great explanation of protecting yourself against such emotional trauma, the Reiki philosophy as I paraphrase:

'Never use your own internal energy to heal others. Always use the eternal energy around you. Gather it and channel it into your subject. Failure to focus and concentrate on the positive chi may tap you of your own spiritual energy, even worse, negative energy may attach to you and attack you. If this happens, you could possibly take on the physical ailments of those you are trying to help another.'

Doesn't this sound much like Romantic Love? It would also be helpful to remember, "Love conquers all." "All," in this context, can refer to "all" external forces attacking the Romantic Love. But "all" can also include both the Lover and the Lovee, couldn't it? This is what Romantic Love meant for Romeo and Juliet. "All" can also refer to "all" of a complete person. This can serve as a warning to Romantic Lovers. The one ingredient that holds you together as a person, or as a couple, may be Romantic Love. This single byproduct is an amalgamation of interrelated and disassociated components reacting against forces and actions birthing a union of two people. This union can be an addicting and exhilarating ride. It may be everlasting or it may cease suddenly for an equally endless number of reasons. This termination may affect the couple by destroying not just the relationship, but simply stated, it may destroy the individuals. If they let it.

By all means pursue Romantic Love, find it, ride it, enjoy it, but always hold a little back of yourself for yourself, in case the ride doesn't last. This is brilliant advice, though tough to heed when applied to your own emotions. I wanted to figure out this concept for myself—I needed to…

~ 22 ~

Beginning Anew

Time dragged on as I recovered from my Romantic Love stupor. This experience left me dazed, confused, and hollow inside. I awoke to a perfectly cloudy, weekend day. I knew it would transform into a cloudless day later as the sun occasionally flashed through the large white fluffy clouds. What a great day for a hike!

I brought my hounds to the newly dedicated state park down the street named, *The Crow's Nest*. This was one of my new favorites, where I spent most of my days off. was a great escape from the disappointments of the world. After some quick preparation, off I went with my backpack of snacks, water, a few emergency tools, a first aid kit, and collapsible dog bowls. This was my therapy.

The state of Virginia purchased this land from a private hunting club. There were no boundary markers beyond the front gate, no paved roads, no traffic, and no budget earmarked for development. A single horizontal pole marked and blocked the entrance to vehicles. There was no parking lot, only a grassy area next to the wood line where people would eventually park, once the park was publicized. As a newly designated park, it wasn't even patrolled. Here, the three of us roamed freely. I actively hoped there would be no disgruntled or uninformed former hunt club members stalking us here in the middle of nowhere. Thankfully, we never had any issues and we never saw anyone else in these woods. It was always just the three of us. That's how we liked it.

Sliding under the horizontal pole barrier entering the park, I let the dogs off-leash. We walked the dirt paths through the rolling hills lined with trees; the dogs usually trotted ahead. Birds chirped and sang melodic tunes in surrounding trees. Squirrels occasionally bounced high overhead, while many other creatures made noise stirring, rustling, and scratching about in the dried fallen leaves. I selected and followed a trail, letting our feet and minds wander.

Hiking for a few hours, we ignored the multitude of other trails intersecting this one. Occasionally, I checked my wrist compass to ensure we were heading in a consistent magnetic direction. I knew this time I wanted to head east toward the Potomac River. I wasn't sure exactly how to get there and which path would lead us there, but it was fun exploring. This was quite the paradox. Sounds familiar, doesn't it? Isn't life often this way? With a pool of many options to choose from, pick one and if it doesn't work out, go back to the last known point, and follow a different path. Or just charge forward, forcing your way through and see where you end up.

This time it struck me that this same concept parallels Romantic Love. It intrigued me, realizing there are two sides to every story, and many more than one perceptible explanation for every outcome. We search until we find a path bringing us to our intended destination, yet not necessarily the final or correct destination.

Arriving at a clearing offering multiple routes, each going in a different direction, I arbitrarily picked one. After a few false leads and returning to the clearing for a restart, we wandered through the woods on yet another trail. The dogs kept looking back at me. At one point I turned in a 360-degree direction, feigning complete disorientation, with my arms up in the air. The younger dog, Sam, saw my actions and started crying in a sad howl. After settling him down, convincing him I was just kidding, I picked a path and continued forward. It was getting easier now since we had narrowed the field of options and had plenty of light left in the day. Onward we pressed, Sam, Cassie and myself, toward the lost Potomac River.

My four-legged hiking partners looked up at me periodically as if questioning where we were going and all I said to them confidently was, "We'll get there. Go! Go and find!" We continued up a hill and came across what looked to be an abandoned Civil War cemetery. After exploring the few rows of Civil War era headstones, appreciating the sacrifices these Soldiers made for their country and paying my respects, we continued along the path, around a corner, and up another hill. When the incline lessened and the ground leveled, I knew this was the right trail! It felt right. After hiking through the woods for another half-hour or so, we finally made it. I hadn't been here before, but seemingly here we were once again. Atop the high ground, I walked over to a cliff edge. Looking down, we were overlooking the waters of the Potomac River, nearly a hundred feet below us.

The sun was still shining between cloud formations through the leaves on the trees. The air was cool, yet not enough to make us shiver as we all sat down for a break after our mini-expedition through the untamed forest. The ground was cold and damp. A slight crisp breeze brushed across my face, cooling me down from the hike, while the sun provided a blanket of warmth peering through the trees overhead. Beginning with a water break, we sat down near the cliff edge overlooking the shimmering waters below.

It was peaceful where we sat, one dog resting on each side of me. Trail mix [without walnuts] provided the perfect snack for all of us. Pouring some of my canteen water into their collapsible portable silicone bowls, I listened and watched as they happily lapped it up. The weather was restfully peaceful, and the harmony of the forest wildlife, serene. We scooted closer to the cliff edge, sitting on an outcropping of rock only 20 feet long by 10 feet wide. The dogs crawled even closer to the edge stretching their necks out, looking down to the river waters below. My heart didn't enjoy this stunt, so I affixed their leashes securing them, preventing potential disaster. They reluctantly stepped back to join me, finishing their water and more of the trail mix I poured for them.

High overhead, a sharp, shrill scream gave way to a rare sight. Two bald eagles soaring above the trees, riding the air currents in tandem. They formed semi-circles frolicking with the wind under their wings, the sun shimmering off their beaks. Occasionally, their wings appeared to brush together while they floated across the sky, skillfully riding the updrafts. They belonged together in the sky and so did we—the three of us together, here on the ground.

Looking at my watch, it was 10:30 am, October 12th. One year ago, I was in Sweden, enjoying the crystal-clear waters of the Baltic Sea on a similarly bright, sunny fall day with idyllic weather. Except then, on my left was the beautiful white Nordic bear-hund, and on my right—in all her splendor and brightness—was Erika. I missed her. I missed being with her. I missed hearing her voice. Her carefree, joyful laugh danced through my thoughts. I missed seeing her smile. I missed watching her walk. I missed our talks. I missed those Lucky jeans and smelling the light bouquet of perfume in the surrounding air when she was near. But mostly, I missed her friendship. In this moment, I realized the totality of all I was missing.

But I was okay with it. I had to be. I was entranced being part of her world and having her as part of mine. I relished being her muse and her being mine. Because of her, I was gifted poetic writings that were spawned and freed from within the hallways of my mind. Why she confided in me, I didn't understand, but I was grateful she chose me to trust. But why she didn't confide in others was beyond my comprehension. The magnitude of this filled me with a sense of satisfaction.

We reintroduced ourselves after 33 years; at the time, she needed me and I needed her. I was there without stipulation of expectation. I was okay with her decision not to tell me about the relationship her Facebook account eventually revealed. I realized at this point, none of us can make someone like us, let alone love us. And it's unfair to expect it. We can't really make anyone happy, unless they meet us halfway and are open to it. Our sole input is only 50 percent of the Romantic Love equation. I made her happy for a brief time when she needed it most, as did she for me. For whatever reason, she moved on. Thinking of my feelings for her, I honestly didn't know what fueled them—the intensity, the power of the emotion, and the unwavering longevity. Perhaps this was why she too couldn't understand how she felt about me and could never convey her feelings in words.

As I reflected on my trip, I loved every second and everything about it. Germany, the fluidity of my seminar, the enchanted castle, hospitable Hans, Layla and her fellow cackling clucking cynics, Poland, personable Peter. Sweden, its small towns, friendly people, animals, diverse border areas, landscapes, historic sites, twisting back roads, unique cultures, customs, courtesies, architecture, food, sights, sounds, smells, and the range of feelings and emotions I experienced daily. I valued the totality and individuality of each memory. I'll remember all these forever. These are the gifts I received from the experiences encountered; these are what I value most. Therefore, focusing primarily on the journey is critical—it must be all about experiencing the journey; not about your preconceived expectations within it or avoiding discovery.

I'm so glad I went to Sweden and elated I took the time to spend with Erika; and grateful she dedicated the time she did for me. I'm glad I took the chance to rekindle our friendship after 33 years, though it was short-lived. There was something I still couldn't figure out. Did I do or say something to upset her during my visit? I'm glad I finally looked her in the eyes and conveyed what eluded me so long ago. After all those years, I did it! I was disciplined enough to follow through with my plan, though not confidently, and extinguished my associated regrets. During those three perfect days in Sweden, I did my 50 percent. I'm glad we ate together, walked through the Swedish woods, laughed and shared, took the time to care, and so glad we both dared. And like my memories of her as a child-teen, I was happy to have these new memories to complement the old; both of which will last forever.

Was it an aberration in my behavior for me to fly off on a moment's notice to chase and wrestle this rainbow? Yes, admittedly, it was not "normal." And it was the first time I did so in the name of Romantic Love. Having done it once, I'd do it again. I still occasionally buy lottery tickets on the miniscule chance I may win, but I don't expect it. But as with everything you can't win if you don't play. And maybe living a perfect fantasy even for a little while, is better than living endlessly in a distorted, cold, emotionally unpromising reality.

My advice to both myself and to others, is to embrace the fantasy and maybe try living it. Attempt to make it your reality. If it doesn't transform from fantasy into reality, at least you still have the fantasy that can provide you with a mental break, a perpetual escape, a better perspective, and an improved outlook regarding your future. That's why they call it taking a chance. I didn't want to wonder for the rest of my life what could have been. I wanted to know. Now I know. And I'm glad for it.

Without risk, there is no reward, right? Defining and adhering to the "normal" in our lives could birth thoughts to be dismissed as fleeting mental games conjured up to deflect boredom and instill some excitement into our otherwise mundane existence. Such a governor or "blow valve" in our minds protects us from self-destruction, and potential harm or impact. But it can also convince us not to pursue our dreams, preventing us from taking any risks and having any fun.

Such a quest during this stage of my journey was, and still is, to find my sense of "normal." But what is normal? To me, Erika was perfectly normal. More normal than anyone I'd ever met. At least she is what societal "normal" used to be. Which incidentally, is the only normal I know and am most comfortable with. But this was not the "normal" I was meeting before venturing to Sweden. Strangely enough, "societal normal" hadn't worked for me up to that point in my life, so I followed my heart, dabbling in the "abnormal action application," which I thought might aptly work. After all, where's the adventure in "normal"? Is it possible to arrive at your "normal" by adventuring through the abnormal? The emotional intensity I remember feeling in school seemed so perceptibly accessible that I jumped on the possibility of rekindling it. It was worth a shot. And now, once again, life would be a daily adventure, alone.

This emotionally and financially risky endeavor didn't exactly work out as I wanted and half-expected, yet, I had one hell of an exciting emotional, spiritual, creative, and physical ride. This entire experience placed me on a different plane of existence. I now know what my emotions are capable of, and what they can do for me. The next similarly charged opportunity might work out for me. In reality, Sweden did work out for me, but only for a few days, weeks, and months. Not for nearly as long as I hoped.

Afterward, I needed to step back, redefine what was "normal" in my life, define my strategy and identify my tactics. Laying out what I wanted, where I wanted to search, and reassess what could be, should be, and what I wanted to be regarding Romantic Love in my life... from scratch.

Being a part of her world entranced me. But ultimately, I realized I was a visitor in her world, and it was not mine. Now, back in my world, this was the "normal" I was familiar with and compelled to accept. Our worlds once again were strangely disparate, separate, and aloof from one another. Based on the choices she made, our worlds are likely to remain apart for eternity. It is said time heals all wounds; this is debatable. It does, however, provide us the tools and ability to adjust to the pain we experience, and overcome it, eventually healing our emotional wounds. From this experience, I learned we don't always get to determine our own reality. But we do get to determine our perception of it, as well as our reaction to it.

As a child, I believed in Santa Claus, Rudolph the red-nosed reindeer, the Easter Bunny, birthday wishes, the Tooth Fairy, and the Viking Princess. The fact that none of these beliefs abided by the laws of physics, didn't matter. They were what I wanted to believe in, and the path I chose. And now, as an adult, the notion of Romantic Love is in this same category. Though the roles and rules of contemporary society have repeatedly proven me wrong, the notion of Romantic Love makes my life much more hopeful, robust, exciting and fun.

From my perspective, Romantic Love is a magical, mystical, calm, euphoric, young, energetic, spontaneous, creative and limitless feeling. It's the ability to transcend your own instincts, caring for another human beyond the realm of solely your own selfish interests. Romantic Love is not typically practical and pragmatic. Romantic Love focuses on the other person, which often counters the instinct of self-preservation. Just plain old love is an emotion of convenience—carefully analyzing and executing actions, preserving and protecting the "self."

In contemporary society, convenience is king. The notion of Romantic Love is mostly chemistry, perception, and reaction. It doesn't necessarily occur in an instant, nor necessarily out of servitude. Romantic Love should be exciting, deliberate, and impulsive. It should contain elements of anticipation and surprise. It should be fun, interesting, comfortable, familiar, satisfying, intriguing, and shared. It should engender confidence, loyalty, and dedication. It should be powerful, persistent, and progressive. Romantic Love should be groomed, inspired, and maintained at all costs.

Romantic Love is where you feel the commitment and unconditional acceptance when there is no expectation of it. It's where you feel energized to share everything within your world, without coercion or expectation to do so. As unlikely as it is to occur, it's where every factor in two separate worlds at some point smoothly, seamlessly, and naturally converge into one.

Perhaps Romantic Love is different for everyone. As such, people may feel and exhibit Romantic Love at different capacities. However, one's responses to romantic actions may be predictable if you come to know the target of your advances. The secret to Romantic Love is to find the person who can, will, and wants to reciprocate your actions. What you do for each other should occur simultaneously, not sequentially; and not as an expectation or reciprocation for previous actions. It must start somewhere, so why not have it begin with you? Knowing this, Romantic Love doesn't have to end or transition into a love of convenience.

In the end, did I get the girl? No, I didn't. Not in the "normal" sense, as I would've preferred. It was, however, an astonishing experience while it lasted. What I did get between the muted vibes and volumes of unanswered questions, were some magnificent photos, a cute tiny wooden Soldier carved with care, reminders of my trips to Germany, Poland, and Sweden, enduring memories of life and beautiful scenery, and a new favorite scarf. Eventually, I found the wooden Soldier wedged behind my bureau, camouflaged by the carpet. The fact he disappeared wasn't fate at all, it was purely coincidence. Or was it? The salted licorice and chewy Swedish raspberry candy chews didn't last long after I returned. But I wasn't worried. I kept the empty boxes and wrappers, so I knew what to get if I wanted more.

Losing contact with my Viking Princess was like outgrowing my childhood teddy bear. Though my perception of her never changed, it was time to stop carrying her around. Her threads never became worn, her stuffing never came out, nor did she ever become overstuffed. Her eyes never popped off, and she showed no major signs of wear and tear; she changed within. We both did. After meeting someone new and becoming familiar with the person inside, sometimes the veneer of image and outer beauty we once found attractive, tarnishes. This can happen when people reveal snapping and demanding personalities, laziness, overactive lifestyles, serious disorders or physical ailments, or even once hidden religious or ideological beliefs and rituals we may eventually find uncomfortable or unacceptable. Or maybe they chew their toenails in their sleep, or don't enjoy doing chores, or don't remember little things that are important to us. Knowing this was a possibility with Erika, once she invited me into her life, we discussed many potentially controversial issues. Despite this, my perspective of her never changed, as I wholeheartedly expected it might. It didn't.

I don't understand why she is so different! Though I wanted to know, I'd most likely never find out. I had to accept the outcome. I had to move on without regret or recourse. She may not be with me physically, but she's still in my memories. She may not know or care, and I'm okay with that.

What does bother me is that I've never been a priority in any woman's life. But I do have a rekindled, now dormant, friendship still out there somewhere. I realize I can't force life to be exactly what I want it to be; I can only do as much as I can to make my reality close to what I want. The final outcome is up to life itself [other people, chance, and spiritual forces of God and/or universal forces] —these include the circumstances you initiate, the events you perpetrate, the people you meet [and may come to know intimately], their reactions to your actions and yours to theirs, to that which you incarnate and what may self-perpetuate. In poetic verse it may look like this:

You Can't Force Life

You can't force life to be exactly as **You** want it to be.

With the actions **You** initiate,
Resulting in circumstances **You** perpetrate,
Life is what happens when those **You** meet react to
The actions **You** incarnate.

You can do only what **You** can, to make **Your** own reality,
As close to what **You** want it to be,
The result is up to life and the universe itself,
With others, in kind, reacting to its insanity.

You can't force life to be exactly as **You** want.

I decided to take a chance on life, and it took me for an intoxicating, energizing ride. I did what I planned on doing and had a wonderful time doing it. I helped Erika figure out a few things in her life, including her washing machine. And she unwittingly helped me figure out a few things in mine. The outcome was not exactly the way I would've planned it, but in life we all must learn to search the unsearched encompassed within our journey. This search begins within us. By identifying our strengths and weaknesses in Socratic form [through questioning ourselves], we derive answers which will bring forth our short, mid- and long-term goals, identifying where we should launch our journey. The start of the search is just that, a start. Starting will inevitably identify a series of diversions and convergences, forcing us to decide which intended or unintended path we will follow. Ultimately, we must prepare to expect the unexpected. And accept it. That's right, sometimes shit happens. Just accept it.

I had my vision of Erika as we looked into each other's eyes at a distance in my formative pre-teen years, and most recently, during our three days in Sweden. I have my memories of the words we shared as our thoughts intertwined among the mystic mist of the frigid Nordic Sea. I have memories of our actions and reactions, and our feelings, hopes and dreams. I'm okay with this; I must be. I assume this is what true Romantic Love is... wanting another person to be truly happy even when that person's perception or perspective of happiness may be different from your own. It may not even include you. It took some time to settle into this reality, and I'm okay with that too. After all, we don't really have a choice not to accept things we cannot affect or change; although I suppose we could ignore them, or lie about them... but what good does that do? In the end, verifiable absolute truth, will prevail. Wouldn't it be a better life if everyone always told the truth in matters of the heart, didn't take offense, and everyone monastically accepted results and moved on?

Those three perfect days came at a time in my life when I really needed someone willing to focus only on me and need only me, if only for a little while. As her muse, it was my responsibility to return the favor. I provided her the encouragement to improve her life and she provided me with memories of how we did it. This brings me tremendous satisfaction—rounded out by memories of our last and newly found pasts on our journeys, though now separate, toward finding happiness.

Maybe my purpose in life is as a muse. It would make sense if these muses were charged with inspiring people while conducting the chores in their daily lives. Perhaps my mission as a muse is to rescue people from their present circumstance, lifting them out of the mires among the arbitrary circles and rings of complications within their lives. Then helping them continue forward. I learned we can't fix anyone by ourselves. We can give them the tools to instill confidence and provide encouragement, helping them on their way. We can open their perspective and provide a glimpse of a brighter reality. But we can't change it for them, especially not if they refuse to change it themselves. They still must do the bulk of the fixing themselves. We all do. Hope and faith alone are the dreams of fools, the fooled, and the hopeless. People like to dream of a perfect reality but often fail to pursue it. Without pursuing or acting on it, you are transforming your dreams of reality not into truthful reality, but into wishes, wasted thoughts, and lost time.

It's the job of the muse to encourage people to follow their dreams and expect the best from themselves, being prepared for any eventual outcome. The challenge is to encourage a metamorphosis from the watcher, hoper, and dreamer into executors. Seeing the glimmer in a person's eye when they are happy, experiencing the elation which follows success, is most compelling. People often convey a certain look when fighting thoughts of their present, overcoming them, and dragging them down into an abyss of hopelessness. The only aspect of life that should be caged are the nightmares that haunt people, restricting and constricting their progress. Though people want to vanquish their fears, it's easier said than done. In matters of the heart, when someone keeps saying... "nothing is impossible" or the converse "anything is possible" what they may intend to say is… "Nothing is impossible, but everything may be improbable." In reality, they may not have the courage to discourage. Life is much easier to accept when understanding all of the facts, as they truly are—without adornment or delay. This enables us to uncover and accept our realities, rebuild, and continue forward. Without knowing all the facts, we face uncovering little truths incrementally, slowly building the complete picture of the absolute truth. This can be heart wrenching. So why use the trickling truth technique? Since all negative events in our lives can be transformed into a positive experience through analysis, comprehension, and acceptance, just rip off the bandage quickly to enable working through the pain quicker.

Some things are destined never to change; but we won't know for sure, until we know. This is the journey… the search… to define our life mission… for which we organize expeditions and pursue quests… and adventures… to uncover answers in our travels. I have always encouraged myself to pursue opportunities from concept development as far into completion as possible. If you never initiate your journey, your unpleasant reality is most likely never going to change. If it is changed or merely perceived to change, it can still be molded into a positive experience. Even momentarily, a positive change can provide you an escape from your present reality. This instills hope for you to change your future through baby steps. Thrive don't survive, dream big, thrive big.

There may never be another person in my life as compelling as Erika, but I pursued the journey to completion. And I enjoyed it. Do you remember President Abraham Lincoln's immortal words—"It's not the years in your life that count, it's the life in your years."

I wanted to share more time with her, but it wasn't in the cards. We both had completely different and separate lives in different parts of the world, within different cultures, speaking different languages, knowing different realities, on different paths. I couldn't stop thinking about her timeless beauty, her character, her newfound search for clarity, and her unspoken abilities beyond my expectation. During my visit, her actions and words reflected someone who was possibly internally torn. I hoped she would find solace in her life and an ability to express herself in the future. Then again, maybe it's better some things are left unsaid.

The last poem I sent her, in a card she never acknowledged receiving, was:

Make It Count

How long you have to live is anybody's guess
Don't squander it in restlessness
Focus on learning, achieving, and growing from your tasks
Then sit back, watch, and make it last

Walk in the sun, snow, and rain
Abundance found in life's where and when, is never the same
Waste not your time merely wanting it to be
Cherish the time you have debt free

"'Tis not the years in your life
But the life in your years," the wise Abraham Lincoln said
Enjoy each second, minute, hour, and day,
For you'll not know when your epitaph will be read

Make it all count toward your legacy
Live in the now, love, laugh, share, and play
Before you breathe your last of life
Realizing too soon, you wished it all away.

Is it ever "too late?" This is debatable. "It's never too late to find out" is a statement more to my liking. I had a feeling those pristine three days would never transform into present reality; they were too perfect and against universal law. If we lived in heaven on earth, what would we look forward to in the afterlife? Those three days were inspiring, the nights were golden, and the memories lasting forever. That is her gift to me. Wishing her well for the rest of her days is my gift to her. I wrote this for myself:

Living In the Present

Leave the past in the past, perhaps where it should be,
Learn from it, remaining in the know,
Look forward to what new days can bring,
Living in the here and now, will help you learn and grow.

Look forward to new experiences,
Your senses will inherently seek,
Remaining aware of all the new,
Another day will reap.

Depending only on YOUR actions,
Looking forward to what new days bring,
Will grow your roots healthy and strong,
Making your heart sing.

At this point, you may think this story is quite unbelievable. And I will tell you the best part of this story is its ending. But we're not quite there yet. You may not feel like this is the best part of this story, nonetheless, it's the most comprehensive part as this quest draws to its seemingly unenviable close. The entire trip now seems so far back in the past, I wasn't sure if any of it really even happened.

So, we'll just say this is nearly a perfect end to nearly a perfect story, in nearly a perfect time in my life—some people, afraid to venture out taking calculated chances, may never take the opportunity to begin their own search. It was my celebration, as well as, the discoveries I relished. Some people are satisfied living within the safety of mediocrity surrounded by the merely acceptable in their lives. Acceptance of such an existence should not be driven by a phobia of facing unknown realities that might be uncovered. This life of avoidance can forever bury a potentially soul waking experience. There is relative comfort in having complete control over your life by keeping the bar low. It limits the possibility of failure. But like in body building, failure is how we grow. When queried about the failures of all his experiments before discovering the light bulb, Thomas Edison commented that he merely found 1,000 ways it wouldn't work, before finding the one that did.

Some choose to live within the perfect fantasy they have created for themselves, rather than face the cornucopia of potentially endless possibilities confronting them. If this is you, I would venture to say you may never get as far into your search for true Romantic Love as you could. Why settle for not expecting to find the perfect match for you? You can easily pursue other goals whatever they are, whenever they arise, searching for Romantic Love along the way.

Whatever the outcome of your search, your growth is inevitable. This story should serve as inspiration for you to seek your soul's satisfaction, accepting whatever outcomes you find on your quests, cherishing the adventure, appreciating the growth, and internalizing your journey as continuously as life itself. For life is a journey, not a destination.

Awareness is The Key Unlocking Your Journey

Within your Search, Quests are taken
Answering questions driven by curiosity itself
Passing through a myriad of destinations
Bending possibilities some have never felt

Expeditions satisfy curiosities
While determination and audacity build the train
Whether ending in success or in failure
Rarely is nothing of depth found in fame

Try and try again
Is what we're all about
Until your search reveals answers
Casting away shadows of doubt

With every answer unearthed
Is a door to another way
Another method of science is
The beginning of a new era or day

It's mostly been done before you say
But not in every way
And not by every person who thinks of it
In his or her own way

The search beyond oneself
Is a responsibility unto each
Exploding the accepted norms of nothingness
Expanding possibilities within one's own reach

Extending outside one's shielded shell
Pursuing an adventurous chance
Living life on earth to its fullest
Is respecting the immortal dance

This chapter of my life closed, temporarily enveloping within it, my dreams of Romantic Love. There will undoubtedly be more dreams to follow. Someday, somehow, somewhere in this vast world in which we live, there exists someone for everyone. One to shower with Romantic Love, to spoil and treat with affection, to appreciate us for what we were, are, and will become with them in our lives. Think I'm kidding?

I leave you with these final thoughts to assist you in pondering your own journey... your life's mission... identifying what you are searching for... designing your own expeditions... framing your quests... following through on your own adventures...

Too Late

Love not sent isn't love at all
How long is one to wait
And, when does it become,
Impossible and just too late?

What happens if you display your heart?
For someone to reciprocate,
And all they say is... "Oh really?"
"That... sounds... just... great."

How long does it take to love someone?
Is it possible to love from the start?
Or does it take years to get to know,
Through trials and tribulations of the mind and heart?

Since people do change,
What's the sense of a long wait?
Trying to find that absolutely perfect person
Who seemingly dropped in, from heaven, by fate?

How much need you know about a partner?
Knowing your own head and heart?
What if there's no instant chemistry?
And no instantaneous spark?

Can you grow to love someone?
Or wait for the perfect time in life?
That's probably how so many people die lonely,
Without the "perfect" husband, without the "perfect" wife.

The universal lifetime couples' secret,
Is that it doesn't matter on whom you decide,
That "special someone" should have a healthy caring heart,
Because the same issues will always arise.

You both must simply care enough,
Meeting each other's needs and wants,
Being best friends together without jealousy and selfishness,
Preventing tension and détente.

When you find that near perfect person,
How long do you wait to respond?
With love or sending them on their way,
Unknowing, there's no magic wand.

These are the questions for which there are no right answers,
Depending on how you live and for how long,
You'll want to be loved for the rest of your life,
And seeking this seems unwrong.

Do you have the same energy, beliefs, and interests?
Do you want the same things for the same amount of time?
Do you have the same capacity to dive right in together?
Sharing the best life has to offer, without thinking "that's mine?"

The Search

Searching the world
For somewhere to belong
Searching the world
For someone with whom to be strong.

Searching the world for someone,
Who will stave away your weak,
For someone who will stay beside and support us,
Forever, without being meek.

Searching for someplace to live,
Searching for someplace to call home,
Searching to be forever unafraid,
Searching to be forever unalone.

Searching for the eternal forever,
Searching for that happiness again,
Searching for friends with whom to celebrate,
With whom to play... remember when...

This search seems to take a lifetime,
And life's journey will too soon end
Where you stop with whom along the way,
Is the whom you'll be forever with... once again.

Looking down into the eyes of my two best friends panting, now restlessly resting beside me among the beauty and resilience of nature's creations, I urged, "Come on doggers, we gotta go. We've got a long hike home and it's getting late." Looking skyward, catching a final glimpse of the majestic birds soaring above, "Goodbye eagles, enjoy your lives together. We're all journeying onward... but for now, me and the doggers, are going home... Come on guys... Let's Focus on our Journey."

Voltaire (1694-1778) once said:

"Illusion is the first of all pleasures"

I contend that…

Illusion is the greatest of all pleasures…

And often, our <u>only</u> one.

My search continues…

Made in the USA
Columbia, SC
11 August 2021

43446230R00257